Arman Ratip, a pianist-composer of avant-garde music, was born in Cyprus. He began his piano lessons with his mother Jale Dervish at the age of five. Later, he recorded two albums for EMI and became well-known in the UK. He performed in North Cyprus, Turkey and in Europe extensively. Ratip is also the author of *How to Play Backgammon* by Hamlyn in the UK, in addition to his two fantasy fiction novels, *The Devil's Feather* and *King Devil*, about his hero Turan Akova and his encounters with the Devil, novels depicting his research on UFOs.

Arman Ratip

The Devil's Feather

AUSTIN MACAULEY PUBLISHERS™

LONDON * CAMBRIDGE * NEW YORK * SHARJAH

A CIP catalogue record for this title is available from the British Library.

ISBN 9781035801602 (Paperback)
ISBN 9781035801619 (ePub e-book)

www.austinmacauley.com

First Published 2023
Austin Macauley Publishers Ltd®
1 Canada Square
Canary Wharf
London
E14 5AA

One

When I first set eyes upon the magnificent eighteenth-century Chateau Ferranti, I had no idea this would conceivably be the beginning of a final resolution, the resolution following years of research on UFOs, research on scores of cases misted by half-truths and notions. It had not been easy to see through the mist.

The train I boarded in Istanbul drew to a halt in Salzburg while I was pondering on the unanswered questions cropping up in the corners of my mind. I took a taxi from the station and thought about the first time I had been to the Chateau four years before.

I had been invited to attend a conference on UFOs. Although I was by no means among the leading UFO experts in the world, good friends in the USA and England somehow thought a Turkish Cypriot from the eastern Mediterranean island of Cyprus would be a worthy advocate of UFOs. I remember meeting Emma Fitzgerald in the Great Hall as I walked towards the beautiful Bosendorfer grand piano. I am a pianist/composer. She was outstandingly, ravishingly beautiful. She was also probably the youngest chairperson to chair a conference on UFOs. For the week the conference lasted, I had only managed to see her three or four times, and on those occasions, our conversations were terminated abruptly—she must have been the busiest woman in the world! She had only been twenty-eight and very beautiful. All the men at the conference were chasing her for one reason or another—and mostly for the other.

I will not deny that I am an unashamed womaniser. There was a covert attraction between us and we never stopped corresponding during those long four years. For the first time in my life, I found myself waiting four years for a woman whom I wanted desperately. For four years, again for the first time in my life, I had written love letters to a woman I scarcely knew.

Now let me return to the reason why I was invited to this all-important conference on UFOs. The island of Cyprus is quite small. The area covering the

Turkish Republic of Northern Cyprus is even smaller: about 3,355 square kilometres, about 1,345 square miles. The chances of UFOs showing an interest in such a small area, an island in the east of the Mediterranean, may appear slim. But how wrong can you be! There had been several sightings, one in Boğaz village in the Kyrenia Mountains area, and the other in the panhandle. The other three or four sightings were in the panhandle as well. But the two I mention were of special interest. A UFO was seen by a family of four in Boğaz village. The strange, saucer-shaped craft hovered in the air for about three minutes and then disappeared. The family pinpointed the exact location of this close encounter. I searched the ground for two days and eventually found a feather-like object. To my amazement, I found another feather-like object in the panhandle. Both feather-like objects were identical. I wrote to Emma about the feathers and sent her several pictures of them. She said a UFO expert was doing some research in the Middle East. The man could perhaps visit Northern Cyprus and bring the feather-like objects to her for examination. The UFO expert came, and after a thorough search in both areas, took off with both feathers. He gave them to Emma and she, in turn, had them examined in the USA. The result was unbelievable. Never in the modern history of UFOs had such objects been found. A button was found on each of the feathers. When it was pressed, they made a crackling sound. No radioactivity was traced, but the sound coming from the feathers was astonishing and faintly disturbing.

Four years later, the second high-level meeting of ufologists from all over the world was convened: the UFO conference in Salzburg, which started at a rattling pace. There had been tremendous international pressure from governments of major countries to stifle the story, but the veil of secrecy had already been lifted with the revelation of secret UFO documents. The visitations of extraterrestrials were no longer a secret. The closely guarded UFO mystery was now irrefutable, a hundred percent proven fact. The so-called sceptics and debunkers with all their theories and denials had been sent scattering like a band of renegades in front of an army of hard facts.

Several matters needed clarification. The sounds coming from the two feathers created images showing the location of the star system somewhere in our own Milky Way galaxy within a radius of forty light-years. This was the star system of the extraterrestrials who visited our solar system. It was a long and complex process. Top scientists from all over the world, including scientists from NASA and people from SETI (The Search for Extraterrestrial Intelligence organisation), together with ufologists, had worked for hours on end to determine the origin of the two alien 'feathers'. Of course, no one had any idea of the power that would emerge from them.

Moments of incidental drama flipping wildly from one fantasy to another, fantasies that had rapidly shown themselves as fact—that was the general atmosphere of the UFO conference at the chateau in Salzburg. Eminent scientists were poised on the verge of a fantastic breakthrough that would stun the world. Confidentiality had been assured throughout the conference. Confidentiality was one of Emma Fitzgerald's fields of expertise. This time around, I was the most important guest at the conference, having made my mark in the history of ufology as the UFO researcher who had found the 'feathers'.

The extent of deliberate deception and the attempt to hide the reality of UFOs had been so great that the presentation of facts had become a belligerent show of force. Distinguished UFO researchers like Stanton Friedman, Don Berliner, Paris Flammone, Jenny Randles, and many others all communicated their cases with utmost precision and waited anxiously for the big moment: the presentation of the results of US scientist Ralph Turner and British scientist Steven Bradley. The two 'feathers' had been examined and the recorded images were now on film, and this evidence concluded the long-running dispute between UFO researchers and debunkers. This was a statement of fact. One could sense the beginnings of a situation of confrontation between the bright light of truth and the dark world of cover-ups, omissions, denials and outright conspiracies to cover up the UFO reality that had been prevalent since the Rosewell incident in 1947.

The conspirators of silence, sceptics discounting encounters between humans and aliens were now back-tracking by the dozen. The remarkable comprehensive study of the 'feathers' would support the conclusion that beyond conjecture, beyond argument, beyond the shadow of any doubt, UFOs were real. But at the same time, no one suspected that a nightmare scenario was about to unfold. The recently declassified secret documents on UFOs revealed that the 1961 Betty and Barney Hill case, in which Betty Hill had seen a star map in the UFO pointing to an extraterrestrial civilisation from the Zeta Reticuli star system thirty-seven light-years from the solar system, was real, was one hundred percent proof of UFO reality.

This discovery of the feathers had ripped the lid off the classic UFO cases such as the Rosewell incident, the Zeta Reticuli incident and many other cases and abductions, revealing them as startlingly true. But the UFO case in hand, that of the 'feathers', would soon let loose an uncompromising, horrific message.

I had attended two conferences in Salzburg within the last four years. But these two conferences were at the venue of the world-famous Salzburg Seminar. Both seminars were on journalism. On both occasions, I had given piano recitals for the guests. This time, I was asked again to perform my 'space music' opus. What a fitting performance for the occasion. I had a chance to see Emma in private in her office on the third day of the conference. The stairway leading up to the second floor was probably the largest I had seen in any chateau with statues of ancient aristocrats staring you in the eye at every level. Finally, I reached the door of her office. I knocked and went inside. She greeted me with tremendous enthusiasm. She was very happy to see me in private, I was sure of that. She was wearing a light blue dress. By no stretch of the imagination can I describe her beauty. Such harmony between her physical beauty and her movements. I was enchanted. I had of course seen her at the start of the conference three days earlier, but that had been an official meeting.

"I kept all your letters," she said, as I stood in front of her desk.

"Why?" I asked as she gestured me to sit down. She rose, walked around the desk towards me. Her beautiful blue eyes sparkled with excitement. I could see and feel it. She sat on the chair next to mine and took my hands into hers.

"Mainly because they express genuine feelings. In fact, they are a work of art, just like your compositions." She pulled me up, guiding me towards the Bosendorfer grand in the corner of the large eighteenth-century room. "Please play the piece you composed for me, the Romance..." I played. These were magic moments of love with compulsive chemical reaction. When I finished, she took a deep breath: "You are responsible for my first musical orgasm," she whispered. "That was beautiful."

"Emma, you inspire me! You are the reason, the source of my inspiration!"

She pulled me up, showering me with kisses, passionate kisses, her arms around my neck. "I want to be in your arms," she murmured, and within seconds our lips met in a long, long kiss. Suddenly she hurried towards the door and locked it. She rushed back into my arms and we made love all afternoon.

One music critic had once said, jokingly, of course, "It's only a matter of time before your music produces a national and international frenzy." I must admit that I had similar visions of grandeur when another critic said, this time seriously, "You are one of the most important 'New Music' composers in the world." This was after a recent piano recital at the famous Georges Enesco Museum Hall in Bucharest, Romania. Clearly, I had made a name for myself, but I needed a lot more publicity, sponsors, concerts and recordings before I could become a true international celebrity. At any rate, I think I have already said more than enough about my musical career.

Now I was on a mission to explore the findings on the 'Feathers'. If you are going to do detective work, you have to have the courage and you have to be able to improvise. Although I had listened to them in another UFO conference not so long ago in Istanbul, and read all their books, I was once again fascinated by the presentations of the world's top UFO experts. At times, it was an agonising process as I was rather impatient to hear the results of the research on the 'Feathers'. I was also rather bemused by the bizarre behaviour of the two scientists who had experimented on the 'Feather'. It was as if the enduring legacy and mystery of the huge amount of research and findings since the Rosewell Incident of 1947 had shifted on to a new unpredictable, terrifying terrain, with unspeakable innuendos leading up to an assault by the forces of globalisation. When I first sensed this, I decided to investigate. I went into the rooms of the two scientists while they were at the conference. In Steven Bradley's room, I stumbled across some papers and notes apparently prepared for the final day of the conference.

When I read the first paragraph, a very disturbing picture was already emerging. The notes in the first paragraph read as follows: "The Masters of the universe have finally arrived. The forces of 'S' will create one earth." It all sounded like a passage from a science fiction novel. At first, I thought my imagination was working overtime and that this was just a misinterpretation on my part, but the next few lines were clearly devising a sequence of steps to 'dominate and conquer and transform the human element'. It continued: "We must now focus on the implementation of the 'S' plan." I did not want to believe it at first. But now, questions popped up, thick and fast. Dominate, conquer and transform the human element? What was all that about? Such scenarios of conquest of the planet Earth by alien civilisations were to be found in films like War of the Worlds, Star Wars and Independence Day. I discounted that possibility for the time being as it sounded ridiculously unbelievable. But what was the 'S' plan?

Why would two of the most distinguished scientists in the world write a report with such fantastic overtones? The daily reports of Ralph Turner and

Steven Bradley were completely at odds with the scientific approach to the most important find in ufology. I took notes from Turner's speech on the second day of the conference. One theme bothered me more than any other. He said, "A world government is probably the next step. This is a global issue which threatens the very foundation of human civilisation on Earth. The size of the challenge that faces the scientific community is so immense and dramatic that we need the great powers of the world to unite under one roof to deal with the problem at hand."

This was a political speech. But what was the problem at hand? Several questions asked by prominent UFO researchers were brushed aside by both Turner and Bradley with such comments as, "The grim realities will present themselves within the next few days when we announce the final report to the conference."

What did they mean by 'transform the human element?' I took note of all the peculiar statements of the two scientists. These could, perhaps, one day form the basis of a curious historical footnote in ufology. Several government agencies from the USA, Britain, Germany, France, Russia and Japan were looking into the matter, emphasising their country's responsibilities for future generations. But their promises were ringing increasingly hollow. At this stage, it was extremely difficult to say that everybody's sensitivity was ostensibly satisfied. Far from it. The agencies of the countries represented here at the conference had earlier promised to form a united front as this new development would most probably lead to the first-ever official extraterrestrial contact with an alien civilisation from another star system. This would be the most important event in the history of the world. But already some differences between the major powers were broadening out into petty arguments as to how this would be perceived internationally. In terms of positive indicators, there was no sign of any effort to adopt a strategy at this crucial moment.

Over fifty people were now more or less imprisoned at Chateau Ferranti with tight security measures in every corner of the grounds. I was the only person one step ahead of the rest of the crowd. I had copied the notes of the two scientists. But I stopped in my tracks after a second secret 'mission' into their rooms. I needed more evidence. I could sense something utterly despicable. The last notes I had gathered from their room suggested not just a world government but a mysterious power to rule over such a world body. What did they mean by this power? The whole thing was absurd and extremely unpleasant. I did not know who to trust. But I had to warn someone of the danger ahead. Communication with the outside world had become impossible as all e-mails, telephone calls were immediately diverted to a centre at the conference. Several top UFO researchers were extremely suspicious of the situation, and most of them knew it demanded immediate action. A definite resentment of the conduct of affairs at the conference was now simmering away. A mundane, routine fear developed into an unpredictable, unstable situation. Every word spoken by the two scientists raised serious questions as to whether Turner and Bradley were in control of all their faculties.

One thing was certain. The eyes, or rather, the look in the eyes of the two scientists had somewhat changed. There was a fit of visible anger and something quite monstrous in their expression. I know it sounds crazy, but I was deeply affected by this peculiarity, this terrifying expression in their eyes. The odd thing about this observation of mine was that only a couple of other people noticed it. Emma was one of them. Thirty-six hours before the final day of the conference, I went into my room and assessed all the 'evidence' that I had gathered during the previous five days at the chateau.

I had nothing concrete, except perhaps the notes of the two scientists that I had stolen from their private rooms, but I was by no means looking for an endorsement of my claims. Two strenuous hours and then finally I decided to share my secret findings with Emma. Once again we met in her office. It was early evening, around 6.30 on the fifth day of the conference.

"Turan," she smiled, but could not hide her expression of worry. "You are very tense these days. What's happening?"

"Remember what I told you yesterday?" I asked, pulling out the notes of the two scientists from my file and handing them to her.

"Yes, I remember," she replied.

"Then please read the notes."

The notes were written in haste on a couple of pages. She read them.

"Agreed, it is strange," she admitted, "but I honestly don't know what to make of it. There is a certain ambiguity in what they say."

"Perhaps. But what about the look in their eyes?" I wanted to trust her. "Emma, the looks are more than strange. The change in their expression occurred right after the first examination of the 'feathers'. Their bizarre behaviour and eye expression after the first examination of the feathers..." I ventured my conclusion. "So this must mean that the whole thing has something to do with the feathers."

"OK, OK," she said, "I noticed the strange look in the eyes, too, but you can't arrest a man because of the look in his eyes…"

I wanted to do something. But the more I thought about it, and the more I talked to Emma, it was apparent that there was very little we could do before the end of the conference.

"Of course. But the peculiarities and the frightening look in their eyes are linked to the feathers. Are we agreed on that?"

She hesitated for a moment before she replied: "Not entirely. We must wait and see."

"Emma, it's as if something or some power is taking over the scientists. Something is generating and growing into a massive force. This invisible power seems to be spreading to other people in the conference. I can feel it."

"But I can't see what we can do about something that you feel, Turan," she insisted, "OK, so you have the notes which are very strange, to say the least. And yes, the looks are frightening and nothing like we have seen before. But that is all. Perhaps we can let the CIA man in on our little secret."

"The question is, can we trust him?"

"I don't know," she admitted, "but as far as I can tell, he hasn't behaved bizarrely, nor has he got the look."

"OK. Let's do it," I said.

Emma called James Saunders, the CIA Chief at the conference, and arranged for us to meet at the bar just before dinner. Saunders was a big man, probably in his early forties. I explained to him what I had found out so far. Emma also stressed the importance of the notes and of the speeches delivered by the two scientists during the conference. He sipped his scotch and listened.

"Let's sit at a table," he suggested, pointing to the far corner of the bar. We followed him and sat down.

"This is very interesting," said Saunders, gulping down his remaining whiskey. I quickly ordered another round. "We clearly have a detective in our midst," he joked, "Mr Akova, you have started something, and now you have to follow it through."

"I will," I said determinedly, "but we need your help. We need the help of professionals. We need to be prepared for unprecedented developments…"

"Wow! Hold on! What unprecedented developments?" Saunders asked with a note of authority. "You haven't much to go on. OK, the notes are strange, I admit, but that isn't enough to go by. We must wait for the final day. We have to see the images and the film. We need absolute proof of the alien civilisation visiting Earth."

"I am not just talking about a visit by extraterrestrials. That has happened many times over the past sixty-odd years. But I am certain there is an alien presence here in this building," I said. He looked at me with disbelief, and I can't say I blamed him.

"Mr Akova, now wait a second. You have no proof of this. So you can't really expect me to believe such a fantastic notion."

Emma cut in, waving both hands: "Don't raise your voices, please," she warned. "Mr Turner is sitting at a table in the other corner of the bar. Don't look now, but he's staring at us."

I stated our case: "We have no communication with the outside world here. All I am asking from you is to just contact your people and tell them there may be an alien presence in this building." Although I thought it was too late by then for the low-key approach, I felt I couldn't justify asking Saunders to raise the alarm. After all, there was still a possibility that my suspicions could be groundless. But he agreed to do as I asked.

The evening before the final day of the conference, I planned our next move with Emma and Saunders. Emma invited both scientists to a meeting in her office while Saunders and I would break into their rooms and investigate once more. This would be a challenge for all of us. For both Emma and me, the most important UFO conference in years had been overshadowed by the bizarre behaviour of the two scientists. This was the moment I had been anticipating since the day my first suspicions proved to be well worth investigating. First we went into Turner's room. We searched the whole room, carefully placing everything back in its original place. This time we could not find the controversial notes I had copied earlier. In the new notes that we found in the drawer, there was no mention of the 'S' plan and not a word about the 'Power'. Bradley's room was very untidy. Both rooms faced the lake to the west of the building. On the desk near the window, there was a whiskey bottle and an empty glass. I read the notes on the desk. This was probably the speech prepared for the final day. Again, there was no mention of the 'S' plan nor of the 'Power'.

Then, all of a sudden, the telephone rang. We did not answer it. And minutes later, Bradley walked into his room. Saunders pulled out his gun. We had just enough time to hide in the cloakroom near the door. The scientist sat on a chair near the desk facing the lake.

He looked up into the sky. We could see him clearly. Two minutes later, Turner came in and pulled up a chair right next to him. Together they opened the metal box with the 'feathers' carefully stored inside. I noticed they had been carrying the metal box with the 'feathers' throughout the conference. We waited intently. The next moment we witnessed was probably the most devastating, unbelievable scene ever to be seen on the face of the earth. An image of the most devilish-looking face appeared on the window facing the lake…It was like the mother of universal evil descending to earth…A horrifying sight of a creature, a demon not unlike the representations of Satan in art throughout the centuries. Approximately seven spine-chilling minutes passed. A nightmarish kaleidoscope of fragmented images appeared on the window, as on a large wide television screen. The morbid psychological impact of the horror intensified with the hair-raising sound coming from the screen.

Suddenly, what looked like a star map appeared to the right of the image of the creature. This was truly unbelievable, but I could see the names of the star systems man had studied for over forty-five years. These were star systems in our own Milky Way Galaxy and within a radius of thirty light-years. The names of the star systems were written in English, a minor, elementary procedure for an advanced alien civilisation. The devilish creature pointed to the star system, Epsilon Eridani. As a UFO researcher, I had studied the stars nearest to our own solar system as I was convinced most of the UFOs visiting earth came from some of these star systems. Desperately, I searched my memory…Yes, I remembered now…Epsilon Eridani was a star in the long straggling constellation of Eridanus, the River. Its potential as a possible centre of advanced life had been recognised for some time. This star was ten and a half light-years from our solar system and would almost certainly be the subject of future attention in the realms of interstellar communication. That was just a fraction of the information available to astronomers and UFO researchers.

A close-up of a large planet in the Epsilon Eridani system was the toughest test yet, for me and the CIA man. There were scores of UFOs flying over the planet. These UFOs were very similar in shape to the ones which had been visiting earth for many years. This was no dream. This was not a figment of the imagination. It was there on the window. Now we had proof. But the proof of what? Was this Satan, the evil monarch of Hell? Was Epsilon Eridani the home of Satan and his demons? Suddenly, I remembered the 'S' plan I had read about in the notes. Perhaps this was the 'Satan Plan'…A plan to conquer the world. A plan for the Devil and his demons to rule over Earth…The traditional image of an evil supreme being, an adversary equal in strength or almost equal in strength to God…It all added up to one thing. These evil beings had come from the star system Epsilon Eridani. Their plan was to dominate the whole world with co-operation from the people who had already been demonised by the Devil. Diavolos, the Devil, had now revealed himself as an extraterrestrial being from another star system. There was no other satisfactory explanation.

Had this ruler of Hell conquered other worlds in the Milky Way Galaxy? The evil being on the screen delivered his first command to the two scientists. "Tomorrow will be the beginning of a new age," said a hoarse voice. A second or two later, the frightening sounds coming from the feathers unleashed ferocious dissonances. Then two red beams appeared from the eyes of the 'Devil' and appeared to pierce the eyes of the scientists. This was a simple operation to bring humans under their power. So, the 'Power' mentioned in the notes was in fact the power of Satan himself…The position and the existence of the Devil over the centuries had been an inconsistent, confusing assortment from innumerable traditions and cultures. Now, Diavolos came with the feathers from outer space and made his presence felt in this beautiful eighteenth-century mansion in Salzburg, Austria. The scientists must have been transformed into extraterrestrial beings. That strange, terrifying look in their eyes, that monstrous expression that mesmerised others into the fold of the Devil and his armies of demons…

In these few minutes when the scientists had already received their share of the Devil's power from the red beams and while both Saunders and I stood motionless in the cloakroom, undecided on what to do next, I remembered a passage I had read a long time before from a book entitled 'The Zarkon Principle'. There was mention of a phenomenon of what ufologists have come to call 'angel hair'. 'Angel hair' is a strange material, as yet undefined, with the appearance of that white silicone fibrous material which is used as artificial snow in Christmas decorations. It had been discovered falling from the sky or lying on the ground shortly after UFO activity. It tends to dissolve or disintegrate soon after its contact with the earth, or more particularly when handled. But the two feathers I had found did not dissolve or disintegrate. The image coming from the feathers and seen on the window was no angel, but just the opposite, it was the 'Devil'.

The image of the 'Devil' disappeared from the window. The two scientists put on their jackets in robot-like fashion and proceeded towards the door. Those few seconds were the longest moments of my life. The two scientists were gone. Now we had to get out of the room without being seen.

"Wait for a second while I check the corridor," Saunders said. He slipped out of the cloakroom and walked slowly towards the door. He opened it gently and peered through to see if there was anyone outside.

After the terrifying images we had seen on the window, we had no doubt about this strange, alien presence in the building. Somehow we had to warn the people outside. But the line had been crossed and several people in the building had already been 'demonised', including the man in charge of the communications centre at the Chateau Ferranti. Somehow, we had to get out of the chateau and warn the world of the danger.

Immediately, we went into Emma's office and explained to her what we had seen in the scientists' room. She was shocked: "My God!" she exclaimed, "Is this really happening?"

"It certainly is," replied Saunders emphatically, "unbelievable but true..."

"But what are we going to do?" she asked.

"You have to get us out of the building this evening."

"But how?" she asked again.

"I don't know," I said, "but you are familiar with the estate and its grounds. Please try to think of something now."

Naturally, we had to get out and return to the building on the same night, so as not to arouse suspicion. It seemed an enormous undertaking, and although Emma, a ufologist herself, was the organiser and coordinator of the UFO conference, she was by no means omnipotent. With the 'Devil' and his demons pulling the strings, she was under scrutiny. Saunders sat in an armchair, downing his whiskey and trying to recover from the shock. I walked towards the window and cast my eyes across the lake. Chateau Ferranti was built right next to the lake. But what about the shores of the lake to the west? Suddenly, I had an idea.

"What about the shores of the lake at the other end? Are they also within the Ferranti estate?" I asked Emma. She moved near me and looked at the lake.

"No. The shores opposite are outside the estate," she said excitedly, as she got my gist.

"OK," I said, "could we cross the lake in a boat at night?"

"I suppose we could…"

"OK," I continued, "this ought to look like a lover's tryst in the boat." I turned to Saunders. "James, can you pick up a girl for the trip? Is there a female out there who you can trust?"

Saunders thought for a moment and then smiled as if re-discovering the possibility of a relationship with a woman.

"Yeah, yeah, there is this American girl, Jane. She is with the 'Los Angeles Globe'." He raised himself from the armchair. "Yeah, I can ask her out…"

"Right, then. That's settled. If we make a foursome, it'll look much better. Emma, you'll arrange for the boat to be ready for us. We make our move after dinner tonight."

My piano recital of 'Space Music' in the Great Hall of the chateau was a tremendous success. One ufologist, closely associated with a record company in the USA, said he would talk to his friend in the States about arranging a series of concerts and a recording of a new CD. He said I was a 'phenomenal performer' and added, "You are one of the most important new music composers in the world." That had been the day before. Now we were having dinner after the sixth day of the conference. The ufologist with the laudatory comments about my music seemed to be as much informed about new music as UFOs. "You have a dynamic, original style instantly recognisable throughout the world…" I must admit his words did the world of good to my ego. But enough about my music and the previous evening. This was the last night of the conference. We had to make our move right after dinner.

I was sitting next to Emma as always while six other guests conversed on the findings which were to be announced on the following day. Sanders had made sure the 'Los Angeles Globe' girl was sitting at our table. All three of us, Emma, Saunders and myself, had to be very wary about the gazes of people at dinner. We did not want to look into the eyes of someone who had already been transposed to the 'Devil's world'. We had, in fact, painstakingly tracked down the names of those who were suspect and jotted down a list of guests who might have been taken over already. This was a small precaution before the final day. One British lady ufologist, Mrs Susan Bridgeport, looked me straight in the eye: "You are really the latest in line of composers of macabre music, aren't you, Mr Akova," she commented drily. "You could call my music macabre, I suppose. But my main source of inspiration for my space music comes from outer space."

It was the last dinner before the final day of the conference. In her final speech as organiser and coordinator of the biggest UFO conference in the world so far, Emma, first of all, thanked the President and Chairman of the Chateau Ferranti which organised seminars on different subjects throughout the year. She added, "I would also like to thank all the ufologists, scientists, members of NASA and SETI and all the guests who have attended and contributed so much to the success of this conference. The ultimate objective of this conference is to present the world with the truth. I would also like to take this opportunity to thank Mr Turan Akova, the world-famous pianist/composer and UFO researcher extraordinaire…It was he who found the feathers and submitted them to the scientific community. Let us hope the findings of our two esteemed scientists, Ralph Turner and Steven Bradley, will be the cornerstone of a new era of official contact with extraterrestrial civilisations and thus open a new page for the benefit and well-being of all mankind on planet Earth."

Emma was the jewel of the evening. She was so exquisite in her dress of pale blue, so delicious that she aroused an irresistible desire in me for all sorts of sexual love games.

"Stay close to me," I whispered to her, "now they all know we are having a love affair, no one will suspect us."

"You…you are a devil!" she responded passionately.

We waltzed to the music of Johann Strauss for at least half an hour. I wanted to preserve those thirty minutes so that I could treasure them for the rest of my life. A grand building with grand views, a grand waltz and a grand situation. This was a great love story with romantic love as its main theme.

Now the time had come to elope in our little love boat. Neither Saunders nor I had any idea how we would eradicate and finally eliminate the powerful threat hanging over mankind at Chateau Ferranti. Our main concern was to warn the outside world. We had no organised strategy, no ideas at all on how to tackle this enormous problem. We only knew that we had to try.

Two

The ball at the Chateau Ferranti was in full swing when Emma left first and I followed. On my way down, on the large eighteenth-century steps, I ran into Heidi Guder, the German ufologist. She was young and beautiful. The lighting was very poor on the steps, but—wait a second…I could still see the red, devilish glitter in her eyes. My God, I said to myself. Immediately, I covered my eyes with my right hand.

"I have a headache. I'm going to fetch some tablets from reception," I mumbled, and moved hurriedly down the steps.

"I must see you later…" she called after me.

"Sure thing," I replied, my heart pounding with fear. That was close. This miss had been as good as a mile, and thank God for it! I had somehow sidestepped the danger of being transformed into the Devil's crew.

Our bold and adventurous move began when Saunders and his girlfriend finally arrived. They jumped into the boat, and we started off heading straight for the opposite side of the lake.

We could see the lights of the French restaurant on the other side. I felt the gentle westerly breeze blowing on my face as I steered the boat towards the restaurant. With all sorts of scenarios forming themselves in my mind, I could foresee a global terror emanating from the Chateau Ferranti and spreading into Austria first, and then into Europe, and finally throughout the rest of the world. The worst part of this episode was that we had no idea how to stop this extraterrestrial threat. After all, the technological might of the USA with its current scientific research and approach to subdue the enemy might not be enough. What about the Greys, those benign UFO beings who had been visiting Earth over the past fifty-seven years? What about their promises to save our planet and human civilisation? Perhaps the Chosen Few, who claimed to be in regular contact with them, could send out an alarm signal to warn of the danger facing Earth.

Once again, in desperation, I could see that my imagination was outstripping the situation. I had to be realistic. These thoughts were totally speculative, but they could be true! The declaration of the Chosen Few that they were in contact with the Greys had rattled the scientific community. In my opinion, the abductions recounted in Professor E. Mack's latest reports were illuminating, to say the least, and I considered it probably one of the most important scientific milestones in the history of ufology. But any credit he might have taken for his impressive research into abductions by UFOs had been obscured by the narrow-minded scientists throughout the world. World-famous scientists had been unsettled by his findings. But in the firmament of ufological reality, Professor Mack's research had been convincing and stood firm against the onslaughts of those sceptics.

How to deliver a death blow to the 'S' plan? That was the question. Fifteen minutes later, we stopped the boat in a small quay, where I noticed two other boats tied up. I put my arm around Emma and walked towards the restaurant. James Saunders and his girl followed. It would be an understatement to say that the restaurant was crowded. The area was packed with young people drinking and listening to the pianist who had a female singer standing beside the white grand piano. We sat at a table in the bar area.

"What will you do?" I asked Saunders. "Who will you contact? And what will you tell them?"

"I'll contact headquarters, tell them what we have seen and let them decide what to do." He replied. "I'll use the phone booth in the corridor."

I could see Saunders in the phone booth. He talked for about five minutes. Suddenly, I saw two suspicious-looking men staring at us and Saunders in the booth. Who were they? They could not have followed us from the chateau; security at the chateau was organised within the grounds.

"Done!" said Saunders with a chuckle as he sat down next to the 'Los Angeles Globe' girl. "I still can't believe this is happening," he added.

"The question is, do they believe you at headquarters?" I commented.

"I can't say for sure whether they believe me or not. But the chief said he would fill in the UFO projects man."

Then I saw the two men approaching our table. "Change the subject!" I whispered urgently to Saunders. The men were total strangers. The taller one stopped beside the table facing me. He spoke with a heavy German accent.

"I am sorry to trouble you, sir. But didn't you come from the chateau?"

"Yes, we came by boat." I replied, "We needed a change of atmosphere."

He pulled out a card, "We are with the Austrian police force. We have been asked to make sure that no one goes in or comes out of the chateau. We saw you arrive in the boat."

"I thought this side of the lake and the restaurant were within the grounds of the chateau," I ventured.

"No, sir. That is not the case." That tall Austrian plainclothes police officer emphasised.

At that moment, Emma cut in. "I am the organiser of the UFO conference," she said, showing him her credentials. "The two gentlemen and the lady are also attending the conference. I am sorry. We didn't realise that security measures were so tight outside the chateau. We will, of course, be returning there shortly."

"Thank you," said the tall man politely, and they walked out of the bar area and returned to their table. I was surprised that they had said nothing about Saunders' phone call.

Our situation in the chateau had already become precarious. But at least the warning was out. We left the restaurant just before midnight. As we stepped out into the moonlight, I spotted three men near the quay.

"James, don't look now, but three men are watching us down near the bay," I warned. "Let's sit at a table now and see what happens."

"Really, Turan, you suspect everyone!" remarked Emma with amused disbelief.

"No, no." James was adamant. As a professional CIA agent, he had to be alert. "He may be right."

I could feel the uneasiness creep into my body and chill my soul. Their movements were strangely robotic and erratic; they seemed scarcely human. Now they started walking towards us. They were about forty metres from our table. Suddenly, the tall, powerfully built man in front draw a gun and started firing at us. I grabbed Emma, pulling her to the ground for cover.

"Get down!" shouted James frantically as the 'Los Angeles Globe' girl went under the table.

James pulled out his gun and fired. He shot the man on the right. Bullets coming from the assailants ricocheted off the table. When one man rushed to our table which was now riddled with bullet holes, I attacked him with a chair in my hand, pushing him down with me. It was a tussle to get the gun off him, but I managed. The gun fell to the ground. Seconds later, he somehow managed to get hold of it again, and aimed it at me. "This is it, old boy," I muttered to myself, "This is the end." At that precise moment, there were gun shots from the main door of the restaurant. Shots were coming from all directions. The man who had been about to shoot me was shot in the head. James finished off the tall man.

The two Austrian officers had come to the rescue, and thank God for that. The Austrian officer who had spoken to us earlier in the restaurant said, "You take your boat and get back to the chateau. We'll take care of the mess here." We stumbled out of the restaurant area and went straight into the boat. The Austrian officers and James, of course, had foiled an attempt on our lives. Obviously, the people at the chateau who had already been transformed into Satan's team had been tipped off. We returned to the chateau.

How on earth was the Austrian Intelligence informed about the developments within the chateau? Apparently, they had their own people at the conference right from the start. Security had been stepped up inside and outside the chateau. But who were the three men after us? And what about those strange movements? Questions, questions…And no answers as yet. Most important of all, we had to find a way to ward off the red beams transforming normal people into alien-controlled creatures. My little encounter with the German girl who almost looked me in the eye on the steps of the chateau proved one thing. If you covered your eyes with your hands, it worked.

We returned to the great hall. The party was now in full swing with Strauss's waltzes being played one after the other. I sat at our table contemplating the whole situation. The attempt on our lives was a serious matter. Obviously, someone or some people in the chateau were aware of our activities. But how? The two scientists had no idea I have been spying on them. So who else was involved? I had no clue.

We had been followed to the restaurant. I did get a glimpse of the three men coming at us while we were ready to leave. They were complete strangers. Emma said they had not been guests at the conference. So this meant that the conference had been infiltrated by men from outside. But who were they?

The negative connotations of the overall episode multiplied. I was in no position to insist on the intervention of the Chosen Few. The scientific community had rejected their claim of contact with the Greys. A year of meticulously organised work by the thirty-six men in various countries and the culmination of their discovery, which determined the future of the human race on planet Earth, had been waived aside as pure fantasy. They always said the Greys would be the saviours of the human race.

We had managed to send out a warning to the appropriate people. Their task was daunting. Nevertheless, they would try and stop the danger. Danger? This was no danger. This would be the end of the world as we knew it. Somehow, a global strategy would have to be implemented to stop Satan's people from conquering the planet. There was no question of believing or not believing what had happened with the feathers.

I had no inkling as to how to stop the transformation of normal people into Satan's crew. One could cover one's eyes and protect them from the red beams once or twice, perhaps—but not always. I also felt guilty for bringing down such big troubles upon the world. How could I have known the demonic powers of the feathers? Emma was disturbed by the events of the evening and retired early. As for myself, I decided to stay on till after midnight. It was 1.30 am when something clicked in my head. Somehow, the vile act of transformation did not take place in a crowd. The demonic aliens would let out their red beams only when they cornered an individual somewhere in the chateau. That was odd. Emma had witnessed one such case the previous evening—forgetful girl! I had nearly become a victim of the German girl on the steps. Perhaps this was significant. Or perhaps it was merely a coincidence.

I went into my room and locked myself in at around 2.00 am. No matter how you looked at it, the prognosis for the future was grim. There was no way to defeat the enemy. I was just an ordinary UFO researcher. The scientists had to think of something, and fast. A warning had to be sent out to the Chosen Few who claimed to have regular contact with the Greys. Perhaps that was the only way out. Eric Clayton was the man to contact in London. He was one of the Chosen Few. Clayton was the man in my thoughts as I switched off the bedside lamp to end a pretty dreadful day. Also in my thoughts was the final day of the conference, which was tomorrow.

In all the seminars that I had attended over the years, I generally had difficulty getting up early in the morning. One had to be in the conference room by 10.00 am. I always had my breakfast at around 10.00, so I was the last person to get into the conference room just before 11.00. The vitriolic speeches by the two scientists astounded the guests. Turner was saying: "This is a great opportunity to reach out for the Golden Age. The source of the power which has descended upon Earth is the star system Epsilon Eridani. They have come to end the frailties of mankind once and for all. No power on earth can challenge them. We have to submit to their will. The powers already vested in me eliminate death itself. These powers will multiply themselves around the world. Representatives of Epsilon Eridani have reached all corners of the world. In each and every country, the powers of those in charge have been whittled away by the magnificent beings of Eridani…"

And so it went on. Turner was already talking about world domination. The claim of eliminating death was a very interesting one. I had heard that the Greys had made the same claim as well. Who wouldn't want to become immortal? It was definitely an attractive proposition for all mankind—but for a price, of course. Submit to the devil's will and you will live forever…Turner had spoken like a true general of the Devil's army.

The final day of the conference reflected a kind of confusion among the guests. Emma ended the conference with a short talk and thanked all the guests. Most of their return air tickets had been already arranged. They began to leave one by one. I booked a flight for London, and Emma decided to come with me. I also telephoned Clayton (the Chosen One) and said I would meet him at my music manager's office. I told him a concert had been arranged at the Purcell Room and that I wanted him to be there. I had to make up a story as all the telephones at the Chateau were bugged and there were spies all over the place. Saunders and his girlfriend decided to come with us to London. I planned to tell Clayton the whole story and ask for his help. Naturally, he would contact all the other 35 Chosen Ones. I was hoping the Greys would be able to suggest a solution to the problem.

With these thoughts in my head, we left the Chateau and took the plane to London. The telepathic communication of the Chosen Ones with the Greys could not easily be written off. Once I had witnessed Clayton make contact with them. It had been an extraordinary session and the messages he had received told of a threat from an extraterrestrial civilisation. This meant that the Greys knew of the presence of the devil's civilisation in the star system Epsilon Eridani. Sure proof of UFOs visiting Earth regularly was one thing, but claiming to be able to contact extraterrestrial beings was quite another. I was not trying to make this sound intimidating by any stretch, but the debunkers and those scientists who repeatedly rejected UFO reality, despite the declassification of secret UFO documents, placed Clayton in a rather difficult position. Some found his claims macabre and comic, others called him a madman. But I had seen him make contact with the Greys once, and I knew he was telling the truth. I telephoned him from the airport and, deviating from my original plan to meet him at the Purcell Room, asked him to meet me at my house in Charles Street, Mayfair. Emma, James and Jane, the 'Los Angeles Globe' girl, were staying at Claridge's, all expenses paid by the UFO Conference. I had invited Emma to stay at my house, but during the flight she had told me of her very busy schedule organising another UFO conference in London. Several people would be working for her, and a whole suite at Claridge's had been reserved and changed into an office with a communications centre at her disposal.

"Hi, Eric," I greeted the Chosen One as I opened the door of my house. "Turan!" he said, "this is just unbelievable!" He was ebullient and excited, as always. Once we had settled down with some coffee, he asked me, "So what do you plan to do?"

"The question is, what do you plan to do?" I asked him and continued, anxious to keep him on the course I had already planned in my head. "Let's sit down and plan this thing, Eric. I personally think this extraterrestrial civilisation of the 'Devil' and his kind is inextricably linked with people in key positions in most countries of the world, people who have been transformed into the Devil's army. I don't think that the technology we have now can stop these creatures. We are heading towards the messy and acrimonious destruction of the human race as we know it. You and the other Chosen Ones, and through you, the Greys are our only hope."

He sat in a chair near the large dinner table in the living room with paper and pen in his hands. "You are right. We have to plan this thing very carefully. First things first. First of all, I have to contact the other 35 who can make contact with the Greys." He took out from his file a list of names and telephone numbers. Within an hour, I had already written out for him exactly what had happened at the chateau. It all sounded like a science fiction story and I for one did not believe for one moment that the public would believe such a story. Nevertheless, we had witnesses. Emma, the CIA man James and his girlfriend had seen it happening. Furthermore, I had recovered the two feathers in their special box. It had not been easy, but I had simply returned to Bradley's room at about 3.00 am and stolen it. These had to be sent to the USA as soon as possible. Hopefully, the scientists in the USA would be able to regenerate the feathers and see the images we had seen in Salzburg. Otherwise, Turner and Bradley, the two scientists who had started this madness, would be summoned, perhaps placed under arrest and forced to cooperate.

No matter how you looked at it, the danger was imminent. We had to find a vital and courageous way to get rid of the 'Devil'.

Eric Clayton had finished contacting the other 35 chosen Few. The primary objective was for all 36 to make contact with the Greys and pass on the message using telepathy. Naturally, contact with the extraterrestrials was no easy task. Sometimes the messages would get through very quickly, sometimes you had to wait for days before receiving any word from the Greys. That is why all 36 people had to try for contact now. We somehow had to devise a strategy in collaboration with the CIA and NASA to fend off and eventually stop the transformation of people into the Devil's army.

A CIA agent from the US Embassy in London was contacted by James, my CIA friend, who had witnessed it all. We gave him the box with the feathers. Emma contacted a UFO expert at NASA and explained the incident at Chateau Ferranti. The UFO experts would examine the images seen through the feathers, the fantastic images we had seen at the chateau. But top scientists had to devise some form of action to render ineffective the look-in-the-eye tactics of the extraterrestrials. States throughout the world would have to cooperate in a massive large-scale operation to fight the enemy before the day of darkness descended upon the earth.

The increasing dominance of the extraterrestrials was apparent as there were reports coming from all around the world. It had been almost three weeks since I arrived in London, and there was still no progress in the investigations trying to determine how these creatures sustained their power on human beings. The origin of these evil ones was Epsilon Eridani. That was already established. Epsilon Eridani, ten and a half light-years from the solar system, was a star in the constellation of Eridanus, the river. Its potential as a probable centre of advanced life had been recognised since the Ozma Project of 1960. Who would have thought this star system was the home of Satan?

There had been numerous media communications all over the world forecasting a war of the extraterrestrials on Earth. Panic had reached an all-time high. But no state on earth, including the USA, could go beyond its limited capabilities against such a powerful adversary: Satan…The psychological impact of the incident was immense. Once an American hawk said, "Non-violence means being defenceless and being defenceless is tantamount to a death sentence…" Could this really be the case for the people of earth? Were we really on the brink of a war between the forces of Satan and the Greys? When would the Greys receive our cry for help?

Three

Finally, it arrived. A Spanish girl in the city of Valencia had received a message from the Greys. Clayton had asked all 36 contactees throughout the world to contact him as soon as any message was received. Maria Valdez Rodriguez, a young Spanish girl in her late twenties, had been abducted once by the Greys. Her account of the abduction when she was only eighteen was extremely plausible. The Greys had promised to 'save' the world. The details of her story were well-publicised by the media and she had later published a book explaining her intimate connection with the extraterrestrials.

Clayton contacted her immediately. He seemed disappointed by her message. "This is nothing but a message of reassurance," he said.

"What do you mean?"

"Well, Turan, let me read you what she has sent me: 'We have the power to destroy the threat of the Eridanian devils. We will make our presence known. You will know we are here…'"

"What do you make of it, Clayton?"

"I don't know," he seemed at a loss for some reason.

"You are the expert," I reminded him, "do they plan to do something?"

"That's just it. The message simply tells us not to worry, that they will deal with it: 'You will know we are here.'"

"Well, what more do you want?"

"I don't know," he replied disconsolately. "It's just a strange message."

"What do you mean by 'strange'?"

"It's nothing like the messages I received before. It's too simple. Almost childish. I mean—it doesn't sound real. For one, in all the messages that the 36 have received up till now, there has been no mention of the power of the Greys. The messages just describe the better—much better—world which the Greys will help to create on Earth. In all the abduction cases, they continue with that same theme. They talk of a better world for the people of Earth. They also tell of the integration of several extraterrestrial civilisations."

"You say it doesn't sound real. Are you really saying that it's a fake?"

"I don't know. But it would be best to talk to Maria."

We decided to fly to Valencia the following day. It was a two-hour flight as we had a connecting flight in Madrid. Eric Clayton was a man I could trust. I first met him almost fifteen years ago when I interviewed him for a Turkish Cypriot daily newspaper. The interview appeared in several national dailies in Turkey and attracted tremendous interest on the subject of UFOs. Clayton expressed particular concern not only about the content of the message, but he insisted that the wording was strange. Weighing up his comments during the flight, I saw that Clayton's uncomfortable response was based on his enormous experience on the subject of contact with the Greys. After all, he was the top man in the Chosen 36.

Looking solemn and resolute, Clayton searched his notes with the hope of finding a similar message to that of Maria.

"No, I can't find anything even remotely similar to her message. I tell you, Turan, there's something wrong here," he said.

"We'll soon find out."

Lashed by torrential rain, the cold, wet streets of Valencia reflected a somewhat grim city, with most of its inhabitants running for shelter. From our taxi, the middle-class suburb where Maria lived, a few miles outside the city centre, looked like a ghost town. We stopped at Maria's house, on the corner of Santiago Street. As we walked towards her garden gate, we were stopped immediately by two policemen.

"This is Maria Valdez Rodriguez's house, isn't it?" I asked. I had never met her, but Clayton knew her well and when the policemen told us she had been murdered, Clayton almost collapsed.

"But how?" I asked.

"She was shot in the head, sir," replied the policeman, "I am sorry, I cannot let you into the house. If you want to go in, you must get permission at the main police station in Caranga Square in the centre of town."

The main police station was a six-storey modern building built next to the old police station. Once there, we asked for the Chief Inspector and he directed us to the office of the detective in charge of the case.

Emilio Casillas greeted us politely and gestured for us to sit down in the two chairs in front of his desk.

"What can I do for you gentlemen?" he asked, offering us cigars.

"We are here to ask about the murder of Maria Valdez Rodriguez. Mr Clayton was a good friend of Maria's." My heart sank. I could see it was going to be difficult to explain Maria's involvement with UFOs, the fact that she was one of the 36 Chosen Few, and about the message she had supposedly sent to Clayton.

I gritted my teeth and began: "What you are about to hear may sound like a science fiction story, but it is the truth. As UFO researchers, we have recently found out about the presence of extraterrestrials on earth. They come from the star system Epsilon Eridani, and they plan to conquer the world. They must, of course, be stopped." Casillas sat there motionless, his eyes wide with disbelief.

"We know that even the most sophisticated weapons cannot stop these space people," I went on, and explained that Maria had been one of the 36 people who were specially empowered to contact the Greys, another two extraterrestrial civilisations coming from Tau Ceti and Zeta Reticuli.

There was a long silence. Our detective was no doubt weighing up the probability of the fantastic news he had just heard from these two strangers.

"And how should I conduct this murder investigation, given all that you say is true? Who are the suspects? Are you actually saying she was murdered by an extraterrestrial?"

"No, not extraterrestrials," Clayton chipped in. "When you are looking for suspects, look for someone with red eyes."

"Red eyes?" Casillas was hiding a smile, and quipped. "Like he had a hangover or something?"

"I promise you, this is a serious matter," I pleaded and explained how I had actually seen ordinary people being taken over, occupied as it were, to become part of the army of the extraterrestrials. "This is the most frightening part of the story," I told him, "these transformations are happening now, everywhere, and unfortunately we have no way of stopping them."

Casillas lit a cigarette and leaned back in his chair thoughtfully. Did he believe us? If he was nervous, he didn't show it. But he clearly had no idea how to deal with such an extraordinary situation. Finally, he spoke:

"Gentlemen, it is very difficult for me to believe such a fairy tale. Where is your proof? Do you have any?"

"We told you," replied Clayton insistently, "we told you we had seen these transformations. Also, at a UFO conference in Salzburg two days ago, we witnessed other more sinister events: the transformation being beamed from the Devil's own eye into the eyes of the two scientists who were in fact examining the Feathers brought to the conference by Mr Akova here."

Casillas gave a bark of laughter: "The Devil's eye? Feathers? What are you talking about?"

"We witnessed the image of Satan as we human beings know it. The red beams from the eyes of this repellent creature pierced the eyes of the two scientists. Within moments, they had been taken over, transformed into agents of the devil," I told him.

The inspector eyed us doubtfully, then leaned forward over his desk and asked gently: "And how do you know they were—er—transformed, as you put it?" I must admit it was a sensible question. After all, he needed hard evidence.

"The eyes of the scientists immediately became red, sir," I replied.

"And the feathers?" he asked quizzically. "What significance do these feathers have?"

I told him about the strange feathers I had found in Cyprus, the island of my birth; of the odd little button which gave them a disturbing crackling noise when pressed, and of the subsequent effect on the top UFO experts to whom they had been sent for research. I described our chilling observations from the cupboard in their room and the subsequent red-eyed zombie look of those the Devil had taken for his own.

We also explained to Casillas that the US and British governments had been informed about the rapid developments after the conference, and that measures were being taken to prevent the transformation of ordinary persons into the Devil's army. Casillas finally grasped the daunting enormity of the situation.

Four

Ralph Turner had been moved to a country house in Gloucester, near Boston, Massachusetts. He was being kept under house arrest. This suited him somewhat, as he wanted to be as far away as possible from his wife and two children. He walked into the bathroom upstairs and looked into the mirror. The redness in his eyes had gone. He had regained self-control of his faculties. This was a predictable pattern; the red eyes would come and go. But once the redness came, then he was controlled by mysterious forces to look into the eyes of others. The telepathic message simply said: "Look into the eyes and transform..." He was appalled at the idea, and yet there was nothing he could do to prevent himself from carrying out the command. He was gripped by fear, but he was determined to fight this devil.

He descended the stairs with a heavy heart and sat in an armchair. His confidence was shattered; he closed his eyes. When finally he woke from his thoughts, he found himself in total darkness. He walked to the light switch, but there appeared to be a power cut. He tumbled back into the armchair, too depressed to investigate. A few minutes later there was a knock on the door. When he opened it, he saw the profile of one of the security officers in the darkness.

"Mr Turner," he said, "there is a power cut, I think." He stepped inside, "I'd like to check downstairs." The security officer opened the door to the basement, and disappeared inside, closing the door behind him. At that precise moment, while Turner was still standing in the doorway, he saw a red beam streaking across the garden. The beam struck one of the security men watching the house. Then the other one fell.

Turner saw a huge blinding light in the sky. It was a UFO, a large UFO—therefore probably from a mothership. He panicked as he saw red beams emitting from the UFO, and stepped into the shadow of the doorway. A third man was hit as he was running towards the house for shelter. The man in the basement rushed up the stairs and was also struck as he opened the basement door. All five security men had been killed by the rays emitted from the UFO. "Now it's my turn," Turner thought. "Now they will kill me, too."

He retreated rapidly into the house, hit a table in his panic, and fell to the floor. As he was about to get up, he was hit again, this time by a white light. He reeled and fell again. The white light hit him a second time, on the face, and he tasted his blood as it trickled from the wound into his mouth. He edged away as far as he could from the white light, but there was no escape. The light grew bigger and brighter. He felt a sharp pain piercing his head. The white light from the UFO had enveloped his whole body, and within seconds he was paralysed and afloat in the air, flying towards the UFO. He looked down towards the house, from which he heard and saw a splintering explosion. The house had been destroyed by a much larger red ray coming from the UFO. This was no ordinary bomb blast. The house appeared to have vaporised from the face of the earth. The door of the UFO was now closed, and he was inside. This was an abduction.

Still paralysed, Turner was taken to another room. "What will they do to me?" was the thought that he could hardly frame for the horror he felt. Seconds after this question, a telepathic reply made itself felt in his brain: "Do not be afraid. You are now with us. But you must do the work you have been assigned to perform. We will make sure you will not hide again."

In the meantime, back in London, Bradley spoke at the press conference: "I was kept under house arrest for almost three days. All this about transforming people into the devil's minions is nonsense! I've never heard such rubbish! Of course, it's true that I examined the feathers! It's also true that some images emanated from the feathers. But to talk of the Devil is pure fantasy! There is no such thing. Yes, extraterrestrials are trying to make contact. Yes, their origin seems to be the star system Epsilon Eridani, but that's all!"

Bradley sneaked away from his press conference in a taxi. Taken by surprise, the Ministry of Defence called an emergency meeting to discuss containing the fall-out from this unexpected publicity. The press conference had focused on Bradley's denial of the evil extraterrestrials. Who would believe such a story anyway? Bradley's mission as conveyed by the Eridanians was explicit: to deny the existence of the devil, but continue the recruitment of people into the world of Satan.

He had no time for his government-sponsored scientific research programme on UFOs; his purpose was to serve the devil, for which he would be rewarded.

They had promised him eternal life. With his denial of everything evil, the argument would dissolve, and Emma Fitzgerald and Turan Akova with the US and British governments would be discredited. The world would rather believe him—a respected scientist with a background of years of specialist UFO research. Those other ufologists, including Clayton, Akova and Fitzgerald would come under fierce criticism from the scientific community.

Once he arrived home, Bradley tried three times to contact his old friend and associate, Turner in America, but without success. After all, they were in this together; they had been chosen to carry forward the work of the Eridanians, and they needed to discuss progress. He had left messages for Turner to call him back and he had sent e-mails, but so far there had been no reply. He sat in his favourite chair in the study and stretched out his legs, savouring his comfort, his future. He was no longer a normal human being anymore—he was Chosen, and he had no wish to remember his old self.

The following day was to be an important one. He would be interviewed by prominent journalists from all over the globe. His vision was optimistic in the extreme, one of grandeur amidst the most powerful extraterrestrial civilisation in space. His complacent manner allowed for no recognition of the problems ahead; he was incapable of understanding the gravity of the situation. He was neither happy nor unhappy. His only focus was the two bright words shining in his mind: 'Eternal Life'.

Five

I returned to London to find the newspapers emblazoning headlines such as 'Devil is a Lie'; 'No Devil from Space'; 'The Devil is a Joke'. The British media had gone to town to highlight Bradley's denial of the presence of the devil. One reporter wrote: *The whole story of the devil was fabricated by Turan Akova, Emma Fitzgerald and James Saunders, the man from the CIA.* We were named in all the papers, openly accused of making up the story. The extent of this deliberate misinformation was enormous.

The all-important meeting at the Ministry of Defence with the UFO experts of the ministry itself was foremost in my mind the next morning. Emma came to my house at about ten o'clock, when I was still in the shower. I hurried out of the bathroom with a strategically placed towel and answered the door.

"Well, Mr Akova, it seems I caught you in the shower," she remarked with a smile. She appeared unexpectedly cheerful considering we were both viewed with such disfavour by the British public after the reports in the newspaper over the previous few days.

"Would you like to join me?" I asked, pulling her to me and kissing her.

"Come on, Turan," she protested lightly, "we have a meeting at eleven and you are still in the shower."

When I finished my ablutions, I joined Emma in the living room where she was busy re-arranging some papers on the table.

"What are those?" I asked.

"A report for the MoD." She replied, handing them to me.

There were four pages of a detailed account of what had occurred in Salzburg. Emma's style was neat and economic; nothing was superfluous.

"Excellent," I said, "but I think we should have a press conference as well. We should involve Saunders, too. After all, the three of us are the only ones who witnessed what happened."

"Yes, you are right. We'll arrange one for tomorrow or the day after. Why don't you call Saunders right away?"

It seemed clear to me that the disappearance without trace of the American scientist in the USA and the blatant denial of the whole story by the British scientist were linked; they seemed pretty much like a two-pronged attack by the Eridanians. Ralph Turner had vanished along with the five agents who were protecting him and I was in no doubt that he had been abducted. So with the abduction of the one and the denial by the other of anything untoward, public confusion was inevitable. This was what the Eridanians wanted, I was sure.

Saunders was at home when I reached him on the telephone.

"Hi, Turan, what's new?"

"You know the story about Bradley, the British scientist? He's denied it all. So we've decided to hold a press conference of our own in London in two days' time. It's his word against ours. It's time for us to present our case to the media, so if you could catch a plane to London to be here when we do it…"

"It'll be difficult, but I could try to be in London by tomorrow evening."

"That would be fine. Do your best. By the way, any news about Turner?"

"No. Not a squeak. The UFO experts here insist that he has been abducted."

"Of course," I said, "what else? But why?"

"I have absolutely no idea," he replied. "Turner and the five agents, and even the whole house just vanished into thin air."

The public's growing frustration and anger at what they thought was our mischievous fabrication needed to be met head on. The three of us, Saunders, Emma and myself, had to restore our credibility in a direct confrontation with the press, with proof of our presence at the Chateau in Salzburg. We had to demonstrate that we were actually there when it happened. This would be best done by referring to the shooting incident at the other end of the lake. It was obvious now that there had already been recruits into the Eridanian camp even before the conference had ended.

The sudden and dramatic disappearance of Turner et al. was another major incident supporting our story. The CIA and the FBI had stepped up their investigation, but the American scientist had simply vanished without a trace. The abduction of Turner had been overshadowed by Bradley's press conference, and the latter's denials were clearly red herrings. In other words, the public would largely believe his story, and the Eridanians, meanwhile, would be free to continue their mission of recruiting humans to their cause.

The next day, thank God, Saunders arrived. I had invited him, Clayton and Emma to my house for lunch. The Turkish Cypriot chef, Hasan Bey and his helpers arrived at around nine that morning. He was a wonderful caterer and owned several classy restaurants in central London, and I always used him when I had guests. I opened the door for him and returned to my bedroom where I was preparing for the day. Soon afterwards, I descended to the dining room where my English breakfast awaited me.

Six

Emma arrived at about 10.30. She was wearing a light blue trouser suit. Her every move increased my desire for her. The two days before our press conference at the Hilton had provided brief breathing space, but she was now her familiar, brisk self, efficiently organising the reports we had submitted to the MoD. Clayton gathered the newspaper reports, all the harsh covering accusing us of creating needless panic, and Saunders brought with him the CIA report on the whole incident. I had to revise my own report. This was not an attempt to prove anything; indeed, as far as I was concerned, it was all so obvious. The truth was there for all to see. We had to demonstrate it once again. We had to lay down all the facts and hopefully show them the spectre of the Eridanian Devil once and for all. This was going to be no easy task.

Brian Lovecroft was the head of his own company, Lovecroft Industries, at Cockfosters in London. A brilliant young scientist in his early thirties, he had risen to the challenge at my detailed description of detail how several people at the conference in Salzburg had been taken over by means of the red rays. He had called me the evening before in a state of eager anticipation, wanting me to pay him a visit. I arrived to find that he had devised an invisible armour to protect humans from the red rays.

"It's an extremely thin layer made up of an indestructible mixture of chemicals, all controlled by a switch!" he explained excitedly. My knowledge of physics is very limited, and he saw that it would be easier to demonstrate this invention: "Here is the switch," he told me. "Now, all you have to do is press the green button and the invisible layer will cover your whole body, from head to toe."

He handed me a small mobile switch that looked like a tiny alarm clock. I pressed the green button. I moved around the room but did not see or feel anything around my body.

"Can you feel it?" Brian asked eagerly, smiling with the air of imminent triumph.

"Well…" I replied uncertainly, and then a thought occurred to me: "Is this thing bullet-proof also? It would come in very handy if it was."

"But of course," he replied happily and stepped backwards. "Now let me throw something at you." He picked up his bag and threw it at my body. The bag hit the layer or whatever it was, but not me, and then fell to the floor.

"Yes, but will it work with the red rays?"

"Well, I tried it with lasers and it worked, so I see no reason why it shouldn't work against the red rays," he replied with conviction.

This was no solution to our problem. I had no intention of suggesting mass production of this invisible protective layer for distribution throughout the world. Indeed, it would provide scant comfort to anyone anywhere in the world which was susceptible to the Eridanian threat. Nevertheless, it had its uses and could be worn by people who were directly involved, such as Emma, Saunders, Clayton and myself, not forgetting the 35 remaining Chosen Few. But despite all our efforts to fight the most lethal and potentially devastating threat to mankind in history, sceptics in the British government appeared to be working overtime to hinder any action whatsoever to fight the adversaries. It did not make sense. It seemed that the Eridanians had already infiltrated the higher echelons not only of the government, but also of the scientific community. I did not want to be embroiled in a wider argument with such narrow-minded people who believed the whole thing was a scam.

No one had any idea about how widespread the recruitment had become. Perhaps hundreds or even thousands had been recruited by now. Although the American and British governments and some European countries had established networks to pinpoint locations of contact with Eridanians, it was impossible to tackle the problem before it actually happened. The problem was so massive and so mysterious.

How could one man's denial reverse the true facts of extraterrestrial presences on planet earth? On the face of it, Bradley's denial of the Salzburg incident seemed like a one-man show, and yet his press conference almost resembled a politically motivated campaign to discredit the certain proof of Eridanian presence. A rigid ulterior motive, combined with a determination to turn the truth on its head with fictitious elaborations seemed designed to transform the least certainty into definite disbelief. It seemed to me like a collaborative effort.

I had to find Bradley. But we were preoccupied with the preparations of the press conference. It was far from clear how the media and public would respond to the truth after Bradley's denial which had received world coverage. We had to do better. I summoned all my journalistic resources and contacts in Britain and the rest of Europe, including Turkey. We could not risk a serious stand-off with the international community.

Seven

The large hall at the Hilton Hotel near Hyde Park Corner could accommodate up to five hundred people. Emma had already guaranteed a rich list of sponsors for the press conference. The International Media Services which took over the organisation at the Hilton was an Anglo-American company operating worldwide, with headquarters in New York. The press conference would be presented in thirty different languages and broadcast live in ninety-seven countries. Emma was as always the prime figure at the gathering. We had to be extremely careful not to allow for any loopholes in our presentations which might weaken our case.

Emma began her opening speech by simply stating the aim of the press conference. "This is not merely a fabricated claim that UFOs are present on Earth. We have come here to tell you the facts. We have indisputable proof of extraterrestrial presence. Visits to Earth of UFOs with their extraterrestrial beings are one thing; but a mysterious force aiming to transform our planet into a colony of the star system Epsilon Eridani is another. We have proof of an unstoppable force coming from this star system, a force which is changing the world and human beings as we know them. The whole human race is in great peril." She explained how American scientist Ralph Turner—a key figure at the Salzburg UFO conference—was in fact one of the two scientists who examined the infamous 'feather' and a witness to the whole episode.

"I cannot understand why he denied the eye-witness account at the conference in Salzburg. As you know, he has disappeared without trace. We suspect he has been abducted by the Eridanians. I have just received fresh news regarding the British scientist, Steven Bradley. Unfortunately, none of the MoD officials have been able to reach him. Police are now investigating his disappearance as well."

She then gave a blow-by-blow account of the Salzburg episode. She stressed the fact that not only she, but Saunders and I, had been present when the feather became operational and the repellent images of the 'devil' had appeared on the windowpane. She continued: "Any hope we had of stopping the danger threatening our planet have been utterly dashed for the moment. But an invisible shield has been devised to protect the people who are directly involved in combating the main players. This is by no means a solution to the problem. The American and British governments together with several agencies are working on how to tackle this enormous challenge."

"Needless to say, this is an ongoing project for NASA. The organisation, SETI (Search for Extraterrestrial Intelligence), continues its research. But most important of all, thirty-five of the thirty-six Chosen Few are trying very hard to establish telepathic communication with the Greys—another extraterrestrial civilisation—who seem to be our only hope of warding off this demonic force."

"One of the thirty-six I mentioned was murdered only last week, after Mr Clayton here, who is among the telepathic communicators, had asked her to try and make contact with the Greys. The remaining thirty-five are in grave danger. The policy of the MoD regarding this matter is deeply regrettable. While the world is moving step by step into the embrace of this evil force, the ministry officials treat it as a simple UFO case, and say that it has been brought to a close with the announcements of Dr Steven Bradley."

"This is indeed a most alarming situation and we have to try to convince the Ministry of the extreme danger we are all in. It is of the utmost importance that we have a united front. The US government is investigating the matter fully. This time, there will be no cover-up. We are also here to give the media the facts, and any member of the media who wishes it will have access to all the information available through our organisation."

"Sharing creative commonality with the media. The media will no doubt play an important role in unravelling the activities of not only the Eridanians, but also of those who have been recruited into the evil conspiracy which is spreading so rapidly throughout the world. The mood is positive, and we have made some strides towards containing the enemy. I am now asking the media to stop bickering with each other and allow these facts to rid them of the last remnants of doubt about extraterrestrial presence on earth. This campaign of incitement against us and against our organisation must stop. We have a tremendous spectrum to cover. The MoD is reneging on their previous promises. Indeed, they had promised to investigate the matter fully. Now they seem reluctant to turn up the heat."

"Now is the time to do just that. Security forces must be put on high alert. There is no other alternative explanation to what has been occurring over the last three weeks. We have reached a dramatic moment in the history of the human race on planet earth."

"We have no time for delay in this enormous struggle. I repeat once more: none of the events told here have been made up. Now, Mr Turan Akova who found the feather in North Cyprus will tell you how it all happened."

I did not want to repeat the same story twice, so I decided to make my speech as brief as I could.

"Emma Fitzgerald has given you a detailed account of the incident. More importantly, she has stressed how the action taken by the US and British and other governments must be co-ordinated, and without delay. The role of the media is equally important. Invisible shields will be available for those members of the media who will carry on with their investigative reporting. We need you."

"We must find the nerve centre of this demonic activity. We must not leave a stone unturned. That could be fatal. We hope to arrange a meeting with the governments concerned. UFO organisations, ufologists, NASA, SETI and all the thirty-five specially gifted people will participate. Naturally, a decision has to be taken at a very high level."

"I know you have many questions. Believe me, we have many questions too."

Saunders, the CIA Chief, did not want to speak at the conference, but he had prepared a report written especially for the media.

"Emma," I motioned her to the centre of the stage once more. "I believe it is question time."

"Yes," she said, looking into the audience, "number 89."

A tall, thin man rose from the ranks.

"Mr Akova," he addressed me. "Why did you pick up this feather-like object in the first place? If you hadn't come across this thing, would we still be in the same danger as we are now?"

"I found it in an area of North Cyprus called the Karpaz. It is a largely uninhabited place on the panhandle of the island. I have been researching UFOs for the past fifteen years. North Cyprus is a very small country. Nevertheless, there had already been some UFO sightings in the area I mentioned. So, I went there and by accident, I found the feather where a UFO had landed. I was reluctant to handle it at first as there are many examples of radioactive material left behind after UFO landings and departures. It was a peculiar object. When I touched it, I knew it was nothing to do with this earth. I put it in a metal box and contacted Emma immediately. As for your second question, yes. I think the feather was left behind for a purpose. Someone, somewhere would have activated it anyway. There have been several reports of the same feather-like objects found in other parts of the world."

Next, a young woman put up her hand: "Two questions. First about Ralph Turner and Steven Bradley, the two scientists. You say you witnessed their transformation via the red beams. But reports so far, following the press conference Bradley gave, have not in any way suggested that any dangerous rays were emitting from him. Why would he stop his recruitment activities at that moment? Or rather, why would he defy the orders given him from the Eridanians? My second question: you say the American scientist Ralph Turner was abducted. Now we hear of the disappearance of Bradley too…Why?"

"This is a mystery for us, also. But let us be thankful that Bradley is no longer active in recruiting people. The reason behind Bradley's move—I mean the press conference where he denied the whole incident and the fact that he did not use his power during or afterwards, points the finger of suspicion even more firmly at the Eridanians. This is speculative as we do not know what their strategy is exactly as far as the two scientists are concerned. For your second question, the answer is simply this: we have more or less conclusive evidence of Ralph Turner's abduction. As for Dr Bradley, yes, he has just disappeared and we suspect that he has been abducted as well, but in neither case do we know why."

A man in the front row, no. 56, put the next question.

"Mr Akova, we have no doubt now that you are telling the truth about the extraordinary episode in Salzburg. You have been kind enough to give the media the full text of your eye-witness accounts. My first question is that now we believe that the 'feather' is being kept under lock and key at the MoD, will the ministry or the government decide to operate the feather once again, so that we can all see the face of the devil? My second question is about the Greys. It is very difficult for anyone to believe that there are thirty-five Chosen Ones who are able to establish telepathic communication with this other extraterrestrial civilisation. Can you prove this communication? And how do you know the so-called Greys will help?"

"The decision to operate the feather once again rests solely with the MoD itself. I believe it can be done. But we must take extreme precautions. Previous contact with the Greys has proved that they are trying to help the human race. Reports of contact by some of the Chosen Ones will be distributed to the media in the next few days."

No. 97, a female journalist commented: "Surely up until now, we have Bradley's word against yours. First of all, Bradley did not deny the incident at the Chateau in Salzburg. In fact, he said contact had been made. But he denied the bit about the red beams. He said there was no such thing. Furthermore, he said there was no such plan on the part of the Eridanians to conquer the world. His actual response to the red beam story was: 'a science fiction story...' We want proof, Mr Akova. So far, you have given us eye-witness accounts of the incident. This is no more than an eye-witness account of an ordinary UFO sighting. Your comments, please."

"What we have given you is much more than an eye-witness account. We have one hundred percent proof which is elaborately described in the text we have given out. Furthermore, we have a murder on our hands, the murder of a Spanish girl who had been in contact with the Greys. Then we have the feather which became operational at the Chateau and we witnessed the whole thing. True, Bradley does not deny what happened at the Chateau, but he does deny the existence of the red beams. Well, we will have proof of that, too, which will be available to the media within the next few days..."

Questions came from left, right and centre, and the press conference lasted more than three hours, including lunch. Conversations with members of the media later on were a major boost to our morale as they seemed to believe the whole story.

I had been hoping for an international outcry after the full coverage of the press conference. The MoD had to act now to get the ball rolling. Sometimes I wondered whether it had been wise to hand the feather over to the British. But Emma was British and she was probably the single most important figure in the world of ufologists. Perhaps a meeting with Lord Wetherby—a friend of the family—would accelerate things and the whole affair would gather fresh impetus in the coming days. It was a lengthy process. But I was single-minded and tried every available channel in my efforts to diminish the threat to the human race. Attack is the best form of defence, I always say; that's how you move things on. When I called Lord Wetherby, his personal secretary, Miss Tibbs, answered.

"Lord Wetherby's residence," sang out a melodious voice at the other end.

"Hello, Linda, this is Turan Akova."

"You don't need to tell me who you are, Turan. I recognise your voice," she replied.

"But we haven't spoken in months," I countered.

"Nonetheless, your voice is unique." Linda was one of the prettiest girls I had met in the UK for months. That may seem a passing comment, but it was actually true.

Eight

Lord Wetherby's London house was in the Bishop's Avenue, right next to the mansion that once belonged to Elizabeth Taylor. His daughter Susan was an old flame, who could become flammable at the slightest touch. She was the embodiment of sexiness loaded with affection.

I brought the car to a halt in front of the large iron gate. There were pine trees on both sides of the road leading up to the enormous mansion. His Lordship had been kind enough to ask me to visit him at the mansion.

"Lord Wetherby is expecting me," I told the man at the gate. He nodded and went back into the small room inside the gatehouse. Two minutes later, the fifteen-foot high gate opened by itself. I drove in, with a wave of thanks to the doorman. The mansion itself was surrounded by a lawn, rolled and watered. This was the first time I had seen the mansion in the daylight. We had had our little escapades in the past, Susan and I, but they had been at night.

I parked the car by the flight of steps leading up to the door. James, the butler, had become a family fixture after thirty years of service. He greeted me with a smile: "How nice to see you again, Mr Akova."

"Nice to see you, too, James," I replied.

"Sir John is waiting for you in the study," he told me as he led the way through the hall and into the study. I was surprised to see another man sitting in the study next to Sir John.

"Turan," Sir John exclaimed, rising from his armchair. "Here is the Turk who came in from the heat," he said, addressing the man sitting opposite. Turning back to me, he chuckled: "What mischief have you been getting yourself into, lately? The extraterrestrials are here to recruit us all? Heavens! What's happening, Turan? You are in the papers once again as the UFO researcher." He then introduced me to the person sitting beside him.

"Lord Fairfax, this is Turan Akova, the world-renowned Turkish Cypriot pianist/composer, amongst other things."

"How do you do?" I gave a slight bow.

"How are you, Mr Akova? Sir John mentioned your name the other day."

I had been hoping to speak to Sir John alone. Lord Fairfax must have sensed my feeling about his presence for he then announced his departure: "I was just leaving. I suppose you want to have a private talk with Sir John." He took a few steps towards the door of the enormous study.

"Nonsense! We have no secrets," protested Lord Wetherby lightly, but he knew I wanted a confidential conversation with him.

Lord Fairfax left and Sir John asked James to bring us coffee. When it was poured, James quietly left us to ourselves, alone at long last. I told Lord Wetherby the whole story.

"Good grief, Turan! This is a most alarming situation!" he exclaimed.

"It is, and I need your help. You know the British government has been somewhat reluctant to act on this matter. I think that as they are holding on to the feather at the MoD, they must act now. First of all, centres should be established in different areas to report any sort of extraterrestrial presence. Secondly, security measures must be taken to tackle the red beams."

"But you say there are a very limited number of shields to protect the people," pointed out Sir John with a heightening sense of anxiety. "How do you propose to protect ordinary people from this danger?"

There was no answer to this question. "I don't know. But the extraterrestrial danger thrives and officialdom within the British government and especially within the ranks of the Defence Ministry are treating this case as a usual fabricated UFO case."

Lord Wetherby was a popular and flamboyant character in the House of Lords. People would listen to him, I was pretty sure of it. "Perhaps you could draft a word of advice, to be presented to the Lords and later in the House of Commons."

"Yes, I see," he replied, "then let me have your reports on the case. I'll prepare a draft from them."

"Sir John, you could suggest the establishment of a Committee of UFO research. But we would have to be prepared to entrust such a committee with unprecedented and far-reaching power."

"Hmm…Definitely…" he responded thoughtfully.

I called Emma and asked her to e-mail all the reports to Sir John. Lord Wetherby had been a close friend of my late father. He was a patron of the arts and had sponsored several of my concerts in the UK. He had undertaken many musical projects and had financed many cultural exchange programmes with Turkey and the Turkish Republic of Northern Cyprus. His wife was charming and an equally memorable character who would preside over the cultural activities of his Lordship with tact. He was a supporter of artistic musical talent in both countries. He was also a smooth-talking, larger-than-life politician. I admired his energy, his know-how, enthusiasm, eloquence, and most of all, his inimitable, aristocratic touch.

Susan was the model of her father. As James walked me to the door, at my departure, Susan called out from the stairs: "You were leaving without seeing me?"

"I had to discuss something important with your father and I didn't know you were at home."

She rushed down while James, who knew of our close friendship, took leave of me with a wink. Seconds later she was in my arms, kissing me. "Where have you been all this time?" She held me tightly and wouldn't let go. "You know I love you," she whispered. She was intensely emotional; the epitome of the art of seduction.

"Susan, I love you, too. But I've been very busy. As you probably know…" She did not let me finish. "I know! I know!" she exclaimed impatiently. "You are one of the key figures in this extraterrestrial thing. But please find time in between to come and visit me," she pleaded passionately. "Promise me you will."

"All right," I sighed, "I promise."

During the next few days there were masses of banner headlines, and exclusive interviews with Emma, Saunders, Clayton and me, in all the newspapers across the UK. We had to put in appearances on all the TV channels. The UK media was debating the most important event in the history of mankind. Some journalists claimed the MoD was on the slippery slope to disaster with the evasion of the matter at hand, and they demanded an immediate change of policy. Our press conference had been a huge success and had received worldwide coverage through the press agencies, and through TV channels in many other countries. Overwhelming evidence of extraterrestrial presence on earth was the key factor in this astounding, significant development. There were no more secrets, no more conspiracies or cover-ups. The major part of the scientific community appeared to be giving us its full support. It was a truly historic occasion.

The timing of the presentation of Lord Wetherby's report in Parliament was perfect. With Lord Wetherby's brilliant tour de force, something of a political taboo had been broken in both the Houses. A committee was formed to discuss it further and it was just a matter of time before Parliament voted to back the policy endorsed by Lord Wetherby. As I had predicted, Parliament voted overwhelmingly the next day to coordinate a research programme by the Committee of UFOs and the MoD. A course of action would be taken in cooperation with the US government. Lord Wetherby, Susan and the committee of fifteen members—a joint committee from the Lords and the Commons—were given shields to protect them from any immediate danger. The worst part of it all was that no one knew from where the danger would spring next, and no one would even dare to guess the level of power and influence the extraterrestrials would have on humans.

Nine

My next mission was to find Bradley. He had disappeared soon after Ralph Turner's abduction. Emma and the others suspected another abduction. But I had a feeling he was in hiding somewhere in London. My first call was at his home in St John's Wood. He too had been under house arrest immediately after his return to the UK. But he had somehow managed to escape the Scotland Yard net surrounding his house. At least, that's what I was told at the Scotland Yard headquarters.

I operated the shield and rang the bell next to an imposing wooden door in the middle of a ten-foot high wall. I could barely hear the bell ringing in the house. The door opened slowly with a creak. A medium-height man with a round face stood in the doorway, staring at me.

"Yes?" his tone was abrupt and ill-mannered.

"My name is Turan Akova. I'm here to see Mrs Bradley," I said, forcing a polite smile.

"One moment," he muttered, expressionless, and shut the door in my face. I waited for about five minutes before it was opened again.

"Follow me," he ordered, as I stepped inside. He led the way with inappropriate haste through a bushy garden. The asphalt path led to a large glass door. Sliding it open, he pointed to an armchair in a large room adorned with Victorian furniture and large paintings on the walls. I recognised Grandma Moses' 'A Beautiful World' on the right above the large fireplace. Her primitive style never failed to captivate me. It was no wonder her popularity continued undiminished in the States, I thought. They even celebrated her birthday every year on 7 September in New York State. This painting reminded me of Whitby in Yorkshire—Dracula country—where an English artist had once introduced me to her.

A thin, good-looking woman, probably in her early fifties, appeared in the doorway on the other side of the sitting room. She looked pale. Her voice exuded remorse, and although she appeared calm and composed, she seemed to be paralysed with grief.

"Please, sit down, Mr Akova," she said finally, taking a few steps in my direction. She turned to the man who had opened the door for me: "Tea, Fletcher," she ordered, and turned back to me: "Would you like some tea, Mr Akova?"

"Yes. Tea's fine," I nodded.

She sat in an armchair opposite me. My first impression of Mrs Bradley was that she was a strange woman. Her eyes were wide open and unblinking. "What can I do for you?" she asked quietly.

"You know why I am here," I ventured.

"Yes, I have a rough idea." Her voice was now becoming tenser by the second, "You are here to ask about my husband's whereabouts."

"We want to help him, Mrs Bradley. As you know, he was the victim of an evil extraterrestrial force. We can help him only if we find him and protect him from this force."

She was clearly exasperated and tried to hide her anger. "It is because of you and your friends that my husband is in a state of total panic." It seemed as though she had a personal grudge against me for some reason. I could understand her predicament. The daunting reality of her husband's condition explained her acrimonious behaviour, and I sympathised with her.

"Yes. I do understand," I said. "But we had no idea the material or feather would produce such devastating results."

She hesitated for a moment and replied with a stronger tone: "I am sure you're right, Mr Akova. But I cannot help you."

"Why not?" I had to ask.

"My husband left the house two days ago with a friend. He said he would contact me. But I have not heard from him since then. I have no idea where he is."

This meant that Steven Bradley had not been abducted after all. Despite this good news, I was severely disappointed.

"Who was the friend?"

"I do not know him well, but he's from the MoD. I think his surname is Giles; I don't know his Christian name."

This man Giles would be my only lead for the time being. "Could you please describe him?"

Mrs Bradley appeared to be more cooperative, but she was still highly emotional: "Thin man, about your height, with glasses."

I asked whether she could remember anything else that might help with my investigation. She thought for a moment and then placed the cup she was holding on the small table between us.

"Yes, there is. I was in the adjoining room when they were conversing just before leaving the house. Yes, yes, I remember overhearing Giles telling my husband that everything would be OK and that he would be under their protection. It seemed as though there was an extraordinary bond between them."

"Why do you think they were so close, Mrs Bradley? I mean, what gave you that impression?"

"It was unusual behaviour on the part of my husband," she remarked thoughtfully. "Mr Akova, my husband has a mind of his own; he has always been an independent person. But with this person, he seemed obedient, submissive even. He deferred to everything Mr Giles said."

"Can you remember anything else? Anything at all as to where they were going?" When I asked this last question, she covered her face with her hands, trying to remember. Then she raised her head with a bemused expression and suddenly frantic, she pointed her finger upward and cried: "Yes, yes I remember now! Giles mentioned the town of Loo in Cornwall. I can't say for sure whether they intended to go there as I didn't hear the end of the conversation."

"Mrs Bradley, I will need a recent photo of your husband. We have to find him and furnish him with the special shield. This is absolutely necessary for his protection. As you know, he was taken over once, and we do not yet know how to erase the extraterrestrial influence on the human brain and in the soul. But scientists are working on it."

I did not want to mention the thirty-five Chosen Ones as almost everyone found it hard to believe that these people were communicating with the Greys. Clayton had asked the Greys this specific question: "How do we erase the red beam from people who have already been mesmerised?" I knew Mrs Bradley would brush aside such fantastic claims. She went upstairs and came down with a photo of her husband. She also gave me a card with their names, address and a telephone number.

"Mr Akova, please call me as soon as you find Steven."

I promised her I would, and left.

The night was very still as I walked towards my Daimler-Sovereign 4.2. It was fairly cold for a November evening. Suddenly I saw two men sitting in a white Rover at the other end of the road. I drove towards Swiss Cottage and then turned back into Mrs Bradley's street. I stopped beside the house. The white Rover passed me and then came to a stop in exactly the same spot as before. I put Stravinsky's Rite of Spring in the CD player and lit a cigarette. I waited for about five minutes and then drove past the white Rover once again in the direction of Swiss Cottage. They followed me.

When I had parked the car outside my house, I called my friend Inspector Mullery at New Scotland Yard.

"Hello, Jim. It's Turan Akova. A white Rover with a registration number of RYG 3498 HLS is parked fifty metres from my house in Charles Street. It's been following me. I'd very much appreciate it if you would apprehend the two men inside and find out who they are and what they want."

"Will do, Mr Akova. I'll call you back."

I entered the house, hurried upstairs and peeked through the curtains of the window overlooking the street. Within fifteen minutes, two cars coming from opposite directions closed in on the Rover. Two plain-clothed policemen got out of each car and approached the Rover. They talked for a minute or two to the occupants, and then the two police cars drove away. Half an hour later, Jim Mullery called.

"Mr Akova, the two men in the white Rover are MI5. They have been instructed to follow you wherever you go for your own protection," he said. I thanked him and hung up. I then called the MI5 chief Sir Michael Pearson and asked him to call his men off.

"I don't need any protection. Believe me, it will only complicate matters."

"OK, Mr Akova," he agreed reluctantly, but added. "Call me if you do need any help, though."

The next morning, Lord Wetherby was catapulted into the post of Chairman of the UFO Research Committees of both the Houses of Parliament. Sir John protested that there had been a lot of backroom dealing, but everyone urged him to take the chair. He said there were several MPs who rebutted the idea but eventually agreed to further investigate the matter.

Emma was in her own house preparing reports for the committee. Clayton, on the other hand, stayed home concentrating on telepathic communication with the Greys. The CIA man, Saunders, coordinated a joint action team with MI5 to stop the spread of extraterrestrial red beams. The whole operation was in full swing to stop the Eridanian danger. How on earth they would do it, I had no idea. The Greys' intervention was my only hope. Nevertheless, the security of the operation could not be jeopardised by the action of any single person.

Now we had unlimited, unrestricted absolute power in the history of UFO research with the full backing of the US and UK governments. It was a story situation with the public at large panicking at times. After all, the extraterrestrial presence was no longer a figment of the imagination but a substantial fact. The formation of the UFO Research Committee headed by Lord Wetherby was a welcome relief. The ufological rhetoric made its mark and there was now a growing impatience among the leaders of the two countries—the USA and the UK. The staunchest allies of these two countries worked overtime putting pressure on their own governments to investigate the matter. The military-technological ability of the US and the UK had been put to the test. It seemed as though the devastating news of extraterrestrial presence had somehow united the fractured, hopelessly divided international community and had prepared them for the difficult days ahead.

Ten

I boarded the train from Paddington Station for Loo in Cornwall. The only clue to the whereabouts of Bradley was this small picturesque town in Cornwall; there was East Loo and West Loo. I had been there once before years ago with a girlfriend and had stayed at her house. At the time, I did not see much of the town as we stayed indoors almost all day and night. I did not have to book a room at the town's most prestigious hotel in West Loo at this time of the year. Nevertheless, the hotel seemed to be almost full and I counted myself lucky to have found a room there.

The Samuelson Hotel was a large family-run hotel by the seaside in West Loo. I arrived in the town at around 1 o'clock, had lunch in the hotel's restaurant and then bought a booklet listing all the hotels and guest houses in Loo. There were about twelve in all. I did not know Bradley very well, but as far as I could gather from his close friends in the scientific community, he was loved and loathed in equal measures. Loved, because he was a good-humoured man, always helping young and talented scientists in his field of research—Space Research; loathed because he was peculiarly undiplomatic, as he could sever his relations with people at the smallest pretext and for no apparent reason.

Who was this Giles character? And why would he bring Bradley to Loo, of all places? I found my head turning with the same questions, and my lack of sleep over the previous few days did not help. So I was happy to retire to the large, comfortable bed in my room, where I soon became oblivious to the world. It was after half-past six in the evening when I finally awoke. I took a quick shower and decided to start my investigation with the hotel itself. There were a man and a woman at the reception desk. The man was busy registering a young couple, but the woman, bespectacled but gratifyingly shapely, smiled as I approached the desk. "Can I help you, sir?" she asked, as I put my hand inside the breast pocket of my jacket and drew out a photo of Bradley.

"I certainly hope so," I replied, leaning on the desk. "I am looking for this man. Is he staying in the hotel?" She took the photo from me and looked at it carefully.

"No," she said, and then raised an eyebrow at me, "are you with the police? What has he done?"

"I am with the UFO Research Organisation," I told her.

"Really? Is this about the stories we have been reading in the papers? Yes, I remember now. You were on television talking about the extraterrestrial presence."

I was surprised to hear her talk about the extraterrestrials coming from the star system Epsilon Eridani. Our press conference at the Hilton the other day must have been very successful. A person in a small town in Cornwall was well aware of the danger threatening humans all over the country.

"Yes, that was me," I said emphatically. "That's the story. I think he's been abducted."

"Abducted by aliens, eh?" She seemed more interested.

"No, not by aliens, but by another person who is working for the aliens," I said.

"This is becoming more interesting by the minute. Now you are saying that there are people who work for the space people." At this point, she seemed to treat the whole affair lightly, I was not going to give her a lecture on UFOs. Nor did I intend to start sifting facts from fiction.

"Where shall I look for him?" I asked her. "What is the most popular place here where everybody goes?"

"I suggest you try The Blue Moon pub about a mile from here to the west," she told me.

The night was very still. I decided to walk to the pub. I always walked on the right-hand side of the road, otherwise in a country like Britain, you would run the risk of being run over by a car coming from behind you. I had walked about a hundred metres when a white Rover passed me by. It was the same white Rover I had seen near the Bradley residence in London. Despite my request to the Chief of MI5 to stop his agents from following me, these two men were still on my trail.

I had no doubt in my mind that these two men in the white Rover were agents of the Eridanians. The Blue Moon was a large Victorian mansion standing on its own on a small hill. It was about seven-thirty and the place was packed. I entered through the large door and walked up to the wide bar in front of me. The pretty barmaid smiled when I planted myself comfortably on a stool.

"What would you like, sir?"

"A bottle of lager, please. I shall pour it myself."

"Of course," she replied, handing me a bottle of Carlsberg and an empty glass.

"Can I offer you a drink?" I asked her. I love to make new friends.

"I'll have the same." She must have been in her late twenties, with curly, light brown hair and large blue eyes. She was wearing a light blue blouse and tight trousers.

"I'm looking for someone. But before you ask me the same question that greets me everywhere I go, no, I am not a policeman. I am a member of the UFO Research Organisation. It is of vital importance that I find this man." I took out the photo of Bradley again and handed it over to her. "And your name is…?" I hinted, not very subtly.

"Gertrude," she murmured as she examined the photo. She looked up at me, "I am not sure," she replied, "the face seems familiar, but you must admit it is quite an ordinary one. And there are hundreds of people coming in here and going out."

"OK, Gertrude. Let me give you a copy of this photo. Here is my telephone number at the hotel where I am staying, and this is my mobile number. Please, give me a call if you see this man. Remember, he will be accompanied by another man."

"Come back around eleven o'clock, when I finish," she told me. "I may have something for you by then." She had been very helpful, so I thanked her and left the pub.

Emma's UFO Research Organisation kept receiving reports from the CIA, MI5 and all the other agencies in other countries investigating extraterrestrial presence. Some of the most startling of these documents simply outlined the fact that human technology was not up to the task yet of stopping the onslaught by the Eridanians. Scientists in the USA, Britain, Germany, Japan and Turkey were working incessantly to formulate a deterrent against the extraterrestrial presence. Exposure to the energy fields of UFOs UFO beings and their red rays simply meant unavoidable wholesale recruitment into their number.

I visited four more hotels and guest houses in West and East Loo during that same evening and left copies of Bradley's photo at each location. It was a painstaking business. When I finally turned my steps back towards the Blue Moon at closing time, I replayed in my head the inviting looks of Gertrude. I was powerless to resist the urge to meet and spend time with her. The pub was on the outskirts of West Loo. Beyond the small hill where the building stood, I could just see a field leading out of the inhabited area of the town.

Suddenly, the street lights and the lights in all the town went off. I was shrouded in darkness. I pulled out my gun—courtesy of MI5—and held my torch in my left hand. I ran towards the rear of the pub as there was a very bright light descending onto the field. Amazing! Unbelievable! But there it was! An extraordinary UFO of large dimensions hovered about ten feet above the ground. I stood motionless. To my left, about fifty feet away stood the two men. I sprang towards them with my torchlight illuminating the area on the left-hand side of the field.

Then I stopped. The two men were not moving a muscle. A very bright, white light from the UFO appeared to have paralysed them, and they stood motionless as statues. Minutes later, a strange figure appeared through the mist. A four-foot-tall UFO being very similar to both bodily and facial structure of the Greys began to communicate to me. "God almighty! The Greys have arrived!" I thought. And I was right. Suddenly my brain was filled with the message emanating from the small figure beside the UFO.

"You are now one of the 36 Chosen Few," was the first message. Then it continued. I was now experiencing the most stunning, breathtaking moment of my life. The telepathic communication surged through my brain cells: "We are here to protect you. The Eridanian danger is being thwarted all over Planet Earth. Bradley is in your hotel, in Room 368. The man with him is Eridanian-controlled. But you and the other 35 Chosen Few now have special powers. Do not be afraid to challenge the Eridanians. Return to the hotel. You will be able to save Bradley. We will contact you again soon."

That evening, everything changed for me; my whole life changed. I had no idea how I was fully equipped with special powers nor how to use them. My telepathic communication with the UFO being had been one of active enjoyment. It had been a remarkable few minutes with illuminating thoughts of jumping into a universal realm. I felt a cold chill. I was speechless. It had been overwhelming. I was no longer a man solely belonging to Planet Earth. It was as if I had been transformed into a human being who both lived on Earth and also in outer space. The joy and thrill of becoming a Chosen One was distinctly supernatural. Red, yellow and white lights sent out images through my brain. My soul had reached the highest level of ecstasy. No, this was not a dream.

The mysterious and startlingly frightening figure disappeared with a very bright light emanating from the bottom of the UFO which sucked it back into the craft. The two men from the white Rover ran in despair down the hill towards the road. As the mothership glided over the crest of the hill, I felt a sudden short twinge. It was as if part of me had flown out into the depths of outer space together with the UFO. But the divine quality of the power I now possessed was so great that it dwarfed any unnatural, negative elements deriving from the chastely and yet enormously manipulative experience of universal observation of extraterrestrial sources. It was like a major metaphysical miraculous act.

The mothership shot up into the night sky probably exceeding the speed of light. Within seconds, it looked like a small star in the heavens. Then it disappeared…I stood motionless for a few minutes and tried to re-live the eerie and yet exuberant manifestation. I walked back to the pub, where, oblivious to the enticing Gertrude, I downed a bottle of lager and headed back to the hotel. No one had seen the incident except the two men from the white Rover. But they had been paralysed at the precise moment of contact with the extraterrestrial.

This time around, the hotel lobby was full of Swedish tourists. I took the lift to the top floor and slowly walked along the carpeted corridor: number 374, 365, 366 and 367…and finally, there it was, room number 368. The door was locked from the inside. I tried to open it again. I honestly do not know how it happened, but this time it opened and I entered the room. Two men sat beside the window, one of them was Bradley. The other man, Giles, set his red eyes on me with an evil blight. The red ray hit the shield and evaporated…he was furious, and let out a shriek, coming at me with fists flying. I hit him twice. He staggered and fell. He was now crying like a stricken animal and fell into the armchair beside him. He rolled his eyes…no more red rays. He was pale and anguished, while Bradley looked on with expressionless eyes.

Giles rushed from the room. In a similar manner to that I had witnessed earlier with the two men from the white Rover, he seemed helpless in the face of total defeat. Bradley slowly rose from the armchair and looked at me. He was in a state of shock. Later, he felt more relaxed.

"Thank you, Mr Akova," he said, appearing to have regained his normal mental faculties. "I suppose I am back to being a normal person, aren't I, Mr Akova?"

It was a moot question. But somehow an unknown force wiped out any prevailing uncertainty. "Yes, you are back to normal, Mr Bradley," I reassured him, as we walked to the door. "I will now take you home."

The event of that evening and the subsequent happenings could not be explained rationally. We had something in common, Bradley and I. He had been recruited into the Eridanian numbers, while I had become a Chosen One of the Greys. We had both achieved the capacity to perceive things from an alien perspective. Obviously, the Greys seemed to be much more powerful than the evil forces of Eridanus as I had already eliminated the challenges of the two men from the white Rover and Giles, too.

We went into my room. This was a luxury suite with a bedroom and a spacious sitting room. "Take a rest for an hour or so, while I make my phone calls, Mr Bradley. Then we'll take the night train to London."

"I'm grateful for all you have done, Mr Akova. Believe me, I will do everything I can to help you." I am sure he now felt rather belligerent. Seconds later, he was huddled up on the bed and closed his eyes.

Both Emma and Clayton were jubilant on hearing the news of my encounter with the UFO. I am sure becoming a Chosen One was a special privilege. I told them of the fascinating enigmatic spectacle descending from the night sky right in front of me/ It was a weird phenomenon but a wonderful experience.

"You could not gaze at the very bright light too long," I explained to Emma, "If you did, it would blind your vision." Clayton, one of the most important UFO experts in the world had been one of the Chosen Few for some years now. He was not a UFO buff. He was the most outspoken, most trusted and best-known scientific ufologist in the world.

"I am very happy for you, Turan," he said in a cool, calm unpretentious manner. "Now you have the power, too."

At first, I did not know what to make of that comment. It is true I had lived through a powerfully pleasant experience that abhorred all leanings towards any sort of psychological interpretation. I felt stronger and healthier. No man on earth could challenge the now inbuilt strength in me.

More important than my conversion into a Chosen One was the intervention of the Greys to fight off and wipe out the Eridanian plan to conquer planet Earth. At long last, they had delivered a message confirming their involvement. From what I gathered from their message, this was a triple force, a massive Grey force coming from the star system Alpha Centauri—a triple star system a mere 4.3

light-years away (25 million miles from our solar system). This star system has two main components—Alpha Centauri A and Alpha Centauri B. The former is brighter and is similar to our sun in respect of size, mass, temperature, and luminosity. Alpha Centauri is slightly larger but fainter, cooler and less massive. The third component has always been something of an enigma. This is the component that lies nearest to us, just 4.0 light-years away. This is Proxima Centauri.

Tau Ceti is 11.6 light-years from our solar system and one of the most favourable stars as far as interstellar communication is concerned. The third-star system was Zeta Reticuli, 37 light-years away from Earth. Now, by some inexplicable mysterious force, I had the knowledge, knowledge of Greys coming from these three star systems. I then called Sanders, the CIA man, and through him, passed on the news of contact with the Greys which we so eagerly awaited. He channelled through the information to NASA, SETI and of course the National Security Agency.

There was a train leaving Loo for London at 11.15 pm. Bradley was ready to go home. The streets of West Loo were deserted as we headed for Bradley's rented car. I drove out of the parking lot and we were now on our way towards East Loo strain station. Suddenly, I saw a bright light in front of us. A saucer-shaped craft moved to our right. I became aware of voices coming from the hovering UFO. I kept stamping on the accelerator, but the car wouldn't move...The UFO became visible in the street light. Two UFOs in one night...This was a saucer-shaped craft but it looked different from the Greys' UFO. The craft in front of us hovering about ten feet from the ground had a smaller dome and was thirty feet in diameter.

Eleven

Bradley was trembling: "It's them. They are here to take me…" he whispered nervously. "Please, Mr Akova. Don't let them take me away…"

"The seat belt. Fasten your seat belt. NOW!" I shouted and got out of the car. Bradley was a bundle of nerves. I helped him strap the belt. "Now lock the doors." Just then, I remembered the message I had received from the Grey being during our short encounter: "Do not be afraid; challenge them." I was now in front of the car facing this curious inexplicable phenomenon. The wildest fantasy of a writer with an extremely original imagination could never have dreamed up two UFO encounters in one night. Now, I was up against the evil force of the Eridanians for the first time.

Suddenly, a very bright light from the bottom of the UFO pierced the asphalt about twenty feet from where I was standing. A willowy figure, tall, lithe and slender appeared before me. I could hear an unpleasant grating sound like the rasp of a saw on wood. Then a fricative sound coming from the thin line which looked like the mouth of the creature. The creature looked like a woman. The figure changed into the most beautiful woman I had ever seen. She was stark naked. This was a woman, a real, down-to-earth, beautiful woman touching her pubic hair. Then she started performing all sorts of erotic but scabrous acts with different parts of her body. It was like an indecent, obscene show. She wielded the paddle herself.

"Don't, Turan," I told myself. The temptation was devastatingly perilous. At first, I thought I would succumb to this devilishly attractive woman. But this was not real. This was a game of the devil. Although I must admit, I was pitching the idea of having sex with this pretty, pretty woman.

Within minutes, the mothership of the Greys appeared on the horizon. It was unbelievable. One thing stuck in my mind. It was as if I was now seeing things from the right perspective. I was sure this was the correct assessment. An inescapable corollary, a natural consequence or result. Then all hell broke loose as the mothership of the Greys fired their extraterrestrial weaponry onto the Eridanian UFO. The figure, which had become the most attractively sexy woman on Earth disappeared. Within a minute, the Eridanian UFO vanished from the face of the earth. Pieces of unknown metal cluttered the road. I just stood there, incredulous. A third UFO encounter in one night. This must be a record, I thought.

The mothership flew up into the night sky. I walked back to the car. Bradley has remained strapped in his seat.

"Are you OK?"

He shrugged. Under tremendous shock, he was a total stranger to empathy. I parked the hired car near the train station and telephoned the hiring company to collect it. The train to London was on time. We sat in a first-class compartment and I ordered whisky. I decided to keep quiet about the three UFO encounters in Loo. The fact that contact had been made with the Greys and that this particular extraterrestrial civilisation would challenge the Eridanian threat was of the utmost importance. I had to discuss this matter with Emma, Clayton, Saunders of the CIA and of course, with the British and American governments…before divulging the whole story to the media. My becoming a Chosen One was personal, but nevertheless an important development. Bradley breathed huskily while he downed his third whisky, "I feel much better now, Mr Akova," he told me.

"Let me tell you something, Mr Bradley. First thing tomorrow, I shall have someone bring you and your wife two shields to protect you from the red rays. Remember one thing. Do not be afraid to challenge them. As soon as they know they cannot touch you, they will disappear."

When we reached Paddington Station, we found London dreary and wet. We took a taxi to Bradley's residence in St John's Wood. Bradley's pathetic superstitions now gave way to a zeal to understand others and the developments around him. He made comments unwittingly and he no longer seemed perplexed.

Mrs Bradley greeted us at the door herself. She was wide-eyed with disbelief and responded with a big smile to her husband's hug. I told them a man would come to the house later to bring the shields and instruct them. I left them encapsulated in their own affairs and headed home in another taxi.

I had a late breakfast and then retired for my 'beauty sleep'. I slept for at least three hours, and awoke at ten past seven in the evening. My inner energy was now fully restored. Earlier I had asked Emma and Eric Clayton to come up to the house. A meeting was essential. So far, the information gleaned from contacts around the world illuminated the paradoxes in relation to the disappearance of the two scientists. There was no word of any Grey contact. They had contacted me first and I had become a Chosen One.

Music is my life. Ever since my first touch of the piano, I had studied music and pianoforte with my mother who was the most famous music and piano teacher on the island. I started composing at the age of seven. Over the years after my musical career had taken off in London with two albums, I had earned a reputation, performing only my own compositions and arrangements. It is interesting to note that one category of music among my compositions was dedicated entirely to extraterrestrial civilisation on other star systems.

I realised that I had not practised for at least two days. Two days of no practice is a long time for a professional pianist. My Bosendorfer grand sat in the corner of the large living room like a swooningly rapturous beauty. I started playing the intro to my third piano concerto. I had been inspired to compose the intro and main theme during a thunderous rainy day. This was six months ago. Then it stopped. The stimulation of the soul for that particular work was no longer there. Never in my whole life did I lack the creative ability to compose. But I always felt the third piano concerto would be a masterpiece. A masterpiece on its own demanding a high level of virtuosity and extraordinary techniques. I played the intro again and again. Then the main theme. No…nothing came…I had been expecting an inspiration to enter my hands and fingers and rejuvenate everything from scratch. But it did not happen. It was as if something somewhere had blocked the flow of a bright new beginning. A solemn and emotional situation. As I played the intro and the main theme yet again, the doorbell rang.

I opened the door. Emma looked gleefully happy. Her big doe-eyes reverberated our intense romantic relationship. She put her arms around my neck and kissed me.

"Turan," she gasped, "you are a Chosen One."

"It was unbelievable. But let's wait for Eric so that I don't have to tell the whole story twice."

Minutes later, Eric arrived. He was equally excited and couldn't wait to hear the full story of my experiences in Cornwall. He had been a Chosen One for some years now and he would be able to understand more than anyone the complicated process of the transformation which embodied those special powers which not only prompted telepathic communication with the Greys but which also forged instructive, fundamentally virile and mysteriously invisible faculties thrashing thoroughly the evil Eridanian forces. *What a way to be,* I thought to myself. When I recounted the three UFO encounters in West Loo, Eric was astounded.

"Turan, this must be the most dramatic experience of your life! But let me tell you this much. Your experience is formidable compared with that of the other 35 Chosen Ones."

Eric Clayton was amiable and laid back. His interpretation had somehow elevated me to a higher level than the other 35. Nevertheless, I did not know whether this was good or bad. But one thing was certain. My positive energies and my positive side were formidable. Therefore the events of that historic evening at West Loo on 28 November epitomised a sort of recharging of an unknown, lethal power which made me acutely aware of the seemingly insurmountable task ahead of us. That power was to be put to the test.

"I suggest we keep quiet about my three encounters in Loo. I'm talking about the media. Of course, we have to tell them that contact has been established with the Greys. I think a full report of the events in Loo should be submitted to the British and American governments. What do you think?"

"The media will want the full story of your contact. Write your reports and we'll forward them to the British and Americans." Emma responded.

Eric walked towards the fireplace. "The fact that contact has been established would put serious pressure on both governments. Well, I hope so, at least. You see, I'm certain that both countries have secret sophisticated weapons. But the crux of the matter is that they will never be able to use them as the adversary is neither here nor there. On the other hand, I believe that the Eridanians have a base somewhere on earth. Maybe three or four bases. How we locate them, I have no idea. I think our best bet would be to try and make contact with the Greys as soon as possible. All the 26 Chosen Ones must ask the same question simultaneously via telepathic communication, the question must be: where are the bases of the Eridanians on Earth?"

Eric paused for a moment and continued: "Turan, this is not the only issue left unresolved. Not one single report has yet emerged from any of the UFO centres throughout the world telling us of any Eridanian contact. We don't have a clue as to the numbers of people transformed into the Eridanian camp. You said yourself that the two men in the white Rover were MI5 agents. This means that even MI5 has been infiltrated. I'm sure there are scores of people throughout the world secretly implementing their sinister plan. I'm afraid there is no prospect of our finding each and every single human being transformed by the Eridanians for the time being. The problem is immense and irregular."

"OK. Let's give the media the full details of my contact with the Greys. I'll write the report tonight for the British and American governments. My third and last point: as you say, Eric, let's arrange a meeting with the 36, ourselves included, and send out a message asking for the location of Eridanian bases on Earth."

So. Now our course of action was threefold:

- To inform the media of my contact with the Greys;
- A fill report of the events at West Loo to be submitted to the British and American governments; and
- To arrange a meeting with the 36 chosen Ones, to convey a message via telepathic communication to the Greys asking them for the locations of the Eridanian bases on Earth.

We were having coffee when the doorbell rang. I opened it, and there she was: a beautiful young girl, beaming with excitement.

"Mr Akova," she said, before I could utter a word, "my name is Jill Evans. Jill with a J. I am a freelance journalist and I also write for the Evening Star. I was at your last concert in the Purcell Room. I was absolutely mesmerised by your music and I am dying to hear you again. I would like to do an interview about you and your music."

"Come in," I said, "take off your coat. We were just having coffee. I will introduce you to Emma and Eric Clayton."

"Mr Akova, before I come in, let me tell you about my second request. A friend who happened to be at the pub in West Loo actually witnessed your encounter with the UFOs, She telephoned me, to let me know. So I thought, perhaps, I could interview you on that subject too…"

"By all means," I grabbed her hand as she walked in. "In fact, I was going to send out a report to several press agencies so that the UFO story gets full coverage in the papers. Perhaps you can do that for me."

"Yes, of course." She seemed exuberant.

"It'll be a scoop for you," I added.

Emma and Eric helped me out with the outline of the report to be sent to the British and American governments. The emphasis was to be on the fact that contact had been established with the Greys. The content of the report was somewhat flexible and yet the broad lines were hard evidence. Emma and Eric left at about quarter to nine, and now Jill Evans had me all to herself.

"I've read all and everything about the Eridanians and the transformation of the people. But how will the Greys stop them? I presume they are everywhere/. How will you find them? You think the Grey and the Eridanians will fight it out here on Earth?" she asked, creepily insinuating a dramatic outcome.

"I don't know."

In the course of unfolding the encounters of that evening, I thought she would be extremely enthusiastic whilst preparing the full story. I also believed her request for an interview about my music was genuine and not just a pretext to get the UFO story.

The UFO Research Organisation was in Marylebone High Street, right next to the BC publications building. Emma had been at the head of the organisation for at least five years. As always, I went to bed at around 3.30 am. The two interviews that I had given to Jill Evans the previous evening had been long and arduous. The fact that she was a very beautiful young woman did not make matters easier either. I was losing concentration admiring her full figure from head to toe. I had frolicked in London for many years and my few hours with Jill Evans had been delicious, as I felt this was the beginning of a mild flirtation. Her two interviews would be broadcast widely over media outlets: not just newspapers and magazines, but on TV channels as well.

When she had finished the interviews, she walked up and down the study and then stood in front of me theatrically gesturing her thoughts. Her style was inimitable. She was a cracker and very intelligent. Her kindness and interest endeared her to me in those few hours that she stayed in my house. It was close to 1.00 am when she left. She promised she would call again in the next few days, and I must say that they glowed with contentment as I kissed her on the cheek.

I was at Marylebone High Street at around 11.30 in the morning. Unimpressed with the slew of reporters, journalists, ufologists and TV men in the hall, I rushed into the lift and went straight up to the fourth floor.

Emma sat behind her desk and seemed to be browsing over some papers. "Turan Bey," she exclaimed, "how does it feel to be rubbing shoulders with the most talented journalist in the country? It's heady stuff, isn't it?" I didn't think she would be jealous, but apparently she was.

"Emma, come on! Are you talking about Jill Evans?"

"Who else?" she said, pointing at a paper in front of her. "I've done some research. She is definitely the most promising young journalist in London."

"She must be," I replied, "two interviews in one evening." Eric sat in the corner, watching us.

"Now, now, children," he smiled, "we have more important things at hand."

Two men and three women sat at the table at the other end of the large room. When I looked at the reports coming in from the UFO contact centres throughout the world, I realised there had not been one single report of a transformation. I sat down with them and we debated the subject. I had a suspicion that the Eridanians had stopped using the transformation process. But why would they contemplate making such a move? I had no idea. There were no other reports suggesting a different approach. Not a single case that would signal a totally different sinister plan.

With the five people at the table who were responsible for preparing reports sent in from various contact centres in different countries, we decided to send out a letter to each and every one of the contact centre heads, emphasising that the red rays had stopped, and that they should look for other contact possibilities. Somehow, we had to find out as much as we could about the Eridanian contact strategy. It would be difficult, but we had to try.

Eric, on the other hand, contacted the remaining 34 Chosen Ones, and asked them to be in London within the following two days. We had to dig more deeply into the Eridanian phenomena. All 36 Chosen Ones would send the same message to the Greys: Show us the bases of the Eridanians on Earth. First and foremost, after the message was sent, we would have to try and locate these bases wherever they might be. Suddenly, I thought of one more lead to follow. The American scientist, Ralph Turner, had disappeared during that attack on his country house. Several agents who had been supposed to protect him had been murdered, but no one could find his body. Turner must have been abducted. IK had a notion that he was being kept prisoner in one of the Eridanian bases here on Earth. Finally, I decided to fly to the USA and interview Turner's family. Perhaps they could give me a lead. It was a long short, but I had to try. Two days later, the remaining 34 chosen Ones arrived in London, making the magic total of 36, with Eric and myself. We sat in the hall at the UFO centre and sent out the message: "Show us the bases of the Eridanians on Earth." I returned to Emma's office and told her about my plan to visit turner's family in Boston, USA.

"Well, it's an angle," she said, "perhaps Turner's family can help you. But remember, we haven't received any word from them since his abduction."

"I know, but we have to start somewhere."

The flight to New York was very pleasant with all those popsies sitting around at the bar. One of them recognised me from my pictures on the cover of my Space Music CD. They were from Texas University, returning home from a trip to the UK. It's nice to be recognised as a celebrity. Does wonders for your ego...

Twelve

There were hundreds of people flooding off planes. I had to get up very early for my flight to New York and slept a couple of hours during the journey. I went out of the terminal building and walked towards the taxi stand. Suddenly, a man stormed by and then stopped in front of me, blocking the way.

He was tall and pale with a beard and moustache, and was wearing a trench coat. It was as if he had practised the sentence before he recited it to me: "Let the shame be forever on our heads for not being able to save the human race…" he paused for a moment and then gestured that I should get into the taxi. "Come to the bar called The George in the Bronx, and I will tell you a secret. I'll be there, waiting for you. An hour from now, I'll be there—waiting for you."

"But who are you? What do you want?" He did not reply to my questions. He just walked away towards the parking lot opposite. A porter approached me. He was very polite.

"Don't take any notice of him, sir. He's a nutcase. He tells everyone the same thing. He invited you to the George in the Bronx, didn't he?"

I nodded. The porter continued: "He claims we are being invaded by extraterrestrials from outer space." I smiled at the porter and boarded the taxi. The train from New York to Boston was at 2.00 pm. I decided to go to the George in the Bronx. Even if he was a madman, I wanted to speak to this man in the trench coat.

The George was a place of cheap liquor and rough scenery. As I walked towards the bar, I saw the man sitting in a corner at the far end at a table on his own. He rose and greeted me.

"Please sit down, Mr Akova," he said, and I was surprised he knew my name.

"So, you know my name…"

"Your picture was in all the papers. I recognised you immediately when I saw you at the airport," he said. "What would you like to drink?"

"Beer," I said.

He ordered the drinks and sat down in front of me.

"The press here is treating your stories in the paper with a little caution…but let us put that aside for the time being. There are other factors, too."

"Such as?" The man seemed quite normal to me.

"Well," he replied thoughtfully, "the US officials here, the CIA, the FBI and the Air Force, they are all legendary in terrorising people who know the truth."

"What is the truth, Mr…?"

"Desmond, Desmond Fowler," he filled me in. "You should not ask me that question, not you of all people. You know the truth."

"But what is your experience in the field of UFOs?" I had to ask the obvious question.

"Mr Akova, these creatures are everywhere. They are amongst us. One night, while I was trying to sleep on a bench in Central Park, I saw two men. They talked in a different language. I played the role of a sleeping tramp and watched them. Their faces suddenly changed into the ugliest creatures I have ever seen in my life. They were definitely not of this world. They passed me by, thinking I was a harmless tramp sleeping it off on a bench. I followed them. They went into an apartment on Fifth Avenue. I waited till morning, then I followed them again. This time, they walked into an office building, again on Fifth Avenue. I went in and made some enquiries of my own. The two men went up to the 16th floor. That's where the New York offices of the Secretary of State for Defence are."

"So you think they have infiltrated those offices?"

"I *know* they have, Mr Akova."

Fowler was not a madman. Perhaps he was a bit eccentric. I could detect the highly intellectual seriousness in his tone.

"What is your profession, Mr Fowler?" I asked him as he brought me another glass of beer.

"That's a long story," he murmured, feeling sorry for himself, "I was a scientist once. But neither NASA where I worked as an engineer, nor SETI approved my project on extraterrestrial presence on Earth. At any rate, soon after it was rejected, I resigned. Now I am unemployed. But Mr Akova, you must believe me. Even now that extraterrestrial presence on Earth has been proven beyond all doubt, there is still a conspiracy of silence. They don't want it known. The creatures are everywhere and they have even taken over in most departments."

I paid for the drinks and gave him my card.

"Contact me any time you want."

"I'm indebted to you for listening to me. You are a kind man, Mr Akova."

"You can reach me any time on my mobile if you come across any important developments."

"Thank you again, Mr Akova."

My train left for Boston at exactly 3.00pm. Fowler's observation that 'they were everywhere' sounded exaggerated to me. But how many in actual numbers? The curious incident in Central Park let me to believe that there might be numerous Eridanians in human form. If there had been that many transformations all over the world, then the Eridanians would not have to use their red rays anymore. Perhaps Fowler was right. Perhaps they had already infiltrated the souls of thousands of people everywhere. The fact that there had been no reports of red rays from any of the UFO centres supported that argument. Maybe the secret invasion was in full force now.

If the silent invasion of the Eridanians had been completed, the prospects of eliminating the dangers ahead were as distant as ever. Even the Greys would have to change their strategy. The Greys would destroy any Eridanian UFO out in the open. Their weaponry and technological power were far superior to that of the Devil's own forces. But even now, the Greys did not know where to strike as the Eridanians had definitely gone underground or transformed themselves into what appeared to be normal human beings.

Ralph Turner's house in Gloucester, Massachusetts, was very easy to find. It stood on its own on a small hill at the end of the road. A young girl in her early twenties opened the door. I could hear jazz, but it was so loud that we had to bellow at each other to be heard.

"I'm looking for Mrs Turner," I shouted.

"She doesn't live here," she replied in a bemused tone.

"This is Ralph Turner's house, isn't it?"

She eyed me with suspicion but asked me in. Obviously, there was someone else in the house as the music was turned down.

"George," she called, "someone's asking for my father."

A young man appeared, looking like a wealthy, flamboyant film star.

"Yes? Can I help you?"

"My name's Turan. Turan Akova. I am with the UFO Centre in London. Mr Turner was helping us right from the start at the UFO Conference in Salzburg.

Later, he came under the control of the Eridanians. He disappeared while he was being protected by CIA agents in his country house."

"Yes, we were told about the incident," he commented.

"Are you his son?"

"Yes," he replied, "and this is my sister."

"Well, George, I think your father was abducted during that incident at the country house."

"Please sit down, Mr Akova. Would you like a drink?"

"I'll have a beer," I said.

He brought one over and sat opposite me.

"Mr Akova, we were not told anything. They just said my father was missing, that's all."

"But the evidence shows otherwise."

"What evidence?"

"Well, the bodies of the murdered agents were found, whereas your father's body was never found."

He was left floundering with this thought for a while, so I continued:

"You know, of course, about alien presence on Earth?"

"Yes, I've read the papers. There were some TV programmes on the topic, as well. They really are here, aren't they, Mr Akova?"

"I'm afraid so," I said, "but let me tell you that we are trying to locate your father. By the way, where is your mother?"

"Mum and Dad divorced some time ago. Mum is married to someone else."

"When was the last time you saw your father?"

"Just before he was taken to the country house."

"Did he mention anything about aliens?"

"Yes, he did. He said they were very frightening."

"Anything else?"

"No, not that I can remember," he replied blankly.

"George, we are trying to locate your father. So try to think. Think carefully back to the time when you last talked to him."

At that moment, the music blared again as it had when I arrived. George flounced out of the room, swearing loudly.

"Brigitte, will you turn that darned thing off!"

The music was turned off and Brigitte, Turner's daughter, walked into the room. She smiled and apologised for her thoughtless behaviour: "I'm sorry," she said quietly.

"Brigitte, we are trying to locate your father. Do you remember him mentioning any person or place before he was taken to the country house?"

"No," she replied.

There was no point in going on. These two hadn't a clue.

"I'll leave you my card. If you remember anything, just contact me." I said and left.

I decided to visit the country house which was burned by the UFO. I called Saunders and he gave me its exact location. I hired a car and drove into the country. Ralph Turner was one of the top scientists in the USA. I'd met the man in Salzberg briefly, but I did not know much about him. From his files, I had gathered that he was a meticulous researcher, and he had also written a book on extraterrestrial civilisations. Saunders said it would be easy to find the location as there were at least a couple of agents stationed by the site of the UFO attack which had destroyed the house.

When I arrived, I could see there was no trace left of the house. As reported earlier, it had vaporised completely. Nevertheless, I had to look around to see if there were any clues remaining after Turner's abduction. The agents stationed there were very cooperative. I asked them whether there was another house nearby, as I could see the roof of a large building beyond the forest surrounding Turner's property. It was a mansion, they told me.

"Anyone living there?" I asked.

"Sometimes, I see people coming and going," said one of the agents.

"I'm trying to locate the scientist, Ralph Turner. He may have been abducted when the UFO destroyed the house."

"We spoke to the owner of the mansion. He said they had seen a man taken into the UFO. So there were eye-witnesses who saw the abduction."

"I think I'll go and have a word with this man," I said, walking towards the building.

"You are welcome to do so, Mr Akova," said the agent.

On this rainy day, the mansion looked grey and forbidding. The wind blew from the west and raindrops fell like needles onto my face as I approached the front door. The place seemed shrouded in mystery. I rang the doorbell. I could hear muffled voices coming from inside. A middle-aged man who looked much older opened the door.

"Yes?"

"My name is Akova," I told him, "I'm here to investigate the disappearance of Mr Ralph Turner, your neighbour."

"I've already spoken to the agents stationed here," he said. "I'll tell you what I saw: a bright white light sucking the man into the UFO."

"Was this man Ralph Tuner?" I asked.

"It must have been," he replied, "because the only bodies around were the disfigured bodies of the agents who had been protecting him, and they were found immediately after the UFO shot up into the sky."

"Are you a friend of Turner's?"

"No, not really. He didn't come here that often. So I didn't know him well enough to call him a friend." It was a glib response.

"Did you have any conversation with him before the abduction?"

"No, Mr Akova. He never visited me and I never went to his house."

As I spoke, I saw a woman appear behind him. She was a dry, sexless person. Her fiery eyes examined me for a minute, and then she spoke:

"Who are you and what do you want?"

The man answered before I had opened my mouth: "This is Mr Akova. He is investigating the abduction of Mr Turner."

"We don't know anything. I presume my husband told you what we saw?"

"Yes," I said, "and thank you for your co-operation." My politeness was met with a blunt rebuff, "There is nothing more we can tell you."

I realised she was a bundle of nerves. Clearly, she did not want to be involved. The front door conversation ended abruptly and I left.

Thirteen

I had hoped the meeting with Turner's family would throw some light upon the possible locations of Eridanian bases. But the children had had no idea. In short, my visit to the USA was a big disappointment. Was I deluding myself with false hopes? An intangible urge led me to believe that somehow there might be a clue somewhere in Boston. It was a long shot. With Bradley, the British scientist, it was a completely different story. Through a stroke of luck, his wife had heard the place name of Loo, and I was able to trace him there in Cornwall. I had hoped for a repeat. But Turner's children were not able to give me anything to go on.

My next step was New York. I decided to investigate Fowler's claims. The next day, I walked to the Waldorf Astoria where I was staying and took a taxi to the George where I had had my first conversation with Fowler. I sat at a table and asked the barman to send Fowler to me as soon as he came in. In the meantime, as it was almost 1.00 pm, I ordered a T-bone steak and some beer. The place was packed with all sorts of people and I had no idea that the George was one of the 'in' places for artists, musicians and even some people from the movie world.

I had made short visits to New York in the past few years. Two piano recitals and two avant-garde jazz and Turkish jazz concerts. One piano recital had been at the UN Centre and the other at Carnegie Hall. The two jazz concerts had been at the same venue, the Justine, Manhattan. My fame as a composer/pianist did not exactly border on the popularity of people like Tom Cruise, but I was now quite well known in music circles in New York, not only in London and Europe. The T-bone steak was good and the mashed potatoes excellent. Minutes later, Fowler came and sat at my table.

"Mr Akova, you came back. I know what you want to ask me. Don't worry. I'll help you. There's a strange empathy between us. So I know."

"I want to get into the apartment of those two people you saw in Central Park. Plus I want to get into the offices of the Secretary of Defence."

"Yes, I knew you'd ask me. I'll help you in any way I can," said Fowler, eyeing my food. I called the waitress, and she came smiling and looking at Fowler: "Yes, sir. This gentleman is a regular. So I know he will have a fillet steak," she told me. She stiffened suddenly, as Fowler's hand found its way to her buttocks.

"What's the matter, honey?" he asked, "something wrong with being a regular here?"

"No, no, Mr Fowler," she replied, suppressing her irritation, "no hands, please." The young thing looked at me, embarrassed.

Fowler replied, in the tone of a true playboy: "But you told me you liked it the last time I touched you…"

The gale blustered all night and it was still raining in New York. Fowler was unabashed, and kept blabbing on about his past conquests. But he had a sense of humour.

"You see, I don't want people prying into my private affairs," he said gloomily, "If I want to talk about something, then I talk about it."

"Where do you live?" I wanted to change the subject.

"An apartment flat not far from here. I inherited it from my mother. My father died a long time ago." The man jumped unpredictably from one subject to another. He was clearly unstable, but he was not abnormal. The bitterness of his rejection by the scientific community kept surfacing during our conversation in moments of irritable and angry protest. Then his mood would suddenly change and he would calm down.

"Mr Akova, I want to help you. I like you Turks. You are honest, brave and reliable," he said.

"You said the apartment of the two men you saw in Central Park is on Fifth Avenue. First, I want to get in there, and then into the offices of the Secretary of State for Defence. You said their office was also on Fifth Avenue."

"Let me see now…" It was a crucial moment for him. Then, all of a sudden, he conjured up a name. "OK. David will do it."

"Who is David?"

"Mr Akova, he's a professional thief. He can get us into both apartments. Easy."

"Listen, Fowler, my aim is to find the bases of the Eridanians. So we must try to find a clue as to where they go. I think they are keeping Ralph Turner at one of their bases. Perhaps after our search in their apartment, we can send this guy after them. Maybe he can follow them when they leave their apartment."

"Right," said Fowler with determination, "first things first. We'll do it tonight."

"We can't get through the front door. There are two security officers in the reception area at all times," said David, a short, skinny fellow whom Fowler had said was a professional thief. "So we go up through the fire escape behind the building." The car was parked about twenty metres from the entrance of the apartment building.

"Listen, guys. I have a shield which protects me from extraterrestrials. Once we get in, you let me into the flat and then you go down and wait in the car for me. I don't want either of you to take any unnecessary risks. But first, I will go through the front door and enquire whether they are in the apartment. If they are, then we have to wait until they leave. Once I'm in, you must ring my mobile immediately, if you see them coming back."

The apartment in front of me looked like a fairly new building with very large glass windows on all floors. I was surprised when one of the security officers opened the door for me with a flourish.

"Good evening, sir," he greeted me with a smile, "can I help you?"

"Good evening," I replied, "I'm looking for the two gentlemen on the fourth floor. I'm sorry, but I don't know their names. I'm a journalist, you see, and I wanted to interview them." I gave the security officer my card.

"I'm sorry, sir," he crossed his arms and spoke with an air of finality, "they come in very late, around midnight, so I'm afraid you will have to come back tomorrow, during the day."

"Ok," I shrugged, "but please give them my card."

"Of course, sir," said the security officer and closed the large glass door behind me.

I returned to the car and drove slowly past the building, making sure that the security officer saw me leaving. In fact, he waved at me as I drove past, and this time I parked the car about a hundred metres from the apartment.

I was lucky. The two men had left and would not be back until midnight. So I had plenty of time to look around the flat. The dominant feature was a huge sweeping staircase, leading to the upper floor. It seemed that the fourth and fifth flats were joined together to form a two-storey flat. The lights on the fourth floor had been left on for some reason. The thick, dark blue velvet curtains were drawn across, covering the full length of the window.

I walked—or rather tiptoed—straight towards the large mahogany desk near the window. Everything seemed so tidy. There was a computer on the desk. Quietly, I looked into the drawers. I found several sheets of paper with incomprehensible messages written all over them:

- *Take out subject number 1…*
- *All subjects must go to Whitby, Yorkshire, England*
- *Mission completed*
- *Target European Union*
- *Riots*
- *Unite and Control*

I made a note of all the sentences on the paper. Whether they were messages or directives, they were very complex, even ambiguous. As I moved slowly towards the staircase, I heard a noise coming from the fifth floor. Quickly I slipped behind the curtains near the desk. Through a chink, I could just see the staircase. Seconds later, a beautiful young woman in a nightgown descended it.

She sat behind the desk and switched on the computer. I was a mere three to four metres away, behind the curtains. This was utterly unexpected. At first, I did not know what to do. But I decided to watch, wait and listen. The computer looked ordinary enough, but I could hear a rich hybrid of intensely exciting sounds coming from it. And there it was! I could barely see the image of the same ugly creature I had seen back at the hotel room in Salzburg. The 'Devil' was on the screen again. A hoarse voice dictated: "Tell the twins to close the office in New York and move back to England." That was it. The message was unambiguous.

"Yes, sir," she blurted out obediently, and shut down the computer. "God damn it!" she suddenly exploded, "I'm sick of moving from one place to another! Sick and tired of it!" As she returned to the stairs, I made a snap decision. Remembering the message received from the Greys at Loo, telling me to dare to challenge them, I came out into the open.

"Good evening. Don't panic. I am here to help you." I said, realising what a nerve-wracking situation it was for both of us. She turned around, her eyes wide with astonishment: "Who the hell are you? How did you get in?" she was frantic, dumbfounded.

"Just calm down and answer this one question. Are you human or Eridanian?"

"What is this?" she snarled, "If I call the police, you'll go to jail for breaking and entering!"

"Don't bother. I'm working with the police and the US security forces are looking for you. But first, answer my question."

"Of course, I'm human," she replied, slightly mollified.

"But you were transformed. By the way, don't bother with the red rays. They don't work on me."

She moved slowly towards the table. I sensed she had no intention of sustaining a verbal tussle. She was speechless.

"If you tell me the truth, then we can help one another. Listen. I'm a UFO researcher, and I've been in this thing right from the beginning in Salzburg. My name is Turan Akova."

"Yes, I see," she seemed more relaxed, but tried to cover her naked body under the flimsy nightgown. "I was transformed, but now I'm no longer under the red rays' influence. Actually, they have stopped using them, because they said they were no longer necessary. So now I'm their prisoner."

"OK. What about the twins?"

"They are Eridanians," she told me.

"Now, do you have any idea about the whereabouts of their bases on Earth?" This was the obvious question. "And who are you?"

"I'm Linda," she replied, "Linda Morgan."

"What happened to the US scientist, Ralph Turner?"

"Mr Akova, please, one question at a time. I do not know where the bases are. But everyone's going back to the UK." She thought for a moment, "Ralph Turner…I read about his abduction in the papers. He's probably being held prisoner like me."

"OK," I said, "do you have any other information that could lead us to the basis?"

She seemed vulnerable, and yet there was no longer the look of huge distrust and fear in her eyes: "One of the messages mentioned Whitby in Yorkshire in the UK. Really that's all."

The minute she uttered the word Whitby, I knew she was telling the truth.

"OK, Linda," I said, "get dressed quickly. You're coming with me."

"Where are you taking me?"

"We're going to England. Don't worry; you'll be safe with us. Come on, get dressed. We have to leave before the twins arrive."

Fowler and David were waiting for me in the car. Fowler let out a laugh when he saw the girl with me: "My, my; I see you've picked up a girl on your way out. You're a fast operator, Turan, aren't you?"

I explained what had happened to both men, "Now we go to the offices of the Secretary of State for Defence," I concluded.

"That's a tricky one," murmured David, "park the car and wait for me a second."

I parked the car about fifty metres from the building. David waltzed off towards the rear and disappeared into a dark alley.

Ten minutes elapsed while we sat in the car, waiting.

"He ought to find a way," sighed Fowler hopefully.

"Do you have to do this?" Linda asked.

"Yes," I replied. "It's the surprise element. I have to be one step ahead. I have to find some clue that will lead us to the bases."

The rain had stopped, but it was a dreary night. It was now almost 10.00 pm and there was still no sign of David.

"Where the hell is he?" Fowler was beginning to get impatient, shifting about in the back seat.

"Do stop fidgeting!" I exclaimed, offering a cigarette.

"God damn it, it's been over twenty minutes. We're sitting ducks here, Turan," he complained, "I'm sure the CIA are keeping the place under surveillance. And what about the aliens? They may be watching us, too."

"Don't be such a wimp, Fowler!"

"OK…OK…I'll shut up."

Two minutes later, at long last, David reappeared: "I think some people are watching the apartment," he told us tensely, "I suggest we drive into the street behind it."

"OK, boys and beautiful girl," I said lightly, hoping to dilute the tension, "we are on the last lap, so don't let the side down."

I glanced at the girl next to me in the car. Poor Linda. She was watching us in blank dismay. She had been transformed, given temporary relief with the reversal of the transformation, abducted by a strange man (me) and told that she would be saved; worst of all, she had seen and experienced the unfolding of horrendous developments. I sensed she did not know what or who to believe. But this was no time to boost her morale, I thought. It would be more appropriate to tell her the whole truth later.

"OK," said David, "pull up the car and come with me." He trod lightly towards a building behind the apartment, and I followed. He opened one of the back doors and we slipped inside. We then took the battered old lift to the fourth floor. As we got out of the lift, David stubbed his left foot on an iron bar left nearby.

"Motherfucker!" he swore. We walked towards a window overlooking the apartment. He limped as he walked on his injured foot. As he tried to open the window, I stood beside him and suddenly spied a strange man outside on the windowsill.

"What the…!" I pulled out my gun. David stayed my hand, "No, don't. He's a friend."

"What the hell is this?" I expostulated.

"He's a fellow thief," explained David, "but I don't know what he's doing here…"

God almighty, I thought. This was completely unexpected. David wasn't too pleased either. He opened the window and helped him in.

"Hey, Chuck, you on a business tour, or what?" He didn't want to show it, but the fact that he had been trumped by a newcomer seemed to have taken the wind out of his sails, and then he added: "Not a word of this to anyone. You're in the business—you know what happens to those who blab."

"OK, OK…" replied the young man with a grin, "I'm gone!"

The window of the apartment was about two metres from where we were standing. He jumped first and opened the other window, I followed. David seemed like a man who laughed in the face of danger. The corridor inside was dark. No one in sight. David opened the door of the apartment, and I stepped in and switched on the light. Now we were in a very large airy room. I searched the room thoroughly. As my hopes of finding any evidence gradually dwindled, I stumbled upon a file marked with the word *Eridanians*…

There were only three papers in the file. The first was a full account of the ghastly scenarios of alien domination, one of them being a point-by-point strategic plan of how Planet Earth would eventually become a colony of Epsilon Eridani, the star system which was now established as the home of the 'Devil'.

Most important of all, it described how billions of dollars had been earmarked by the US government and the European Union to transform the world into one dominant power with a world government in control. Clearly, infiltration of major powers on earth, such as the USA, Britain and other countries, had been far more widespread than I had estimated. I was devastated by the enormity of the dangers lying ahead. The second page was all about Whitby. It was uncanny, but the Eridanians, for some unknown reason, had chosen the hunting ground of Bram Stoker's Count Dracula as their first base. I had visited Whitby years before with friends, and I knew the town well.

We left the building in one piece. It was obvious that my next mission would be centred on Whitby back in the UK. It was around quarter past eleven. I wanted to give Fowler and David a treat before I left for London the following day. The Win-Win Casino/Hotel/ Entertainment Centre just outside Manhattan was the place to go.

"Right, beautiful lady and gentlemen. Tonight you will be my guests. We'll have dinner and gamble a little…"

The Win-Win Hotel and Casino opened its glitzy doors onto an indoor paradise of beauty, music, joy and laughter. This was one of those new types of mega-resorts where the hospitality industry blends seamlessly with the entertainment industry. While we were having dinner in the up-market restaurant of the hotel, a trio of piano, double bass and drums played some exquisite jazz. I then discovered that Linda had a huge passion for music. Later, we gambled a little. I won about 5,000 US$ on the roulette table, and gave 2,500$ each to Fowler and David, and then we headed for the hotel…

Linda was a bit tipsy when I escorted her to her room, which was next to mine. Believe it or not, she happened to be a fervent admirer of my music. Her extreme admiration of my musical talent coupled with my, according to her, adroit handling of the crisis in New York, were two significant motivating factors for her to cosy up to me.

"Let's go to bed," she murmured in my ear, and then she kissed me on the lips. After a long kiss, she stopped to take a breath: "Let's take a shower first," she suggested. We made love in the shower, on the sofa, on the dining table and later, in bed.

It would be impertinent to imply that she was a pushover. In fact, by nature, she seemed rather proud. In New York, after our first meeting, I did actually check her identity. She proved to be a genuine human being, rather than an

Eridanian, whose parents lived in New York. And she had just completed a doctorate in musicology.

Fourteen

Back in London, I delivered Linda into Emma's safe hands. Linda was more than willing to work for the research centre. I wrote a long report about my contacts in New York for the record, and Emma was quite impressed by my findings.

"Well done, Turan," she said, "now we know where their base is. Whitby is a very interesting town. But I've been keeping myself busy as well, in the meantime. I have finally convinced the British government to arrange a top-level meeting with the US government here in London."

"How did you manage that?" It was my turn to be impressed. I knew that the current Labour government was not very supportive of our efforts to create a united strategy to eliminate the extraterrestrial threat hanging over the world. But the report of my latest findings in New York pointed clearly to a mammoth new crisis which struck at the soft underbelly of the current timid policy of 'wait and see'.

"Sir John Lubbock, a Liberal MP, has a keen interest and he helped a good deal," said Emma.

Sir John Lubbock was an indeterminate Liberal, wallowing in luxurious wealth. Having met the man on several occasions, I suspected his judgement was warped by self-interest. Nevertheless, he made a lot of noise in Parliament and his last onslaught on Labour and the Conservatives about the extraterrestrial crisis and their unbelievably reactionary, ad hoc policies disguised by their traditional, understated manner, created a furore among the majority of British MPs.

Our prevailing motive was the Pentagon's long-term strategy in unison with that of the British government. We had already reached a point where joint action by the US and Britain would become a significant marker for our future struggle between good and evil.

Over the next couple of days, I realised that the latest developments had made little difference to the public perception of the extraterrestrial danger. At the UFO

Research Centre, we were all strung out with work and stress. Although the CIA, FBI and various members of the US government hinted at more coercive action, they did not know where to strike. The residue of support for the UFO Research Centre was kept alive by official announcements from the British and US governments admitting the visitations of UFOs.

The deliberate disclosure of secret information from the defence sectors of both governments was totally unexpected and out of character. These were the latest in a series of damaging leaks which did not help matters at all. I suspected secret Eridanian hands at work, with the intention of creating confusion and chaos. Coupled with this confusion, was the fact that we were all in danger of falling into the trap of being misled by false messages.

Both the Greys and the Eridanians had solved the tremendous problems inherent in interstellar travel. Direct messages were sent to several star systems in the Milky Way Galaxy, but not a single message had been received from any of these extraterrestrial civilisations. Furthermore, since my direct contact with the Greys in West Loo, not a single message had been received by the remaining 35 Chosen Ones....So we were now witnessing a kind of insularity growing in society, especially in political circles close to the government.

The British Labour government had already earned the unsavoury reputation of being European Litter louts as far as UFO information was concerned. The Conservative opposition's reaction was boredom. In the midst of all this inactivity, Sir John Lubbock's initiative was most welcome indeed. His views on other matters might be unpalatable, but his criticism in the House of Commons against the government's inability to implement crucially significant measures for the protection of the public at large, and the stalling tactics of both the Labour and Conservative parties in the face of the 'most important challenge in the history of mankind...' as he put it, renewed enormous pressure on the government. Lubbock's dramatic offensive received widespread publicity in the mass media both in the UK and abroad. He continued to struggle undaunted by the fierce opposition from the sceptics. He was impervious to threats, and we were treated to the unusual sight of a single Liberal MP gathering huge support, not only in Parliament, but from the public.

I sat in my office on a cold, rainy December morning, examining a recent report sent to me at my London address. The sender was an American ufologist, Bill Stockton, whom I had met at a UFO conference in Istanbul some years earlier. The report was about Area 51 in the Nevada desert. Area 51 had always been an unsolved mystery for ufologists. There were claims that the USA was developing alien technology in this secret underground base. How they would use this enormous technology was another matter of course. Nevertheless, I wanted to explore the possibility of such an important development, and that is why I wrote to Bill, asking for the result of his own investigations on Area 51.

The report read as follows:

There is a part of the United States the size of Switzerland that appears blank on every map. This is Area 51, the secret base where UFOs are kept. Area 51 is in the Nevada Desert, northwest of Las Vegas. It is a prohibited area and the sign says: USE OF DEADLY FORCE AUTHORISED. The air space is restricted also.

Although nothing is shown on the map, there is plenty there. There are roads, buildings, bunkers and a massive runway six miles long. At night, the Groom Lake area is ablaze with light. The closed area is officially known as Nellis Air Force Range and Nuclear Test Site. It is home to Area 51. It is generally agreed by ufologists that, if the government did have a UFO or a batch of aliens, this is where they would keep them.

Ever since Area 51 was established, it has been the centre of UFO sightings. The authorities issue regular denials. But one of their own men said that not only were there UFOs flying in the airspace above Area 51, but that the USA was developing alien technology in an underground plant there.

This man's name was Robert 'Bob' Lazar. A child prodigy who had developed a hydrogen-fuelled car and made a jet-powered car and motorbike that had a top speed of 350 mph. In 1988, he was given a government contract and sent to work at Area 51. He was shocked and frightened by what he saw and he felt that the American people had a right to know what was going on there. He went on television and revealed that the US government had nine flying saucers in Area 51 and was secretly developing alien technology for its own purposes. Knowing the sensitivity of what he was saying, he used the alias 'Dennis'. He was filmed only in silhouette, and his voice was electronically distorted. This did not work. Both he and his wife had already received death threats. After his car was shot at, Lazar realised he would be safer if he came out into the open, and in November 1989, he gave details of the top secret S4 site, where the alien craft were stored. It was next to Papoose Lake, one of the many dry lakes inside Area 51. An underground complex, it occupied the inside of the whole Papoose Mountain Range. Lazar became convinced that it came from another world. When Lazar got down to work, his suspicions were confirmed. The briefing papers he read were full of UFO information. Among them, there were pictures of little grey beings with large, hairless heads, undergoing autopsies. The briefing papers said the aliens were from Zeta Reticuli, a star system frequently mentioned as the home of aliens. All this left no doubt in Lazar's mind that he was working with an alien craft built with alien materials by aliens. Lazar also believed that there were aliens working in S4. One day, he saw two men in white lab coats looking down and talking to something small with long arms. He saw the alien…

The last couple of paragraphs from the report read as follows:

Read on, Turan Akova, this is an interesting case…

Serious research on the possibility of UFOs coming from the nearest star system to our own solar system is in its 14th year: the SETI project scanning the nearest star to the solar system in our own Milky Way Galaxy. The nearest star system to ours is, of course, the star system Alpha Centauri, only 4.5 light-years from Planet Earth. Alpha Centauri is a triple star system. The two most massive components are G class and K glass stars revolving around a common centre of gravity. The third component, the renowned Proxima Centaura is an M class dwarf.

Richard Miller was telepathically asked to go to an isolated place near Ann Arbor in Michigan. Shortly afterwards, an extremely large disc-shaped UFO landed nearby. Miller was taken in. The UFO being who was probably the commander of the mothership said his name was Soltec and that his home planet was Centurus of the Alpha Centauri system. He told Miller there were 680 planets and different civilisations of the same number, only in the Milky Way Galaxy.

Both the Area 51 and Alpha Centauri reports were very interesting indeed. UFO projects, including SETI, had been impeded by a reduction of funds all over the world. But we had gone far beyond the stage where scientists and ordinary people pondered about the possibility of the existence of extraterrestrial civilisations in the star systems in our own Milky Way Galaxy. Through the mass media, not only in the USA and Britain, but in almost every country in the world, millions of people were now aware of the presence on Earth, the presence of extraterrestrials.

With Whitby on my mind, I tidied up my desk and lay on the large couch near the window. I closed my eyes, rethinking the latest situation. Why would the Eridanians choose Whitby as a base? Whitby features in Bram Stoker's classic novel, 'Dracula'. The undead Prince of Darkness is supposed to hang around St Mary's graveyard for bed and breakfast in this famous novel. Bram Stoker actually wrote part of 'Dracula' in Whitby which features in the story before the Count flees to his happy haunting grounds in Transylvania.

But what could that possibly have to do with the 21st-century extraterrestrial presence on Earth? I looked up Bram Stoker's biography but could find nothing that pointed to UFOs. Stoker, an Irish novelist, was born in 1847 and died in 1912. His only work which remains world-famous is, of course, 'Dracula', which has undergone many adaptations since, especially in the cinema. I decided to dig out more information about Stoker before I left for Whitby. I asked one of the secretaries to search for a relative on the internet. Eventually, after two hours of research, she came up with some valuable information. Apparently, Patrick Stoker, the grandson of Bram Stoker's cousin, David Stoker, lived in Whitby, which was a surprise. What a stroke of luck, I thought. He was now almost seventy. According to the information on the internet, he had been promoting his famous uncle's work for years. Deirdre, the secretary who had been doing the search, walked into the room yet again with the printouts. Enthusiastic people are so much more engaging than those without any enthusiasm, and she has all the enthusiasm in the world.

"Mr Akova," she leaped forward and almost fell into my arms.

"Careful, Deirdre," I laughed, "you almost embraced me…"

She was a wisp of a girl and I was surprised to see that she blushed.

"Patrick Stoker inherited the house where Bram lived and wrote 'Dracula'. As I said, he is promoting the works of his uncle and has now found sponsors for a new film. His comments about the film are as follows: 'Tammer Films and Entertainment,—an Anglo-American film company,—will start shooting early December. This will be even better than Ford Coppola's 1992 epic which was admittedly a masterpiece. The director of this new film will be Steven Spielberg. Some top Hollywood names have been suggested for the title role. A decision is to be made soon.'"

This was all very interesting, but I failed to see how Bram Stoker, his cousin and a new film about Dracula and Whitby could tie in with extraterrestrial presence in this Yorkshire town. Why should the Eridanians choose Whitby, of all places, as a base?

During the next ten hours, both Deirdre and I research more and more. The results of our research were as follows:

Most contemporary reviewers were full of unstinting praise for Bram Stoker's 'Dracula', which appeared in 1897. Their descriptions ranged from 'the sensation of the season' to 'the most blood-curdling novel of the century'. Even the 'Christian World' called it 'one of the most enthralling and unique romances every written'.

Bram Stoker's best novel after 'Dracula' was 'The Jewel of the Seven Stars' (1903). This novel could perhaps suggest remote connections to extraterrestrial presence. Also 'Seven Stars' is another pointer to outer space. It was written at the turn of the century, at the height of the enthusiasm for Egyptian archaeology. Thorough research into the creation of the pyramids during the last quarter of the 20th century almost certainly reveals an extraterrestrial technology used during the age of the Pharaohs. At any rate, the occult jewel of the title holds the secret of an ancient Egyptian queen determined to resurrect herself 5,000 years after her death.

Another possible extraterrestrial connection appears in Stoker's 'Lady of the Shroud', a late novel. It is a heady mix of the prediction of HG Wells. The fantastic ending (missing from the abridged versions) predicts aerial warfare five years before the outbreak of the First World War in Europe. The redefinition of demonic possession was probably another clue to extraterrestrials in Bram Stoker's 'Dracula'.

Bram Stoker had been a genial man who wrote novels and stories while toiling eighteen hours a day for twenty-six years as manager to the greatest actor of his age, Sir Henry Irving (1838—-1905), famous for his Shakespearian roles. And that was it, for the time being, regarding Bram Stoker.

I also asked Deirdre to do some research on Whitby. I had a few hours' kip before I started my journey there.

Before I left the UFO Research Centre in London, I checked the list of all sightings in the UK during the 20th century. No UFO sighting had been reported in Whitby. In the few reports I had found in the archives from the 19th century—

during Bram Stoker's lifetime—not a single UFO sighting had been reported. So I drew a blank there.

Another possibility connecting Whitby with UFOs was a more recent map drawn up by several scientists, dividing the earth into seven regions, with the sightings reported in these regions. Whitby was in Region 2, which covered Northern Europe. This was a topographical map indicating locations within this region where sightings had been reported, doubling over the last twenty years. One alignment seemed to be incontrovertible. There was a straight line passing through a suburb of Paris, then onto Calais, then Folkestone, Cambridge and finally to Hull, where it stopped. Whitby could have been the last point on the straight line, but it was not listed. There were vertical and horizontal lines crossing from one region into another. The regions on this world map were divided like this: Region 1 covered North America; Region 2, Northern Europe; Region 3, South America; Region 4, Southern Europe; Region 5, Africa; Region 6, Asia; and Region 7: Australia. Two lines from Region 4 crossed over England but once again stopped at the very edge of Whitby. Even a line from distant Asia passed through northern England, ending near the border of Yorkshire. Whitby seemed like a forbidden small area on the map. The mystery continued. Region 2 and Region 4 were the two areas on which I chose to concentrate. After careful examination, I realised that Whitby was the only small area where lines simply stopped somewhere on the border of Yorkshire or in another area in northern England.

Was it merely coincidental that Whitby was omitted completely in a map full of web-like lines? The meeting and intersection of the alignments varied, and there were at least fourteen multi-radial apexes where three to six alignments met and ended. Close examination of the map indicated other curious features of the strongly marked patterns: parallel and almost parallel lines creating triangles and rectangles. Once again, Whitby failed to lie on or within the borders established by the alignments.

There had been no sightings in Whitby, and that was strange. Actually, it was mind-boggling. Why no sightings there? Why would the extraterrestrials choose Whitby as a base?

Fifteen

I parked the rented car outside the cottage in Church Street. An old girlfriend had given me the key and had told me I could stay for as long as I wished. I slept for a couple of hours and then walked out at around 8.15 pm. It was a dreary, gloomy evening, with sudden rushed of wind blowing gusts of rain. I went straight into the Board Inn, whose landlord was Joe Shaw, whom I had met years before, on my last visit to Whitby with two British journalists. The Dracula Society meets every year at the Board Inn, and I knew that this time of the year, early December, was roughly the time of their annual meeting.

It was Friday, and despite the rainy weather, there were quite a few people there. I walked straight to the bar where an old man stood looking suspiciously in my direction. It was Joe.

"Mr Shaw, I presume?" I recognised him immediately; he was a tubby man with a red face and eyes of an indeterminate colour.

"Yes?" His eyes ran over my face once more. "You'd better come into the light."

I stepped under the light near the corner of the bar where he was standing.

"Wait a second…" he let out a hearty laugh, "you're that Turkish journalist on the track of Dracula." He stopped, and concentrated on my face once again…"Mr A—…"

"Akova, Turan Akova," I said.

"Turan Akova. Yes, yes, of course I remember you. Why, we have pictures of you in our special album. I remember, I'd given you the big black cross to protect you from the Count…" Joe was a good man with a sense of humour. "You'd lost your pendant in the cemetery; your camera jammed, your car burst into flames, and a great black dog attacked you on the 199 steps…"

"Right," I replied, "that was me!"

"Well, now, Turan Akova," he said, somewhat amused, "the last time you were following the footsteps of Dracula. What's your mission now?"

"Do you remember I told you I was a UFO researcher?" I asked him, "That's why I'm here now."

"I see," he laughed, "so now you're here to prove that the old Count was an extraterrestrial, eh?"

"This is a very serious matter, Joe. The media has reported the whole thing on TV and in the newspapers. I'm talking about an extraterrestrial presence on Earth."

"Oh, yes. I've read about it, and saw a TV programme on it as well." And then he asked the obvious question, "But why Whitby? We've had no UFOs here, I can tell you that much."

"Exactly. That is precisely why I am here."

"Wait a second," he was confused. "There have been no UFO reports here, so you are here to investigate that…?"

"Not exactly," I explained. "Listen, I don't want to cause unnecessary panic, but I am almost sure there is a secret extraterrestrial presence in Whitby. Joe, this isn't just a wild guess. Investigations in the US and here in Britain point out an extraterrestrial presence here. Strange as it may seem, Whitby may become famous yet again for a totally different reason."

Joe's watery eyes focussed on me with disbelief: "Turan, are you saying we are about to welcome our extraterrestrial friends to Whitby?"

"No," I replied, "I'm afraid the extraterrestrials I'm talking about are no friends…" I stopped. I had said enough for the time being, I thought, so moved swiftly on to another subject.

"Joe, I have two requests. First, I'd like to meet Patrick Stoker, Bram Stoker's cousin. I believe he lives here in the same house as Bram lived. Secondly, I want to become a member of the Dracula Society here in Whitby. Can you help me?"

"Of course, my friend," He poured me another bottle of lager into a new glass. "This one's on me, old boy. I remembered you were a lager drinker from the bottle, see? Actually, you're in luck. The Dracula Society meets on Monday. Patrick Stoker is its President—so we will kill two birds with one stone."

Joe introduced me to a couple of people in the pub and asked me to meet him there at 11,20 the following morning.

"Don't tell anyone, Joe, but I'm going now for a stroll in the cemetery. So I'd very much appreciate it if you could let me have the big, black cross…"

"You're crazy, Truan!" Joe chuckled, "the mad Turk from North Cyprus!"

The rain had almost stopped when I started slowly climbing the 199 steps to St Mary's graveyard. I did put on my shield just in case of an encounter and I armed myself with a torch. As I entered the graveyard, the large, old grey gravestones seemed to rise in dark shadow. The weeds grew in wanton profusion. The tall black shadow behind a tombstone that I had seen on that cold, windy December evening had perhaps been a figment of my imagination. But it happened again, as it had done years before on my last visit to the graveyard. The esoteric, hideous, dreadful and formidable evil power was there, in this misty old cemetery. The evil presence was there, in the cold, bristling, devastatingly unwelcoming wind. It could not be seen, but you could feel it in your bones…something sinister out of centuries-long past…the evil monarch, Satan, was now ready to unleash his deadly horror. I felt it. It is hard to explain, but many would probably interpret these intuitions and this experience as a product of an over-excited imagination. A sustained evil air of suspense signalled through the pulses of my brain and soil. How do you describe evil? More importantly, how do you see evil? A classic story of the undead Prince of Darkness and the graveyard with large, grey tombstones on a misty, windy, rainy evening…a perfect setting. Why would any man in his right mind venture into the darkness to a cemetery on a cold, wet and windy evening?

I'll tell you why. My mission of the moment was to locate the Eridanian base at Whitby. I was not even sure whether such a base had in fact been established in Whitby. But all the results of my investigations pointed there. How do you go about finding such a base? I had no idea, but I had to search the whole area. I also had to find the link, if any, between the Whitby area where sightings were conspicuously absent, and the Bram Stoker Dracula angle with extraterrestrials. It seemed like an impossible task. But I was determined not to leave Whitby before I had solved this mystery. At any rate, much depended on the findings of my investigation.

Strange thoughts emerged through a sudden and unexpected telepathic communication with the Greys. The thought of communicating with them had not entered my mind—not at this juncture, anyway. But it was there. The message from the Greys was as follows: "The Universe is the arena for two equal gods: the good god as we imagine it though religion and faith, and the evil, dark, supreme being equal or almost equal to and an adversary of the good god. The contest between the two is eternal. The crux of the matter is that the origin of each is in deep space…The supernatural can only be combated by the supernatural. Nevertheless, their armies both have supernatural powers. The struggle continues..."

This message was like a general information text about God and the Devil. There was nothing there that could help me during my search for the Eridanian base. Or was there? I read through the message again. No, nothing.

As I scrambled through the tombstones, the mist thickened and I could barely see the walls of the church. Weeds grew densely, and some of the tombstones were almost half-sunken into the ground, slanting at different angles, yet still defying the five hundred and fifty years of the harsh climactic conditions that battered this windy will facing the North Sea.

I could hear only the sound of the wind. Eventually, I reached a pathway leading straight to the front door of the church. I had not asked for a key from the Welsh parish priest, Father Thomas from Aberystwyth. After all, who would want to get into the church after midnight? But get in, I had to, somehow.

The device was an old lock with a bolt and a keyhole. I unlocked it with ease and entered the church. The beam of my torch illuminated stained glass windows to the left and right. I found a candlestick and lit it and turned off my torch. Now I could see the pews, and as I moved forward, the altar, the altar-cloth, the vestry door and even the choir stall loomed dimly in the flickering light of my candle. There was nothing here. Perhaps I had been too hasty in coming to Whitby. Perhaps I had anticipated them. I walked down into the large crypt, where I noted two large tables and a few chairs. I searched every corner of it in the hope of finding some clue that would lead me to the base. But there was nothing...nothing...

I had been mystically prepared and selected for the experience but had so far drawn a blank. St Mary's was a well-cared-for church, but its crypt was a sea of dust. As I climbed back up the stairs, my idea of a possible subterranean base under the church dissolved and I dismissed it as a fixation. I knew very little about the character of the Eridanian extraterrestrials, but from what I had observed, they had transcended mortality, their totally unexpected behaviour— mostly beyond human understanding—erupted at random, at the same time devouring meticulously the brain of a normal man.

So, I half-expected the surprise element to dominate almost each and every pattern of movement, activity and eventually the above supernatural satanic power to emerge unsuspectingly and deliver a deadly blow to human life as we know it. *Very dramatic,* I thought to myself. Almost like a passage from a science fiction novel. But nevertheless true. There was no reason for carrying on to the point of delirium. I simply had to keep cool, and go on with the search. But why at night, you may ask. To answer that question, I will recount what a top British UFO researcher told me years ago: almost 95 percent of all sightings around the world have occurred at night. They work at night. No one knew why. That was twelve years ago. It is interesting to note that, over the years, still no UFO expert has come up with a conclusive reason for this.

I left the cemetery at about 1.30 am. I felt a bit disillusioned that I had been unable to find any shred of evidence that could lead to the base of the Eridanians. On my way down the 199 steps, the sound of thunder echoed through the dark clouds and seemed to close in over the hill where St Mary's stood. Lightning flashed brilliantly in the night sky. The light rain turned into a heavy downpour as I reached the last few steps. I hurried for shelter under an archway not far from the pub. My Burberry trench coat was just right for this weather. I waited for about five minutes, until the rain had almost stopped. I walked along Henrietta Street towards Tate Hill Pier. Suddenly, a tall man in a black cloak appeared on the pavement. Under the feeble lamplight, this strange, tall figure hurried away in a frenzy and disappeared in the vicinity of the 199 steps and the Board Inn…With esoteric, scientific topics on my mind and the magnificent angelic encounters that I had experienced in Loo, it would hardly be surprising if I took this normal man hurrying away in the rain and heading towards his house for Count Dracula returning from his hunting ground at the cemetery.

The next morning, I knocked on the door of Joe's Board Inn at around 10.55 am. Minutes later, some members of the Dracula Society arrived. Joe did the introductions, and the all-important man—Patrick Stoker—walked in at exactly 11.00 am. I introduced myself to Stoker before the meeting began.

"Mr Akova," he said, extending his hand, "I heard about your last visit to Whitby, but we didn't get a chance to meet then."

"It was a short visit, and I was with some journalist friends."

He seemed a pleasant character and his intelligent blue eyes scanned my face incessantly as if to discover why I was so interested in becoming a member of the society.

"So I hear you want to become a member," he said, gesturing me to a door near the far end of the pub.

"Yes, but more important than that, I would like to have a private meeting with you. It is of the utmost importance."

"I think that could be arranged," he answered, smiling, "how about lunch at my house after the meeting?"

"Great," I said. "I look forward to it."

When we entered the grounds of the Stoker mansion, I noticed the narrow paths running through the very large garden where all kinds of flowers formed a kaleidoscope of colour. I wondered for a moment whether the narrow pathways formed a pentagon, a geometrical figure which had been used as a magic symbol—a symbol of the Devil. Once again, I was ludicrously eager to find a sign of some sort. You would need a helicopter to fly over the mansion and see if there really was a pentagon there, drawn as it were, by the paths.

The Stoker mansion was a fairly modern, very large building up on a hill to the west of the town. It had large windows and a spectacular glass dome right at the top of the house.

"The glass dome at the top, what is it for?" I asked.

"I have been an astronomer for many years. I have my own telescope up there. Mr Akova, I'm well aware of the latest developments. I am referring, of course, to extraterrestrial presence. Tell me, why are you here in Whitby?"

As I was about to answer his question, a tall man opened the large, white door. He was probably the butler.

"Good afternoon, sir," he said with a majestic bow, "lunch will be served when you are ready, sir."

I handed my Burberry to the butler (he must have been at least six foot four inches tall) and followed Stoker into the dining room. The whole place was beautifully decorated with Victorian furniture and antiques. The modern house with its nineteenth century interior exuding the inevitable Victorian atmosphere somehow merged into one coherent whole. Suddenly, I thought about my search in the church the previous evening. There had been nothing there, except the purity of religious symbolism.

After our lunch, we adjourned into the drawing room for coffee. I sat on a large armchair and started asking my questions.

"Mr Stoker, I'm sure you're well-informed about the presence of extraterrestrials. But the issue at hand is much more critical than it appears. These creatures are amongst us in human form. You asked me earlier, why Whitby. You see, the evidence I gathered in the USA clearly shows that the extraterrestrials are planning some sort of meeting here in Whitby. So in actual fact, I'm putting the same question to you: why Whitby? What is the connection between extraterrestrials and Whitby? I know there have been no UFO sightings here at all. It seems strange but this part of England is the only area where there have been no reports of sightings over the years—"

"Let me ask you something, Mr Akova. How will you stop them? Is it really possible to fight these space people? You say they are among us in great numbers. So isn't it already too late? Do you really have proof that they are amongst us in human form?"

"Yes, I have proof. What's more, I have witnessed the transformation of normal human beings into Eridanian-controlled beings. There is a whole army of them all over the world. Frankly, I don't know how to stop them. But we are getting help from the Greys—extraterrestrial civilisations from Alpha Centauri, Tau Ceti and Zeta Reticuli. Perhaps if we could find their base or bases, then we'll find a way to destroy the threat."

"Are you serious about the Greys?"

"Of course, I'm serious. I'm not the only one in telepathic communication with them. There are 35 others all over the world."

"Mr Akova," he moved near the table, to pour himself some more coffee, "you must admit it is extremely difficult for anyone, including myself, to believe this fantastic story. It is wonderfully chilling: Satanic terror and domination of the planet Earth by another extraterrestrial civilisation. But who would believe such a story? Come on, be realistic. This is like passages from a science fiction novel…"

I was sick and tired of hearing the same lines about science fiction novels. Such views created a lot of indignation.

"Mr Stoker, you have to believe me. In fact, those who are involved and the officialdom of the USA and Britain have long gone past the stage of believing. I can present you with scores of official documents, facts about Eridanian presence on earth. But I'm afraid there is no time for that." I was trying hard to swallow my disappointment.

Over the next few minutes, Patrick Stoker's attitude seemed to change with my continual insistence. I wanted him to believe.

"I'm sure there is a connection somewhere. But how or where I do not know. This is where I need your help. Whitby, Bram Stoker and Dracula. In other words, Whitby is famous because of Bram Stoker and his classic novel 'Dracula'. What has happened so far, first at the Salzburg UFO Conference, and then here in England and the USA, has shown us the Devil. We have seen clear images of this creature that emerged from the feathers that I found. This means that the Devil—depicted through the centuries from the beginning the mankind's history on earth—was and is the extraterrestrial being from the star system Epsilon Eridani. Although Prince Vlad in Transylvania was reputed to be a vampire through the legends and stories told since the sixteenth century, this character possessed satanic powers. All this adds up to a theory, a theory which may link Dracula to the extraterrestrial Satan from the star system Epsilon Eridani. Perhaps Whitby is the home of the satanic leader who lived here through the centuries as a recluse. I know it sounds crazy or fantastic, but that's the only connection I can think of for the time being."

Patrick Stoker raised himself from his armchair and strolled towards the fireplace, his eyes darting all over the room and then finally focussing on me with an expression of reserved amazement. It was as if he were uncovering an intricate plot. He sighed and was now ready to speak.

"Now I'm going to show you old writings from the time of Bram Stoker. These were written before he started writing 'Dracula'. His allusions in the notes are chilling and diabolic. In fact, the whole content of Bram Stoker's notes is full of morbid psychological horror. They were written a couple of years before the 'Dracula' was published."

We went into the library. The right had side of the room was full of books: volumes of publications from the 19th century. Patrick Stoker took out a set of keys from his pocket and walked towards the large desk near the window. He unlocked the drawer on the right and pulled out a large file.

"Very few people have read these notes of Bram's, Mr Akova. When I first read them, I didn't know what to believe. But now, after what you've told me, it somehow makes sense. Perhaps you're right. Perhaps the connection is here in these notes. You can sit here." He indicated a chair behind the desk, "I'll leave you alone." He stopped near the door, "You can pour yourself a drink—you may need one." He said grimly, pointing to a small table laden with glasses and bottles of whisky, brandy and other drinks. He left, closing the door behind him.

When I opened the old green file and read the first few lines, I felt haunted by a sinister atmosphere. The notes were handwritten.

I saw the light again tonight for the second time, descending upon the graveyard...It is very large. No, it's not a star. Why does it appear always above the graveyard? I have no idea.

Peculiar sudden zig-zags over St Mary's. What is this strange glowing object? It appears suddenly without warning. And then it disappears, shooting off into the night sky. I must investigate. I must go up to the graveyard at night and see what it really is...

I went to the graveyard and a very bright light appeared again. It was a very peculiar aberration hovering briefly twenty feet from the ground. A dark superstructure was visible behind the bright light. I was hiding behind a large tombstone when I saw this tall figure emerging from the saucer-shaped metallic object. The tall figure moved away from the object which hissed. Suddenly it rose and spun at a terrific speed. Now it was about sixty feet from the ground and seconds later, it shot off sharply in the blink of an eye. It was out of sight in seconds. The tall figure just stood there, motionless.

As I moved from behind the large tombstone, he saw me. That dark, cloudy December evening, I saw his eyes and I swear they were red. When I looked into them, I could not move. He approached me and now he was just a few feet away. I was terrified, but could not move a muscle. I had lost all dominion over my body. I wanted to run but I could not.

Do not be afraid, he told me in a hoarse voice. I have come a long way. I come from another world. You have been investigating my life story in Transylvania. I arrived there in the sixteenth century in the same vessel that you saw tonight. I will remain on Earth until we have transformed the humans to a higher level. That is my mission. Do not be afraid. Just return home and write the story of Count Dracula.

When I returned home that night, I felt so tired that I fell on the couch immediately and slept like a baby. I awoke at about 4.00 am covered with sweat and trembling with fear. A nightmare of Count Dracula was a particularly unpleasant experience. In my dream, I was running away from the Count and the saucer-shaped craft. Three beautiful women stopped me on my way down. I could not move. They pulled me by the arms and I was helplessly being drawn into a sexual encounter. Then the fangs appeared in their mouths. One of them was about to sink those fangs into my neck. That's when I awoke.

Then I thought about the previous encounter with the Count at the graveyard. Was it a dream? I do not remember going into the graveyard that night, so the episode near St Mary's could also have been a dream, I'm not sure. But what Count Dracula told me on that cold evening at the graveyard simply stuck in the corner of my mind. To this day, I have great difficulty believing what happened to me on that fearful night. It was probably a dream. But I am not sure.

The notations seemed to indicate a sighting and then the landing of the saucer-shaped craft in the graveyard. The tall figure who had arrived with the craft was none other than Count Dracula.

Sixteen

I was the second person to read the private notes of Bram Stoker. Frankly, I was doubly surprised Patrick had entrusted such a sensitive, historic family document to a foreign journalist. I would not let out such a fantastic story to the media as I knew the sceptics in the scientific community would seize this opportunity to ridicule even the most undisputed facts about extraterrestrial presence. Telling the world that count Dracula was an extraterrestrial landing in Transylvania in Romania 450 years ago and that the Count had also met Bram Stoker in Whitby, would be carrying it all too far.

After two hours of reading and re-reading and examining these notes, I realised that the UFO encounter at the cemetery and Stoker's dramatic meeting of the Count in 1897 was a further stroke of inspiration for the author, culminating in a real visit to Whitby by the Count. The overlapping account of his story in the classic novel, however, tells the story of the evil vampire and does not touch on any subject remotely connected with extraterrestrials. Clearly, the vampire story was fiction, but why didn't Stoker mention the real extraterrestrial Count Dracula in his novel? It didn't make sense. The Count would have been more offended by the terrible character Stoker had created in the book. Or was the author specifically instructed by the count not to mention his extraterrestrial origin? Or had the author become the Devil's disciple? Was he one of the first humans to be transformed?

Or perhaps Stoker did not want to play second fiddle to HG Wells's 'War of the Worlds' published in the same year, with an extraterrestrial theme. These unanswered questions cloaked in a shroud of mystery were impossible to explain.

But whatever his reasons, Bram Stoker did not say a word in his lifetime about the extraterrestrial presence in Whitby in 1897. Patrick Stoker said he had found the notes by accident and there were no specific instructions by the author as to what should be done with them. Bram Stoker died leaving a mystery behind him.

This all-important incident in Bram Stoker's life unmistakably conveyed a resolute determination on the part of the author to keep quiet about the whole thing. But why? Was he afraid? Had he been threatened by the count? Was he afraid of ridicule? Another question cropped up in my mind. Why had I been lured to Whitby? Of course, my investigations in New York had led me here, yet why was Patrick Stoker so willing to divulge such a closely kept family secret to a complete stranger?

What I had discovered had opened a new chapter with ghastly dimensions. Count Dracula, the extraterrestrial Prince of Darkness, was back in Whitby. And this time, for real…Now I knew why the evil devils from Epsilon Eridani—the invaders—had decided to meet up in Whitby. They would gather around their leader, Count Dracula. Disinclined to leave anything to chance, I had to investigate this possibility. So far I had found nothing at the graveyard or inside St Mary's, the obvious place to look for a trace of the extraterrestrials. The secret notes of Bram Stoker had been handed to me without the slightest hesitation by Patrick Stoker. This, in itself, suggested a somewhat cunningly contrived plan to keep me in Whitby. Or was I becoming suspicious of everyone and everything?

Patrick Stoker opened the door of the library and walked towards me slowly with a drink in his right hand. As I glanced out of the large window, I saw lightning flash somewhere above the North Sea. I realised only then that the day had turned into evening. His presence removed the suspicions lurking in my mind as I raised myself stiffly from the chair behind the desk.

"Would you like a drink, Turan?" His tone was friendly. "I may call you Turan, may I not?"

"Yes, of course you may. I'll have a beer, thanks." I was still flirting with the idea of asking some direct questions. Why would he trust a total stranger and a foreigner to boot with the private notes of Bram Stoker?

"Those notes have raised a lot of questions," I ventured as he strolled behind the bar and took out a bottle of English bitter. Handing it to me, he asked, "Such as?"

"Well, my first question is how can you trust a total stranger like me with the secret notes of Bram Stoker? As far as I can gather, you are the only person who knows of their existence and you have kept this a well-guarded secret for all these years. Why didn't you open up and tell this amazing story to the world?

After all, this could have been a perfect publicity stunt for a new project, perhaps..."

Patrick Stoker listened dispassionately but intently. His invariable courtesy revolved around a likeable personality and dramatic finesse.

"My handing you these notes may seem strange on first impression, but I wanted to help you. I have always been interested in extraterrestrial civilisations and the possibility of UFOs visiting Earth. You see, I follow the news and ever since the discovery of these notes, my interest has grown into an obsession, if you like...Especially after recent developments and the official announcement of the British and American governments accepting extraterrestrial presence and backing up that acceptance with hard data and physical evidence. So I decided to redouble my efforts to investigate the possibility of extraterrestrial presence here in Whitby. It struck me as very strange that not a single UFO sighting has been reported in this area. But you received a lot of coverage in the media and I knew of course that you were one of the key figures in this unbelievable saga."

I had to interrupt. "You had met me for the first time and yet you did not seem at all surprised to see me here in Whitby? Why?"

"Turan," he said, thoughtfully sipping his whiskey, "you are right. I was half-expecting you here in Whitby. Let me explain why. During the last six weeks, some members of the Dracula Society have been acting very strangely. I've known these people for years, and it just doesn't add up. Their behaviour is of a somewhat robotic nature. The look in their eyes carries a deep red fury. I read about the transformation of scores of people all around the world, and I feel the Eridanian aliens have taken control of their minds and bodies. But I have not been able to pin down a single shred of evidence to prove this. So I contacted the MoD and explained my suspicions. My theory was brushed aside with an e-mail—the sort of official letter which they send out to hundreds of people who are claiming an extraterrestrial presence in their area or country."

"At any rate, the disinclination of the MoD to take the matter up forced me to send the same report to the US Secretary of State for Defence in Washington. A reply from them, once again an official letter, said they had channelled through my information to their New York office."

"The New York office sent out an e-mail saying that Emma Fitzgerald and Turan Akova of the UFO Research Centre would look into the matter."

Patrick gulped down his whiskey and poured himself another. Now the pieces began to fall into place. The person at the New York offices of the Defence

Department sent a letter to Patrick to tell him that Emma and I would investigate the strange happenings in Whitby, but the London office of the UFO Research Centre never received any information about Patrick's account of extraterrestrial presence in Whitby. I had entered the New York offices of the Secretary of State for Defence on my own initiative and found the documents with the words 'Go to Whitby' written in capital letters all over them. Was this a coincidence or was I lured into those offices in New York which eventually would lead me to Whitby? How and why?

"So, Patrick, let's see now. I told you that my investigations in the New York offices of the Defence Department had led me to Whitby. You say that you received a letter from the same office telling you that Emma and I would look into the matter. At any rate, we have two situations here which might be interconnected. But the New York office didn't send out any information regarding your story to the UFO Centre in London. I am here only because of the result of my investigations in New York. So this means, perhaps, that somebody somewhere along the way wanted me to get into the New York office and lure me to Whitby. Why?"

I thought for a moment while Patrick stared at me, speechless. I knew the answer to my own question. I was one of the 36 Chosen Ones, and therefore one of the main threats to their presence on earth. This may sound conceited, but ever since this multi-faceted mystery had begun, I had been in the field most of the time, challenging the Eridanian extraterrestrials. The culmination came when I was inducted into the fold by the Greys in Loo, as one of the Chosen 36. From then on, I had become almost invincible. So I had more or less walked into a trap. But why Whitby?

The only reason why I had been tempted to come to Whitby was perhaps Count Dracula, whom I saw as a possible leader of the Eridanians. I had no silly notions about the powers that I possessed, endowed by the Greys. But after the night when I was in contact with them in Loo, I knew the Eridanians had not been able to touch me so far. Perhaps I was the only human being on Earth that could challenge the Eridanians. The primary reason behind this scheme of bringing me to Whitby could have been a plan to finish me off with the powers of their great leader, Count Dracula.

But surely an alien civilisation with such unbelievable powers would be able to destroy their adversary anywhere in the world. So why Whitby?

Patrick finally broke the silence: "So you think somebody in New York led you into the New York Office of the Defence Department, where you saw the message 'Go to Whitby' written in their documents, upon which you came here. It's obvious that someone wants you here. Why, I simply cannot say."

"I know why, Patrick. The Eridanians know full well my profound knowledge and my powers as one of the Chosen 36. I think they have already arranged a meeting with their leader, who must be Count Dracula. Bram Stoker's notes clearly suggest that the Count arrived on Earth—in Transylvania—back in the 16th Century. Bram also saw him arrive in a UFO up there in the graveyard at St Mary's. I know it sounds fantastic, but I have to check this theory."

I continued as if to reach out for something beyond human understanding. "Patrick, I still cannot answer the question: why Whitby? Perhaps you can arrange another meeting with the members of the Dracula Society. What about a cocktail party and an informal piano recital by yours truly?"

"I think that's an excellent idea," replied Patrick, as he poured yet another drink for himself, "how about tomorrow evening?"

"Suits me fine," I said, "but where will you get a grand piano?"

"Oh, that can be arranged…"

"OK, Patrick," I stood up, "I had better go now."

"Come up to my house at around seven. We'll have your piano recital here in my house in the large hall." he said as he walked me to the door.

Confusion reigned over this visit to Whitby. I managed a glimpse at the eyes of the tall butler as he opened the front door of the house to let me out. They were strange. Their expression was one of anxiety and horror. Maybe I was imagining it…but there was definitely something strange about the man.

Nobody could envisage the consequences of an alien invasion. But I sensed another sinister motive somewhere along the line. It was as if I had my back against the wall. My confidence had evaporated somewhat, and I felt weak. It was around 8.30 pm when I walked into a restaurant, High Society, near the bridge. An insignificant-looking little man greeted me at the entrance and introduced me to a young and beautiful woman, who was the manageress.

"Good evening, sir," she said and looked at me again with recognition, "Mr Akova!" She seemed to be in a playful mood, "I recognise you, now, Mr Akova. I was at your Purcell Room recital in London. I am Gilda." And then with a gorgeous smile, she added: "It was a magnificent performance."

"Thank you, but how did you recognise me?"

"Mr Akova, you are world-famous. You are a musical genius." As we strolled through the restaurant to a table, she showered me with compliments.

"I am looking for a lonely table just for one," I said.

"You need not be lonely, Mr Akova." She definitely had a sharp mind: "I will come and sit with you later." Her eyes gleamed with anticipation.

"I shall look forward to that. You are very kind."

I sat at a table by a window and ordered. I needed to be alone and re-think the situation. What was so special about Whitby? What was the connection between Whitby and the extraterrestrials? Just when I'd finished my dinner, Gilda joined me at the table. On the windowsill by my table and on all the other windowsills, there were carved ornaments, pieces of china and vases. It was a pretty restaurant.

"Mr Akova," she was definitely a seductive woman, "I also know about your research on UFOs. The presence of extraterrestrials is the most talked about subject these days."

"So you are interested," I said, realising that she had a genuine and independent view on the subject, "so what do you think is happening in Whitby?"

"There are a lot of shady characters in Whitby these days," she ventured, "I can't point a finger at anyone, but I have this nasty feeling in the pit of my stomach."

"Why? Who are these shady characters you talk of?"

"I don't know. But let me tell you this much. My brother, who is a member of the Dracula Society here in Whitby keeps talking about local people—I mean members of the Dracula Society. He says their behaviour is very strange."

"Patrick Stoker said the same thing." I commented. "By the way, I have a piano recital at Patrick's house tomorrow evening. This is when I hope to find some kind of omen which will tell me more about Whitby."

I looked into those beautiful blue eyes, "What are you doing after you close the restaurant?"

"Nothing special," she whispered, "and you?"

"I could invite you to my cottage for a drink…"

Our conversation suddenly moved from flying saucers into a blatant flirtation. The little man brought us a couple more brandies.

"That would be nice…" she said, "we are taking giant strides towards a beautiful relationship…"

She moved closer and her knees touched mine under the table.

"You know, you're absolutely right." I agreed, "Positive energies, that's what it's all about. And we have to accentuate the positive."

She now seemed exuberant and definitely ready for take-off:

"I am perfectly, unquestionably very relaxed."

"That will help me tremendously as I am trying to solve a mystery."

"I adore mysteries," she glanced at four people, two couples, actually, who were just leaving the restaurant.

"Excuse me a moment," she said and walked with them to the door.

She was back in a flash. "We can go now."

"You know, Gilda...nobody told me where to find you. It was sheer intuition..."

"I love your intuitions..." she smiled and we left the restaurant.

As soon as I closed the door of the cottage, I was enthralled by her beauty. It was captivating, melting ecstasy as I pulled her towards me and we kissed...She was an extremely interesting person with a degree in psychology. She was also quite well informed about UFOs. She had read most of the recent books on UFOs and followed the news of extraterrestrial presence with intense concern. The scale of the crisis of satanic terror somehow inspired her. I told her the latest developments and explained why I was here.

"I don't think the Eridanians have bases here in Whitby," she said finally, as if she had calculated an immensely complex mathematical problem and reached a solution that was indisputably correct.

"And how did you come to that conclusion?" I asked.

"I don't know. But a base here would be too obvious. You said the aliens behave in a peculiar manner. They are totally unpredictable and have absolutely nothing in common with known human behaviour patterns."

"But what's happening in Whitby? Why do they want me here? And what is the connection between Whitby and the extraterrestrials?"

"I don't know, Turan." She said, "But I will do some research for you."

"You must come to Patrick's house for my recital. You know of course that the sole purpose of this recital is to bring together all the members of the Dracula Society. Patrick says some of them are suspect, and might perhaps let us in on some secret information about the Eridanians."

Gilda rose from the bed and while she made coffee in the kitchen, I lay thinking of the Greys. A telepathic communication seemed infinitely remote, but

I had to try. Then it happened just as she strolled back with two white cups in her hands.

"Gilda, please sit down and keep quiet."

She was astonished. "Please just give me a pen and paper."

She put the cups on the small table beside the large bed, "You'll find both in my briefcase," I told her.

The feeling was very reminiscent of my first encounter at Loo. So I knew I was about to be contacted by the Greys. All my efforts and attention were exclusively and intensely focussed on one thing: communication with the Greys. The question I put to them was simple: "What is the connection between Whitby and the extraterrestrials?" I was now sure that the Greys would wade in and shower me with instruction. However, what I received back telepathically was not what I expected. Something whizzed through my brain, and I wrote down two sentences.

A building earmarked for demolition
Play your composition Alpha Centauri

My concentration during this cryptic communication was extreme. I sat on the edge of the bed staring straight into the wall. Gilda was frightened at first, her unease mounting almost to a panic.

"Are you all right?" she cried.

"I'm fine, Gilda. Just be quiet for a few more minutes."

She stood motionless with a minimal expression of defiance. Then in an apparently dramatic gesture, she held both my hands. This was my second telepathic communication, but I don't know how it happened. My concentration had wavered for a few seconds at Gilda's dismay, as she read the notes I had jotted down on the paper. Maybe she thought I had suffered some kind of fit.

"What has happened? What's wrong, Turan? Are you OK?"

"I'm fine," I reassured her, and squeezed her hands. "Listen, my dear, I'm going to tell you something and I need your help."

She sat in the armchair opposite me, "I'm listening."

"What I am going to say may seem very strange, incredible, even, but you will have to trust me. I am in telepathic communication with the Greys—the extraterrestrials from the star systems Alpha Centauri and Zeta Reticuli. They are the only ones who can challenge the power of the Eridanians. You've seen my notes. We have to find the building earmarked for demolition here in Whitby. Can you think of any such building off-hand?"

Gilda seemed more relaxed, "Let me see now," she said, getting up and pacing the room. "I don't know. I can't think of anything at the moment. Perhaps we should ask the council tomorrow."

"OK. We can do that tomorrow, but what about now? You're a local. Think of all the streets here in Whitby. After all, this is a small town."

She stopped her pacing and nodded to herself, then turned to me and said: "There is a rumour floating around, about a new hotel to be built here in Whitby on a site to the west of the town. There is a very large, old building on that site." She repeated, "It is a very large old building," and then she smiled suggestively: "But couldn't you wait until tomorrow?"

"No. We have to go there tonight. I can't risk prevaricating on any instruction received from the Greys."

It was a cold night. At around fifteen minutes past midnight, we left the cottage. Gilda drove her seventies model Daimler-Sovereign 4.2 into a road which led to the west of the town. I had no idea what was happening. But the messages, or rather the words I had received from the Greys were quite clear. I was supposed to find something at 'an old building marked for demolition'. The second sentence was a simple instruction: I was to play my own composition Alpha Centauri at my piano recital the following evening. Perhaps this would be my first breakthrough in Whitby.

"Gilda, maybe there are several other buildings that are down for demolition?"

"I don't think so," she said firmly, "but we will find out tomorrow from the council."

The street lamp on the narrow road illuminated part of the old building. It looked like an old nineteenth-century mansion with many rooms. We parked the car about fifty metres from the gate. There was a twelve-foot wall around the building. Slithering precariously in a muddy dirt track, we reached the gate. It was open. The door of the building was also open. The whole seemed in ruins. I held a torch in my left hand and the gun in my right. We walked slowly into a very large hall and proceeded towards the other side of the house. Suddenly, I heard a squeaking coming from the entrance into the hall.

"Did you hear that?"

"Probably rats." said Gilda.

But it was no rat. A black figure with a lit candle appeared at the other end of the hall. It looked like a weird apparition. The figure walked slowly towards us, his footsteps echoed in the empty hall. The beam of my torch forced him to cover his eyes. As he walked nearer to where we were standing, he spoke angrily to us: "This is my home, and you are trespassing."

As I moved the torch from one hand to the other, he saw the gun. He mumbled incoherently, shaking his head. He had long hair and a beard.

"What's the gun for?"

"Nothing," I said, "just a precaution."

"Why are you here?"

"I was hoping you would give me some information about the extraterrestrials."

"Flying saucers, eh? Well, there is nothing anyone can do anymore. They've taken over." He spoke in perfect Queen's English and he seemed to be in deep despair.

"Excuse me, sir, but who are you?"

"Sir Peter Dankworth. I've just arrived. Only two days ago. You see, I was away for fifty years. They abducted me fifty years ago. I was fifty then and I am still fifty. Isn't that wonderful?" he gave a mirthless laugh.

Was he really abducted fifty years ago? Why was he here? Why was I sent into this derelict building? Maybe we were in the wrong house. I doubted that very much as the man spoke of UFOs and of his abduction all those years ago. If true, he was most definitely the first human to have stayed such a long time in the wilderness of deep space.

"Where did they take you?"

"The star system Epsilon Eridani. The Devil's planet. The devils rule over there. It was horrific, but I survived. They realised they had no use for me. So they brought me back. This is my home."

"But this is a building earmarked for demolition."

"Yes, yes. You have passed the test. Those are the exact words," he said, clearly indicating some sort of foreknowledge of my arrival.

Two shadows moved near the door. A big black dog appeared beside Sir Peter, snarling unpleasantly.

"The information you need is in my inside pocket—" he said. But just then the two shadows closed in and I shouted: "Get down, quick!" A shot was fired. The dog bolted in terror at the sound of the gun. Sir Peter fell, clutching his left shoulder. He had been hit. I fired six shots in the direction of the shadows, but they had apparently disappeared...

We helped Sir Peter into the car and drove him straight to the hospital where he was treated for his gun wound. In the car, he quickly gave me the piece of paper from his pocket. Although he seemed normal, from time to time I sensed much darker emotions, and the fear in his eyes which was so disturbing had been very apparent from the outset. I felt sure he could help me to uncover the plot I had been trying to untangle. Sir Peter told us he had a son, Adrian. The boy had been eight when he was abducted in 1956. He told us that Adrian was now living in London, his only remaining relative. But he refused to believe his father's story.

Sir Peter also told us that he lived in a flat in Whitby. After his disappearance, his son had sold the big mansion there. The whole episode was astonishing. When I asked him how he was enticed into meeting me at the old mansion, he replied simply, "I don't know, Mr Akova. There are many things that I don't understand."

"Did you speak to anyone before coming to your old home tonight?"

"No."

"But you had written information ready for me."

"Yes."

"Perhaps a telepathic communication simply instructed you to meet me there tonight."

He was taken aback at the thought, "I don't know. But whatever it was, I think this was an audacious scheme, Mr Akova. I am sure this is a war of attrition. You had better prepare yourself for a mounting extraterrestrial storm. Elements of it are lurking menacingly in every corner of the world..."

"You rest now," I told him, "we'll talk tomorrow." And we left the hospital.

Seventeen

The information on the paper was yet another puzzle. It was handwritten. Gilda and I read it back at the cottage.

There are three points of massive extraterrestrial presence in England. The first is West Loo in Cornwall. You have already been there. The second is Whitby, where you now are. Your final destination is Stonehenge. Go to Stonehenge. You will have a powerful tool when you measure it against the special powers of the other Chosen 35. You are their leader. Charlie Booth, the crop circles man, will answer all your questions. You will find him at Samantha's Pub near the river at Avebury.

The next day, we visited Sir Peter in his flat somewhere in the centre of town. I asked him about the message. Obviously, the Greys had sent it, but why hadn't they sent it to me direct? Sir Peter was not among the Chosen 36, which meant that he was incapable of telepathic communication with the Greys. So how on earth had he received it?

"It was given to me, Mr Akova," he murmured finally, "It was terrible. I had become one of them." With his eyes fixed on mine, I saw he was now re-living a dark, nightmarish past: fifty Earth years in a remote (11.6 light years from our solar system) star system called Epsilon Eridani. God knows how many Eridanian years...

"Did you see the person who gave it to you?"

"No. At least, it was too dark and I had had a bit too much to drink."

"Could you describe him?"

He tried to remember, "He was very tall; perhaps 6 foot 6 inches. I did not see his face. He didn't utter a word. Just handed it over and disappeared."

"What about your son?"

"I saw him once when he came here two days ago. But he didn't believe me...can't forgive me...can't forgive me for leaving him and his mother all those years ago. You see, he had heard rumours about another woman. Of course, there had been a few 'other women' in my time, but no one knew anything about them. I would never leave my family. It is so sad. He is the only family I have, but he doesn't believe me."

"Come, now. In the wake of extraterrestrial infiltration, I am sure he will eventually come to terms with the truth. There have been quite a few significant developments over the past five months. Now the whole world knows they are here."

A lot of valuable information emerged from my long conversation with Sir Peter. He said that the Planet Eridanus in the star system Epsilon Eridani was very similar to our Earth. However, their technology was far beyond the understanding of any human brain. And they suffered from a constant water shortage. He had no clue how this extraterrestrial civilisation had become immortal.

"Shambling mutants, products of alien copulations, Mr Akova," he said, "but I think the water shortage on their planet is acute."

Sir Peter also told me that the Eridanians were 5,000 Earth years ahead of our civilisation. The devilish creatures had been visiting Earth since the dawn of man. He said the Eridanians were ferocious, violent and savage, despite remarkable technological developments in their society. The solar system and planet Earth comprised one more destination in their long struggle to find a new home in the Milky Way galaxy.

"My son's disparaging remarks about my long space adventure are sad. But I do not want to dwell on it. I look forward to our next meeting," he said despondently. Clearly, he was disorientated. Well, what would you expect after an absence of fifty years? Throughout all my investigations into abduction cases, I had never heard of anyone who had been kept prisoner for fifty years in another star system. It was a unique case, and Sir Peter was probably the only human who had experienced this. But he had survived the battering and torture of the devils, albeit at some cost to his mental health, and had been returned to Earth. But why?

Ever since the first evidence of extraterrestrial presence, I have seen and experienced first-hand some fantastic incidents. There had been no point in trying to convince people what was really happening. The impact of the official announcements confirming UFO visitations and alien presence soon dissipated after the first couple of months, while the public were largely dismissive of the dangers of extraterrestrial presence and Eridanian domination, considering it a science fiction fantasy. This attitude was encouraged by the gnomes of Whitehall, the White House and Brussels—and that was the real danger.

The Eridanian extraterrestrials seemed to have recruited many thousands of people into their camp in all parts of the world. There was no sign of an all-out attack to destroy human civilisation on Earth. The mighty military forces of the USA and other countries could not galvanise themselves into action as there was no target to hit. We were not yet able to find the bases of the alien race here on Earth. The last message I had received from the Greys spoke of massive extraterrestrial presence in Whitby, West Loo and finally Stonehenge. The major countries of Europe and the EU itself had a fallacious view of the current situation and were not able to address the real problem. It was virtually impossible to trace an invincible army of aliens, now in human form.

Gilda now stayed with me at the cottage. She was a wonderfully intuitive girl with original ideas. At around mid-morning, I received an e-mail from Emma saying that the UFO Centre in London was being inundated with enquiries about Whitby. Clearly, someone had leaked out a story of extraterrestrial presence in Whitby to the media.

I told Emma to send out a press release to the media denying any presence in Whitby. This would save me from answering the questions of an army of reporters looking for sensationalist stories. Of course, no one yet knew of Count Dracula's extraterrestrial origins, but any journalist worth his salt would find out about that, too. The Eridanian strategy had a peculiar and unpredictable pattern. Were there several bases on Earth sucking in masses of water—that was a possibility. But where? The slimy ways of the devil, that's what it was…The furtive transformations of humans continued. In earlier experiences, one could tell those who had been transformed into Eridanians from their red eyes. Evidently, the 'red eye' operation had been cancelled out. Now it was impossible to tell who was who…no one could pinpoint a pattern, aspect of behaviour or mark that could identify the 'devils'. But we could still ward off the evil by challenging them. The message I had received in Cornwall had simply said: "Do not be afraid: challenge them." That was indubitably the best course of action for the time being.

The 'Grey help' as I called it was neither here nor there. The Grey extraterrestrials should have been able to terminate the Eridanian threat with their supreme technology. But no. Apart from the occasional telepathic communications and messages, not a single shred of evidence could be detected to link the Greys to a struggle against the Eridanians. That was another mystery…Why didn't the Greys show themselves? Why didn't they wage open war against the Eridanians? Why did they send bits of information and leave it to me to solve the puzzle? Perhaps they had their own reasons. But there was no way I could determine their reasoning, which was beyond human understanding…

The Greys were sending me on a merry-go-round between three points in England, West Loo, Whitby and finally Stonehenge. The last message had said that Charlie Booth, the crop circles man, would answer all my questions at Samantha's pub in Avebury near Marlborough. The message also spoke of massive extraterrestrial presence in all three points. So far, I had not come across a single Eridanian-controlled human in Whitby. Even if I had, I wouldn't have known what to do about it. The Greys said I had special powers and that I should challenge them. Well and good. But with those 'special powers', I could protect only the people with me and myself. That was all. How could millions of people protect themselves from the Eridanian threat? There was no answer to that question yet.

The English breakfast at Gilda's restaurant was perfect. I was grateful to this young, yet cultivated and loveable woman. Our fast-growing relationship—it had only been 36 hours—and our exchange of ideas had enriched my theories and pumped positive energy into my resolute decisiveness to counter the dangers ahead. But I had to be careful not to do anything rash. I had to wait for the right moment to arrive.

Patrick Stoker was an outstanding organiser. My piano recital at his mansion would start at 8.00 pm, and the dinner/cocktail party at 9.30 pm.

We arrived at the Mansion at around 6.30 pm. The Great Hall could sit at least 170 people. A Bosendorfer Grand had been brought into the Stoker residence at around lunchtime. Stoker said the piano tuner had come and gone. From what I gathered from the locals, including Gilda, Patrick was famous for his charm, wit and resourcefulness.

"Good evening, Turan," he said, and almost leapt for joy when he saw Gilda. "What a lovely surprise!" he exclaimed. He was presumably a fervent admirer of the beautiful lady standing beside me. "I see you've already become good friends."

"It was inevitable," said Gilda.

"I bet it was," Patrick murmured, as he ushered us into the hall and asked a waitress to serve us drinks. While Gilda and Patrick conversed, my mind was fixed on a telepathic call to the Greys. I wanted the Greys to make contact with me immediately after the piano recital. I walked to the end of the hall behind the small stage where the Bosendorfer stood, and opened the large glass door into the back garden. There was a very large garden at the rear of the house. The chances of a telepathic communication with the Greys after the concert were very slim, but I had to try.

Slowly, people started arriving. All the members of the Dracula Society were expected. Every single member of the society seemed normal, except for one man. He was very tall; probably about 6 foot 8 inches. He spoke with an Eastern European accent, and his English was perfect. He wore a black robe over a black suit. Could this man be the undead Prince of Darkness? Was he the extraterrestrial devil from Epsilon Eridani who had landed in Romania almost five centuries ago? Perhaps he wanted to speak to me. Maybe all the people in the hall were fully under his control. Perhaps he wanted to challenge my powers. I suppose he thought I was a key figure throughout the episode. A human who had acquired special powers through his worst enemies—the Greys…If indeed he was the Count, he might try to destroy the threat that stood in his way. That would appeal to his lurid taste.

He stood in the centre of the hall with a young, beautiful girl beside him. At that moment, I realised they were both staring at me. I decided to walk over and introduce myself. I shook hands first with him, and then with the girl.

"I am Turan Akova, the pianist/composer playing for you this evening."

"I know who you are, Mr Akova," said the tall man, smiling weirdly…

"And you are…?" I persisted.

He answered without hesitation: "Draco, Peter Draco. And this is Angela Holsworth."

The girl smiled, "You have been very much in the news, Mr Akova. I mean about the extraterrestrials. I'm dying to hear your latest exploits."

"I'll be only too pleased to fill you in," I replied, sipping my lager. Her eyes twinkled while I was asking Draco the next question.

"What line of business are you in, Mr Draco?" My persistence made him feel rather uneasy, I could tell.

"Oh, I travel a lot. Early retirement, you see. Now I'm spending the family fortune."

"Mr Draco, are you at all interested in what's happening in the world at present? I'm referring to extraterrestrial presence."

"Oh, yes, definitely. I think the human race can no longer fight the technological power of the Eridanians. Look around you, Mr Akova. All these people here are in fact terribly resigned to their fate."

"So you think there is no hope for the human race. Perhaps you think we ought to surrender." I did not want to make any disparaging remarks but Draco seemed to be a very strange character and his attitude upset me a great deal.

"Mr Akova, I have no wish to upset you. But I have already been asked the same question by many members of the Dracula Society, and they have put me in an invidious position. I have to tell them the truth."

Patrick Stoker waved a hand and then joined in the conversation.

"Turan, it's ten to eight. People can't wait to hear your space music."

"OK, Patrick," I said, as I watched the tall man walk away from us.

"Patrick, do you know who that tall man is?"

"He says his name is Draco. I met him only a few days ago. A strange character, eh?"

Patrick did not seem at all bothered by Draco and that seemed strange to me. Could it be that Patrick too had been transformed into the Eridanian world? Or was my imagination getting the better of me? With the disappearance of the red eyes symptom of the transformed, I was no longer able to detect a single sign that would uncover the Eridanians amongst us. They all seemed like shady characters with an apparent detached, unemotional style. I had the feeling that underlying that style, their mental processes were complicated. Over the few months of my encounters with these creatures, or the humans who had been transformed, I had not detected even a minimal expression of resistance. The essential part of their character seemed to be clouded by a climate of fear. When you approached them, they behaved like normal humans. But the satanic terror was there. I could feel it in my bones.

Patrick's hall was very much like a small concert hall. All the people there were seated. I walked onto the small stage and introduced myself to thunderous applause.

"I am a Turkish Cypriot from North Cyprus. I will play for you tonight some of my space music compositions. These pieces are dedicated to the good extraterrestrials who have been visiting planet Earth since 1947, Earth time. My inspiration comes from somewhere up there. This is new music, avant-garde music, which shakes up the status quo, and breaks new ground with novel and progressive ideas. And it is frequently dramatic, adventurous, mysterious and sometimes humorous."

"It is a great adventure…Avant-garde music focuses not only on innovative music with introductions to new ideas and techniques, especially for the piano, but it also concentrates mainly on improvised music."

After the applause for my introduction, I started playing. The first part of the recital included Alpha Centauri, Avant-Garde 1, Avant Garde 2, Seven Stars and Vega. After an interval of 15–20 minutes, the remaining five compositions, Taksim, Zeta Reticuli, Moonlight in Neptune, Space Fantasy and Sirius. The atmosphere in the hall was great. This was one of my best performances ever. Perhaps Gilda had inspired me. When I finished playing, there was a tremendous demand for an encore. I played the new composition Alpha Centauri once again. When I had finished, I hurried out into the large garden…

A saucer-shaped UFO was hovering about fifteen feet above the garden. A very bright white light appeared from the bottom of the craft. Seconds later, I was drawn up into the UFO. The oval craft had a raised central console. I was taken by four Greys into a large room. There, to my amazement, stood an identical black Bosendorfer grand piano, placed in the middle of the room. One of the Greys walked up to it and sat on the stool. He had six fingers on each hand, which were longer than those of humans. First, he devoured me with his eyes, and then he started playing my Alpha Centauri space music composition. I stood, astonished at this remarkable sight. It was like a trick played on me out of sheer devilment. The whole thing was phenomenal: my composition Alpha Centauri was performed brilliantly by the little grey being. When he had finished playing, the small creatures in the UFO scurried about me. At first, I had a distinct sense of unease, but moments later, two Greys who looked taller than the others started growling in their own language, and transmitted a telepathic message into my brain. The message was as follows: "You are a genius. The first human to compose and dedicate music to the extraterrestrials. You are the Chosen One. The leader of the 36 Chosen Ones. Have no fear. You have the power to eliminate the threat of the Eridanians. Do not be afraid of their leader, Count Dracula. But beware the tricks of the Devil. Go to Stonehenge and complete the triangle. There, you will find the answer…"

Right after this telepathic communication, I was pushed unceremoniously out of the UFO and onto the lawn in the garden. Seconds later, the UFO soared away into the night sky. The people in the hall were still applauding my performance. The little grey beings with large hairless heads and big almond-shaped eyes had set up a screen between their craft and the hall. No one had seen what had just happened in the garden—except for the tall, mysterious man called Draco. He stood just outside the large French window which led into the garden.

"Yes, Mr Akova, I am Count Dracula, the Eridanian leader. I saw it all. Your meeting with the little Greys." He seemed unduly reticent. "Your attempts to fight the might of the Eridanians are futile. I am offering you the hand of peace. Already, thousands of humans have joined us. Some of these humans are very important people at the helm. They control the power on Earth. So do not expect any help from the USA or Britain, or from the European Union. Once you join us, you will have a very different understanding of nature and the meaning of the universe and human life…With us, eternal life is not just a promise, it's a fact. You, your family and the people you love will have eternal life."

The supreme evil being stood motionless. I recoiled in horror as the count made his move. This was no regular fight. It was, I suppose, a demonstration of deadly demonic movements. A very powerful force pushed me down onto the lawn in the garden. I was now lying on the ground about ten metres from the Count. I had put on my protection device before coming to Patrick's mansion. It seemed as though the particular faculties of his body and mind joined together to wipe out anything and everything all around him and perhaps further beyond. It was definitely a force not previously known, seen, felt or heard of in the world. Two words dominated my brain, "Challenge him!" With a brave and bold leap, I flew in the air and struck him with my two feet. I continued to fight undaunted by the enormously solid, sturdy and yet elusive lights and strikes emanating from this diabolic creature. The count's second attack was a debacle: the red, yellow and bright white lights sizzling towards me with terrific speed ricocheted back on him, probably inflicting great physical and mental pain as he stepped back in a shroud of smoke. He was now crouching and reinforcing himself with his unnatural, uncanny demonic powers. I heard weird shrieks in the darkness as the count rose once again. I walked slowly towards him, getting ready to strike. But he conjured up the fastest trick I had ever seen in my life. He flew in the air, and disappeared in the woods beyond the garden…I stood there waiting for his reappearance, but he had vanished.

Patrick stood at the edge of the large glass door, scared out of his wits. A recurrence of a more powerful attack by the Count was a frightening possibility.

But nothing happened. Lord Cecil Summerville who was among the guests, a true Englishman—noble, taciturn, stiff upper lip, arrogant sometimes to the point of contempt—stood near Patrick as I walked into the hall.

"What the devil is going on?" he asked, slightly disorientated by Patrick's behaviour and panic. He may have been proud and haughty, but he was also correct and courteous. "I say, old chap, you seem to be in tatters. Red-eyed fury enmeshing and defeating his challengers, eh? That's the old Count Dracula, isn't it? Your next Dracula film project fell through, though, didn't it? I was so taken up with the music that I almost completely forgot my feeble interest in UFOs and the old count. So what's been happening?"

Patrick was in no state to reply. But Jeremy Jones, a fusty old professor whom I had met earlier, almost carried the tipsy baronet back to the bar.

"Have another drink, Cecil," he said to his Lordship. Several other people who had gathered around Patrick looked on in amazement. Summerville's naïve attitude provoked their derision. Gilda held my arm and we walked towards the bar. She handed me a large brandy. The members of the Dracula Society circled around me with congratulatory statements about my pianistic accomplishments, and my extraordinary talent as a composer.

Later, Gilda and I sat ourselves in large red upholstered chairs with gilt arms at the far end of the hall. The lord returned, a stooping figure with clumsy movements, he mumbled something barely understandable.

"An unusual artistic experience, old boy," he jerked his arm away from the beautiful girl who had been with Count Dracula and continued impudently: "This lovely lady," he pointed to Draco's girlfriend, "she wants to get to know you better, if you understand my meaning." He laughed, winking at me. "She immediately recognised your unusual and extraordinary gifts."

"My name is Stella. I'm sorry we were not properly introduced by Draco. He's disappeared again." Obviously she had no idea about the dramatic and violent fight between me and the count. She must have been transformed. But it didn't show. The vast chasm separating humans from Eridanians somehow appeared diminished by a clever trick of the Devil. You could not tell the difference. She held my hand and squeezed it. The lord broke the magic once again:

"Now. You bring your girl—whassername? Oh, yes, Gilda—and Stella will come too. We'll make a foursome at my place. How about that, then?"

"That would be nice," Stella said, still holding my hand.

"Come on, Turan," the lord was insistent. I wanted to accept his invitation because I thought I might get Stella to divulge her transformation, if indeed she was transformed. The lord was very unbending in his demands. "I'll give you an hour to talk to your admirers and then we go," he said, finally.

"OK." I said.

All four of us left Patrick's mansion after an hour or so. The lord's chauffeur-driven Rolls was waiting outside. The chauffeur, a man of improbable ugliness ushered us into the blue Rolls Royce. I sat between Gilda and Stella. Stella was incredibly sexy, affectionate and full of childlike gaiety. Gilda held my hand and didn't want to let go in case Stella took over: a flattering rivalry between two gorgeous women. I had a lucky gift of always seeing the bright side to any fearful situation in which I found myself. My natural confidence and optimism triumphed over unpleasant thoughts. The Count had disappeared without a trace. I still had no clue as to how the process operated, by which humans were transformed into Eridanians. I could not yet link anyone to a specific plot.

It was a boisterous party and we had all imbibed a few drinks at Patrick's mansion. I realised right after long conversations with various members of the Dracula Society that almost all lived unconventional lives. The whole atmosphere at the party spelled of universal apathy. The uncertainty of everyone as to whether they would still be alive to see the next day was dominant in more ways than one. They all seemed relaxed, uttering words like, "Who knows what will happen to us tomorrow." And, "No death. Nobody wants to talk about death. But how will we survive?" I could sense a great nervous tension among the people I talked to. But I had to continue the investigation, despite my frustration.

It was virtually impossible to harangue Lord Summerville in my usual way. He was unstoppable. I laughed at the thought of him being transformed, as he would run rings round the Devil with his mannerisms and tacky verbosity. The man was tactless but humorous. The Rolls came to a stop near a large, probably 15 foot tall, iron gate.

"This is my estate, Turan," said Cecil, "one hundred acres of land. There," he pointed to a large mansion twice the size of Patrick's, "there's my palace." It was indeed a very large building. The Rolls swished by a pine forest and we finally reached the residence. It lay just a few miles to the west of Whitby, standing on a small hill. The outward appearance looked Victorian, but I could not see it clearly as the lighting around it was very poor. A middle-aged butler opened the door with two women servants practically running out to greet their master. I remember looking at my watch as we entered this 'palace'. It was 11.30 pm.

"Let's have a drink at the bar," said Cecil affably. He took off his coat and lit a large cigar. The women servants took our coats also. In the central part of the hall, near the wall, there was a large, very large fireplace. The burning wood started to give out yellow and orange flames. The hall was warm. I think there was central heating all over the house.

"Let them come in!" shouted Cecil from behind the bar.

"Yes, your lordship," uttered the butler obediently.

Suddenly, from a side door close to where we were standing, a brass band of about eight men in shabby uniforms playing a familiar old English tune walked in. This, I suppose, was another surprise from a man with a weird sense of humour.

"How do you like my band, Mr Akova?" he cried unsteadily—he was clearly on the way out. Stella helped him to an armchair near the fireplace. He was asleep in five minutes.

"Gilda," I whispered, "sit by the fireplace and wait for me. I have to talk to Stella in private."

"Be careful, Turan," she warned, and sat beside Lord Summerville.

"Come with me, Stella," I took her by the arm and walked out. The band had finished playing and the butler paid them off handsomely.

"At long last! A private session with the musical genius of the century!" she exclaimed, smiling and squeezing my hand. Cecil had told me back at the party that she sometimes enjoyed singing in her pretty soprano voice. Crazy as it may seem, I shuddered at the thought of accompanying her on the piano, but she insisted that I did. I had to give her whatever she wanted, as I needed desperately to make her talk about the Count and the Eridanian transformation process.

She put her hands into mine while we sat near the piano. They were soft and perfumed.

"You think I have sold my soul to the devil, eh?" she said suddenly, without any warning.

"Well, haven't you?"

"I don't know what happened to me. It's like magic. It gives me great pleasure. At the same time, I was forced into it by Draco."

"Forced into what, Stella?"

"Forced into becoming one of them," her angry glance said everything.

"You mean forced into becoming an Eridanian?" I asked.

"Yes, damn it! Do I have to spell it out for you?"

I felt something akin to pity. She was in an agony of indecision. She was a seductive woman and I knew she was stubbornly determined to go to bed with me.

"Take me upstairs, Turan," she whispered.

"I need your help, Stella."

"I am now relaxed and free from his devilish grip." She murmured into my ear, "I need your help too."

Her warm, sexy movements aroused turbulent moods, passions and thoughts in my body, soul and brain. We mounted the stairs and I opened the first door on the right. The room looked like a study and there was another fireplace in the corner.

"You must tell me about the process of transformation, Stella. You must tell me how we can stop it now!" I said fiercely.

"Turan," she almost cried. Her soft voice reduced the tension immediately, "Turan, be nice to me."

"I will, I will…"

"Don't worry. I will tell you what I know." We were now going round in circles, "First of all, I must tell you this. Eternal life with the devils of Eridanus is a fact. It's no fake allure. I met a man only two days ago, a man who was 797 years old."

"Tell me how they operate."

She pressed her beautiful body against me: "Turan, hold me. I'll whisper what I know into your ear."

I did just that while she started talking into my ear.

"Turan, it's something to do with the eyes. They have special powers in their eyes."

"Any red rays coming out of the eyes?" I had to ask her this as the red rays were the first real phenomenon I had observed in the process of transformation right from the start.

"No," she said emphatically, "no red rays. It's a kind of hypnosis. Probably a very advanced technological hypnosis. They stare into your eyes and within two minutes, you are transformed."

"So how come you are able to talk to me and tell me all this? Aren't you supposed to be under their full control?"

"My initiation is not yet complete. I have only been with him for a couple of days. Last night, he said he had a special treat for me. I don't know what that means, Turan, but I am terrified."

"Don't be afraid. Neither the Count nor anyone else can touch you while you are with me."

"But what will happen when you leave?"

"Don't worry. I'll tell you what to do when I leave."

I kissed her gently, soothing her nerves. She wanted to be loved. Her desire for sex was voracious. She undressed and slipped under the covers. After an hour of athletic and extremely passionate love-making, we lay in bed, smoking.

Suddenly, the lights went out. A terrific wind blew the balcony door open, and there he was. The tall dark figure of Count Dracula stood on the balcony. Immediately I put on my protection device and held Stella's hands firmly in my own. Everything in the room moved: the chairs, the table, the curtains, the two armchairs and the bed all crashing about into each other. Everything in the room flew over our heads with tremendous speed. I pulled Stella out of bed and onto the floor. The image of Dracula was even more dreadful with the light coming from the flames in the fireplace.

I heard a very loud noise coming from the balcony. A strange, high-pitched noise. The tall figure on the balcony stood motionless except for his long arms, which he moved very much like a karate expert as if he were directing the missiles which came hurtling down above our heads. Stella was not only agitated by his sudden appearance, but she was by now trembling violently with fear. This noise was enough to drive anyone to lose his mind. I crawled back into the darkness and then stood up near the bed. Trying my best to summon up my special powers (whatever they were!), I held up both arms, pointing at the Count. Draco gave a harsh cry and once again flew out into the pitch-black darkness. All the furniture and the rest of the stuff in the room fell to the floor. A gust of wind blew the curtains up once more and then dropped to a mere breeze from the north. Minutes later, the lights came on again. Stella, crouched beside the bed, looked up at me weakly. Thankfully, the hideous monster had disappeared for a second time.

"Come with me." Stella pulled my hand and rushed towards the door. She had hinted before that she might take me to a place in Whitby, but had not said where or what it was.

"Where are we going?" I asked, hoping against hope that she would lead me to something rather more tangible than the look in the eyes of the Eridanians. Quivering with tension, she slammed the door shut and we ran downstairs: "Just shut up and follow me!" she snapped. "I will take you somewhere where you will see how they operate."

Richardson, the butler, finally succeeded in procuring a taxi after a long twenty-minute wait at the door. I had told Gilda to wait for me. I could see drab houses lining the road as we went west out of Whitby. Then we arrived at the gate of another large mansion with striking individuality. It was in a pine forest and brilliantly lit to project the Victorian architecture at its best. Stella told the two minders at the door that I was a friend.

"Members only," stated the big man on the right, flexing his muscles. He made a contemptuous gesture, trying to hold me back.

"Listen," Stella lowered her voice threateningly, "he is a friend of Draco's— and that means he is a friend of mine…doesn't it?"

I met his gaze just once and he became speechless. The other man became more articulate as we entered.

"Listen, Miss," he pleaded, "you take responsibility for him, right? Otherwise we have to throw you out."

Stella adopted a more soothing manner: "You want me to tell Draco about this?"

"No." he mumbled, "he's not here, anyway."

Once again, I looked into the eyes of this second man, and he stepped aside, letting us in.

Stella led the way into a hall. There were at least a hundred people all dressed in black and standing as if at a ceremony. They all looked in the same direction, a fixed gaze at the stage. As Stella pulled me by the arm towards the stairs by the door, I could feel a centrifugal force driving the people outwards and away from the circular ceremonial centre. We climbed the stairs and hid behind the seats at the edge of the balcony. From this point, we had a bird's eye view of the hall. This was a place of communion. We sat on the floor. Stella explained to me in a low voice: "There is a substance called 'maro' which they brought in from Eridanus, the largest planet in the Epsilon Eridani star system. They need to mix maro with water and take it regularly to survive. This mixture of maro and water is also used as one of the ways of transforming humans into Eridanians."

"In other words, they are contaminating the water supply."

"Yes," she concurred, "they are doing this all over the world."

"We have to find an antidote that will destroy this maro substance. And we have to find it now."

"Yes, my darling…" she purred, in her warm, winsome voice. "You had better contact all the scientists you know to do just that. But first, you have to get a handful of that substance."

"Ah, but that is your job, Stella."

"Who? Me?" she blurted out, startled out of her newfound complacency to contemplation of such a mission.

"Well," she continued, rallying, "I suppose I could slip into the crowd, as I am, after all, a member. But I do not think Draco will take lying down the fact that I was in bed with you only an hour ago."

"He will not see you. I will make sure of that."

"But how, Turan?"

"I will create a decoy. An old trick. But it works every time, if you improvise."

Suddenly, the crowd started singing on just four different notes. It was like a sermon sung in harmony. The very tall figurer of Count Dracula appeared on stage. The singing stopped abruptly. The audience was completely mesmerised by the Count's speech. The harsh bass voice reverberated through the hall:

"The universe was created out of a primordial ball of matter. We Eridanians have dominated several galaxies. Now we look at our own galaxy, what the humans call the Milky Way. We are the masters and we are in control. It is of the utmost importance that we control Planet Earth and the whole solar system. We have the substance and Earth has the water. So we can do it. Take the substance, maro, and mix it with the water; do it now, and do it everywhere…This is one way to deal with the inferior humans. There will be other plans that I will divulge to you in due course."

At this point, a prismatic transparent object with bright, clear colours appeared above the Count's head. The substance, maro, was right in the centre of the circular hall. Stella was already down among the crowd. I pulled out my gun and started firing at the prismatic transparent object. Obviously this was an Eridanian tool, but I had no idea why it appeared right above Draco's head. His reaction reverberated against the walls:

"The enemy is here. Seek him out and destroy him."

There was panic in the hall and the crowd scattered in all directions. I went and disappeared into the crowd, trying to be elusive. I could see Stella grabbing the substance and putting it into her skirt. In spite of the skirmishes, we managed to get out of the building…

A taxi was waiting outside. We jumped in and went straight back to Lord Summerville's mansion. Cold winds swept in from the North Sea as we entered the house. There were about ten people still drinking and enjoying the party. It was now a quarter past one in the morning. Patrick approached and spluttered a few words of apology: "Turan, I'm so sorry. I wasn't able to find you." I had no plausible explanation to offer.

"Patrick, I had to persevere in my efforts to uncover the secrets of the Eridanians. Stella helped a great deal."

Gilda stepped forward and took my hand. The rest of the crowd gathered around, commenting on the concert. The flattery and toadying they forced on me was one of the trials of becoming a favourite of the public.

"There was an unexpected tirade against the existence of UFOs by a couple whom I've never met before." Gilda told me.

"She is referring to the remarks of the gentry here," said Patrick calmly, and added a few more epithets regarding their background. His flamboyant style contrasted with that of the so-called cream of the aristocracy. His remarks were not charitable, but Patrick could not stand such people who rejected out of hand the very idea of extraterrestrial presence.

Now I had reached a stage where I had just about managed to chart the progress of the movements of the Eridanians. I could not trust anyone, except maybe Gilda. Stella also had been saved at the last minute.

"Gilda," I said, "Stella is coming with us to London. She will be in constant danger here. Patrick, Draco is our man. He is Count Dracula, the Eridanian leader. I am sending you ten protection devices from London by hand. He will give you instructions on how to use this device. They cannot touch you as long as you wear it."

I thanked Patrick and left the house with Gilda and Stella. We went back to the cottage. It was about 2.15 in the morning, by the time we retired into separate bedrooms.

After the journey from Yorkshire to London in a hired car, I embarked this time on a mission to Stonehenge. Stonehenge, Stonehenge, here I come…

I have always gone to unusual lengths to fight against acts of blatant injustice. This was no mere injustice, however, this was a clandestine invasion of Earth by extraterrestrials who had arrived from the Seat of the Devil. Having investigated the pattern whereby the Eridanian extraterrestrials had firmly established themselves, it was quite apparent that a slick take-over had occurred. They had done it smoothly, efficiently and apparently effortlessly. These were creatures who acted on an enormous scale. The substance of maro with which they had contaminated water all over the world had already been sent to at least twelve scientists from the USA to Britain; from Germany to Japan; from Turkey to Peru. But even if these scientists did find a liquid solution to eliminate the effect of maro, this was no practical way to deal with the situation. Imagine enormous amounts of this antidote being taken to all the countries in the world and planted into the water systems of each and every city to destroy maro! It couldn't be done. Perhaps the best course would have been to destroy maro itself. But we did not know where the stocks were kept. No, I was pretty sure there had to be another, much simpler, way to eliminate the seemingly indestructible force of the Eridanians.

Nevertheless, information about maro was immediately communicated to the world media. It would be superfluous to expect some sort of total victory against the Eridanians. No one could anticipate the way of the devil. It is true, of course, that the discovery excited everyone, not least the media. It was obvious that the delirium could not last.

Eighteen

The train left Paddington Station at 12.15 pm. It was approximately two and a half hours' drive to Great Bedwyn. I had planned a visit to Sir John Talbot at Marlborough before heading on to Stonehenge. He had already arrived in his royal blue Daimler Sovereign 4.2 and was waiting for me at the station. I had met Sir John before in North Cyprus and he had introduced me to the Marlborough International Jazz Festival where I had performed the previous year. He had been a UFO buff for many years, doing his own research. He had called immediately after my departure from Whitby and said he had some vital information about the extraterrestrials. Sir John was a man of considerable influence in the upper echelons of government. He lived a life of affluence with his wife, a charming lady who had been kind enough to drive me in her own car to Stonehenge the previous year.

The minute I entered the car, this cool, calm English gentleman started excitedly, "Turan, Thomas Matthews, a close friend of mine, was at Stonehenge the other day. He was the last to leave and as he walked past the monument, he found a metal box. In it, there were two feathers, just like the feathers you found in North Cyprus. I think you ought to see this man and the box."

"OK," I said, "you can take me to him right away."

The feather that I had found back in North Cyprus was also kept in a box, in the USA. But later it had been stolen. I was completely snowed under by the contaminated water business, the count's devilish new plan, of which I knew nothing and now the discovery of two more feathers in a metal box! The West Loo—Whitby—Stonehenge triangle was another mystery. The only connection between these three points was the extraterrestrial presence. There had to be something else. Something concrete. After sending the latest information to the London office, e-mails were coming in thick and fast.

Thomas Matthews' house was on the road leading to Avebury. The detached house was in a cul-de-sac about fifty metres from the main road. It was a sunny afternoon. We walked along a pathway in the middle of a well-kept garden. An Alsatian sat in front of the door which was slightly ajar. The dog's long, loud howling was quite unusual as it just sat there and did not make a move towards us. Sir John called out for Mr Matthews.

"Thomas," he paused the door open and entered. I followed him. Just then, a woman came running towards us in a state of panic.

"They beat him!" she cried.

A man sat in an armchair at the other end of the room.

"Sir John," he gasped, pale with shock and utter incredulity, "two men threatened to kill me unless I gave them the box. I'm sorry. I should've listened to you and handed it over to the authorities."

"Call the police," said Sir John to Mrs Matthews.

"I already have."

It was obvious that our adversaries were one step ahead. The Eridanians had people working for them all over the place. Perhaps the metal box with the feathers sent out signals on its own. One thing was certain. These boxes with the feathers must have been invaluable to the extraterrestrials. A power source diffusing, spreading out innumerable cosmic streams contaminating the brains of humans. This was just another theory. How to retrieve at least one of the boxes with the feathers? That was the question. The count might have both boxes…

Nagging her husband incessantly, Mrs Matthews bent over to wipe the blood from her husband's face. "I told you," she sniped, "I told you not to get mixed up with these people and metal boxes and feathers."

He was clearly exasperated by her insistence. A twinkle in his eyes belied the gravity of his demeanour. He did not even bother to answer back. The local police took the description of the two men and left.

Sweeping over Stonehenge with an army helicopter with Sir John at sunset, I looked for evidence that could prove the presence of extraterrestrials. The bird's eye view of Stonehenge was spectacular, but there was nothing to suggest any unusual presence. The filming and photography of the age-old pre-historic site was complete.

Stonehenge is the most outstanding and mysterious prehistoric monument in England. It is said that ancient people, 5,000 years ago, mapped the course of the sun and the moon to build this extraordinary centre of one of the world's earliest cultures. The large stones in the circle are Sarson stones brought from the Marlborough Downs thirty kilometres away. The smaller stones, known as the

Bluestones, were brought from the mystical Preseli Mountains in Wales, 385 kilometres away.

Sir John was instrumental in securing permission for me to visit the site at night. I walked around Stonehenge under a very clear night sky. As I stood in the middle of the circle, I shivered at the sight of seven images. These were clear figures of extraterrestrials. The presence was there. This was an unnatural radiation of a very bright light…

The seven figures were almost transparent. A blinding white light shone all over the site. The figures looked like Halloween freaks. They were tall and thin with ugly faces. I felt sure they were the emissaries of the Devil. I had my protective device on me. I found myself surrounded by the aliens and the danger was imminent. The slanting eyes focussed on my eyes, they stood there motionless. One came forward. A very thin figure whose diabolical face was all lights. Now I could see the tight-fitting white outfit he was wearing. I was going through a shock of helplessness.

I felt powerless, inferior and at the same time, enraged. Now the alien was just a few feet away from me. The eyes were big and dark and deeply set in the somewhat triangular longish face. The nose was retroussé and wide. This was a traumatic experience and nothing like my encounters with the Greys…The encounter with the devil was beyond words. It was like an evil force blasting into my soul. I had to stop this demonic attack. The word 'challenge' multiplied itself with capital letters in the corners of my mind. It was a very difficult, demanding and stimulating task, but I had to do it. I had to ward off the seven demons with energy and determination. I felt I had accessed the source of creative energy that could protect me from the danger staring me in the face.

Was this some sort of concentrated action by the Eridanian extraterrestrials to destroy the powers I had acquired through my contacts with the Greys? I had no idea. They just stood there, staring at me. And I stared back. Minutes later, all seven disappeared with a sudden thrust into the night sky…

All along, I had argued that it was impossible to determine the peculiar behaviour of the extraterrestrials. What I had experienced at Stonehenge was a big mystery from whatever angle you looked at. Would they eliminate me once and for all? Were they trying to transform me also? Or perhaps both attempts on both accounts were repulsed by the powerful force with which I had been armed. The power given to me by the Greys as the leader of the Chosen 36.

Humans have the problem of seeing things with human eyes. They try to understand things with the human brain. They sometimes evaluate and define the behaviour of the extraterrestrials, some of the UFO encounters and extraordinary experiences as benevolent, kind and friendly. We see them as very advanced space civilisations who perhaps want to save us from ourselves. On the other hand, we see them also as malevolent. As evil aliens, whose sole aim is to conquer Earth and wipe out humankind. The Eridanian devils' strategy was based on the gradual conquest of Earth and the human race with the transformation of the brain and souls of humans into their own devilish form and characteristics. The Greys, on the other hand, wanted to save the human race not only from themselves but from the evil forces of the Devil from the star system Epsilon Eridani.

Two different extraterrestrial civilisations, Epsilon Eridani—the devil and his armies descended on Earth, coming from this star system 10.5 light years' distance from the Solar System, and Alpha Centauri, one of the homes of the Greys—the nearest star system to the Solar System—a mere 4.3 light-years away. The other home of the Greys was Zeta Reticuli, 37 light-years from us. So the Greys came from two star systems at least 32 light-years apart. That was another mystery. How could the same extraterrestrial civilisation come from two different star systems so far away from each other? But the records showed that the Greys came originally from these two star systems...

Both these star systems were in our own Milky Way Galaxy. There are in fact 46 nearest stars similar to the sun within a radius of 54 light-years that are single or part of a wide multiple star system. They have no known irregularities or variations, and are between 0.4 and 2.0 times the luminosity of the sun. Thus a planet basically identical to Earth could be orbiting around any one of them. So this means that there are probably some more extraterrestrial civilisations within that radius of 54 light-years.

On my way back to Marlborough in Sir John's car, I remembered all these data from my studies on extraterrestrial civilisations. At the current time, we were regularly visited by two extraterrestrial civilisations—the devils from Epsilon Eridani and the 'good' extraterrestrials from Alpha Centauri and Zeta Reticuli. But what did they want from us?

Dr Steven Greer—the Director of the Centre for the Study of Extraterrestrial Intelligences—after a comprehensive survey of documents and case studies, reached the conclusion that there are seven principal activities of the extraterrestrials which may answer the question, "What do they want?" These are:

1. General reconnaissance of the Earth and its civilisations;
2. Study of human psychology;
3. Assessment of human development;
4. Monitoring the space programmes with particular interest in parts directed towards establishing colonies in space;
5. Limited interaction with humans to pass on information about themselves and to accustom us to their presence.

I would add to that Dr John E. Mack's theory. He sees abduction as a form of benevolent biological intervention. Extraterrestrials are creating a hybrid species to preserve human DNA, because humankind faces extinction owing to our wilful destruction of the environment.

Some ufologists suggest the aliens who have been studying and observing planet earth for over 60 years are now ready for an invasion. They say the chances of the survival of the human race if such an attack began, are very low indeed...Some go even further to suggest that *while we know very little about the aliens, SETI (Search of Extraterrestrial Intelligence) is beaming out messages into space actually handing over information to the extraterrestrials. They tell anyone out there who cares to listen the position of our Solar System in the Milky Way Galaxy, the position of planet earth within the solar system, the total population of the earth, the average height of humans, the structure of our DNA and the atomic numbers of carbon, hydrogen, oxygen, nitrogen and phosphorus—the elements of which we are made. No invading force in history has been given such vital intelligence.* (Extract from The World's Greatest UFO and Alien Encounters).

The present situation was far worse than all the scenarios predicted by some ufologists. There was a bewildering array of theories on how to eradicate the evil Eridanians. Scientists all over the world worked overtime on strategies that would at least defend the human race and prevent the transformation of humans into Eridanian form. But that seemed like an impossible task. The Devil and its emissaries had some form of power that was definitely beyond the understanding of humans. With a technology vastly superior to our own, there would be no contest in a war, and our puny weaponry would be no match against such superior forces.

Sir John dropped me off at my hotel in the main street of Marlborough and promised to make an appointment with the Crop Circles man, Charlie Boyle, for the next day. The Ivey House was a pleasant, small hotel with very efficient personnel. Room 20 was reserved for me. All the knowledge I had gathered during the last twenty years of research and reading on UFOs, extraterrestrial intelligences and star systems in our own Milky Way galaxy repeated themselves throughout the night in my mind. Finally, at about 2.00 am, I was really very tired and slept like a baby until 9 the following morning.

Our appointment with Charlie Boyle was at 6.00 pm. Sir John drove his car through Marlborough and then into Avebury. Samantha's Pub was on the Kennet and Avon Canal which runs from Reading to Bath and has a spectacular series of 29 locks. Charlie Boyle was the author of several books mainly on country life. Sir John told me it had been about a year ago that Charlie's interest switched to UFOs and crop circles in particular. He had become quite well-known in Wiltshire. His eye witness account of three saucer-shaped metallic objects hovering over a field of wheat forging markings was published in the local paper. When Sir John had told him of the extraterrestrial presence in Whitby, West Loo and Stonehenge, and that I was a key figure carrying out the investigation into this alien presence, he was doubly interested. He told Sir John over the phone that he had followed the story in the papers and on television. He said that he was sure there was a link between crop circles and the devilish extraterrestrial Eridanians.

Charlie was at Samantha's Pub. We found him in the backroom, and by the looks of it, he had come well prepared with documents and large photographs of crop circles. He raised c himself from the table while Sir John walked to the bar to get the beers.

"How do you do," said Charlie politely.

"I am Turan Akova, a Turkish Cypriot from North Cyprus."

"Pleased to meet you, Mr Akova," He said, "I have read about you in the papers. I also watched your interviews on TV. Is it really that bad? I mean, is the silent invasion by the extraterrestrials true?"

"Yes," I replied, "I'm afraid so. And worst of all, we are not able to stop them."

Sir John came back with the beers. Lady Pamela sat near the window and I sat opposite Charlie Boyle. Charlie shuffled the papers around on the desk and produced a very large picture of a crop circle.

"Well, I don't know how or why, but there must be a connection. I'm positive these crop circles are made by the extraterrestrials. Why, I do not know. Now look at this picture. This is probably the best and biggest crop circle in the area."

He put the large photograph on the table. We all got up to take a good look at it; it was really an amazing configuration. Charlie continued excitedly: "This gigantic crop circle was approximately 600 ft in diameter and the shapes within it defied all conventional interpretation. I'm sure you'll agree it would not be possible for any man-made machine to make such a complicated and perfect figure. Was it some kind of insect? Was it depicting a conjunction of stars or planets? This circle appeared below Windmill Hill—one of the oldest prehistoric encampments in the UK, I think from 3,700 BC. Visitors to this formation used their mobile phones and cameras to report a whole series of inexplicable effects whilst standing inside the circle. This photo was taken by a photographer who works with me." He paused for a moment, and then continued, "What I experienced about five days ago is absolute proof that these circles are made by the extraterrestrials. I took photos of the tramline markings I saw appearing in a field of wheat with three mysterious white metallic saucer-shaped objects actually making them. It was early evening, around 6.30 when I was cycling past a field just below West Woods when I noticed three moving white metallic saucer-shaped objects suspended above the field so that the tops of the wheat were bent over...I swear, Mr Akova, this was no dream or hallucination. I stopped instantly and concentrated on what I was looking at. I had never seen UFOs before. But these were UFOs, I am sure. I'd never seen anything like them before. Three saucer-shaped craft above the field. They were a metallic white, somewhat oblong and domed on the upper surface, with smooth contours and no edges. Two of them moved slowly through the wheat and down the slope of the field, leaving a trail behind them. The third one rose slightly above the other two for a few minutes and then dropped back to the same level. All three UFOs were about three feet above the crop. The size of the UFOs must have been about four feet across and six feet in length. I felt they had some purpose or other...I sat there watching in amazement, and took some pictures. I will show them to you in a minute."

He put a red file on the table. This was really a serious matter and his story was very impressive indeed. Charlie lit a cigarette: "Mr Akova, Sir John, as I said, I considered some possibilities. Possibilities such as a scientific crop research, or perhaps a trial of new spraying equipment, or even people playing around in the field itself. No. Not a chance. No farmer would break his wheat where there were already tractor tracks through the crop for them to operate in. I think the UFO beings in these strange crafts were aware of my presence. Some mysterious power stopped me from trying to get closer. Every time I had the urge to do so, something—some power tantamount to a command, a telepathic communication, if you like—stopped me. Something coming from the UFOs told me not to get any closer. The next day, I visited the same spot. A crop formation had appeared in the same field…"

It has been at least 20 years since crop circles appeared in England. This meant that the Eridanians had already been here over 20 years before. I had no idea whether there had been any transformations during the past twenty years. The likelihood of an extraterrestrial presence of the current magnitude was quite improbable as there had been no evidence to point in that direction. The crop circles were in the vicinity of Stonehenge, one of the points forming the triangle with West Loo and Whitby. But I was more concerned with the box that had been stolen from Thomas Matthews. Right from the start, we had formulated an instantaneous communication system with most of the intelligence agencies throughout the world. Already, MI5, 6 and 7 were combing the area to find the two men who had attacked Matthews. Not only did I have access to all the information on UFO close encounters or extraterrestrial presence while they were being processed, but I was an accredited, officially recognised representative of the UFO Centre in London. This meant that the police, intelligence agencies, government officials, ministers, members of parliament, prime ministers and even presidents would cooperate and try to help whenever possible. It was just a matter of time before the police apprehended the two men.

It was just past 8.30 pm when I received a telephone call from the local police in Marlborough. Two MI5 agents and two policemen from the Marlborough Police Station traced a call made from a house not far from Sir John's house near the large parking lot. The two men were arrested and brought over to the station. The police had searched the house and found nothing. But the neighbour next door said he had seen a third man in a red Toyota jeep. The third man had not got out of the car, he said, and the two men had handed him a package in a plastic bag. Then he had driven off in great haste.

Obviously, the all-important box was given to the third mystery man in the red jeep. It would be naïve to think that such a disappearing act was a fluke. Immediately after the apprehension of the two men, a computerised search detected only five red Toyota jeeps registered in Marlborough, with the names and addresses of the owners. Four of the owners were cleared of any suspicion as the cars had been parked in their homes. All four owners were interviewed all the same, just to make sure. The fifth Toyota had somehow disappeared into thin air. While the MI5 agents and the police went off to locate the red Toyota, I had other ideas…

By now, I was accustomed to the ways of the devilish Eridanians. I stopped dithering and decided to search the house where the two men had been arrested. Perhaps the third mystery man in the red Toyota jeep was yet another decoy. I parked the car at least a hundred metres from the house. I was surprised to see that the police had not cordoned off the premises for some unknown reason. There was a For Sale sign right next to the garden gate. It was a cold evening and the moon was covered with black clouds. While I tiptoed into the garden from a side entrance, the night sky cleared once again above the windswept hillside and the half-moon shone through.

The lights were on in the front room of the house and I could see the shadow of a man behind the curtains. The front porch was rather sordid. I stepped in as the door was open. An exotic creature stood there smiling at me. A beautiful seductive woman wearing a white, transparent dress. I was immediately taken by her beauty. She was very slick and libidinous but did not move a muscle. A faint smile flickered across the beautiful face. The eyes were very strange and glassy with no expression. As I took a step towards this strange beauty, two very tall men appeared behind her. She walked back, made a sharp movement with her right hand and simply evaporated. Another game of the devil. The two apes who looked like world champions in pumping iron jumped on me…

Several blows rained on my body, and I fell to the floor. I did not feel any pain as I was wearing the protective device. Nevertheless, these two heavies had the upper hand for a long minute at least, as I struggled to get up. I hit the man nearest to me, but he did not budge. I could see the other man grabbing the box on the table. As I tried to stop him, I stumbled and fell face down on the sharp edge of a metal table. The two men who looked like twins ran out of the house.

I took out my gun and fired at their legs. One of them fell while the other disappeared into the nearby forest. He had managed to escape with the box. Within seconds, the police had arrived. They took the wounded man into a van, and I ran into the forest with gun in hand. I asked the police to send in more men and surround the area. It had started to rain heavily. I took out the torch in my pocket. Police with Alsatians had already surrounded the small forest to the north of the area. The strong light from the torch flashed all over in front of me. Then I spotted the big man. I fired to warning shots. He stopped suddenly. The box and the untidy bundle of files slipped from his hands in the streaming rain, onto the wet, muddy ground…

"Stop!" I shouted, "or I will shoot to kill!"

Several police officers with guns were just now a few metres behind him. His stooping figure and his clumsy movements were surprisingly very much unlike the character of the man I had encountered in the house. He was ready to surrender. I grabbed the box and collected all the files he had dropped. The big man tottered visibly as the police pushed him into the van. Now, I had the box. One thing was certain: the box generated a special power—the power of the devil. It would be presumptuous to assume that our scientists would be able to control or destroy this power. Nevertheless, we had to try. No one—including myself—knew how many of these boxes had arrived on Earth during the latest secret onslaught of the Eridanians. The one I had found in North Cyprus had been the first. There were three more: in West Loo, Whitby and Stonehenge. I had managed to get one box out of the West Loo—Whitby—Stonehenge triangle, but there could be other boxes in other countries. On the other hand, there was not a single report from anywhere in the world on mysterious boxes and feathers. The mystery surrounding the West Loo—Whitby—Stonehenge triangle was unsolved. All that had occurred at these three points in England re-echoed interminably in my brain. While Emma, back at the UFO Centre in London, noted down every single detail of our findings with scrupulous accuracy.

Marlborough Police had already interviewed the two men. But I decided to interrogate them myself. I walked into the room on my own. The two men sat behind a table.

"Who sent you to get the box with the feather?" I asked. The man on the right answered with an ill-mannered, bad-tempered and insufferable insolence.

"Who the hell are you? The police have no right to hold us here. You have no proof of anything."

I tried to keep calm. He lashed out at me again with intense fury: "I wouldn't tell you even if I knew, but I can say this much. It's like winning the lottery, the amount of money we've been paid to do the job…" He paused for a moment, "Listen, don't ask me where the money is. We have no intention of parting with that kind of cash."

"But you have failed," I interrupted him. "Now, we have the box. So you are in serious trouble. They will get the money back, all right. In the meantime, I've been told by the police that you will be charged with assault, stealing and breaking and entering…Also, there is one more thing. Do you know what they do with those who fail?"

The man on the left looked despondent. These two men did not show any symptoms of transformation. They were probably just hired to do the job. The Police Chief at Marlborough Station had already delivered a firm warning to the two men. I think they were both aggravated that they would be charged for the crimes they had committed. My comment on their failure and the fact that they would be hunted down by the Eridanians had frightened the life out of them.

The man on the left seemed more sensible as he got up from his chair and approached me: "Sir, I think you are right. We will need police protection," he said apologetically, "but honestly, we did not see the man who ordered us to steal the box. The message was delivered by telephone. We were staying at the King's Arms Hotel. The money—a million pounds each—was delivered to reception there. The receptionist did not see who brought the bag with the cash."

I believed him. The violent behaviour of the other man had been subdued by his friend. It was almost a quarter past ten when I left the police station.

Nineteen

I was starving. The nice lady at the hotel—the receptionist—ordered a fillet steak, mashed potatoes and brussels sprouts, and I sat at a table overlooking the courtyard. It was a splendid dinner, but after the apple pie and custard the food lay heavy on my stomach. I placed the box with the feather in my old Samsonite briefcase and held it beside me at all times. The next day, I said my goodbyes to Sir John and his family and left by train for London.

Back to the scurry and scramble of city life. But I loved London. I had spent fifteen years, off and on, in London, first during my student days, then as a pianist/composer and journalist. In fact, my musical career took off there. It was time to sit down and reflect upon all our findings. We also had to develop a new strategy against the devil and its armies who had become a vital force in social and political life.

During my absence, Emma's research was inextricably intertwined with one half of the equation. An equation that would show us the way to uncover the new strategies of the Eridanians. Emma had infiltrated the homes, the offices and the activities of prominent people in politics. After her initial contacts, she managed to gain the confidence of several influential people in the government. It was through these people that she came across a secret, cunning plan that pumped disinformation to the media and to the public at large. The message was simple, that extraterrestrial presence and the secret invasion of the so-called extraterrestrial forces were stories made up by ufologists wanting to disrupt the smooth running strategies of the world powers, and particularly of the European Union, with the ultimate purpose of uniting peoples and countries under one roof in a multi-racial society in peace with itself. It was unbelievable, but news stories, articles and TV documentaries focused mainly on nation-state protagonists who wanted to dismantle efforts towards a negotiating process for the political union of the EU.

Television coverage of UFOs and extraterrestrial presence had become rather sparse. It seemed as though a media black-out preventing the release of information on the subject had become operational, especially in England. This new development could not be lightly brushed aside. Emma was rather worried and was busy setting up a meeting of ufologists.

"Invite some of the Americans, also," I said.

"Yes, I will." She walked into her room at the centre, and I followed.

"Turan, it's an extremely delicate situation. They seem to have control of the mass media in almost all European countries. And the worst part of all this is that we don't know who to trust anymore. It's like total surrender. The government here and the EU Commission seem to have resigned themselves to accepting the terms put forward by the Eridanians. I sent two private detectives to Brussels. They were able to wangle a press invitation at the headquarters of the Commission. Posing as journalists, they placed a recording device into the main meeting room. The whole meeting between the Eridanians and the EU Commission was recorded. Clearly, an accord between the two is imminent. Britain, Germany, France and Italy were represented at the meeting at the highest level. There is strong evidence from the recording from which I gathered that a covert group within the EU is engaged in the back-engineering of alien spacecraft. This group, which is clearly on the payroll of the Eridanians says there is nothing intrinsically wrong in acquiring alien technology. But, Turan, whether they learn the technology of the Eridanians or not does not matter very much as the aim of this evil extraterrestrial civilisation is a secret invasion and full control of planet Earth. Once they have full control, it won't matter whether the EU learns the technology or not. Remember, it's not just the technology that the Eridanians are offering. They have already promised everlasting life."

"Emma, the Americans have been working on back-engineering at Area 51 for years. Confirmed reports say these alien spacecraft at this secret base belong to the Greys. The Americans are developing an alien technology, that of the Greys, at both Area 51 and S-4 secret bases. I suspect the Grey technology has not been fully developed despite a lengthy period of time since the Rosewell incident in 1947. But the Greys have not yet come out into the open. They want to help us, but their presence is always surrounded by mystery and uncertainty. Without their help, I do not think humankind can survive. Whenever I made contact with them, I have been told to challenge the Eridanians. As you know, the Chosen 36 have been equipped by the Greys with special powers. But the

Greys appear only when I try to contact them through telepathic communication. Although I'm sure they are well aware of the current situation, common sense tells us that the Americans may be lagging behind the EU as far as alien technology is concerned. At any rate, if the EU has agreed to the Eridanian terms, there isn't much we can do on that account."

But we had to do something. I knew exactly what to do. We had to inform the Americans. This new development was totally unexpected. Emma's investigations had uncovered a new and complicated problem. If announced, the Eridanian strategy would succeed in entrenching a division between countries who were determined to stop the secret invasion of the aliens, and those who had already succumbed to their will. The EU would use this new technology in their space programme. I listened to the tapes. What surprised me most of all was the fact that there were billions of dollars involved. How on earth would an extraterrestrial civilisation accumulate such enormous sums of earthy money. Clearly, the aliens had wealthy allies all over the world. The monies to be paid to the EU would increase this organisation's budget tenfold, thus creating the most powerful financial giant on earth.

At the meeting organised by our UFO centre, the USA was represented by two men: one of the top political advisers to the President and the CIA Chief. I thought the immediate release of this vital secret information would send alarm signals of EU domination in a world where the US had been—at least, until now—the supreme power. The EU was now on the verge of becoming the number one space organisation with Eridanian technology. The US would not tolerate such a development. Our confidence was profoundly shaken by the fact that there were high-ranking officials representing the major EU member states who had become puppets of the Eridanians, one way or the other. Now the USA and we, the UFO Centre, had to decide whether to announce our findings about the secret meeting between EU officials and the Eridanians, thus facing more ridicule from the mass media which was already biased against us, as a result of the propaganda, or whether to keep it a closely guarded secret.

While the American representative insisted on the full disclosure of the secret meeting between the EU Commission and the Eridanians, the British Foreign Minister, Stephen Leyton, said such a disclosure would ultimately affect relations between the EU and the USA, and suggested stalling for time.

"Already they have infiltrated the EU at prime minister level. According to the information from the meeting, billions of dollars have gone into the EU budget. This suggests they have control of powerful multi-national companies."

"This is a huge drain on many multi-national company's resources. None of them can survive for much longer, unless of course, they are collaborating with a counterfeit money organisation. At any rate, I think we ought to organise a meeting of the prime ministers of Britain, France, Germany and Italy, and have them listen to the tapes. Once they know they have been cornered, they will be forced to resign. From then on, we take matters into our own hands. But we have to act fast. Fast enough to avert the Eridanian handover of space technology to the EU."

The foreign ministers of France, Germany and Italy agreed. The Americans were a bit reluctant to accept such a proposition at first, but they also agreed in the end. The content of the tapes could not be construed as just very serious accusations. It was sure proof of the sell-out of the EU to the Eridanians. Stephen Leyton said he would arrange the meeting of the four prime ministers within the next couple of days.

The attempt of the Eridanians to take control of the EU was a shocking new revelation. Everyone at the UFO Centre, the British Foreign Minister Leyton and the Americans in particular was annoyed beyond reason. If this was leaked to the press, it would most certainly lead to the disintegration of the European Union. How could the four major EU member states, namely Britain, France, Germany and Italy, have been drawn into such a trap.

The implementation of the concept of political integration and political union of all member states of the European Union was a long and complicated process, and yet the European Commission, probably under the influence of the aliens, wanted to double the speed of the process. But the reports I had received from experts in the EU suggested this move towards the sharing of power between the national governments and the Eridanian-controlled Brussels was still in its infancy. The reports also said a power struggle was going on between the aliens and high-ranking EU officials. There was a move towards a reformation of integration and political union and the outlines of an evolving confederation began to emerge in the formation of the European state structure.

No matter what happened in Brussels in the next few days, we had to watch out for the big four, namely Britain, France, Germany and Italy. The leaders of these four major countries would determine the future of the European Union. The Eridanian strategy was, as far as I could tell, domination by infiltration.

The meeting of the four prime ministers went as planned. I was present, with Emma, and of course, the Americans were there, too. Steven Leyton was next in line in the Labour Party to succeed the ousted prime minister. The resignation of all the four prime ministers caused a furore in the media and no one could really understand what was happening in Brussels.

It was now apparent that many officials in the European Union had been lured by the promises of the Eridanians. This was by no means a secret meeting of the four prime ministers and the aliens. There were others to take over where the four prime ministers had left off. I had to carry out a thorough investigation in the European Union itself. But first of all, I decided to pay a visit to the offices of the two private detectives Emma had hired. Emma's achievement had been quite extraordinary. No one would even begin to imagine a takeover of the European Union by the Eridanians. But Emma had her own suspicions, and eventually she was proved right.

The roar of the train reverberated in the long tunnel just before reaching Brussels. My visit to the Massey and Massey Private Detective Agency in King's Cross, London had proved very fruitful indeed as the two brothers had given me a few important contacts in Brussels. The first was Phillippe Trousoutte, a Frenchman who lived there. The report described him as a scientist of international stature with a spotless reputation. He was not suspected of any collaboration with the Eridanians. The other was a high-ranking official in charge of foreign affairs in the EC. Sifting through the EU documents in the file, I found her. She was only thirty-five; young, considering her important office at the Commission. These were the two people I was supposed to trust.

The aim of my investigation into the EU was not just to extract information leading to the ringleaders of the plot to overtake this vast organisation, but to find out if they had the box with the feather. Apart from the one I had found in Marlborough, the other two were still missing. The secret of the box with the feather was still a mystery to us all. The scientists in the USA and Britain were not yet able to decipher the special powers of the feather. The diabolic cunning of the devil sent out conflicting messages, and the pattern of the Eridanian strategy was completely unpredictable. We hardly knew what to expect next...

The Devil's strategy was unpredictable and impulsive. A ghoulish behaviour, if you like. Somehow, the power of the feather would generate indomitable and changeable, and yet, undetectable action. This was a strange characteristic. The main difficulty was that the feather could not be destroyed. So far, the tests conducted on it had proved a waste of time. They maintained there was nothing emanating from it, and it was highly likely that they would conclude that this evil extraterrestrial toy was dead…

If the power of the feather was now extinct, how would the Eridanians regenerate the power they needed to carry on with the secret invasion? Was the feather in the box the only tool of this evil technology? Apart from the transformation by the red beams piercing into the eyes of humans, no one had witnessed any other pernicious effect from the feather. So perhaps this meant some form of interrelated dynamic was in force to ensure the devil's control over humans. But I could not trace any signs of such visible action on the part of the Eridanians.

I did not know Brussels very well, although I had been there a couple of times in the past. The taxi took me from the station through one of the seedier parts of the city. It was a gloomy, murky, early winter evening with no moon. My contact in Brussels was an old friend of Emma's, a woman who worked for the Foreign Relations Committee of the EC. Her name was Julia Van Weddingsen. As arranged, she arrived at the Brussels Hilton where I was staying at around 8.30 pm. While I lit a cigarette in the smoking area, I could see a good-looking woman in her mid-forties approaching the reception desk.

"Mr Turan Akova is expecting me," she said to the man behind the reception desk. I had met the man with the black glasses at reception only an hour before. The woman, according to Emma, had a reputation of the highest academic standards.

I walked up to the reception desk and introduced myself.

"Julia Van Weddingsen?"

"Yes," she extended a hand.

"I am Akova, and I would like to invite you to dinner."

"You don't waste much time."

"The man at the reception desk said the restaurant here at the hotel is very good. Shall we try it?"

"Why not?" she gave me a mischievous smile.

"I don't have to fill you in about the current state of affairs. I'm sure Emma told you everything." I said as we sat at the table. "The two British detectives were not able to identify the two men who were representing the Eridanians.

Well, they only got a glimpse of the people getting out of the room. I am talking about the meeting between the now ex-prime ministers of Britain, France, Germany and Italy and the Eridanians. One detective gave me a description of a very tall man. This matches that of the man I met in Whitby, who turned out to be Count Dracula, or Draco."

"This is really too fantastic. No one would believe it, really," she said in a French accent, "you think he is the Dracula who came from Romania?"

"I don't think so, Julia. I know so. I met him in Whitby myself. He is definitely an Eridanian. The leader of this alien race."

"But how can you be sure?"

"I'm sure because he told me so. The secret notes of the famous author, Bram Stoker, who created the literary character of Dracula tells us the same story. I found the notes in Whitby." Apparently, Emma hadn't told her of my Whitby adventures.

"Well, how can I help you?"

"The lack of progress so far in trying to stop the Eridanian infiltration has been very dispiriting. It's an awkward problem. We don't know who we are looking for—except for Draco, of course—and we don't know how to stop them. The European Union seems to be the centre of activity at the moment." She thought for a moment and looked at me with unswerving eye contact. Her eyes were impressive and penetrating.

"Emma told me of her investigation into the matter," she said despondently, "I take it this is a top secret investigation on your part. And that's how it should be. Otherwise the disclosure of such fantastic news would create panic and focus worldwide attention of the ramifications of the plot to take over the European Union. I fear that the firm hold on power of the people at the helm may be slipping."

Julia Van Weddingsen was well aware of the changes within the European Union. She had done her own investigating. She said many people in the EU believed the advanced civilisation coming to earth from Epsilon Eridani would save the world from destruction. They think this is it…Unite with the Eridanians for a far more advanced civilisation. Of course, neither she nor any of the others had any knowledge of the Greys from Alpha Centauri and Zeta Reticuli who were far more advanced than the Eridanians.

"None of these people believe the story about the Devil and evil forces from Epsilon Eridani. The devil arriving on earth with his armies! Come on, Turan! Who would believe that?"

"Whether they believe it or not, it is true."

"But think of all the past publicity! Think of all that news in the papers and on TV about the evil forces of the devil being unleashed! No one did believe it."

She was right, of course. The general public believed the alien technology of the Eridanians would end all the major problems on Earth. Instability—the hallmark of society in less developed areas—would cease to exist in a united world, or such was the general belief.

"We have to get through to these people at the top and convince them of the dangers ahead. The Devil and the evil forces want to invade Earth. This is a secret invasion. All the governments would have to capitulate in the end. The people of the world would have to face a lifetime of slavery!"

"But how do we convince people that the 'Devil' who exists in myths is real and belongs to an extraterrestrial civilisation from the star system Epsilon Eridani? Only Bram Stoker who has been dead for a long time, you and perhaps a few other people have actually seen the Devil. But you have no picture of film of him, so this means you have no proof."

Once again, she was right. We could go on arguing forever. Even documented evidence with pictures or films would not be enough. I realised that arguing about the Devil's existence would not help matters.

"Let us tell the people in power that the aim of the Eridanians is simply the conquest of planet Earth. We have to tell them that we will be nothing more than lice on this planet, fully under the control of this alien civilisation. No more talk of the devil; just this." I suggested.

"OK. But even then, you'd have to seek out their evil tactics, and prove they are the enemy of mankind."

"I need your help, Julia. I need to meet people in the EC. People who may be suspect. I have to investigate their activities in the hope of finding evidence to prove their collaboration with the Eridanians."

"Yes. I see..." she said thoughtfully.

I urged Julia to try and locate the box with the feather that was somewhere on the EC premises. I was convinced that there was some sort of special power the Eridanians derived from the feather. Furthermore, a unanimous vote by the 27-member organisation to discourage or disengage any attempts for a new agreement with the Eridanians would put pressure on the Commission to clean up their already tarnished image, caused by the resignations of the prime ministers of the big four. The British Parliament under the leadership of its new prime minister resumed its debate on alien presence and that was official. The public at large now accepted the fact of alien presence on Earth. There was no question about that. The American President also made the following declaration:

"The arrival of extraterrestrials on our planet is the most important event in the history of mankind." Official statements from the White House said there was no cause for alarm and that the USA and its allies were now ready to seek an agreement for the co-operation between the Eridanians and the peoples of Earth.

Watching events unfold, I realised that I was the only man with the secret of the 'Devil's' presence on Earth. The people who trusted me and believed in me numbered no more than twenty. By all indications, the policies of the US and British governments would rest upon monumental decisions on whether they would cooperate with the Eridanians. The EU seemed to be one step ahead in falling into the trap set by the Eridanians. A complete domination of the EU by the aliens hanged in the balance. I felt like a solitary soldier in the battlefield fighting against enormous odds. Russia, China and Japan demanded a meeting at the UN.

The current situation resembled that of a world which was merely indulging in a public relations exercise, overriding the cries of, "The extraterrestrials are here!"; "The peoples of the world must unite to ward off the danger!" There had been an abrupt departure from the panic-stricken media reports which had sent out harsh messages during the previous two months. The majority of the people were now exposed to the mysterious Eridanian power which spread like an infectious disease. People were now entirely devoid of resistance against this evil alien force.

I had a very rough ride ahead of me. But I would never give up and surrender. I was firmly and stubbornly determined to fight. But how? How do you fight an enormous power which has already dominated almost the whole European continent? How do you convince people in key positions that the alien Eridanian force is evil and its sole aim is the domination of the whole world? A CIA agent, a friend in the USA, said that Washington had its own suspicions. They had been working on a 'Grey' alien technology for almost sixty years. "Now is the time for the US to show its 'Grey Power'!" he had enthused. But there was no sign of any such activity on the part of the US government.

The EU was in a far worse situation. It seemed as though the Eridanians had destroyed the very fabric of decision-making. Julia said the extremely upbeat mood of the people she worked with was quite disconcerting. No one seemed to care anymore. None of the officials seemed to entertain such grand plans as the United States of Europe, or any way forward beyond a purely economic vision. Major difficulties in the field of common, foreign and security policies added to the flaws in the decision-making process. Now it seemed as though blocks in progress in every area had spread throughout the EU.

The EU, incorporating a political dimension which had transcended the earlier, essentially economic approach, had now become an organisation with two very striking manifestations: the formulation of a defence policy which had been a priority now had simply ceased to exist. Secondly, the implementation of a pluralist culture had become a goal for the immediate future. The most important and significant example of the ongoing widespread inactivity within the different departments was the inauspicious and sometimes antagonistic attitude towards member states, threatening policy changes in relations between member states and other foreign countries. Julia's observations during a whole week included a notable decrease in specific interests and aims. Leaders of member states and their governments were now willing and able to adjust their aspirations by turning to an overwhelmingly powerful high authority, an authority that dominated the EU and yet was non-existent in any form or shape. This high authority was none other than the evil Eridanian extraterrestrials.

While Julia was busy carrying out a thorough investigation into her own department and others with a staff of about fifty who worked under her, I decided it would be apt to do a piano recital of my latest works—mainly new music—in Brussels. I asked for an appointment to see the Belgian Minister of Culture. As a pianist/composer, I would be able to move in circles within the Belgian government and meet some of the high-ranging officials within the EU. It had been over three months since this whole episode began with the advent of the Eridanians and there had been many reports and interviews on TV and in newspapers and magazines. My name and face had become quite well-known throughout this period. The pianist/composer was not really a cover. It was me, the real me. Mr Pierre Gubeis, the Belgian Culture Minister, greeted me warmly.

"Turan Akova," he exclaimed, "you are a colossus among today's pianist/composers. I have all your CDs. I am particularly interested in your Space Music. I take it you are a new music specialist?"

"Yes,"—the handshake continued while he spoke.

"*Alors*, Monsieur Akova, what can I do for you?"

"First of all," I said, "I want to thank you for receiving me with such short notice. I would like to do a piano recital at the Salon de Meis. I am here in Brussels for only a few days, and I know it is difficult to arrange a concert at such short notice, but—"

He interrupted immediately, "Let's sit down and have some coffee while I look at the programme."

He sat behind a large desk as a pretty young secretary walked in.

"This is Mr Akova, the world-famous pianist/composer," he introduced me to his secretary, "and this is Denise." Minutes later, she brought the coffee.

"Now then," he looked at the programme, "here we are. I think we can give a Christmas present to the aficionados of new music in Brussels."

"I do hope it's not Christmas Day, but I can't afford to be choosy," I remarked.

"No, no…this is the 24th of December. Yes, we'll arrange it for you…"

Twenty

As I walked in the corridor of the eighth floor, towards the lift, I saw an old man. He must have been in his eighties. The face looked familiar.

"Mr Akova," he had a gravelly voice, "I saw you going into the office of the minister and I waited for you. My name is Jorge Belette."

When the face was anchored by the name, I remembered. He was a famous author. His last book, 'Our fathers in Space', just released, was a sequel to his best seller 'Origins of Man'. I remembered reading Our Fathers in Space. His theory was based on the arrival of at least four different extraterrestrial civilisations on Planet Earth before the dawn of man. He claimed that no one could explain the difference between the physiognomy of the Chinese/Japanese/ Koreans and that of the Europeans and the Africans. He claimed each belonged to a different extraterrestrial civilisation arriving on Planet Earth from different star systems in the Milky Way Galaxy.

"Yes, Mr Belette. I read your last novel with great interest."

"Mr Akova, perhaps you'd like to walk with me," he was thoughtful and looked rather worried.

"As you wish," I replied, and wondered why people came at me all the time. Of course, the main reason was the full coverage on TV and in newspapers of the Eridanian extraterrestrial arrival.

"Mr Akova, I don't like to talk about my age."

"Same here," I agreed.

He continued, "I am ninety-seven years old. But I feel very energetic. In fact, I feel like a young man."

He was surprisingly sprightly for an old man of ninety-seven…

"Mr Akova, something strange is happening to my body and my brain."

"Mr Belette, do you know what's been happening in the world?"

"Yes, I know the extraterrestrials are here. I read all about the Eridanians."

"Then you must know about the transformations of humans."

"Yes, I do," he said, "but I have simply no idea how or what happened."

"Have you been in contact with any people here, who perhaps seem strange in some way to you? People who talk of the great change and benefits for all humankind with the extraterrestrials?"

"Yes, I want to talk to you about that. But more importantly, I think I am onto something which may throw some light onto your investigations."

Belette's two-storey house was about a hundred metres from the Ministry of Culture. When we entered the house, he went straight to his computer on a large table at the other side of the sitting room.

"I found the information on the internet," he said, sitting down behind the desk and scribbling a few notes on paper.

"Now then," he gazed upon the documents in front of him. "First of all, both men are Italian and they come from Florence. The first man said his name was Lorenzo de Medici. The second introduced himself as Luigi Gonzagga III. They arrived at the EU Commission's headquarters about a week ago as special representatives of the Italian government. I met them at the farewell cocktail reception held in the conference room at the EU Commission headquarters of a Belgian member of the Foreign Relations committee. They introduced me to a very tall man, by the name of Draco. I do not know who he is. My Belgian friend said all three had been present at a special meeting at the EU Commission, which he had also attended. He said that these three men had initially offered an agreement to be signed between the EU and the aliens."

I was surprised the old man knew so much. "Since you've come so far in this investigation, you must know the agreement was rejected, and the prime ministers of Britain, France, Germany and Italy resigned soon after the meeting." I ventured.

"Yes," he replied emphatically, "I know about the resignations, but have no idea how they came about."

"At any rate, please continue." The reasons behind his suspicions made sense.

"Well, Mr Akova, I'm sure you have heard of the de Medici family. It was one of the most famous in Italy. Lorenzo was born in 1449 and died in 1492, the grandson of Cosimo de Medici. I thought this man I met at the cocktail party was from the de Medici family, but when I made further enquiries, I realised that Anna Maria Luisa who was born in 1667 and died in 1743 was the last in line in that family. It ended with her. Then I thought perhaps there were other families using the same surname. I made enquiries. Believe me, this was a painstaking job. There were twenty-six other de Medicis all over Italy. Some of them dead. But none of them live in Florence. As for our other man, Luigi Gonzaga III, there are only five Gonzagas in Italy and none of them live in Florence. So our man Luigi—nicknamed 'Il Turco' is the one and only Gonzaga to live in Florence. Believe it or not, the real Luigi Gonzaga III who lived in Florence in the fifteenth century had in fact the same nickname. I find that very odd. You are a Turk. Do you know why he was called 'Il Turco'?"

"I've no idea," I replied, "I have heard of the de Medicis. As you know, Caterina Cornaro who was alive during that same period was the Queen of Cyprus from 1474 until 1489. Later in 1571 when the Turks invaded Cyprus, Cornaro's cousin, also called Caterina, married a member of my own family back in 1572 in Cyprus. As you know, I am a Turkish Cypriot and we have a well-documented family tree. But I can't think why he was called 'Il Turco'. Well, here's another mystery," he said, and produced some photos from a white envelope. "Photos were taken of all the people who attended the meeting." Bellette pulled one out. "There, in this picture, the two men I mention, Medici and Gonzaga are standing side by side." He pointed a finger to the right of the photo, "There's more. A fellow author who is also Belgian did a lot of research on mysterious incidents covering at least 600 years going back into the 14th century. He said there was a story about a saucer-shaped object landing in Florence in the fifteenth century. This man, whom I trust implicitly, said that the secret documents of this incident are in the Vatican Library. But the Vatican refused him access to their secret Archives Section where they are lodged. Mr Akova, this is all very strange. I think you ought to investigate these two men."

"Yes, definitely. But I want to ask you about this author friend of yours. Why was he refused access?"

Bellette scribbled down the name of Cardinal Giovanni Messi on a piece of paper and handed it to me. "Mr Akova, this cardinal is, of course, in the Vatican. But even he was not able to get my friend into the library. You can try asking him."

"What else can you tell me about these two men?"

The old man thought for a moment, "I had a chance to talk to Lorenzo de Medici. He was convinced that everyone was at their wit's end, by dint of his intrigues. A conceited man. It was a bizarre evening, at that reception. An English official there said it was just another bizarre night in the chaotic but rarely dull life of Lorenzo de Medici. The man destroys everything he touches…"

"Tell me, Monsieur Bellette, how did you find me? I mean, here I was at the Ministry of Culture, and suddenly and very conveniently you run into me. How did that happen? Surely it was not a coincidence? Furthermore, you give me this information which is vital in our struggle against the evil forces of Eridanus. How come?"

"You're right. It looks very suspicious," he acknowledged, and continued unruffled, "you have every reason to believe I'm inventing this story—but no, this is the truth. I'll tell you exactly what happened. This morning, I was sitting at home feeling sorry for myself. Imagine! I'm ninety-seven and yet I feel like thirty-five. Despite this energy and sudden youthfulness permeating my whole being, physical and mental, I felt so desperately entangled in a web, the nature of which I could not even begin to understand. I contacted our own UFO Centre in Brussels. You see, we have a bureau here too. I have ten young people working for me, and we are in regular contact with your UFO Centre in London. The London centre informed me you were coming here, and told us about your hotel reservation. So this morning, I followed you to the Ministry of Culture."

"I was really very depressed, but I am sure you'll agree that self-pity is a very unattractive emotion. Of course, I had already decided to see you, so our meeting was not such a remarkable stroke of good fortune, nor was it a coincidence. There are no coincidences in this world, Mr Akova. I know, I know…I'm giving you a rather sombre picture of the world. But we have already become the slaves of the alien force. I hope my explanation is satisfactory."

"Monsieur Bellette, you will appreciate that I have to check out every person I meet. I can't trust anyone these days. We have not lost yet."

"I admire your courage, Mr Akova…"

Bellette had the photos of de Medici and Gonzaga enlarged and later accompanied me to the hotel. I promised to keep him posted on my findings in Rome and Florence. In my room, I telephoned my old Italian friend from our student days in London. Tonio Maldini was one of the most famous journalists in Italy. He had regular weekly columns in a couple of daily newspapers, but he had always been freelance. He was well-known for his investigations into the EU institutions and how the Italian people were affected by them. Maldini was also a good friend of the crème de la crème of Italy, and an international playboy. He would often be seen with wealthy socialites moving from one fashionable resort to another. Tonio's phone just kept ringing. It was midday. He was a late riser, like me. Eventually, his voice, husky with sleep, responded, *"Pronto?"*

"Hey, old friend! The last time we met was at the French Riviera last year, when you introduced me to the girlfriend of your girlfriend…"

"Turan, the Turk who came in from the heat! Where have you been, buddy? I know, I know, you are very busy tracking down UFOs. Very interesting indeed. I haven't had time to do any research on these flying saucers. But you, my friend, you are very much the man of the moment…Are the extraterrestrials really invading Earth?"

"Yes, they are, Tonio, and this is no joke. But I will tell you all about it when I arrive in Rome tonight. I hope you have time to see me. I need your help."

"Of course, old man, I have all the time in the world for you."

Tonio's villa was about a mile from the Spanish Steps, 137 of them descending down the slope of the Pincian Hill, joining the church of Santa Trinita dei Monti with Piazza di Spagna and Via dei Condotti below. He met me at the airport in his ostentatiously expensive Ferrari with all sorts of gimmicks. I'd been to his house many times before. It was large, surrounded by a twenty-foot wall. Tonio was a very successful journalist, but he had also inherited a lot of money from his family. He would never let me stay in a hotel, whenever I came to Rome. His fifteen-room mansion was like a small hotel anyway. He had servants looking after him and the place, and I had been present at some of his more memorable all-night parties there.

"My home is your home, Turan," he said, smiling, as we arrived at the house. A tall man and three young ladies approached the car. One girl took my small suitcase, while Tonio gave instructions to the tall man who was the butler.

"Prepare the suite in the west wing for my friend, Turan," he said, and added, "Giuseppe, you remember Turan Akova, my Turkish Cypriot friend? He was here last year."

Giuseppe responded with a polite gesture, nodding to his employer, "Yes, sir, I remember."

Tonio Maldini had published three books, fictional and yet factual novels about the most famous Italian families of the twentieth century. I had read one of them. His literary style was full of elegance and wit. This first book had sold over two million copies in Italy alone. It had also been translated into English.

"So, what are you doing in Rome? It's a girl, is it? *Ma certo*, it must be a girl, eh!" The ground was covered in a pristine layer of snow. We walked up the steps while two yellow stone lions stared at us from both sides.

"I'm afraid not, this time, Tony," I replied.

"Well, let's have a drink first," he said, "and we can talk about it before we go out to dinner."

He went behind the bar in the left-hand corner of the great hall; "I know," he called to me, "you'll have a beer with a head on it." He poured himself a whisky. "So tell me what's been happening?"

"Tonio, I need your help. You know it's been almost four months since the alien presence has come into the open. Now it's official. The aliens—or rather the Eridanian aliens—are evil. There is no doubt about that. We are fighting to save the world from them, but with no success so far. Technologically, they are thousands of years ahead of us. There is widespread infiltration in the European Union. The Eridanians were ready to sign an agreement with the EU, which was averted at the last moment. You've heard about the resignations of the prime ministers of the big four? Anyway, to cut a long story short, there are two men in Brussels at present—though they could be anywhere. They are Eridanians but they are also Italian."

"Italian aliens," he smiled at the thought, "this is very interesting."

"I know it sounds unbelievable. But it is true. The funny part of this story is that the names of the two Italians are Lorenzo de Medici and Luigi Gonzaga III—also nicknamed Il Turco. As you well know, there are the names of famous personages from the Renaissance era in Florence. I have checked the history of the families. The family line of the de Medicis ended with Anna Maria Luisa who was married to Johann Wilhelm. She had had no children and died in 1743. Gonzaga died in 1478. He never married, so no children. So, neither of these had any descendants extending into the 21st century."

"But there may be other people with the same family name?" he challenged.

"A Belgian author friend has made enquiries. Twenty-six de Medicis and 5 Gonzagas in the whole of Italy. Some of them are dead. But none are from Florence."

"Why Florence?" Tonio's knowledge of Italian families stood him in good stead.

"Because that's where they said they were from. First of all, we have to check with the department of births and deaths. We have to find out if they have birth certificates. Secondly, once again, we have to see if they have identity cards and passports."

"OK, that's easy. What else?"

"We have to go to the Vatican Library. There is a secret vault where they keep the most confidential documents. Of the two I am looking for, one dates back to the time of Dante Alighieri. This document describes the landing of a UFO in Florence. The second is an account of the arrival of yet another UFO in Florence during the time of Lorenzo de Medici and Luigi Gonzaga III. I will probably have to be disguised as a priest. A dumb priest, as I don't speak Italian!"

"We'll have to forge an Italian identity for you. I'll talk to Cardinal Giovanni Messi who is a friend of the family. I'm sure he will give me the information about the secret vault." But it was clear that Tonio also had another idea, "Wait a second! I know the man who will help us. Cardinal Tommaso Tenco. He is a revolutionary guy. Tenco recently denounced the hypocrisy of the Vatican. He's done everything incognito, nevertheless the big boys there have their spies out and he's already been deprived of every support."

"But Tonio, if the Vatican have put their people onto him, we may have a problem."

"No, no, it's OK. Tenco is a clever chap. He will take the risk. Don't worry," said Tonio.

My suspicions over the identities of Medici and Gonzaga were proven right. There was no record of birth for either man. The passport office in Rome had no record of passports issued in their names either. Tonio had a lot of influence with the police and government. He was simply making enquiries about two famous families for his new book. For some unknown and inexplicable reason, the Rome police did not even bother to find out why these two men had no identity cards or passports. These evil Eridanian would pass from one form to another, and perhaps they had no need for such trivialities as passports and identity cards. I personally thought the Head of the Police Department in Rome would come under suspicion of collaborating with the aliens. But I had no time to investigate each and every person who was supposedly in allegiance with the Eridanians.

A clear picture was emerging in my mind of the three men, Draco, who was in fact the real Dracula who had arrived in Romania back in the 14th century, Lorenzo de Medici. And Luigi Gonzaga III. These were the three key figures, the three leaders of the Eridanian star people, the devils described in many historical documents. I had to find their weak points and strike. It was, of course, virtually impossible to challenge them on my own. But I had to try. Everything hinged on the outcome of my investigations.

Despite his outspoken criticism of Vatican policy, the youngest cardinal in the Vatican, Tommaso Tenco was unduly sceptical about our mission. For him, this would be downright robbery. Tonio explained and pleased with him for more than two hours, "Listen, Tommaso," he urged, "Mr Akova cannot read the documents in question. You can. We cannot take them out and make photo copies of them, to do that, we have to get in and get out twice. We cannot take that risk. You enter with Turan, read the ancient documents, take notes and then you can translate them into English or Italian. We need the information in those two documents. You are the only one who can enter with Turan."

Tommaso gave me an incredulous stare, and asked: "What's the point of getting you into the vault if you cannot read the documents, Mr Akova?"

A sensible question, I thought. So I told him my reason: "I have a very small camera, and I want to take some pictures of the documents, just in case."

Soon afterwards, Tommaso Tenco made his decision. We went to his house, and I was dressed up as a priest. With the help of his friends in the Interior Ministry, Tonio was able to have an identity card issued in the name of Alberto Donatini, a priest from a church in Padua. Anyone could get into the Vatican Library, but to go further through the corridors which led to the vault under the old Basilica, one had to show one's identity.

Gianlorenzo Bernini—Italian architect, sculptor and painter and master of the Baroque style—was responsible for much of the completion of St Peter's, including the magnificent colonnaded piazza. When we entered the Vatican Library just before closing time, I gasped at the riotous frescoed decoration adorning the vaulted arches of the library. How on earth Tenco had obtained the key to the secret vault I'll never know. The secret Vatican archives were in the vault of St Peter's, which was also the burial site of St Peter, one of the twelve disciples of Jesus.

Research on the Vatican Library said that the Secret Vatican Archives had been separated from the library back at the beginning of the seventeenth century. The Secret Archives contained about 150,000 items. But the vault was within this secret archive section. Among the most famous possessions of the library was the Codex Vaticanus—the oldest known manuscript of the Bible. This and several other documents were kept in a secret vault. There were two Swiss guards and a Papal official near the door that led into the Secret Archive Section. The

Swiss had been serving at the Holy See since 1505. Tommaso Tenco murmured something in Italian and the Papal Official let us through into the secret section. Tommaso closed the large door behind us. The room itself was quite small and the secret vault was right in front of us. Tommaso had permission to look at the archives. There were scores of them. The vault was right in front of us. The door was not locked and the papal official could come in at any time to check what we were doing. So Tommaso had to act swiftly.

The dusty old room evoked admiration, smells and even sounds coming to the present day from times back in the 14th century. For me, it was the ultimate experience. Tommaso opened the vault with the key and took out a bunch of old documents. An ancient seal with the Papal insignia of the 14th century strung together the documents. Tommaso Tenco was extremely careful undoing the string attached to the wax seal. The Dante document describing a UFO landing in Florence in 1290 was easy to find, as it was among the first few documents. He made notes of it while I took three pictures of the documents. For me, the UFO landing in Florence on the day Lorenzo de Medici died was the all-important one. In this document, there was an eye-witness account of the UFO landing by at least three men who were close to de Medici. The tower of the church Santa Reparata had allegedly been struck by lightning as de Medici was dying. The eye witnesses claimed he was abducted by UFO beings from his deathbed. Apparently, the lightning was the UFO that had landed on the grounds of his house. While Tommaso Tenco was taking notes, and I was preparing to take pictures, I heard the sound of footsteps behind the door.

"Quick," said Tommaso, "pull out a document from the side. Any document, just open it and put it on the table."

He put the secret documents in the vault just in time, as the door opened and the official entered. He said something and Tommaso Tenco replied in Italian. The official looked at both of us doubtfully and then went out, closing the door behind him.

"We have a few minutes," said Tommaso, while he opened the vault again and took his notes. I took the pictures of the second document. The mission was complete.

The River Tiber winds through Rome much as the Seine through Paris and the Thames through London. When we left the Vatican Library, we crossed over the bridge of Sant'Angelo which led to the Castel Sant'Angelo, built by the Emperor Hadrian, as a mausoleum for Roman rulers. Quite frankly, I did not understand why Tommaso Tenco took the same road back to the Vatican Library. "Why are we going back?" I asked him.

"It's OK," said the young cardinal, "I forgot to report to the official in the library. All cardinals have to report in if they go into the secret archives section of the library. Just wait for me here; I'll be back in two minutes."

From where I was standing, I could see the basilica, the large, oblong-shaped church with the double row of columns inside and the apse at one end. The apse was a semi-circular or many-sided recess with an arched or domed roof. I pondered about the latest situation. Now, the files of the three men (Eridanians): namely, Draco whom I had encountered in Whitby and whose arrival in Romania in the 14th century was well-documented in Bram Stoker's secret essays; Lorenzo de Medici, a member of the famous Italian Medici family, and Luigi Gonzaga III (Il Turco), were now almost complete. I had to send out my reports to the Americans and the British.

All three Eridanians were here on Earth on a mission in which lying, intrigue, murder and the transformation of humans into Eridanians were one of their main devilish traits. The victims of Draco (Count Dracula) brought to light a much more sinister side of the so-called King of the Vampires, or Prince of Darkness. He had recruited many people into the Eridanian camp and no one knew the extent of the damage. At first, these three men had embarked on a mission of transformation of humans, but later their strategy tended to be at odds with this stance. Rage and suspicion possessed mend's minds. Those who had been transformed did not actually know what was happening to them. The devils moved in unpredictable and mysterious ways. They were in the highest societies of most European countries. Their parties had already become famous for their sumptuousness. Those who attended these parties were now completely under their influence. They had become the slaves of this devil.

As there had never been a single example of a clash between the military might of the USA and the Eridanians, it was quite unnecessary for the moment to dwell upon such a mammoth confrontation which might indeed destroy human civilisation on Earth. Neither the USA, Britain nor any of the other powers had a specific target to aim at. The Eridanians has so far proved themselves completely and utterly elusive.

But why the Medici family? Why was one member of this renowned Italian family—a family which had in fact ruled Florence during most of the Italian renaissance—an Eridanian from the star system Epsilon Eridani? Why had a family with such finesse and individuality been blotted by the mark of the devil? Why was an avid patron of the arts, Lorenzo the Magnificent, a religious man, a cultured individual who had loved the arts and led a very active life, now known as one of the evil patrons of the Devil who had descended on Earth? I could only deduce that, as a man fascinated by technology, he had been abducted by aliens while on his deathbed; that the immortal beings of Epsilon Eridani had prepared an ever-lasting mission for him: the conquest of Planet Earth.

And what about Gonzaga? Luigi Gonzaga III (Il Turco), was a famous soldier who had apparently acquired his nickname after defeating the Turks in a sea battle. He also had been a patron of the arts. And, I surmised, he also was now an Eridanian who had arrived in Florence probably together with Lorenzo de Medici.

I looked at my watch. It had already been fifteen minutes since Tomaso Tenco had returned to sign off. I felt strange and oddly conspicuous standing on the pavement beside a small park, dressed as a priest. Yet another fifteen minutes elapsed when I decided to call Tonio on the mobile that he had given me. He said he would be there in ten minutes.

It was almost quarter past six and quite dark when I felt the chill of a breeze rustling the leaves of a tree nearby. Suddenly, two police cars raced towards the big piazza with their sirens echoing along the boulevard. People stopped and looked, some coming to see what was happening. Tonio arrived, and we walked towards the Vatican Library. The motionless body of a priest lay on the ground. There were no visible signs of life. It was disfigured, but recognisable. It was the body of Tommaso Tenco. The police had just cordoned off the area, but fortunately we had managed to slip through. Then it happened. A bright light descended from the night sky and fell on Tenco's body. And the body simply disappeared. Tonio and I looked at each other in disbelief. The police officers had begun to panic, and Tonio pulled my arm, whispering: "Come on. We'd better get out of here."

When we got home, I took off my priestly disguise and threw it into the large fireplace, where a log fire was already ablaze. I added the identity card of Alberto Donatini, and after pouring a whisky for Tonio and myself, sat heavily down in an armchair, the weight of what had happened reluctantly dawning.

"You think we'll have a problem with the people who gave me the false identity?" I asked.

Tonio ignored my question and turned on the television: "Look! You're already in the news. My God, but they're fast, aren't they?"

The news told of a mystery man with the name of Alberto Donatini who had been seen in the Vatican Library with Tommaso Tanco. There was no mention of the spectacular disappearance of Tenco's body. The only man who had seen my face had been the Vatican official at the entrance to the Secret Archives section. Within half an hour, television channels all over Italy had broadcast a photofit, or rather a drawing of the face of Alberto Donatini, the priest from Padua. Thank God, the drawing bore no resemblance whatsoever to my face. Nevertheless, the Eridanians had spies everywhere. Obviously, these people had been informed of my arrival in Rome, and it would be easy for them to implicate Turan Akova in what had occurred.

"Tonio," I felt I had to seek his advice, "what should I do now? I mean, we could perhaps go to the Ministry of the Interior, and see your friend there. We could tell him exactly what happened. And you could explain the importance of my mission, and so on...Look, I never meant that you should get into any trouble over this. It's obvious that you didn't tell them why or for whom you needed this false identity. But the official at the entrance to the Secret Archives knows that Tommaso and I were there together. So the police will obviously start asking questions. The most important secret we have to guard with our lives is that Tenco managed to open the vault to allow me to photograph the relevant documents, while he took notes. Nothing was found near Tenco's body—which means that the notes he had taken disappeared with him."

"OK," said Tonio, "yes, I agree. We tell the police and the Ministry that you needed this false identity as you are so well known as Turan Akova that they would have immediately cottoned on to you, to find out why you were wanting to get to that particular section of the Vatican Library. Yes. I think that's the best possible way. I will tell the police that Tommaso Tenco—whom I knew—was simply trying to help."

Tonio was right. (Well, after all, it had been my idea!) Perhaps that was the best way. But what was bothering me was the possibility of Eridanian controlled officials in the Italian police force and the Ministry of the Interior. I confessed this worry to Tonio, who dismissed it nonchalantly: "You worry too much, Turan," he smiled, "don't worry. I can deal with it."

When we entered the Rome police headquarters, we were greeted at the door by the Chief Commissioner, Signor Eduardo Bellini: "Eh, Tonio, I have not seen you in a long time," he said with his sharp eye appraising me, "and this is your friend, Turan Akova."

"That's right," confirmed Tonio, holding me rather protectively by the arm.

Once in Bellini's office, we explained in detail what had happened. It turned out that Bellini was well-informed about alien presence and my investigations throughout Europe.

"I know, I know. If it was up to me, I would let you go, believe me," he said with a worried frown on his thin face, "but the Minister Signor Pietro Savona will be here in a few minutes. This is the first time he's ever visited this place. I don't know how, but he seems to know more than I do about all this. So be careful when you talk to him. You may have a problem."

The Minister arrived. The moment he started talking about alien presence and the Eridanians, I knew that he was obsessed with extraterrestrial presence to the point of madness, and the scepticism borne with it foreshadowed many of the critique's narrow-minded views on Eridanians which would form the core of the supporters of an agreement with the aliens.

"Mr Maldini," he frowned at Tonio, "you should be arrested for forgery," and then he glanced fiercely at me, "and as for your friend here, Mr Akova..." he drew a breath and addressed me directly, "you used a forged identity to enter the Secret Archives of the Vatican Library; you too could be arrested for that. What is more, however, is that you, Mr Akova, are a prime suspect in this murder case."

Tonio, somewhat amused, couldn't resist protesting at this, "But why should he want to murder someone who was helping him?"

"Let me just ask you this," replied Bellini, through his teeth, determined to punish us for a crime we had not committed, "why would Mr Akova want to get to the secret archives with a forged identity, when he could have gone in with his own true identity."

"You know how it is, Mr Bellini," Tonio countered, "It is almost impossible for a foreigner to get in."

Bellini seemed a cold-hearted bastard, with his absolute loyalty to the letter of the law. And I was equally absolutely certain that he was on the payroll of the Eridanians. He turned to the Chief of Police and said, "I think you should place both of them under house arrest until we find the murderer."

Bellini left without even saying goodbye, and the police chief had no option but to carry out this veiled order. Tonio wasted no time and called the newly reinstated Prime Minister of Italy. Nicolo Bicci had been prime minister twice in twelve years, and was now back in power after the resignation of the last premier.

Tonio was a close friend of Bicci. He told me Bicci was an individual of unusual insight. He was back by popular demand and his perception and understanding of the nature of the current chaos in Italy was next to none. Tonio trusted him.

The Minister of the Interior, Mr Savona, whom I suspected was an Eridanian controlled human, would most certainly try to pin this murder on me. So we could not just sit around, waiting for them to catch the culprit. It was around a quarter past eight when Tonio telephoned the private residence of the Premier. From the tone of his voice, I could sense a positive reaction from the Prime Minister. It was a long conversation, lasting about seven minutes at least.

"*Grazie mille*," said Tonio, and hung up. He clapped his hands in the air, "Let's have a drink. And then we get ready to go!"

"Go where, Tonio? What happened? What did he say?"

"You won't believe this, but Bicci is lifting the house arrest. Right now, he is issuing a special permit for you to investigate anywhere in Italy. Turan, he has all the detailed information about your investigations. He is a great supporter of your fight against the Eridanians. He said he had received the latest reports from your UFO Centre in London and from a lady in Brussels. Also, we are invited to have dinner with him tonight at his home. He is sending a car to collect us."

"Tonio…" I replied, amazed at all this, "aren't I lucky to have a friend like you!"

"You most certainly are," he replied, grinning smugly.

Tonio's handling of the situation had been admirable. Emma in London and Julia in Brussels had done their work with remarkable precision. But Tommaso Tenco's murder and his body's sudden disappearance with the light from the sky was just another example of the enormous powers of the aliens.

The murder disturbed me deeply. But it would be senseless to try to find the murderer. Tommaso Tenco had simply been recruited into the world of the devil. A Vatican cardinal murdered on the doorstep of the pinnacle of Christendom! Tenco had been a revolutionary critic of Vatican policies and his murder aroused a lot of controversy in Italy. But not a word was written or spoken about the sudden disappearance of the youngest Cardinal of the Vatican after the murder. No word was mentioned in the media of the mysterious light which had struck the body and wiped it from the face of the Earth leaving no trace.

The dinner at the Italian Prime Minister's private home was a lavish affair. Premier Bicci, a friendly, jovial fellow, dismissed any possibility of the Interior Minister overriding his decision to lift the house arrest, and enquired bemusedly, "How do we stop this evil alien force, Mr Akova?"

"I do not know, your Excellency. There is no specific target to hit. If there was such a target, the Americans would have already done it."

"*Si, certo*; the Americans do not waste much time in such a situation, do they?"

After dinner, we all adjourned to the salon. Bicci assured me that he had absolute power over the government in Italy. His lovely wife and two young children, a boy and a girl both studying at university, were also present. The man was a believer in joie de vivre, and his family were delightfully vivacious. Tonio was no stranger to Bicci. His wealth and reputation gave him entry to the upper classes.

"Is there anything else I can do for you, Mr Akova?"

"Well, yes, there is," I ventured, "I am going to Florence, and I would like to be sure of the cooperation of the officials there."

"What is happening in Florence?" he asked.

"I think there was an extraterrestrial visitation to Florence some 600 years ago. It seems that the Eridanian aliens' first landing on Planet Earth coincides with the Renaissance and somehow the Medici and Gonzaga families are involved. I am already investigating the activities of two Florentines." I did not want to go into detail, but the premier was very curious.

"And who are these two men?" he asked.

"Lorenzo de Medici and Luigi Gonzaga III. It seems they are using the names of these two prominent figures. It's very complicated at the moment, but I will of course inform you of my findings."

"Very interesting indeed," murmured Bicci, as a beautiful white cat jumped onto my lap. Amidst the contented purrs of the friendly cat, the conversation switched to Tonio's artistic, literary and scientific pursuits. Signora Bicci watched me stroking the white cat, and then uttered a few words in Italian: "Come, Bianca, leave the gentlemen alone. You are a spoiled cat, aren't you?"

"It's OK. I love cats."

It was just after midnight when we left Premier Bicci's home. One of his chauffeurs started the car. The engine sputtered feebly for a moment and then stopped. The driver apologised and said he would get the other car. We stood in the cold, waiting for him while he talked to another man standing beside a Jaguar. He returned with the Jag and we headed for Tonio's place.

"Keep an eye on these two men," I told Tonio.

"Why?"

"I don't know. I just have a feeling. Perhaps it's nothing. I think you should tell Bicci to have them investigated."

"You're suspicious of everything and everyone," complained Tonio.

"Well, we don't want any of the devil's disciples to harm the Premier, do we? It may well be my imagination, but it's better to be safe than sorry. So please warn Bicci."

"OK," he sighed, "If you say so."

When we approached Tonio's house, there was a man sitting by the gate. It was dark and I could not see his face at first. The driver asked Tonio if we needed any help. Tonio replied that he would deal with it, and the driver left.

Tonio called to the man at the gate in Italian. He answered in perfect English, only a few metres away from us. Seconds later we could see his face. It was unbelievable. The man staring at us with blank, expressionless eyes was Tommaso Tenco.

"I have been reincarnated, Mr Akova," he murmured, grasping my arm, "say a prayer for the souls in purgatory, Mr Akova."

He seemed to be in agony but he continued to speak in a low voice. The disfigured body I had seen right after his murder near the piazza had apparently been transformed back to its normal condition.

"The culture of death is null and void. Death does not exist in their world. I am in their world. Please do not try to save me, Mr Akova…" Clearly Tenco was deranged.

"Who hit you, Tenco? Please tell me."

"I don't know," he looked at Tonio, "*In nomine Patris, et Filii, et Spiritus Sancti…*" His sporadic utterances returned to normal, but only briefly.

"Here you are, Mr Akova. The notes I took in the secret vault. Can you really help me, Mr Akova?"

"Yes. I can and I will," I promised, trying to comfort his disturbed soul, "we'll find a new home for you. Don't go to your old one. Tonio here will find you a new home. When they try to contact you again, just challenge them. Stay put and challenge them."

"But Mr Akova, the gods of Eridanus are here. They've already taken over so many."

Tonio was flabbergasted. He stood staring at the man. Minutes later, he was on his mobile to someone who would find Tenco a new home. He called his butler, gave him his car keys and asked him to take Tenco to an address somewhere in Rome.

This was my first experience of a remarkable reincarnation. Tommaso Tenco, the youngest Cardinal in the Vatican had returned from the dead. Tonio had a big story to sell to the media. He managed to get hold of the photos of Tenco's dead body, and had also taken some pictures of him while we were conversing at the gate. Within an hour, he had written the story: CARDINAL RESURRECTED FROM THE DEAD.

"Of course, you can publish it tomorrow!" yelled Tonio when the head of an American newspaper in Rome hesitated about publishing it, "change the front page!" Tonio told him, purple with rage, "this is the biggest news since the resurrection of Christ!"

The next day, I woke up at around 10.30. Tonio had already gone out, the butler told me. It was obviously to be a busy day for him. The purists were shocked by the news. The Vatican denied any knowledge of Tenco's reincarnation in an official statement to the media and said that the young cardinal has been suspected a week before the incident. The whole text was full of derogatory connotations. Meanwhile, I was interviewed five times by five different Italian TV channels.

Twenty-One

I took the train to Florence at 7.45 in the evening. I had visited this beautiful city once before, but only for a long week-end with an English girlfriend. I had not seen much. Florence had been the most important centre of the Italian Renaissance, and great figures such as Dante, Leonardo da Vinci and Michelangelo all spent time here. Today, it was still a major cultural centre. Florence was the cradle of the Italian Renaissance. I took a taxi from the station and asked the driver to take me to the Bianca Hotel. That was where I had stayed with my girlfriend. It was the best in town. The road swept around the Ponte Vecchio. Many of the bridges across the River Arno had been built by the Romans, but the Ponte Vecchio was unique with its multitude of shops built on either side, upheld by stilts.

Nostalgia at its peak. I remembered that long weekend, the romantic moments, and of course, Jill...The majestic fountain of Neptune, a masterpiece of marble at the terminus of a still-functioning Roman aqueduct. We had had long walks after midnight and had often stopped by that fountain.

I had a few drinks at the bar and then retired into my room at around 12.30 am. I had it all planned in my mind. I had to find the portraits of Lorenzo de Medici and Luigi Gonzaga III. Then I had to take pictures of the paintings, enlarge them and compare them with the photos of the two characters. There were no descendants of the Medici family or the Gonzagas. The Medici line had ended with Anna Maria Luisa in 1743. The Gonzagas on the other hand had vanished from the face of the earth much earlier than that date. I felt there was a connection between Florence and the extraterrestrials and I had to find out where they could be located in the city.

The next day at around 10.30 in the morning, I crossed the Arno and walked towards the huge Pitti Palace, lavishly decorated with the Medici family's former private collection. This is where I would find the paintings of both men. Adjoining the Pitti Palace stood the Boboli Gardens, elaborately landscaped with many interesting sculptures. Pitti Palace was once the residence of the Medici family. The Uffizi Gallery, which would be my next stop was not so far from the San Lorenzo, a monument to the Medicis. This was the most famous palace in Florence. At the Pitti Palace, I was given permission to take pictures of the portraits of Lorenzo de Medici and Luigi Gonzaga III.

I took several pictures and moved straight to the Uffizi Gallery. The Uffizi had probably one of the richest collections of paintings in the world, and a 1,500,000 volume library. I found Lorenzo de Medici's portrait together with other famous members of his family in one section of the gallery. Gonzaga was in other section. Once again, I took my pictures.

Later I passed by the crowning architectural jewel of Florence—the domed cathedral of the city, Santa Maria del Fiore, known as the Duomo. This magnificent dome, which gave the cathedral its colloquial name, was built by Filippo Brunelleschi. Tonio had given me the best available information on all these historical monuments in Florence not for tourist purposes, but to try to seek out more clues leading to the secrets of the Eridanians which could indeed be hidden among the centuries-old palaces, galleries, etc. It was a long shot, but I had to try. I must say my mind was set on other possibilities. Perhaps a relative, a cousin or someone who was a distant relative could still be living in Florence. But of course, the main purpose of my visit was to establish the fact that the photos and paintings of the two men were identical. If Lorenzo de Medici and Luigi Gonzaga III were Eridanians who had arrived on planet Earth back in the 15th century, both men would be over 550 years old. The old count (Count Dracula) would be more or less the same age.

Now I had to find a photographer to enlarge the photos I had taken. It was around 1.00 pm, when I realised how hungry I was. I went into the first restaurant I saw not far from the Boboli Gardens. Ascoli Restaurant seemed to be quite upmarket and I was looking forward to eating some cannelloni. I sat at a table near the window. Right opposite sat the most beautiful girl I had seen in months. I was spellbound from the moment I had noticed her—she looked like a woman from a Renaissance painting. Stop it, Turan, I said to myself. I had become so fixated on the Renaissance that even normal people appeared to have emerged from the 15th century.

She smiled, her beautiful blue eyes sending out messages of love. Well, I am an optimist. I smiled back and walked over to her table.

"Are you alone?" I asked.

"Yes."

"Then perhaps we could lunch together."

"Why not?" she replied, gesturing to the opposite seat, "my name is Lola."

"Mine is Akova, Turan Akova. I am a Turkish Cypriot pianist/composer amongst other things. Are you a local?"

She gazed into my eyes enquiringly while the waiter took our orders.

"Yes, I am. Full name: Lola Santini. I am also a musician."

"Well, well, how lovely. But tell me, can this be love at first sight?"

"I have no idea," she laughed, "but I do know that your manner is one of an accomplished womaniser." A sudden ray of the Florentine sun brought out the gold light in her long, blond hair.

"You speak perfect English." I commented.

"You, too." She said quietly, and then our food arrived.

She told me she had graduated from the Conservatoire in Rome, and was now performing in operas. She was also a pianist. What a wonderful coincidence, I thought. Suddenly, she put down her fork and stared at me intently.

"Now I remember," she cried, as if she had found a long-lost friend, "you are very much in the news with the UFOs. I know, I know. The extraterrestrials are here. I also believe they are here. But what are you doing in Florence?"

I explained my findings to her so far, on Lorenzo de Medici and Luigi Gonzaga III. She was astounded. The visitation of extraterrestrials on planet Earth was one thing. But the arrival of three men, namely Count Dracula and the two most famous Italians of the Renaissance back in the 15th century was very hard to believe. Despite the complications in my story, she wanted to help my investigations in Florence.

"Lola, many people, probably thousands, have been transformed by the Eridanians. Most of these are prey to fear and remorse." I also told her of the pictures I had taken of the two men in Brussels, which I was going to compare with my photos of their portraits. She was very excited. We were so rapt in our conversation that we did not realise that we were the last ones left in the restaurant.

As we walked out into the street, I asked Lola to take me to a professional photo shop. We were offered coffee while we waited for half an hour. The photos were brilliant. She invited me to her house and said she might be able to locate some people who were relatives of the Medici and Gonzaga families. The house was really a large villa.

"My parents are on holiday. And my sister is with her boyfriend in Venice. You will play your latest compositions for me, won't you?" she asked.

"Of course, I will," I assured her, "you know, Lola, have you realised how time flies when we are together? We must try to make it stand still." The simple irony of this touch of inspiration was unrivalled by any close relationships that I had had with other women in recent months. Take it easy, Turan, I told myself. Just play it by ear, as you always do, and don't jump to conclusions.

As we entered the house, it began to rain. A terrific thunderstorm, lightning and heavy rain with strong winds swept the city of Florence, illuminating the whole area with glimpses of the houses nearby and sometimes the horizon itself. The fireplace in the hall had a blazing fire, and it was very warm inside. The housekeeper asked if we needed anything else, and left. We drank one of the finest Italian red wines and settled into a large armchair near the fireplace.

Verdi's Requiem and later his opera, La Traviata, graced the hall with its inimitable splendour.

"Who is the conductor?" I had to ask.

"Frederico Barzini. He lives here in Florence and he is a friend of the family. He is noted for his interpretations of Verdi," she told me.

"Lola, can we compare the paintings with the photos now?"

"Yes, Mr Akova," she murmured light-heartedly.

In the study, we put the photos given to me in Brussels and the pictures of the paintings I had taken in the galleries side by side on the table. The likenesses were identical.

"Amazing! Unbelievable!" she exploded with excitement. "But is it possible that it might just be a strong resemblance rather than the same identities?"

"Even if that were true, why use their names? Furthermore, there is no record of their birth; they have no proof of identity, nothing…"

"What do they live on?" Lola was very anxious to know more.

"They were both very well off during their lifetimes. It is always possible that the Eridanians arrived on Earth in the fifteenth century and replaced the two men, reproducing their physical features, thus disguising themselves in human form. Remember the extraterrestrial Eridanian aliens are extremely advanced in this transformation business. There is only one way to find out whether they replaced them or not. We have to open the graves of Lorenzo de Medici and Luigi Gonzaga III, and see if their remains are still there. Do you think we can do that, Lola?"

"I suppose so," she replied, reluctantly, "but what about the authorities?"

"We have no problem there as the Premier—your Premier's—instructions will be obeyed to the letter. His instructions are to help me investigate the matter and to assist me in every possible way. But we will have to keep it quiet."

"OK, but what about Gonzaga? What's his story?"

"Il Turco's ups and downs were countless during the power struggles of the period. He lost a great deal of his popularity and power towards the end of his life as he was completely outwitted by his adversaries. Nevertheless, he was appeased by being allowed to retain the fortunes of his family. This is the information I have gathered during my research on the two men." I told her.

"Very interesting. You seem to know more than I do," she said regretfully.

"His rivals made Gonzaga's presence in every court in Europe irksome by a few very subtle slurs on his character. You see, the man was a playboy and he had one too many affairs with married women in the aristocracy."

My conversation with Lola continued over dinner.

"Turan, what about the Greys and the Eridanians? Are you able to compare their technological powers?"

"The Greys have the edge over the Eridanians. I had the experience of a showdown between the two in the UK and the Greys had the upper hand, while the demonic Eridanians performed the most elaborate disappearing act ever."

"Then why don't they help us?" was Lola's next sensible question. "You say you have telepathic communication with the Greys, and you also say you are one of the chosen 36 on Earth—in fact, the leader of the 36. So, send a message and ask for help." She was right, of course, but she had no idea about the complex process of telepathic communication with the Greys. I explained.

"Mostly, even the combined energies and telepathic powers of all the chosen 36 had no response from the Greys. We have no way of knowing whether they receive all our messages. The messages I received from the Greys so far—and I have successes in communicating with them on three occasions on my own—were precise and to the point, but lacked any sort of full strategy that could wipe out the forces of the devil. The messages simply told me to challenge them."

"In fact, I think the patterns of thought and actions of both extraterrestrial civilisations are beyond human understanding. Their level of intelligence and their special powers are so immensely superior and varied when compared with our own that once again, it would be impossible to understand their movements and exploits. Add to that the fact that they are around 5,000 Earth years ahead of us with their technology and you have a full picture of their situation."

She responded with one word: "Hopeless…"

We had to go to the cemetery at night and preferably after midnight for the simple reason of avoiding the crowds of people visiting their loved ones. Two men were assigned to perform the delicate operation of opening up the tomb of Lorenzo de Medici. It was in the crypt of the San Lorenzo Church in Florence. A monument had also been erected during the time of his death. This was the family vault, although Medici's tomb had been kept separate from the rest. The night sky darkened as another storm approached.

It was a full moon. But it soon disappeared behind the dark clouds. The possibility of evil forces lurking behind each tombstone made Lola tremble with fear. The sound of the rushing wind and thunder turned it into a fearsome night, as the two men led the way to the door of the small church in the middle of the cemetery. One of the men turned the key in the lock and the large door opened with a creak reminiscent of a scene in a horror movie. Suddenly, Lola grabbed my hand for the first time, and squeezed it gratefully.

The premier had to arrange for a DNA specialist to come with us to the cemetery. That way, we would have a valid pretext for the opening of the tombs of both men. Lorenzo de Medici was interred here in the family mausoleum. For Luigi Gonzaga III's tomb, we would have to travel to the family vault in Mantua. There would be a DNA examination, a purely scientific study of the bodies. The tomb was opened after about thirty-five minutes. I pointed the big torch inside it; there was nothing inside. No body. The DNA specialist and the other two men who had opened the tomb were shocked into speechlessness. I was not surprised. He had been abducted by the alien Eridanians back in the 15th century.

Lola exited the mausoleum hastily, breathless with terror. Now there was no doubt in my mind that Lorenzo de Medici had been abducted by the aliens back then, only to return to Earth in the 21st century, armed with the powers of the devil. There was no question of any body-snatchers stealing the remains of this famous ruler of Florence. The mausoleum was always kept locked, and even we had had to get special permission on the pretext of a scientific DNA examination of the remains of Lorenzo de Medici.

The next day we left early evening for Mantua, the burial place of Luigi Gonzaga III. This time, it was a still night at the cemetery there. The two men and the DNA specialist went in first. The crypt of the Gonzaga family was underneath the church. The atmosphere cracked with tension as the first man opened the tomb. Once again, he had to work hard for at least half an hour to open the ancient tomb without damaging it. Then it opened with a creak. The horrified gaze of the man startled everyone except me. It was as I had expected. This tomb, too, was empty. Just at that moment, I heard very strange sounds coming from outside the church. I opened the door and looked into the darkness of the cemetery. There were black figures jumping up and about all over the place, appearing and then disappearing. A triumphant chorus of demons celebrating the fate of Luigi Gonzaga III, il Turco. Lola was right behind me, looking outside, anxious to see who was making these strange noises.

"Get back into the Church, quick!" I shouted at the three men who wanted to look out also, "Lola, get back…I will deal with this." I pushed them back in and closed the door behind me. We had been followed all the way from Florence to Mantua. The devils were here in the cemetery. As always, I had the shield with me. The protective device. I ran towards these with the torch in my right hand. They did not like the light. It was a terrifying experience, like a wild ride into the depths of hell. But I had to challenge them, it was the only way to get rid of them…Two of the demons attacked me, not knowing the powers I possessed. I hit them both. Then I took out my gun. I fired a few shots. For them, this was just a game. No bullet could harm them. I ran after them. The tall figures were black and ugly. Soon after the shots, I was able to repulse them. Within seconds, they had disappeared.

I waited for another ten minutes outside the church to make sure they had gone, and then I returned inside. Lola and the three men were astonished by my courage. Of course, they had no idea that the Greys had given me the power to challenge these devils. Shortly afterwards, we left the small church and hastened away towards the gate of the cemetery. I looked behind me. From the hillside, I could see the city glowing in the light.

The three men travelled with us all the way back to Florence. It was a tiring two days for Lola. I took her home in a taxi and went back to my hotel. She needed time to ponder about the awful facts about the two historical figures.

I was now in a difficult position. I had established the true identities of Medici and Gonzaga. With Count Dracula heading the list, these two were added on as prime enemies. Now I had to deal with three enormously powerful figures who wanted to bring the world under Eridanian control. But how, I did not know. The transformation of humans all over the world was continuing. Many countries had no idea who was under Eridanian control. The silent invasion continued, and some countries had been completely overrun by the aliens.

My love and affection for Lola was deep and sincere, and it was returned in equal measure, but she did not seem ready for a serious relationship. Somebody somewhere must have told her I was notorious as a seducer. Within a short period of time, I had become extremely fond of her, but she seemed to be constantly inhibited, never relaxed.

In my hotel room, I found philosophical comfort in reminiscing about the last two days in Florence and Mantua. Three men. No, not men. Three devils. The devils that men feared so much since the early ages, were now physically present on Earth, devouring mankind. Three creatures who with some extraterrestrial technology had entered the bodies of Prince Vlad, Lorenzo de Medici and Luigi Gonzaga III and turned the world into their playground. Three men who had appeared as humans but were inexorably determined to turn mankind into slaves. Slaves to be ruled by demons, who could not be killed, arrested or imprisoned. Three men, whose inexplicably enormous powers could not be challenged by any power on earth.

With the exception of the very pleasant and beautiful Lola, there was nothing to comfort me during my investigations in Florence. I found myself lying in bed in my hotel, feeling hopelessly unhappy. Then I had an idea. I turned the pages of the telephone book and found a company who hired out pianos. I told them to bring a white grad piano near Lola's home. Later, at dawn, I serenaded Lola beneath her balcony, playing my romantic compositions on the white grand. She was delightfully surprised and threw flowers down at me from above.

The people from the piano hiring company waited for me to finish my serenade while Lola applauded my performance with great enthusiasm. Later, she invited me in. We had breakfast and talked for at least an hour. I was also delighted and surprised when she took my hand and led me upstairs to her bedroom. We lay in bed smoking, gazing at each other lovingly. She straightened up in bed, showing the contours of her breasts under the sheet.

"You meet beautiful women all the time, don't you?" she asked.

"Yes. I'm lucky, I suppose," I replied, looking admiringly at her form.

"No. It's not that you're lucky. They just can't resist you. That's how you are. I mean, you don't have to do anything." And she showered me with kisses.

"How do you feel when you end a relationship? Do you feel unhappy?"

"Yes…and no. Yes, because I know that these moments are very special. Sometime in the future, when and if we meet, it will be very difficult to relive the magic of our first meeting. No, because I always stay in touch with the very special people in my life."

We spent the rest of the day in the house. Lola insisted that she would find some distant relatives of the Medici family in Florence. With proof of Lorenzo de Medici's extraterrestrial background, I doubted whether I could add anything new to my investigations. But I wanted to stay for a few days more in Florence just to be with her. She rejoiced at my decision and immediately afterwards, looked up some names in the telephone directory.

During the next few hours, I kept myself busy writing a report for the Italian Premier on Lola's computer. He believed in me and now I had proof of Medici's and Gonzaga's abductions back in the 15th century. Bicci believed I was the only man who could stave off the danger of an imminent invasion of the world by aliens. Outlining the details of the abductions, and the opening of the tombs, I assured the premier that these famous Italian figures of the Renaissance were oblivious of what had happened. Their tarnished reputations would be restored once I had had the opportunity to challenge the powers of the Eridanians.

The DNA specialist and the two men who had opened the tombs were ordered to keep quiet. I asked Lola also not to mention a word of what she had seen. Her background seemed to be domestic comfort and convention, but with my sudden arrival into her life, she had taken the plunge into investigating the extraterrestrial presence in Florence. Interestingly enough, she had found a report on the internet about the missing body of a Medici minor. Scientists in the report had said that the corpse of the four-year-old heir of the Medici family had mysteriously disappeared. Instead, they had found the remains of a one-year-old child in what was supposed to be the tomb of the Medici heir, Filippino, the son of Grand Duke Francesco I (1541—1587). It was lucky that the reason they had not tried to exhume Lorenzo de Medici's body was that it lay beneath beautiful Michelangelo tombstones too fragile to move. "Thank God for that." I said, "Otherwise they would have found out there were no remains of Lorenzo de Medici in the tomb."

We spent the weekend together and then on Monday morning I left for Brussels. It had been an eventful few days in Florence and Lola had made it all the more interesting. I caught the 11.00 am flight with a connection from Rome to Brussels and Lola was there to see me off. She promised to visit me in London.

I had telephoned Emma earlier and she had told me that a meeting was to be arranged for the near future to evaluate our latest finds and then to determine a new strategy.

Twenty-Two

My recital in Brussels was a much-acclaimed performance. New music had become very popular in Europe and there was a lot of interest in my 'Space' music compositions.

"The sonority and dynamics of your playing is amazing," said one music critic after the concert. Over a thousand people attended the recital which was televised live in all EU member countries. I left Brussels for London the next day.

Back in London, there was a sign of renewed commitment on the part of the British government. Emma said that the British prime minister was insisting on a meeting to discuss the latest situation.

"At long last, they have seen the danger. There's an international outcry against the EU. Reports from various sources say that Eridanians are springing up around the country like mushrooms."

She was right. There was no doubt about the increase in the population of Eridanians all over the world. These were Eridanian controlled humans. But so far, scientists had been unable to formulate an effective theory as an antidote to discriminate real humans from Eridanian humans. They lived the life of a normal human being but served the evil purposes of the Eridanians. Another unanswered question was whether the arch-demons, Draco, Medici and Gonzaga, where the three main sources of power for the aliens.

Invitations were sent out to high-ranking officials in the governments of Britain, France, Italy, Germany and of course, the USA. We insisted that they all had to be interviewed by the UFO Centre in London before they would be allowed to attend. We did not want any Eridanian-controlled people in the meeting. Clayton and I were considered to be the only two experts who could tell the difference between a normal human and an Eridanian-controlled one. This was just a precautionary measure, but neither Clayton nor I had any idea if we would be able to tell the difference. But we had to try.

So in all, we had five officials representing their governments to be interviewed. "Let me try something with the first one," I said to Clayton as the first candidate walked into our office. He was the British Under-Secretary at the Foreign Office. A tall, well-dressed man with—of course—a stiff upper lip. The moment he sat down, I became like an eagle ready to swoop down on his prey.

"We will challenge the Eridanian power. These devils will perish in the end. I know how to kick them out of this world!" The British diplomat from the old school remained calm and composed. His stern face forbore from confrontation.

"Stop making such empty threats, Mr Akova. I well know what we are up against. There is no need to behave disrespectfully," he responded, and I knew he was a normal human being. Our brief interview at an end, he was permitted to go.

Suddenly, I felt a strange and powerful source of energy flood my body.

"Clayton, something's happening to me." I whispered, full of wonder.

Poor Clayton looked worried sick for a moment. "Just sit down and watch me," I urged him, "an extra-special power has just come to me. Watch. I'll move that table over there by just looking at it." And miraculous as it may seem, that is what happened. I looked at the table and it moved.

"How the—?" exclaimed Clayton, his eyes wide with disbelief.

"I don't know," I chuckled, "but call in the next one before it leaves me as suddenly as it came."

Clayton opened the door and called in the Frenchman. He sat down.

"I will destroy the diabolic plans of the Eridanians. The puppets of the Eridanians will disappear from the face of the Earth." The special energy was there within me, and I knew the Greys had contacted me once again.

The Frenchman rose immediately and backed away from me. Utterly unmanned and in terror, he shrieked for help. The shock was great and he seemed to have become demented. With a furious roar, more bestial than human, he made a hasty retreat.

Clayton was astounded. He shut the door behind the Frenchman and hurried back to me.

"What's happening, Turan?"

"I don't know. But it's something different from the experience I had with my encounter with Count Dracula in Whitby. I feel as though I am letting out some kind of emanation that has an odour. Can you smell it?"

Clayton moved in closer, sniffing the air.

"Yes…it smells terrible. Where did that come from?"

"I don't know, Peter, but it seems that anyone who has anything to do with the Eridanians is repelled by this odour."

The Italian, German and American officials came in one after the other. The behaviour of all three was normal.

Ten minutes later, the awful odour was gone. Just as well, I said to myself. No woman would come anywhere near me smelling like that. The Greys were obviously playing around with us humans. Their contacts always helped but they never—up until now, anyway—offered a permanent solution. A solution to end Eridanian domination in the world. Perhaps they were not able to challenge the power of the Eridanians. That was a hair-raising thought…But my guess was that the Greys' technology was far superior when compared with that of the Eridanians. If that was the case, then why had they not destroyed the Eridanian presence on Earth? It was a mystery.

Emma contacted the French Foreign Office and asked them to send a new representative to the meeting, which was set for the following day in our offices. Emma, Clayton and I had already decided to ask for a resumption of talks with the Eridanians. Such a proposal would bring out into the open the aim of the aliens. Then the US, British, German, Italian and French governments would appoint an ad hoc committee to deal with the affair.

The next day, the French representative arrived. There was no odour this time, and the man seemed quite normal. In her opening speech, Emma reiterated the dangers of Eridanian infiltration, especially in governments, and added, "Their aim is to control the whole world. We cannot be absolutely certain, but we think some countries in Europe have already succumbed to their power. We are also investigating the activities of some of the largest multi-national companies in the world. Our investigators say billions of dollars have been spent by these companies with the sole aim of recruiting more and more people into the Eridanian fold. Ordinary people with small, regular incomes have been furnished with enormous financial rewards and instructed to take part in such well-known programmes as the 'global partnership for development'. In actual fact, this is a plan to unite the world under Eridanian control. With promises of immortality and large sums of money, people have become easy prey for the aliens."

The French representative interrupted Emma with a question: "What's this promise of immortality?"

"Well, we've had cases of people being promised just that. Furthermore, and this is an eye-witness account, Mr Akova here witnessed the resurrection of a dead man. First the body disappeared, and then it reappeared a couple of hours later."

The Frenchman looked aghast at me, but before he could speak, the American butted in: "Why can't we just use every weapon available to us, and destroy the bastards? Where do they get their power from, Mr Akova? You've encountered these devils. They must have bases here on earth. Why can't we just bomb them off the face of the earth?"

"I'm afraid that's not possible," I replied, "at first, we thought they had bases. But later, we found out there were no such places. They came from the star system Epsilon Eridani. They arrived here on Earth at different times with a mission. So far I have proof that Count Dracula, also known as Draco, Lorenzo de Medici and Luigi Gonzaga III—the latter two from the Renaissance period— are the three Eridanian leaders. I am sure there are others, though."

"So..." the American persisted, "let's send out some agents to finish them off."

"We can't do that. They can't be killed." I told him. This time, it was the American who went berserk, "What do you mean they can't be killed. If bullets can't kill them, then we blast them with missiles."

"Nothing, and by that I mean no weapon can destroy these creatures. That is why we have to talk to the three Eridanian leaders I have just mentioned. That is why we have to find out the source of their power. If we can find their source of power, then we can destroy them. Otherwise, our case is hopeless..."

"And how do you propose to find the source?" asked the British representative. He had a point, because none of us had any idea where to look. He continued, "You, Mr Akova, have a special power. You don't risk your life when you challenge them. Miraculously, you are protected by Grey power, so they cannot eliminate you. But the other Chosen 35 are not so fortunate. They are in no position to challenge them, and that includes Mr Clayton here. So this means that you are the only one who can fight them. One man against an army of Eridanians. It is indeed hopeless."

All of us at the centre knew that without Grey help, it would be impossible to eradicate the devil's armies. But so far, the messages I had received from them had not revealed any specific strategy aimed at ending Eridanian control in the world. Perhaps a mighty war between the Greys and the Eridanians would destroy planet earth as we know it. Such a war with the sophisticated weapons of two extraterrestrial civilisations would indeed destroy the world and mankind. Perhaps that was the reason behind the Grey's reticence in recommending a way out of the extremely difficult situation we were in. I had no idea. Which is why I wanted to suggest a meeting with the Eridanians. To buy more time. But the danger of becoming slaves of the aliens was coming closer by the hour.

Another alarming development which had come out into the open was the fact that the Eridanians now controlled most of the financial world. The largest multi-national companies in the world were now under their control. That had been the conclusion of the reports by the investigators of the UFO Centre in London. According to these reports which had been sent to headquarters from various capitals of EU member states, the economies of these states were on the verge of collapse. This topic would be on the agenda in all the important meetings between the leaders of the big four in the EU and the US President.

I was asked time and again why I wanted a meeting with the evil Eridanians. Did I have the power to rid the devil from all societies? If we were indeed powerless against the might of the aliens, one man's challenge might ignite a much wider conflict. I would then be responsible for submitting mankind to the Eridanians. There was no one who could help resolve the crisis. I had many supporters, but almost half the people at the helm in their own countries opposed my strategy.

Although they opposed my strategy, they were unable to present the remotest idea for a possible alternative. The world was being drawn into a situation in which there would be no choice but capitulation. The collapse of the economies of European countries, the USA and other countries would bring about incalculable chaos and the destruction of human civilisation. Surely the Earth people did not deserve such a catastrophe. The devil had presented itself formally once in a meeting with the European leaders. But governments of European countries had rejected the offer of superior space travel technology.

The creatures which had arrived on Earth had no recognisable deity. Their images, which we had acquired through the feathers found in different parts of the world (I had found the first one in North Cyprus)—were those of the devil known to mankind: the devil of the dark, evil forces, undefeatable and as elusive as ever. This evil force could neither be diluted nor eliminated. Panic at the shocking realisation of alien domination was spreading by the day.

A feeling of insecurity engulfed all the people present at the next all-important meeting, except, of course, the devils themselves. Namely Draco, Lorenzo de Medici and Luigi Gonzaga III. These creatures were so advanced that they spoke English like Englishmen. I could not help but admire Emma's elaborate and sophisticated analysis of the current situation. But this was no ordinary meeting. No one, with the exception of the American representative perhaps, who thought the USA could somehow deter the adversary from its uncompromising stance with its military might, believed that the three alien leaders would sway from their current dominant position. Emma proposed a compromise, a compromise to cooperate with the Eridanians. The aliens would help end fatal diseases such as AIDS and cancer, scrutinise all human traditional weaknesses and offer solutions that would result in a much more advanced lifestyle in countries all over the world.

But the Eridanians would have none of that. Draco rose from his chair with the air of a supreme being.

"We are here to rule over Planet Earth and make it a better place to live in. We are here to help you in the way we want. Not the way you want. You humans are not in a position to bargain for anything. There may be a few pockets of resistance…" he glanced in my direction with a sinister smile, and continued, "such as Mr Akova, here. But soon, you humans will realise that you cannot challenge our power. We will rule and you will carry out our orders."

The British Premier protested, "How could you envisage such a black future for mankind? Yours is an advanced, supreme extraterrestrial civilisation. We are not your property to do as you like with."

"You are our property. And now is the time to claim that property."

"In other words," I said, trying to remain calm, "the whole population of the world will become your slaves."

"You may call it slavery. We view you as inferior, backward creatures."

"But this is so evil…" the French Premier gasped.

Rattled by my behaviour, Draco snapped back immediately, "Yes, we are evil. You call us devils. Hell is our star system Epsilon Eridani, and the word evil means supreme in our civilisation…Numerous other civilisations in the Milky Way Galaxy are in alliance with us. But we are supreme…We are the rulers…"

"What about the Greys? They are more advanced than you are."

"They can't touch us here on Earth, or anywhere else in the universe. We are supreme. The Chosen 36 humans' telepathic contact under your leadership, Mr Akova, is a trivial matter." Draco casually dismissed the Greys' power with a shrug, and then added, "We have a superspecial purpose. Even your God in the Bible cannot challenge our power. You have no solutions for the basic needs of your people. We are highly advanced, we study your human race as you study rats in a maze. Your DNA is very interesting. There are innumerable combinations of our genes and your genes that fit our specialised needs. We have been colonising other planets in many other star systems. Your Earth is just another planet on our list."

The Italian Premier looked at the two famous Renaissance characters, de Medici and Gonzaga, "You have brought shame to your country and people," he murmured quietly, and then took a few steps closer to the two men, his eyes narrowing: "But you are no longer the real Medici and Gonzaga now, are you?"

"Yes, we are," came the reply from Lorenzo de Medici, "the only difference is that we are far more advanced that we were. Now we have a task of the utmost importance: the advancement of humankind."

The Italian Premier's answer to that was prompt: "You mean the surrender of mankind to the Devil? Ha!"

The German Chancellor had been listening to all of us with great interest: "With your space technology, you could take us to the stars, as slaves, probably."

The Eridanians kept quiet while the US President retorted angrily: "There is no point in continuing this meeting." He got up and walked to the door. Then he turned back, looking at Draco: "We will fight back…" he said finally.

A widespread dissemination of disinformation would serve no one. Millions of people were aware of the danger. But many thousands had succumbed to the tempting gift of immortality. The frightful, slobbering Eridanians had promised them an iron-clad, indestructible life. The Eridanians were masters of deceit and intrigue. They could not only control normal human beings, but change into human form themselves. No one could tell the difference. They saw themselves as the ultimate example of power. They could overcome any challenge to their stature.

The shocking realisation that a far superior alien force was in control in most parts of the world now began to sink in. The staggering news of the disintegration and eventual demise of the EU was now a real possibility. It was a truly shocking situation. Man was reduced to a position of subservience. The mission of the

Eridanian aliens was to tempt humans into the Devil's Kingdom which seemed to be impregnable. The silent invasion had created an atmosphere of menace and fear.

The meeting had one purpose only—to stop the Eridanian infiltration. But we had failed. Furthermore, we were not able to find out their source of power. The gravity of the situation had finally dawned on the world leaders. But it seemed too late. One could foresee a stock market crash of gigantic proportions, a drop in the value of shares on the stock market, especially in defence shares. No manmade military hardware could destroy the alien force. When I looked into the near future, I could also see the lay-off of thousands of employees and the bankruptcy of service and support businesses. The greatest depression in the history of the world was at hand…

The people in the room left one by one in an atmosphere of stunned horror. This was probably the most dramatic moment for all the leaders of the world. There was no question of a compromise with the Eridanians. Confrontation with the evil ones would result in complete and utter defeat. The military knew full well the task was beyond them. They would fight and lose…

The USA would have it their way. In other words, confrontation rather than compromise. But they had no chance against the power of the Eridanians. Man had become a mere pawn in the struggle for supremacy. It was just a matter of time before the truth surfaced about the hopeless situation. No one could suppress the truth. The British Premier was quite adamant in his insistence that I contact the Greys and ask for help. He encouraged this possible contact with all the force of his eloquence. Clayton agreed also. Personally, I was convinced that the Greys had a very good reason for not intervening at the present time.

The American President was still defiant: "Let us find their bases and destroy them!" I told him that so far, we had not found a shred of evidence pointing to any bases on earth. He came up with outrageous bargains to outweigh the advantages of the Eridanians. I told him that the aliens would not listen to such offers. We were not in a bargaining position. The long and the short of it was that now there was nothing we could do, except to try and contact the Greys for help. I suggested a meeting of the Chosen 36. With the combined efforts of these people, we could perhaps reach out and deliver a message. An urgent message, explaining mankind's desperate fight for survival. A telepathic communication with the Greys would rekindle our hopes.

No matter how you looked at it, this was a grim, unrelenting state of affairs. The news of the failure of the world leaders to reach an accommodation with the aliens was devastating. Panic-stricken crowds in many capitals in EU member states protested against the outcome of the top-level talks, unaware of the real reasons behind the deadlock. I contacted several of our investigators to see if they had any new clues leading to any particular locations of UFO activity in England, France and Italy. I had to look for a base once again.

Could the Eridanian devils survive on Earth for a lengthy period of time without contacting their own kind? Ever since the beginning of extraterrestrial visitations in the modern UFO era, initiated by the Rosewell crash in the USA, not a single case had been reported of aliens staying on Earth and planning to take control over humankind. The Greys who had been visiting Earth for the past sixty years and who were the kind of alien frequently seen in different locations, did not show any movement towards colonising Earth. The data amassed over the years, especially in the USA, did not indicate a Grey invasion of the Earth.

One of our investigators had succeeded in photocopying the most secret documents in the EU, specifically from the 'Secrecy Missions' department of the EU. Trawling through EU secret documents of UFO sightings, I was convinced that there had been a cover-up…a cover-up of secret agreements with the Eridanians. These had been kept under wraps for more than ten years. This meant that the Eridanians had arrived on Earth more than ten years earlier, long before I found the feather in North Cyprus.

The secret EU documents revealed shocking evidence of alien insemination. So now we had the problem of solving the mystery not only of the Eridanians but of the Hybrids amongst us. Enough evidence had seeped through the EU secret documents I examined to convince me of the presence of the Hybrids, especially in England and France. But they would just be products of the superior Eridanian beings, and they would most certainly be under their control. The fact remained that the Devil had a civilisation of its own in the crucible of the universe, and that civilisation came from the star Epsilon Eridani in the long-struggling constellation of Eridanus, the river. This star was in fact one of the two stars at which the 85-foot radio telescope at Green Bank, Virginia, was directed during the Project Ozma experiment of 1960. A star system 10.5 light-years from the solar system.

The devilish plans of the Eridanians had stifled all argument that the good Greys would eventually descend upon the Earth and save mankind form the

Eridanians. A force from outer space that would eliminate the centres of evil on Earth. But there was no sign of the Greys. The Chosen 36 would try to communicate with them, but there was no guarantee that they would respond to our call. Each extraterrestrial civilisation had its own material, physiological, psychological and mental differences. The human mind had no capacity to understand advanced extraterrestrial civilisations. The Eridanian invasion was the greatest challenge ever to confront mankind. The Eridanians on the one hand seeking to enslave the human race and the Greys on the other, promising to save the world. The magnitude of the problem made my mind reel.

I decided to investigate further into the machinations of the EU. I had a few contacts in Brussels and the first man who sprang to mind was a German economist, Heinrich Stabler, who had resigned from his post in the Commission quite recently. In our brief telephone conversation, he said he had gone into partnership with a Belgian firm based in Brussels. I had mentioned my investigations into Eridanian activity within the EU before I had left London. We arranged to meet at a restaurant in the city centre the next day. My mind was set on the EU. I had a hunch. I had no idea why, but my instincts told me it should be further investigated.

The food in the restaurant was good. Surprisingly, Stabler had invited his secretary to lunch with us, and added, "I am sure she will be able to help you in your investigations."

"Thank you," I said, turning towards Stabler, "sir, why did you leave the Commission?"

"Well, Turan, I'm sure you are much better informed about this dreadful business of Eridanian control over the EU. Now the economic and political events are no longer under the control of the European Commission. The economic order especially, which once benefitted all the members, is defunct. Chaos reigns over the European Commission. The new premiers of the big four are hopelessly entangled in an effort to save the EU from the extraterrestrials. The enormous danger of fragmentation is no longer a secret. At least, four member states are on the verge of leaving the EU. I can predict an unprecedented wave of disintegration. Yes, I'm afraid I can see it all happening. The collapse of the EU."

"Yes, I heard about the massive takeover of EU finances by the Eridanians," I said.

"Absolutely. The EU as we used to know it no longer exists," he said emphatically, "the organisation is still there. But the aliens have taken over. The major powers in the EU are leading us in different directions. The financial machine has collapsed. The value of the Euro is zero. Not even member states use it anymore. The dream of a unified pluralist culture is gone. There are so many disparate cultures now scattered all over Europe."

"Did you meet any of these aliens?"

"Oh, yes, Sure," said Heinrich, "and believe me, I had to do whatever they ordered me to do."

"Such as, for example?" I asked.

"Transfer money into their own accounts."

"Heinrich, did any one of the aliens try to bring you under their spell? I am sure you have heard about the mysterious powers of the Eridanians emanating from their eyes. It seems to me they are no longer using this power to transform people."

"Yes, I've heard about it, but they are no longer using this method. Eridanians use human eyes as a window through which they can monitor human thoughts."

"Do they have a meeting place? Or do they gather around in a secret place? Did you hear of such a secret meeting place for Eridanians?"

Elsa, the secretary, who was a charming girl by the way, spoke for the first time, "Yes. I have heard of such a place. I was writing a report on my computer, when, quite by accident, I saw an e-mail on the screen. It read as follows: '*The next meeting will be on the 3 March at the Chateau Villeneuve*'. I looked it up in a book of chateaux. Chateau Villeneuve is about 90 kilometres to the west of Paris…"

"Thank you, Elsa, that kind of information is vital. Today is the fifth. So the meeting was two days ago. Nevertheless, this is one place I have to visit." I said.

"Heinrich, can you think of any of the people that you worked with at the Commission who could throw some light on the activities of the Eridanians?"

"Yes, I can think of two. A man and a woman. But Turan, these people are very much under the control of the Eridanians. How can you possibly hope to get any information out of them?"

"I can. I have special powers. Powers that nullify the spell the devil has put on them. Don't ask me where that power came from. It's the Greys. They are helping me. I have experienced this before and it works. The minute they come into contact with me, it happens automatically. So give me the names of these two people."

"The man is British. His name is Michael Snow. He's been living in Brussels for a number of years. His wife is Belgian. The woman is French: Valerie Dubois. She is the head of the French Delegation in Brussels. I will give you their contact details later."

Heinrich thought for a moment and continued, "They are good friends of mine. Turan, you must remember that we worked together for at least three years." He gave me their addresses and telephone numbers. It was clear from the geographical evidence that the UFO Centre had gathered so far that the main bulk of aliens were in fact in Europe. For reasons unknown to us, they had chosen the EU and Europe as the first bastion of their force. The Eridanians had moved in from the periphery and were closer to the core. The challenge of the big four in the EU was keeping them out for the time being. But how long would it last? It is interesting to note that in countries like Turkey, Syria, Lebanon, Israel and Egypt, there was very little evidence of the alien presence.

Our network of investigators was mainly in Europe as almost all cases of alien presence came from that continent. The number of Eridanian controlled EU officials was growing by the day. Back in my hotel, I looked at the list to see if the two names Heinrich had given me were included. Hut the list consisted of officials whose collaboration with the Eridanians was established beyond question. There could be many more who had become the slaves of the aliens after the list was completed. At the same time, there were very few murder cases or violent actions involving the Eridanians. There was, of course, the murder of the priest in Rome, which I had more or less witnessed. But the man had been resurrected and now was a slave of the aliens.

The power of the Devil was so advanced that probably there was no need for violent action. They would simply take control and make humans the devil's slaves. That train of thought was dominant. The devils moved from one place to another, they assumed different forms, could not be killed or destroyed. So they had no reason to kill humans. Humans would be used as slaves. So far, their actions had helped to substantiate this theory. The only good sign in the struggle against the Eridanians was the sharply increased awareness of the great dangers that lay ahead. People in Britain, France, Germany and Italy had been very well informed through their respective media.

Michael Snow was in his late forties. He invited me to dinner at his house when I told him I was a friend of Heinrich's. Apparently, he had heard of me in my pianist/composer capacity and had read about my research on UFOs. His wife, Marie, a beautiful woman in her thirties, was a Belgian citizen, but her father was British. A young woman of about 27 was also present. She was Marie's sister who lived in England but was on a visit to Brussels.

"Heinrich told me about your investigations here in Brussels," he said, "frankly, I admire your courage. You are a Turk, aren't you?"

"A Turkish Cypriot," I replied, "I am especially interested in gathering as much information as I can about the Eridanians. I feel the aliens have a power source somewhere in Europe. I'm trying to find that spot."

"I am sure Heinrich told you about Chateau Villeneuve."

"Yes, I plan to visit the chateau in the next few days." I said.

"Good. I know this chateau is an important meeting place for the Eridanians," he said enthusiastically.

He downed his brandy and continued, "Mr Akova, I was astounded by the ontologically shattering nature of the information that I received."

"Surely an ontological argument is something of the past, when we were not sure about their physical existence. The Eridanians here are a physical reality." I said.

"Yes, that's true," he admitted, "Mr Akova, what about the bases? You say they must have bases in Europe. But why Europe?"

"I am convinced that the first part of their plan was to dominate the European Union. There have been many reports from our own investigators of Eridanian controlled areas within the EU. When I say our investigators, I mean the investigators of the UFO Centre in London, of which there are about fifty. The Eridanians must have a source of power which they have established somewhere in Europe…I am sure spaceships from their star system Epsilon Eridani arrive regularly to feed from this special source. After all, they are alien to our world and their existence here on Earth probably depends on it."

"But this is just a theory, isn't it?" he asked.

"Yes, true…but we have nothing else to go on. We have to find the bases and we have to find the source that even now remains unknown."

"If indeed there is such a source," said Michael dryly.

"OK so we don't know, but we have do something. We have to try."

"Right. Try we will. And I will help you as much as I can." He was now drinking his third brandy. He poured one for me, too, and then handed me a large white envelope.

"You see, I have been working on my own for two months now. The aliens did not suspect such an obedient official. That's how I chose to appear to them, so as not to attract attention," he explained, and continued, "In that envelope, you will find a list of at least seventy people of different nationalities. All these people are collaborating with the Eridanians. I think I can arrange for them to come to a meeting in one place. Then you move in with the police and arrest them. Just put them in prison, away from the evil force."

Michael Snow's list of collaborators was a complete surprise. But I could sense he had no qualms about his own personal investigation into the matter.

"Fantastic," I said, "let me know when you arrange the meeting. The police will do the rest."

"The Chief of Police is a friend of mine, so I can arrange that as well. But I want you to be there, too," he said.

I made photocopies of the list and also of my own list and handed over the full names to Snow. He accompanied me to the hotel and we had a few drinks there also. He said he would call me after a couple of days and left. In my room, I thought about the whole situation. The life of the planet was under a profound threat. After years of locking horns with the debunkers, we had now reached a precarious and unpredictable period of time in the life of the Planet Earth. No single or combined power could break the stranglehold of the Devil.

Twenty-Three

Michael Snow's arrangement of the meeting was perfect. Around sixty people were present at the cocktail party at the Hotel Centrale. Scores of policemen moved into the hall after about an hour. At first, the crowd panicked but Michael calmed them down and told them they had to go with the police for routine questioning. No one resisted. Eventually, they were packed into police vans waiting outside the hotel.

"So what's next?" I asked Michael, offering him a drink at the bar.

"It's all been arranged. They will all be charged with conspiring against the European Commission."

"I didn't realise it was a crime," I commented.

"If it involves transferring money from EU funds into another account, it is."

"Well done."

"Of course, they will be kept in for more than a week. After weeks of interrogation, I don't think any of these people will work for the Eridanians any longer. Remember, these are ordinary civil servants of different nationalities who have been more or less forced to collaborate with the enemy."

"Michael, if there is a real Eridanian among them, he or she will most probably use all its power for a disappearing act. You know, they do this all the time."

"Let them. It doesn't really matter. At least, the devils will know that we have challenged them and have released sixty people."

All movements and actions of the devils were too outlandish for the rational mind. The arrest of those sixty people at the Hotel Centrale was discreetly hushed up. But the devils knew only too well what was happening. The media, on the other hand, did not yet have the courage to blow the lid off the discovery of the Eridanian domination of the European Union…This would only provoke senseless tirades about the current situation embellished with misleading information. A new story, however, had leaked into the papers and onto the TV

194

news channels which was all about the well-meaning actions of the Eridanians who wanted to help mankind. This version had absolutely no foundation whatsoever.

The Eridanians could make disappear all atomic particles of which flesh and matter were composed. They could perform this operation at a whim. One scientist told me the ultra-vibratory rate through which the molecular and cellular composition of matter was altered was child's play for the Eridanians. They could animate and make inanimate. They were visible in one form, invisible in the next. Stimulated by the diligent research of our investigators, amongst whom there were some top scientists, we could determine the alien behaviour in a richer and broader perspective. It was an unnerving experience. However, the scientists could examine swiftly and unerringly the behaviour patterns of the Eridanians.

The alien devils would eventually bring destruction and calamity to Planet Earth. Nevertheless, we had to be prepared for such a dreaded contingency. The scientists would have to prevent the eventual eradication of mankind.

Valerie Dubois—the French lady—was somewhat distant and cold. When I asked her about the activities of the Eridanians within the European Commission, she responded with a distinctly perplexed attitude.

"Their presence undermines the sovereignty of the European Commission," she said, finally eyeing me with suspicion.

"Well, we know that. But can you give me any information about their source of power, and where it comes from?"

"It's a certain fact, Mr Akova, that no one knows where they get their power from. I think they have unlimited powers within themselves which the human mind cannot comprehend. I do not think they need power from any source."

"That's one way of looking at it. On the other hand, I have reason to believe that they have to get more power from a source somewhere in Europe. At least, that is the conclusion our scientists have reached." I said.

"Clearly, your scientists know more about this than I do," she pointed out coldly, "so why are you asking me?" Her attitude was distinctly discouraging.

"Am I right in assuming that you are in regular contact with the Eridanians?"

"Yes. But I just do my job. I do not ask any questions."

"You are head of the French delegation for—"

"—Space research," she said.

"That's very interesting. Heinrich didn't tell me that," I told her, "perhaps we could talk about space research some other time. You could tell me all about your findings."

"Perhaps," she replied with a small smile, the first in half an hour. Perhaps she was relaxing a little.

"Let's have dinner...perhaps this evening...?" I let my sentence trail vaguely.

"Yes, I would like that," she inclined her head in affirmation. She was clearly very reserved and cautious.

She told me that the Eridanians were clinical and authoritative.

"Even though they have taken human form, I can tell the difference," she added.

"How?"

"Well, you can feel the alien presence. They dominate your whole being. An other-worldly evil force is always present. I don't know how else to explain it."

The more I made her talk, the more I realised how little she knew about the aliens. Nevertheless, I could not dismiss any source of information that could lead to more knowledge about them. Valerie Dubois seemed eager to please. She sat behind her desk, tossing out papers she had pulled from her drawer. Then with a sudden move, she grabbed one paper, held it up and started to read it:

"Here! I have something for you. It's not very important, but at least it's a lead." She relaxed her grip on the paper and started to read it aloud.

The contents consisted of astronomical data about three star system: Alpha Centauri, Tau Ceti and Zeta Reticuli. The first two were among our closest stellar neighbours. Zeta Reticuli, on the other hand, was a bit further out—37 light-years away from our solar system. 'Project Statler' named after the scientist who conceived it, was primarily sending out signals to these three star systems.

She handed over the paper which had atomic numbers of principal biochemical elements, the DNA double helix, with vertical and horizontal units. It was like a cosmic tongue. She got up and stood beside me.

"You see it all in the figures which were sent to us by Herr Statler, the German scientist, who claims he's found a much faster way of beaming out these messages to the three star systems. At any rate, you can read the full contents later. Now, here's the lead. Two Eridanians who come into my office every now and again asked me to send this report to the secretary of the Foreign Press

Association at Carlton House Terrace in London. The secretary's name is Frank Dorchester."

"Interesting," I said, "why would a superior technology such as the Eridanians want to know about this project?" "Who is Statler? And how come the world and the Americans especially are not aware of this system which can transmit beams to other star systems in such a short time? Such an important development would fall like a bombshell into the scientific community. How long does it take for Statler's beams to go to another star system?"

She thought for a moment and then spelled out a figure which was astounding—unbelievable—to say the least.

"He claims his signals system programme, which is operable now, can transmit signals to these three star systems within 35 days. I know it sounds impossible, since the most advanced signal transmitting system the Americans have developed so far transmit signals for one hundred days for each star system and the signals only reach their destinations after 35 years...I'm sure you'll read Statler's full report. He explains everything in great detail...But from 35 years down to 35 days is, I'm sure you'll agree, a remarkable achievement if it's true."

"Valerie," I said, "this is getting a bit complicated. Frankly, it actually doesn't make any sense. OK. Now let's examine the facts. Eric Statler is one of the leading scientists at the European Space Agency. The Statler Project is a new project. Whether the Americans, British or any other scientific space research centres are aware of it or not, we don't yet know anything. The evidence we have gathered so far through American and British sources clearly singles out these three star systems, namely Alpha Centauri, Tau Ceti and Zeta Reticuli as the homes of the Greys, the extraterrestrial civilisation trying to help us. I personally have proof of this through contacts with the Greys themselves. Now, the question that springs to mind is this: is the EU Space Agency trying to contact the Greys for help? And if it is, why would the Eridanians simply eliminate Statler and dispose of the Statler Project? Instead of this course of action, they have asked you to send the Statler Project to Frank Dorchester at the Foreign Press Association in London."

Valerie Dubois looked desperately confused. She sat beside me, hands clasped together and then finally spoke.

"I don't know. Although I am involved with space research, the action plan of the European Space Agency is top secret. I am just one more official doing what I'm told to do."

"Perhaps the Eridanians will try another game through the media. After all, the media big shots of the European countries are represented at the Foreign Press Association. What about Statler? Could you arrange a meeting?"

"Yes," she said, "In fact, he is here in Brussels at the moment."

"Valerie, I do appreciate all your help. Could we go and see Statler now?"

We had to wait at least forty-five minutes for the meeting, but while we waited, I asked Valerie about the two Eridanians who has asked her to send the Statler Project to Frank Dorchester at the Foreign Press Association in London. She told me that one of them had been a very tall man called Draco, and that the name of the other was Lorenzo de Medici. She said they had spoken perfect English and had both been with the European Commission. I was not surprised about the fact that these two were quite openly manipulating the affairs of the EU.

Eric Statler was probably in his early fifties. A man of medium height, well-built, with a clean-shaven head. He actually looked more like a wrestler than a scientist. After the formal introductions, I asked him about his project.

"Beaming signals to the three star systems and reaching all three in just 35 days? This is a remarkable achievement. If I may say so, it is quite incredible. When will the project become operational?"

"I cannot divulge such information, Mr Akova. This is top secret."

"You are, of course, aware of the extraterrestrial presence of the Eridanians and the fact that they are very much in control of almost all the institutions of the EU."

Statler simply nodded, and I continued, "Not only the Americans, but the renowned Scottish scientist and astronautics expert, John McFay, have developed a system of beaming signals to the three star systems. But these signals take 35 years to reach their destination."

He moved his hands nervously on the table, and then raised himself from the large chair. "You are well-informed, Mr Akova," he said, smiling.

"Mr Statler, are any of the Eridanians involved with this project?"

"I don't know. I have been working on it for almost six months."

"But why? The Eridanians are astonishingly, unbelievably technologically advanced. In fact, their interstellar communications systems are so advanced that they can communicate with any one of the star systems in our own galaxy. So why do you think they are interested in your project which is a midget compared with the mammoth technological know-how of their own civilisation?"

"Again, I don't know, Mr Akova. And quite frankly, I shouldn't be talking to you at all. This project is, as I said earlier, top secret." Statler was repeating himself, and I suspected he was under Eridanian control. Normally, I would have been able to detect patterns of behaviour in Eridanianised humans, but with Statler, there was no sign of any Eridanian characteristics.

"One final question, Mr Statler. Who is Frank Dorchester?"

He was now totally confused and replied bemusedly: "I don't know."

Either he was determined not to say a word of what he knew, or he was simply telling the truth. I thought the latter was a real possibility. All animation had gone from his face. But the fact remained that an insignificant official of the European Space Agency, Valerie Dubois, had been instructed to send the 'secret' project to Frank Dorchester at the Foreign Press Association in London. And who had issued those instructions? Draco and Lorenzo de Medici...The two Eridanian extraterrestrials in human form, who were conducting the secret invasion of Earth and the subjugation of humankind.

The whole affair had now become an open secret. There was no more talk of the devil. The tangled mesh of Eridanian power seemed to control most of Europe and the EU in particular. The whole picture of darkness, doom and slavery of mankind that would be brought about by extraterrestrial presence was being manipulated to the public, and promoted hypnotically as a 'Golden Age' by the Eridanians. Mankind would apparently be raised to a much higher plane by this highly advanced civilisation. They had somehow persuaded people that all fatal illnesses would be eradicated from Earth, that economic, social and political problems would cease to exist; and man would take one more step towards immortality. The increasingly technology-driven society would gradually succumb to the powers of the Eridanians. No one would be able to control the alien agenda.

This was indeed the most perplexing evil and yet scientific mystery of our times. The barriers of time and distance were great. Mankind had been eagerly awaiting the advent of the 'good' extraterrestrials—namely the Greys—to rescue Planet Earth and to save mankind from destroying itself. But from the dark oceans of space, the galactic empires and celestial dynasties, the Devil had come. Satan, that great extraterrestrial devil, was slowly but surely devouring man's will to live a normal life on Earth. The noisy negativists allied with the evil extraterrestrial Eridanians had become the creators of turbulent times. It was of paramount urgency to awaken the fighting spirit of mankind which had been lulled into passivity. The evil Eridanians, now in their thousands, were in control of most of the EU member states, and they were in human form. Superficially, they appeared to be working for the benefit of mankind, but in reality, they were spreading a false expectation of a world full of happiness, through the media and the internet. Mind to mind communication had somehow tamed fears of these supreme extraterrestrials. Many people seemed ready to accept a life together with the Eridanians and had lost their bias against the extraterrestrials. The behaviour patterns of the devils were totally unpredictable and contrary.

Twenty-Four

I travelled by train from Brussels to Paris. I slept for a couple of hours at the Imperial Hotel near the Gare du Nord. Chateau Villeneuve was approximately a hundred kilometres west of Paris. I did manage to find a small book on the chateaux of France, in which I read that it had been built in 1897 by Baron Fleuvert and had been preserved as a historical monument after the First World War. The Fleuverts came originally from the Netherlands in 1790 and had lived in France from that date onwards. The directions in the book recommended that you go to Versailles and then travel about twenty kilometres to get there. I rented a car and started off quite early in the morning. On the road map, I had taken from the hotel, Versailles was shown as the nearest town to the chateau.

Whilst on the way to Versailles, I realised once again that I was no nearer to finding the power source of the Eridanians. But I had to follow up every single lead. Apparently, this chateau was a meeting place of the Eridanians and their collaborators. So maybe this was the place to search for evidence leading up to the source of Eridanian power. Now that the Eridanians had succeeded in creating a positive, beneficent image of themselves, it would be extremely difficult to tell the world that these same Eridanian extraterrestrials were evil and their sole aim was the domination of planet earth. So I had to find the power source of the Eridanians and prove, once again, that the devils had come to earth for one reason only: to take full control of mankind throughout the world. How could anyone dismiss such evidence as inconclusive?

But even with proof, hopes of a full-scale challenge to outwit them with earth technology were very slim. Eridanian infiltration into the EU was massive. The aliens were everywhere and it was now almost impossible to tell who was who, where or why. Their plan was unfolding in great depth, they were fluent in all European languages and had developed overnight a behaviour pattern which was astoundingly similar to that of human behaviour. There was no discernible material difference. The chain of reasoning to find a solution to this critical problem was gone. How could anyone find any sensible reason behind all this unpredictable and shocking activity—a reason, a link, even, or evidence that would lead to the power source which remained unknown...

We were simply not able to grasp their purposes as they moved from one range of activities promoting good relations with humankind, to another contrary, incomprehensible course of action. The implications of such actions were far-reaching. Humankind was helpless against such advanced beings, the impact of the eventual disintegration and domination of the EU by the aliens would be devastating. The extrapolations of probabilities were immense. Top scientists in the USA and Europe had slid from to a state of panic to one of fatalism.

I turned slowly from a narrow lane into the main road leading to Versailles. My eyes on the road, I mulled over almost all the events since I had found the Devil's feather back in my own country. This was no ordinary mystery, no detective story in which you could put the pieces together and solve the case. True, my investigations following the painstaking research by the team at the UFO Centre in London, had taken me from Salzburg to the UK, the USA and then back to Europe. Throughout these travels, I had discovered new facts, had some unbelievable, fantastic experiences—and I don't mean just with women— and most important of all, through the Grey power that I had acquired, I had challenged the leaders of the Eridanians. I was in short one of the few people who possessed knowledge that could eventually rid the world of the Devil and his armies.

And yet, I felt like a plaything thrown from one place to another by the inexplicable phenomenon and constantly changing strategies of the aliens which were far beyond the understanding of the human mind. It was like fighting a losing battle. At first, the whole world was aware of the great dangers ahead through interlink, internet and all the other media. People had been presented with ineradicable proof of Eridanian presence and their evil schemes to reduce mankind to a mere puppet of the alien force. But, within a very short period, that had all changed. Now the Eridanians controlled not only most of the EU and the governments of the member states, but the entire system of communication and the media. A new picture of advanced extraterrestrials working for the benefit of all humankind had emerged. Masses of people had been hypnotised into believing that these Eridanian extraterrestrials were in fact the saviours of Planet Earth...

The intense struggle we had been undergoing appeared pitifully sporadic and hopelessly inadequate. But together with Emma and all the other members of the UFO Centre, we would never give up. The greatly falsified account of the intentions of the Eridanian extraterrestrials had contaminated all levels of society in Europe. But it was our duty to act to reverse the effect of this poisonous deception. But how? Perhaps we could force the Eridanians to show their true evil face. Once again, everything rested upon our investigations to find the Eridanian power source, which would, I surmised be somewhere in Europe, perhaps in England.

The imposing western façade of the great palace of Versailles had 375 windows, according to the hotel guidebook. Many of these were in the hall of mirrors, where the World War I treaty had been signed. The palace had once housed 10,000 people. The gardens of Versailles have always been a popular Sunday outing for Parisians, but I was in no mood for that. Besides, this was only Wednesday. Within an hour, I had reached the road with a big signpost pointing northwest: Chateau Villeneuve.

I reached the gates of the chateau at midday. There were several cars in the large car park. About a dozen tourists were admiring the large hall on the ground floor and later I joined them on the upper floor. A tourist guide who also confessed to being the housekeeper was dressed in a blue uniform and spoke in French and English. I stayed behind, venturing into the large bedrooms and balconies, when the tourist guide was looking the other way. The rear of the large chateau looked on yellow fields of wheat. There was a heavily forested hill a couple of miles to the west of the chateau. While the crowd and the guide, who was apparently on duty at the chateau and lived on the premises, disappeared into another room, I went into the lavatory. I waited until they returned through the same corridor and walked downstairs. I could see no reason why the Eridanians would choose this chateau as a meeting place. Perhaps there was no reason; or it might have been merely because it was secluded.

Having found nothing of any importance, I left the chateau in the late afternoon. I stopped the car at the gate, when I saw a white van go past me in the opposite direction. I reversed and drove back to the spot where I had parked the car earlier. I saw about ten men carrying large boxes of wine and trays of food into the chateau. At that moment, the guide/housekeeper approached the car.

"Can I help you, sir?"

"I would like to stay on and join the party. You think you can let me in?" I took out five one hundred dollar bills and discreetly passed them to him. "You see, I know there is a party at the chateau tonight and I am meeting a girl…"

"Well, I don't know…*C'est une partie privée.* You must have an invitation," he mumbled. I passed over another five hundred dollars, and this time he smiled and nodded, "*Bien sûr, monsieur*, please join the party."

"I'm going to explore the grounds," I told him, "and I'll surprise my girlfriend later inside."

"*Tres bien, monsieur*," he gave a slight bow, "you can stay the night, *si vous voulez*." He looked at me knowingly and winked.

I moved away. I had been lucky that it had proved so easy. The man obviously could not have cared less who attended the party. At that moment, my mobile rang. It was Valerie.

"Yes, I am here. I'll meet you at the party," I said, moving further out of earshot, though the Frenchman made me a thumbs-up sign and gave me another knowing wink.

"What party? How did you know about the party?" Valerie asked, her voice rising slightly with repressed panic.

"It's OK. I found out about it just now, and the housekeeper is going to see to it that I can attend—for a small fee, of course. How did you find out about it?"

"I met a man here at the office. Draco, he said his name was. And he invited me. I declined."

"That's the Eridanian leader."

I walked around the large building. It was now almost 8.30 pm, and dark. The wind buffeted me when I reached the back of the chateau. Once inside, I found myself in a labyrinth of dark corridors. The carpets were thick, the lights dim. I had to move fast and find a strategic spot to view the large hall. I thought that would be the most likely place to hold a meeting. I was not even sure if they would have a meeting at all. Now I had the opportunity to find out. I was completely convinced that the Eridanians restored their youthful, vigorous appearance on earth by some process of refuelling their bodies with an energy imported from their own star system. At least, that was the information I had gathered from the scientists who had studied the structure and function of molecules associated with living organisms. But how could such alien beings change their totally different body structures into that of the normal human beings of Planet Earth? That was the big mystery. That was a physical, scientific impossibility for Earth technology. Furthermore, all evidence pointed to a permanent presence of the aliens on earth. In other words, their aim was to colonise earth, and rule over humans forever…

The public at large no longer believed that Satan or the supreme evil being as described in hundreds of writings and books over the centuries, from biblical times until modern times, was the extraterrestrial devil from the star system Epsilon Eridani. Widespread publicity through the media which the Eridanians controlled in EU member states built up an attractive but completely fabricated image of the extraterrestrials. The deceit was perfectly organised. People believed a superior civilisation has arrived on Earth to save mankind from self-destruction…

The USA, Britain and some other countries outside the EU were trying desperately to show the world the true face of the evil extraterrestrials. But the struggle to inform the world of the facts, backed up with the proof of Eridanian aliens' dreadful and foul plans for mankind seemed quite impossible, especially since the contorting changes in the behaviour of the demons had stopped abruptly. When comparing the rhetoric and reality behind the current situation, rhetoric weighed heavily against the truth.

I sat on the floor in the corner of an indoor balcony above the great hall. All the guests were now in the hall, sipping their drinks. Everything seemed perfectly normal. There were approximately a hundred people, and I immediately recognised the tall figure of the savage fiend, Draco…Then I saw Lorenzo de Medici chatting over his shoulder to a lady in pink. Luigi Gonzaga III was there too. The great Satan and his deputies to preside over a meeting of the evil extraterrestrials. But what kind of meeting was this? Naturally, I did not expect to see an ordinary meeting with speeches and proposals in the traditional way. I was lucky to have found this strategic point on a small balcony above the hall.

Much earlier, before the arrival of the guests, I had placed seven very sensitive recording devices around the large hall: three under the tables in the centre, and four in the corners of the hall. I put on the protection shield and checked my gun before I placed it back in its holster. With the tiny control mechanism, I could hear Draco, Lorenzo de Medici and others making small talk. Then all of a sudden, Draco raised both hands and shouted in a coarse voice, "The time has come…"

De Medici and Gonzaga stood beside him. All the people in the hall looked up at Draco and his two deputies. The music had stopped and you could have heard a pin drop. During those two minutes of total silence, I could just hear a strange hissing coming from the rear. As this rather disturbing sound grew louder, Draco, de Medici, Gonzaga and all the guests moved in unison towards the large door leading to the courtyard behind the chateau. Suddenly, the lights went out. I rushed downstairs and into the hall…

Window casements rattled with the sound waves. Walls trembled and the doors groaned on their hinges. This was like an earthquake shaking up the old chateau, From behind a large curtain, I could see three very bright lights above the field behind the chateau. What I saw would make stout hearts quail…Three large, spherical spaceships hovered above the field…Immediately, I took out the small video camera and filmed the whole sequence of events that followed…With Draco at the head, everyone stood in a row for at least half a minute facing the three rays of a very bright white light emerging from the UFOs.

Could this be what I had been looking for? Could it be that the amazing power of the Eridanians came from their own UFOs which arrived at pre-determined destinations on Earth? Was this how they recharged their bodies? Did they need this power at regular intervals? What did Draco mean, when he called out to his fellow aliens, "The time has come…"? The time had come for what? The three large UFOs and the field on which they had landed emanated a strong sense of evil…I could feel it. This was proof. I had everything on film, and also the recordings of their conversations. Would this be proof enough to sway public opinion against them?

Despite the very bright lights of the UFOs, I was in pitch-darkness behind the large curtains in the hall. But I had to get out of the chateau as there was every possibility of the lights coming back on…I walked back through the hall and headed towards the main door. Then I crept round the large chateau hiding behind the bushes to the left of the UFOs. Almost an hour later, the operation was complete. As the UFOs started their preliminary hovering, I threw myself on the ground and lay there in the bushes until they took off with a thunderous roar. Everyone in the field stood facing the UFOs, hands outstretched towards the night sky. Draco called to them once again: "Now, we return to England!" I lay there in the bushes and glanced at my watch. I waited there for at least an hour. A very uncomfortable hour. I rose stiffly, and hobbled to the west side of the chateau when I heard cars moving out of the car park. I saw Draco getting into the large black limousine. They left at about midnight. I went inside, removed the recording devices and headed for my car.

What had Draco meant by, "Now, we return to England!" Why England and where in England? I had driven about five miles towards Paris when I parked the car at a large petrol station where there was a restaurant. I had a bite to eat there and resumed my journey at 1.30 am. I replayed a conversation I had held with the receptionist before I left my hotel to come to the chateau. During his time off, he had joined me at the bar and asked if I could need a companion later on in the evening. In the same conversation, he volunteered his life story: how he had been employed at the Ritz in Paris, his meeting with Catherine Deneuve, and so on…and finally, why he had decided to come to this hotel. His background was somewhat dubious, to say the least.

Now, as I walked in at 3.45 in the morning, he was on duty at reception.

"Good morning, Monsieur Akova. You had a good time at the chateau?" He handed me a piece of paper, "A message for you," he grinned.

"Thanks. I'll see you tomorrow," I said, eager to go to my room and listen to the recordings. Most of them turned out to be incomprehensible, although it was obvious that the language was English. Then I heard Draco's unmistakably harsh voice: "Statler and Dorchester will do the rest…" Then a falsetto-like voice added: "We must deal with the government people and the UFO Centre in London. I don't understand how such a private organisation can—…" Then I heard a crackling, and the recording ended there.

Clearly the intention to 'deal with us' was a clear and ominous threat, more immediate than any I had encountered previously. I had to warn Emma and our colleagues right away. I called Robert at reception and asked him to make a flight reservation for me to leave first thing in the morning. Dorchester, the secretary of the Foreign Press Association in London was next on my list…

The Foreign Press Association was an important centre for the foreign media in London. Many journalists from all over the world had become members over the years and had formed extremely fruitful liaisons with each other. I had been a member during my first years as London Correspondent for Turkish Cypriot newspapers, and quite frankly, I was rather surprised to see that the FPA had kept to its old building. It had been the home of William Gladstone, the British Statesman who had dominated politics for over thirty years with his great rival, Disraeli, in the nineteenth century. It had been refurbished Victorian style, in the manner of a typical old British aristocratic home. Approaching the two curving staircases, one to the right and one to the left, I looked into the eyes of

Gladstone's statue, rising authoritatively as always between the two. I had made an appointment, and was met by Dorchester's secretary upstairs.

"My name is Akova," I said to the neatly turned-out girl, who smiled at me in a warm welcome. Her eyes were of an extraordinary bluish-purple colour, and quite beautiful. She shook my hand, "Gabriella Milton," she replied, and led me towards a door to the right. "Mr Dorchester is waiting for you."

Frank Dorchester was a good-looking man, probably in his early forties. Gabriella closed the door behind me, with an encouraging wink and mischievous smile: "See you later," she whispered. Her manner was rather promising…

"Mr Turan Akova. I was informed of your arrival. And of course, we know a lot about you. Not only as a pianist/composer, but as a member of the UFO Research Centre in London. I must admit the thought of meeting you had flashed through my mind on several occasions. Well now, here we are…"

I did not want to ask how or from where he had been informed of my arrival in London. He offered me a drink, and continued: "Your performance in Brussels was broadcast recently on TV. Fantastic. I believe you have a piano recital in the Purcell Room sometime this month. Your space music seems to be of tremendous interest. But you also made a name for yourself as a jazz pianist also…?"

"Yes, thank you." I said, but went straight to the point, "Mr Dorchester, I am here on a task of the utmost importance."

"Yes, I know. The aliens…Or the Eridanians to be exact. Rest assured, I will do everything I can to help you," he said.

This remark was superfluous; and at that moment, I remembered Draco's words at the Chateau Villeneuve, "Statler and Dorchester will do the rest…"

"Mr Dorchester, I should like to ask you something."

"Oh, do call me Frank," he interrupted, looking keenly interested.

"OK, Frank. Why would Eric Statler, a stop scientist at the EU Space Centre want to give you the full details of his project; a project which is apparently capable of beaming out signals to three star systems, Alpha Centauri, Tau Ceti and Zeta Reticuli, signals which apparently arrive in just 35 days?"

This crucial question did not seem to bother him in the least. He placed his drink on the small table beside his armchair, and spoke softly: "Well, Mr Akova, this project is no longer a secret. In fact, we all know now and we all fully understand why the alien presence—by which I mean the Eridanians, of course—has already proved to be highly beneficial to all mankind. It's almost like magic. First of all cancer, then AIDS, and every kind of insoluble health problem have ceased to exist. Secondly, the whole socio-political structure is about to change. Every single nation is ready to move on to a much higher plain through the advanced spiritual and technological miracles of the Eridanians." He paused for a moment a gulped down his whisky. "To answer your question. As the head of the FPA, I have been instructed to inform the masses here in Britain of the new world order. I will tell them that we now have the technology to reach out to the stars. This is not science fiction, Mr Akova. This is the simple truth. Through the advantages of the unbelievable Eridanian technology, the whole EU—with the exception of Britain—has gained superiority over the rest of the world. This is truly amazing, Mr Akova. The spiritual and technological overflow will elevate us to the edge of the infinite."

"Frank Dorchester, are you aware of the fact that the aim of the alien Eridanians is the domination of Planet Earth? We have proof of the evil force scheming to push mankind into slavery. Now they are doing it with a different strategy. People in Europe have been led to believe that the creation of a wonderful world is at hand."

He looked at me suspiciously, "Mr Akova, I must say, you have a rare grasp of the conspirator's mind. We all know about your UFO Centre's research. You are the Turkish Cypriot who found what you call the devil's feather in North Cyprus. We all know of the plight of the Americans and the British and your organisation to prove to the world that the—er—Devil—" he smiled in amusement, "is roaming the earth with his armies to conquer mankind. I am sorry, Mr Akova, but no one believes that story any longer. Now, we have no longer any need to drift into protectionism or deal with the crisis of globalisation, or global warming. Now, we have this superior technology dominating throughout the EU…"

"Mr Dorchester, you will sing a different tune when you see the evidence which proves beyond shadow of a doubt that you are wrong about all this. But tell me, how do you plan to deal with us poor UFO Centre people and the British government?"

"Top-level talks," he replied, with a sinister smile. "Surely a man of your stature…come now, Mr Akova, you surely don't believe that conflict is bubbling beneath the surface…No, no. There will be no more wars, no conflicts…"

"But why would the Eridanians want to send out signals to the three star systems? I presume these messages are to be addressed to the Greys?"

"You are absolutely right, Mr Akova. The Eridanians want to reach an accord with the Greys after Earth centuries of armed conflict between these two extraterrestrial civilisations. Isn't it wonderful? Peace on Planet Earth and peace in the Milky Way Galaxy. Exactly like your Ataturk's 'Peace at home and peace in the world', wouldn't you say?" he commented suavely.

"For God's sake, Dorchester! Don't you realise the evil aliens are in control in the EU and precarious conditions in every single institution of the organisation have developed that will soon be too late to reverse. The next Eridanian move will be to create a robotic society and lead the masses to slavery, to serve Satan…!"

He rose from his chair, raising both hands as if to try to ward off the truth, "Mr Akova, populism grows in a vacuum. Politics which claims to represent the interests of ordinary people is now the way of the world. Surely, this is feasible in terms of the way the world is…"

Mine was a shrewd argument, but Dorchester was so stubbornly determined to prove his point, that I had no doubt he had become a puppet of the Eridanians. The man sounded like a character from a science fiction novel. The superior technology and all the benefits the Eridanians were promising to offer mankind had entrapped him into believing that this was the beginning of a new golden age for Earth people. Through the mass media in Europe and Britain, they had embarked on a publicity campaign that had shaken the core of mankind's existence on earth. Top-level talks? Peace? It was not difficult to imagine what sort of outrageous, unacceptable proposals would be dictated to the British government. The talks would be designed to entice people to join the Eridanians. Who could resist this temptation, when there was a promise of cures for cancer, AIDS and financial prosperity for all—not forgetting the space technology that would carry mankind to other star systems…

Somehow the Americans, the British and our own people at the UFO Centre would have to think fast and create a plan to outweigh the enemy's advantages. Dorchester's openness about the whole affair had not failed to amaze me. He was the first person I had met who supported wholeheartedly the presence of the alien Eridanians and was now the chief instigator and promoter of the Eridanian 'doctrine' if you could call it that. I wanted to ask him two more questions before I left.

"So what about Draco? Who is he?"

"Vladimir Draco…" For the first time, Dorchester hesitated. But then he recovered himself and replied, "He has been dubbed Romania's most eccentric tycoon."

I could see there was no point in revealing Draco's true identity to him. Dorchester continued: "He is the chairman of numerous multi-national companies in Europe. In fact, he is the top man."

"One final question, Mr Dorchester. When do you plan to make direct contact with the Greys via the Statler project?"

"That I do not yet know," he replied, this time without faltering, "but rest assured, we will contact you and we would like you to be present. We will also contact you during our top-level talks with the British government."

I left Dorchester's room and closed the door behind me. Gabriella was there, ready to greet me. She was very pretty and it seemed to me as if she was yearning for sympathetic attention and admiration. I rose to the challenge without effort, saying, "Here is my card. Perhaps we may meet again. I would like some more information about the FPA."

"Yes," she said, handing me her own card, "I would like that."

The whole new strategy of the Eridanians was now crystal clear in my mind. All the member states of the EU had yielded by now to the aliens. Multi-national companies headed by Draco, de Medici and Gonzaga plus other giant financial organisations—including the banks in each and every member state under Eridanian domination—had taken over EU finances. With the exception of a few private TV companies and newspapers in France, Italy and Germany, the media in Europe was under the iron rule of the aliens. The armies of the 'big boys' in the EU had succumbed to the new technology and weaponry of the extraterrestrials. The EU states had moved from individual defence systems to a common defence system, and were now helpless when it came to the crucial matter of their own security. The Commission had handed over power to the evil Eridanians. But Britain somehow managed to resist the sudden and drastic changes brought about by the aliens. Now, the Eridanians' goal was to take control of the British government and people.

Britain was to become part of this integrated Eridanian system. The aliens would achieve this through the British government. They would, of course, impose their superior technology here as well as they had so successfully done in Europe. The importance of the nation-state of Britain, its sovereignty, would be diminished…British economic power would also be eroded. The aliens would then have full control over Britain also. I could see that Dorchester was the key figure in the media world in Britain. His mission was to disseminate propaganda so effectively and efficiently that it would bring about the final, silent and subversive invasion of Britain.

Twenty-Five

At the centre, I filled Emma in with the new strategy of the Eridanians. While I was discussing Frank Dorchester's activities, Clayton walked in with a piece of paper in his hand. He seemed rather distressed.

"Turan," he said, and looked at Emma, "I haven't told you about this, either. A man was found murdered in his home late last night. The police gave me this note, as they found out he was a UFO researcher. His name was Clive Jenkins. He was with the *Radio Times.* I checked the list. He was one of the Chosen 36. The police report says officers from Scotland Yard were astounded by the sudden disappearance of the body. They found this note in his room. Here, I'll read it to you: it says, 'I consigned my soul to perdition—everlasting punishment of the wicked after death—as I became a slave of Satan. Now I am immortal with the evil one. I am not worthy of the Chosen 36, and my place has been taken by James Bradbury, grandson of Lord Bradbury...'"

"Remember the disappearance of the body of the priest near the Vatican? That's what's happened with him. He is now serving the Eridanians and will most probably reappear within the next couple of days. But what about James Bradbury?" I asked.

"Wait for it. You won't believe this. A double murder. Unfortunately, James Bradbury was also found murdered in his home in Mayfair. He was murdered within hours of his appointment as one of the Chosen 36."

"My God, this is terrible!" Emma exclaimed, while Clayton continued.

"Apparently, there are at least four people who are being questioned by the police. The circumstances of James Bradbury's murder are rather weird. This is inside information which I have received from a friend who knew him personally. James was very popular with the ladies. On the evening of the murder, he was lured into a house in Hampstead where he was supposed to meet three other friends. One of these 'friends', Michael Rodgers—a journalist, is one

213

of the four being questioned, and I've been told he is a prime suspect. The two other men and the woman are being held in custody for further questioning."

Clayton was a perfectionist and the research he had done so far had left no stone unturned.

"The woman has a watertight alibi which indicates that she was not in the house at the exact time of the murder," said Clayton, "let me give you the big picture. James Bradbury is known to have initiated a steady stream of anti-EU activities in London. Later, he was in collaboration with the Eridanians. He wanted to witness direct contact with the Greys. The four being held by the police admit to seeing the Eridanians using their technology to contact the three star systems. It is at this stage that the picture darkens."

"What do you mean, Clayton?"

"Just this. We don't know who murdered Bradbury or why," he stated.

"Well, one possibility is this: the Eridanians found out he was a spy for the British government and that he had got hold of the technology for direct contact with the Greys…" I ventured. I was not sure that this was not too obvious. Clayton was more practical and less emotional than me. Then Emma stood up, facing me.

"Turan, wait a second. These murders don't add up. The aliens have switched their strategy from violent attacks and an extraterrestrial power show in favour of an amiable superior being who in fact can live here on Earth in human form and help mankind to reach a much higher plain. I don't think the Eridanians would want to damage that image."

She was right. But I had to investigate and find the truth. My first port of call was to the residence of James Bradbury's parents. Lord Bradbury had two other sons and a daughter. He was more than willing to cooperate.

"Mr Akova," he said, while we were served tea in the large sitting room of their country house in Hertfordshire, "James's reputation was tarnished. He lived in a society that was a haven for drug dealers. He was very interested in UFOs and had done his own research. Ever since the first official announcement of alien presence, he had dug harder into the mystery of the 'Devil' and his demons. Actually, he was planning to write a book about it. I will, of course, let you have his notes later on. I know for a fact that his aim was to prove that the Eridanians were evil. After the Eridanians' sudden change of approach which convinced the people of their benevolence and harmlessness, he decided to join their clan, as it were, and learn more about their very advanced technology."

"Did he know Clive Jenkins, the man found murdered the day before your son's murder? Also, did he know or maybe you might know, a journalist called Michael Rodgers?" I asked Lord Bradbury.

"Clive Jenkins…No. But I did read the report about his murder in the papers. But I do remember vaguely the name Michael Rodgers. Every week they had parties, all night parties in one place or another. James was always the life and soul of parties. But he was also deeply involved with surveying Eridanian activity throughout Britain. It seems it was impossible for him to extract himself. The ability to confront your remorse and act upon it is a rare quality, Mr Akova. I think James had been ready to act, and divulge all he had discovered about the Eridanians. I have no idea who murdered him. But I intend to find out." Lord Bradbury's face clouded, and his voice sank to a whisper. He clearly felt the loss of his eldest son most keenly, despite his polite and civilised manner.

"I am investigating the murder," I told him.

"More tea?" asked Lady Bradbury as their two other sons and daughter entered the sitting room.

"You see," said Lord Bradbury, looking remarkably calm and composed, "James's was a clandestine operation. I think he was onto something extremely important, but unfortunately, he didn't have time to write about it."

"But why do you think he was onto something very important?"

"He spoke to me just a day before the murder. I remember the exact words— after all, they were the last words of my beloved son. He said, "Father, I don't mean to alarm you, but this is a matter of extreme urgency…" I asked him what matter he was talking about, but he didn't say. He only said he had arranged to have a meeting with the Prime Minister and tell him all. Mr Akova, he was drunk and to be honest, I thought it was largely the alcohol talking. He went to bed. And that was the last time I saw him."

I was introduced to Lord Bradbury's children and stayed on for another fifteen minutes. As I got up, Lord Bradbury fetched James's notes, as he had promised. I left his Hertfordshire mansion with a sense of unease and vulnerability.

At any time, we could expect some sort of assault on the UFO Centre, I felt. I was sure such surprise attack was imminent. I could feel it in my bones. And the idea was not very comforting. God knows what sort of plan the Eridanians were devising to get rid of the UFO Centre. The aliens had already managed to weaken the British government. The organs of the government had subsequently been replaced by unelected NGOs. This was illustrative of the success of their strategy. But first of all, I had to investigate the murder of James Bradbury.

I found Michael Rodgers at the Press Club. This was a new centre for journalists in Lower Regent Street. The Press Club was in a five-storey building. Emma had gathered all the information available about Rodgers. Although his CV had stated that he was a journalist, he was not employed by any of the newspapers, magazines or TV stations. He seemed to be working freelance. His father, David Rodgers, had been with the Foreign Office for many years, and Michael had joined the FO soon after graduating from the London School of Economics. He was married with two children, a boy and a girl. The Rodgers family was quite well known in London, as their association with the FO went back a few generations.

Rodgers met me on the ground floor in a pub-like bar. The music was so loud that we had to bellow at each other in order to be heard.

"Mr Akova," he said, "I recognised you from the picture in your poster. The Purcell Room concert. How do you do?"

"Hello, Mr Rodgers."

"Let's go up to the restaurant," said Rodgers, leading the way to the lift, "the food is rather good here."

"Right," I mumbled, following him to the lift.

We sat at a window table. The room was pleasantly decorated. After ordering our meals, I put aside my scruples about good manners and small talk, and said: "Let's dispense with the formalities, Mr Rodgers, and get to the point. I am investigating the murder of your friend James Bradbury, and I hope you can help me. From what I've gathered so far, there had been no major police manhunt. The four people under suspicion have all been released. This is a hushed up case, isn't it?"

"As you probably know, Mr Akova, there is a vicious feud between those who support the Eridanians and those who want to keep Britain away from them. Bradbury was opposed to any sort of agreement with the Eridanians and the Eridanian-controlled EU. He believed Britain to be in crisis, threatened from above by an alien takeover and the supranational structures of the EU, the development of which is itself linked to the alien Eridanian globalisation of the British economy; and threatened below by the fragmentary forces of British NGOs. There was even a possibility of wiping out those key figures who opposed and rejected the advanced technology of the aliens. MI5 was involved—…"

I interrupted, unable to resist my hunch: "You're from MI5, aren't you."

"Yes," said Rodgers, smiling, "I know that you know that from your friend Major Blount, so I won't deny it. Bradbury had become uncontrollable. I know beyond any doubt that the developments leading to his murder were perpetrated by MI5."

"Are you saying that James was murdered by MI5?"

"No, that is not what I said," replied Rodgers. "The MI5 are fully accountable for their strategies. James had already burnt his boats. Someone somewhere decided he had become too much of a threat to the Eridanian plan to take over Britain. Of that I am sure. But who? That I don't know. Mr Akova, I was in the room with two other journalist colleagues when two masked men walked in and shot Bradbury."

"But surely, if MI5 had been following James's activities closely, they would now have some idea who planned the murder," I said.

Rodgers responded immediately, "No. I was always with Brad bury and my job was to keep him under surveillance at all times. I'm afraid I failed."

"But are you saying that there is someone in MI5 who planned the murder?"

"I think so. But I can't be sure." He said. "You see, James's philosophy was confrontation rather than compromise. He often told me he was haunted by nightmares and the horrors of extraterrestrial war. I know, that just a couple of days before he was murdered, he was in a frightful rush to see the Prime Minister. He said he had witnessed activities detrimental to the British Foreign Office and the interests of Britain as a whole."

"Did he tell you anything about his findings?"

Rodgers thought for a moment, trying hard to remember.

"No, unfortunately. But wait a second. He was always talking about a woman. Yes, I remember now. A Scottish girl from Falkirk who lived in London. He said she was helping him. I remember her name because it was so Scottish: Fiona McIntosh. On his last day, he was shaken and bewildered apparently by his discoveries."

Rodgers had given me enough to go on with the investigation. Apparently Bradbury's murder had become an all-important new development that could reflect upon Eridanian activity in Britain. But what had Bradbury uncovered that was so important? Why had he wanted to see the Prime Minister? I interviewed the other two journalists who had been present in the room at the time of the murder. They both told me the same story. Two masked men walked in and shot the man. This was certainly not a run-of-the-mill case. My next stop would have to be the home of Fiona McIntosh—James Bradbury's girlfriend from the north.

The address given to me by Rodgers was Dover Street, near Green Park. A woman of about 35 opened the door of a penthouse in an eight-storey building. She was Fiona McIntosh.

"Fiona McIntosh?" I asked, as she opened the door. She eyed me suspiciously, "Yes?"

"My name is Turan Akova. Could I have a few minutes of your time? It is important." I said.

"Yes, Mr Akova. I have heard a great deal about you." She opened the door wider and let me pass inside, before leading the way into a large sitting room. Her beautiful scent lingered in the room.

"This must be a difficult time for you. I mean, regarding the murder of James Bradbury."

"Yes, it is terrible. He was a good friend." She motioned me to a chair, and asked: "Can I offer you a drink?"

"A beer, thank you," I said, and she moved towards a small bar near the corner of the room.

"Miss McIntosh, I must be blunt. Were you intimate with James Bradbury?" I felt embarrassed asking this question, and she winced at my words. Finally, she overcame her embarrassment with a sudden shake of her beautiful blonde hair. "Yes," she replied simply, trying to hide her tears. She was silent for a few seconds, her throat working hard to hold her sobs at bay, and then sat in the armchair opposite mine, "We were planning to marry."

"I'm sorry. I had no idea. But please understand, I will find his murderers. Miss McIntosh, I need your help. You've been together for how long?"

"Just over six months," she replied.

"I presume he talked to you about his activities regarding the aliens?"

She sipped her drink, staring at me with a certain ferocious look of a woman ready to do anything to catch the murderer of her lover. Any man would be struck by that look.

"Yes." She lit a cigarette and offered me one too. "He said he had managed to join the aliens. His aim was to find out how and when the Eridanians were planning to take over Britain."

"So what did he find out during his short-lived infiltration into their camp?"

"I don't know, Mr Akova. But wait a second; I remember he said he had witnessed a direct contact with a star system—I think he said Alpha Centauri."

"Yes, go on."

"Mr Akova, James was convinced that the aliens didn't suspect him of spying for the British government. But apparently someone somewhere knew of his secret activities and found out about his true loyalties."

"Did he tell you anything at all about any other findings? Did he name any names?"

"No, no names. But a day before his murder, he said there was a higher authority. A higher authority which ruled over the British government, MI5, the lot. He said these few people right at the top were responsible for the worsening lawlessness and chaos in the country. This was the way of the aliens. He had seen the same pattern on several occasions. Now he was sure. He said he was going to see the Prime Minister. I remember his exact words. He said this was the bleak view of the current situation." She was reliving the whole episode over again.

"When he talked about the few people at the top, did he give any indication as to their identities? Or where they were?"

She thought, trying very hard to remember the details, I supposed.

"I think he said MI5 took orders from this higher authority. Yes, that's what he said."

"Fiona, please, try to give me a lead."

She looked confused, but all of a sudden, she raised her voice. "Yes. I remember him telling me about Carlton House Terrace. Yes, yes, I remember. He said this was the most important mission of his life…"

Fiona had given me two leads. The first was the Higher Authority; and the second, Carlton House Terrace. I had to find Major Blount, one of the commanders of MI5, and ask for his help in my investigations at Carlton House Terrace. Major Blount was in his late sixties and an old friend of the family. He had helped me a great deal with my studies in England and in those days, I had had no idea that he was with MI5. During his long career, he had been challenged by some of his rivals, but there was enough fuel left from that fight to keep him in power. He was a true English gentleman. His family dated back eight hundred years, a long line of baronets: a family of wealth and social position throughout the centuries. During my student days, Major Blount used to call me the 'mad Turk from North Cyprus'…A polite and honest man.

I met him in his house in Curzon Street, Mayfair. James, his butler, ushered me into the living room. "The Major will be with you presently," he intoned.

Minutes later, Major Blount entered the room as lively as ever, and with that broad familiar smile on his face, "Turan, how nice to see you," he said.

"John, it's been quite some time since I last saw you, you and the family. You are OK?"

"Yes, we are fine. So, tell me what's been happening."

"Well, with the domination of the EU by the aliens, you know of course that Britain has become the last bastion of democracy and freedom. Now even that is being threatened by the increasing infiltration into the British government itself, and I suspect even the MI5 is no exception. I am investigating the murder of James Bradbury. He was onto something extremely important. You see, he spent a lot of time with the aliens but was finally found out and he had to flee in a hurry. Unfortunately, he had no protection from us—I mean, the UFO Centre or the Ministry of Defence. We simply didn't know about his activities until it was too late. As you know, he was murdered just a couple of days ago."

"Yes," said Major Blount, "shocking business."

I was eager to open up to him. He was the sort of person who could influence developments favourably and a brilliant strategist. So I told him the whole story and mentioned the two leads of the Higher Authority and Carlton House Terrace.

His intelligent blue eyes stared at me first, and then he pursed his lips, saying thoughtfully: "I've never heard of this Higher Authority," he remarked quietly, "and Carlton House Terrace?"

"His girlfriend, Fiona McIntosh, said he had mentioned this Higher Authority and Carlton House Terrace just a day before the murder. By the way, Michael Rodgers, one of your men and two other journalists actually witnessed the murder. Two masked men walked into the house of a friend, to which Bradbury had been invited and killed the man in cold blood."

"In whose house was the murder committed?"

"Rodger's house," I replied.

He was confused. "A Higher Authority, eh? The finances of MI5 have been effectively sliced off during the last six months. So I don't see how the MoD can afford a Higher Authority."

"You know, of course, that the aliens are now in control of all the EU finances. They seem to be spending a lot of money here in Britain also."

"What are you saying, Turan?"

"Only that there is a possibility of money coming into Britain from the alien-controlled EU and these aliens may be spending it to exert control over certain people in this country."

"The current strains on the MoD and MI5 stem from the financial cuts in our budget. So the money you are talking about does not come into the MI5."

"What about the Higher Authority, John? Do you think such an authority exists, giving orders within the MI5?"

"I don't know, Turan. But I will most certainly make some enquiries. This is an extremely threatening situation."

"What about Carlton House Terrace?"

Sir John thought for half a minute, and then started counting the places he knew at Carlton House Terrace.

"Well, the Foreign Press Association is there. It's been there for years. Right next door used to be Crockford's, a casino, but I rather think that has moved somewhere else. I don't know who's got the building now. Maybe it's a company. But let me get a full list of all the occupants there."

He picked up the phone and called his secretary. Ten minutes later, the butler brought in a printout from the computer.

"Here you are, sir," he said, "the information you requested."

Major Blount took the paper and started reading it aloud: "Let me see, now…the Foreign Press Association—oh, Crockford's is still there, I see—then there is another old building. After the steps down to the Mall, we have a large mansion which was at one time interestingly enough, occupied by MI5. Now Lady Sarah, the widow of the late Baron Gilchrist and her two daughters reside in this lovely house. Further down, there is a large building which is in part used by the Foreign Press Association."

"I know. You're talking about No 1. Members of the FPA who wanted to work during the evening would get the key from No. 1," I said. "I used to get the key from a man who was there at night. I used to work at night."

"I know your late nights, Turan," said Sir John, smiling. "I can check for you, but I suppose you have to visit all of them. The FPA and Dorchester you've seen already. That's too obvious. But at any rate, you say that Dorchester is openly promoting the Eridanian doctrine and collaborating with them. So really, there isn't much you can do there. But I think Lady Sarah is the most interesting one—not forgetting the two daughters. Recently, she organised a meeting of 'social entrepreneurs'. That's what they call them nowadays: large businesses high finance with lots of risk. Lady Sarah is a very active woman."

"I think she will be my first call," I said.

There was nothing to link MI5 to the so-called Higher Authority. I drove straight into the parking precinct of the big mansion of Lady Sarah Gilchrist. Within minutes, two men appeared from both sides of the large Victorian door. I stepped out of the car.

"My name is Turan Akova, and I would like to see Lady Sarah," I said. One man stayed with me while the other went in and closed the door behind him. Minutes later, he reappeared.

"Lady Sarah will see you now, sir," he said, and showed me into a large drawing-room. Major Blount had told me she was in her late sixties. But the woman who greeted me in her drawing-room looked much younger.

"Turan Akova, pianist/composer, journalist/writer, private eye, UFO researcher and vampire hunter. Yes, Turan Akova, a man I have always wanted to meet!" she exclaimed charmingly, holding out her hand.

"I'm honoured." I said, kissing the hand obediently. She seemed very amiable and had a lovely smile. She was wearing a turquoise brooch on her white dress, and was exquisitely attractive.

"Do sit down, Mr Akova. My two girls will be coming in shortly, and I would like you to meet them also."

"Thank you," I said, sinking into a luxuriously soft armchair.

"We have a piano in the hall," she bubbled, "I hope you will play something for us. I watched your recital in Brussels live on TV. It was a bravura performance. You really are a musical genius, Mr Akova!"

"Thank you," I repeated, "you are most kind."

"Please, make yourself at home. Would you like a sherry?"

"Yes, thank you,"—my third thank you in thirty seconds!

When we were finally settled, she gazed at me enquiringly and asked the obvious question: "So, what can I do for you, Mr Akova?"

"Frankly, I don't know quite where to begin. This is about the murder of James Bradbury, and the two leads he left behind, which I am trying to follow up. He apparently mentioned a Higher Authority, it seems that several men have taken over the British Government, including MI5, and are at present the decision-making body governing Britain today. He also mentioned Carlton House Terrace. It is quite possibly that the Higher Authority's meeting place is in fact in this Terrace. But I don't know. As you know, the aliens have taken over the EU, and Britain is still the only EU member country still resisting alien domination."

"Very dramatic, Mr Akova," she observed lightly.

"Yes, it is rather…" I agreed, "you see, two masked men murdered Bradbury. There were three journalists present at the scene; one of them works for MI5— that much I've established. I have spoken to him, but he wasn't able to help me much. Major Blount, on the other hand, is an old family friend, and he's trying to help."

"Oh, yes, I know the Major. Lovely man!" she said enthusiastically.

"If I find Bradbury's murderers, then I might have a clue about the identity of the Higher Authority. He was onto something vital concerning the Eridanians, and these men may have been collaborators. On the other hand, it is quite likely that they may have their own plans for the future of Britain."

"Dreadful business," she said, "I mean, the murder of James Bradbury. Let me think…No. I can't say I've heard of any Higher Authority. Mr Akova, don't you think Britain is fighting a lost cause? I mean, what chance do we have against the mighty Eridanians? Shouldn't we rather cooperate with them?"

"Lady Sarah, UFO Centre has produced hard evidence that these extraterrestrials are evil; that their leader is the Devil himself."

She let out a short laugh, "Mr Akova, really, who would believe such a story!"—but she looked shaken.

"Lady Sarah, we have proof. Mankind will eventually succumb to their power and be pushed into slavery."

"Well, the opinions of the collaborators are exactly the opposite of that. They are accusing the government of sheer stubbornness, because they are turning down a great opportunity to link up with the Eridanians' sophisticated technology."

"Not true. The British government is doing the right thing. The American government is doing the same. At any rate, let me ask you about the meeting of Social Entrepreneurs here in your house. How did that come about?"

"But Mr Akova, what does that have to do with anything?"

"Nowadays, many multi-million dollar concerns are controlled by the aliens. The economic and financial dimension of their activities could be fatal for Britain."

She looked worried. "Well, this meeting was suggested by a friend. The Chairman of Viser, the multi-national company here in Carlton House Terrace." She stopped and clasped her hands with shock.

"Good heavens, Mr Akova, Viser is in Carlton House Terrace! Do you think it is a coincidence?"

"I don't know. Who is this chairman?"

"His name is Peter Arvatel. I met him at a party and he suggested the meeting."

"Did you talk about anything else?"

"Why, yes, now that you mention it. He said he supported an accord with the aliens."

Suddenly, she called out to the butler, "George, when do the brains arrive?"

The butler replied immediately: "They are parking the car just now, milady."

"I always call my girls the brains. They are so clever, Mr Akova!"

"Christine and Catherine," she announced proudly, presenting her daughters, "and this is Mr Akova, my darlings. Of course, you know he is a brilliant pianist/composer."

"Yes," said Christine, sizing me up. She had her mother's looks. Catherine came closer and shook my hand.

We talked about alien presence, music, entertainment, business, and so on. They were both very lively, beautiful girls.

"How do you suppose it will all end, Mr Akova?" asked Catherine.

"I don't know. All I know is that if I find Bradbury's murderers, it could lead me to the so-called Higher Authority. But I do feel the mystery is hidden somewhere in Carlton House Terrace."

"How exciting!" said Christine, "satanic terror in the bustling city of London. We give you our full support. I think you are absolutely right. These Eridanians, I think they have an evil plan. People talk of their foul tactics. They've brought some drastic changes into our society. Their activities which are distinctly devilish are frequently mentioned in the same breath, as deceit, arrogance murder, suspicion and above all, a plan to dominate the world. That's what we have heard so far."

"Well, you've heard right. I must say, you're very well informed." I said to Christine. They were not twins, but they were very much alike. We had dinner at the house. I played some of my compositions for the ladies and then departed at about midnight, leaving my card in case they wanted to contact me.

At home, I found a report from Clayton in my e-mail, a report prepared by him and by other experts in British politics and economics. Clayton had written that it might throw some light on the activities of the Eridanians. The report read as follows:

Today interdependence is an omen, a sign of the end of the state system as we know it. Complex interdependence (the web that entangles) is a dominant image presented by the aliens. Today, we live in a world where a range of issues competes for the attention of the decision-makers. The decision-making process has been taken over in the EU by the Eridanians. They want to do the same here in Britain. The aliens concentrate on a mixed-actor system and the focus is on the twin forces of transnationalism and interdependence. This is their way. They complicate the issues at hand and then spring a surprise when you least expect it. The element of surprise is always there. A nation-state is a stumbling block for the aliens. They want as many states as possible to unite under one roof. The EU was on the way to becoming a federal superstate, anyway. So the Eridanian take-over at the EU was relatively easy as the European Commission and the big boys of the EU such as Germany, France and Italy succumbed to their enormous power-politics when the key figures at the commission were recruited into the Eridanian camp. Despite all the arguments for a nation-state, a country as strong as Britain, not only in terms of politics, but especially economically, can survive and continue as an independent state. But the fact remains that the first of these twin forces, that is to say, transnationalism has removed the state from centre stage and the second, which is interdependence, forces us to look at the links between societies and to stress the importance of economic matters in foreign policy.

Together, these twin forces refocus analysis away from national control and the balance of power towards management of the structural situation of complex interdependence. The Eridanian aim is to reach a peak of economic integration and complex interdependence, and they seem to be moving fast towards a final victory. The primary objective of the aliens is the acquisition of power and the dominant instrument is the highly advanced technological power and economic capability. These are the evil ways of the Eridanians.

For the aliens, transnational actors working across state boundaries are also important. Multi-national corporations and transnational banks are the important actors in their system. Force—and they do have a mighty force—is not the only significant instrument. Economic manipulation is also a dominant tool. Now the Eridanians are dominant in Europe—east and west—with extremely powerful and highly advanced weapons. Their technology is so advanced that mankind cannot even dream of achieving such intricate scientific development in the next 3,000 Earth years.

Now the question remains, will Britain survive despite the onslaught of the Eridanians to take over the country? The EU has already succumbed to an authority at the top—the aliens—governing this huge community of partnership of states. A covert infiltration is creeping into the British system. The British government has not yet decided how to handle this problem...

Clayton was an expert on preparing exclusive reports, and this was no exception. He was also very well informed in EU affairs. The report focused on certain areas in which alien activity was particularly intense. This general overview of the current situation could help the British government to implement new measures against the Eridanian infiltration. For me, everything else except the mystery behind the Bradbury murder, and what he had uncovered relating to Eridanian technology, had become secondary.

The next morning I was back in Carlton House Terrace, this time to see the Chairman of Viser. Peter Arvatel's secretary was a middle-aged woman. She looked surprised to see me.

"I'm afraid I don't have an appointment, but I have to see Mr Arvatel." I gave her my card.

"Wait here, please," she said, raising herself from her chair behind the desk. She knocked on the chairman's door and went in. She was back within a minute.

"Mr Arvatel will see you now," she said coldly.

I walked into an office in which everything was upholstered in black leather. Chairs, armchairs, even the tables were partly covered in black leather. Mr Arvatel was a tall man with a long face and a thin moustache. He was wearing a black suit with a red tie.

"Good morning, Mr Akova," he said, in a relaxed, easy tone, "do please sit down. Can I get you some coffee?"

"Yes, please," I replied, "I apologise for coming without making an appointment."

"That's all right, Mr Akova," he had already ordered the coffee. When the secretary left the room, I caught him looking at me anxiously. I could sense a bit of tension. But it was only a feeling.

"Well, to be quite honest, the reason I've come to see you is because you are in Carlton House Terrace." That sounded a bit strange, but no matter. I was sticking to my policy of always sticking to the truth, however unlikely it sounded.

"Goodness gracious me! What on earth do you mean?"

"Only that Carlton House Terrace is an important lead in my investigations into the murder of James Bradbury. The other equally important lead is the Higher Authority." I enunciated the words slowly, laying emphasis on 'Higher Authority'.

He looked genuinely puzzled. I continued, realising there was no point in beating about the bush.

"Mr Arvatel, I don't know where your loyalties lie, but I will give you the facts and then perhaps you can help me…"

"I will most certainly try," he said.

"Well, both Major Blount of MI5 and Lady Sarah suggested I talk to you about this matter. I am sure you are well aware of the alien presence in Europe and in England. The EU is already under their control. Britain is struggling to keep them out. The Eridanians are moving fast to a confederation or federal 'United States of Europe', but the real aim of the aliens here is complete control of all Europe. The plan is the plan of the Devil and his demons…"

Once more, the mere mention of the word 'Devil' was met with disbelief.

"Mr Akova. I'm not at all sure about this. I mean, this talk of the devil…"

"It's not just talk, Mr Arvatel. At any rate, I will not go into that right now. The fact remains that the campaign being implemented by the aliens to dominate Britain is an open secret, and from what I have gathered so far, this 'Higher Authority' is the decision-making body above the British government. What do you know about this?"

"Well, during our meeting at Lady Sarah's house, some people did mention top-level talks between a higher authority and the British government." He stopped for a moment, and then continued, "There was mention of Lord Fitzpatrick in the House of Lords!"

"What about the murder of James Bradbury? Anything to link the Higher Authority with the murder?"

"No, not really," he said, getting up and walking towards the large window. "But I think Lord Fitzpatrick may be able to help you on that one. I read about the murder in the papers. It was on TV too."

He stood by the window and then turned and stared at me, clearly reassessing the situation.

"Mr Akova, I think we have no other choice but to cooperate with the aliens, Surely, it is both impractical and at the same time quite impossible to suggest that Britain on its own can challenge this indestructible force, this powerful multi-dimensional army of aliens who, within a short period of time, have mastered all the features of humans and fully super-imposed their own exceptionally progressive extraterrestrial faculties upon the brain and soul of man…"

"I think challenge is the key word, here, Mr Arvatel. Don't forget the Anglo-American entente. The mighty USA, the most powerful country on Earth is working on new technologies to stop the alien insurgency in Britain and the USA. But let me come back to Lord Fitzpatrick. Do you think he is one of the members of the Higher Authority?"

"He may be, Mr Akova," he said, "but I cannot say the so-called Higher Authority is cooperating with the aliens."

"Why?"

"Mr Akova, the EU has developed into a multi-brained entity in which the centres of political decision-making and economic activity have been consciously scattered throughout its member states. You are right, of course, in saying that the aliens are in full control and they have now consolidated their position in the European Commission itself, dictating policy to all its members, including Germany, France and Italy. From what I hear, however, the Higher Authority is trying very hard to ward off this dangerous and unpleasant institutional mayhem which is in fact spreading into British society, and setting the conditions to fully integrate our country into the fold. The Higher Authority seems to be on the side of those fighting Eridanian domination."

"Britain has a political system endowed with democratic procedures and institutions. So this country will resist the alien invasion. I have two questions: Why was James Bradbury murdered? Was he really in possession of an Eridanian secret or some other secret that would shake the world? I have established that he had decided to infiltrate the aliens, the better to spy on them. He managed to survive, but then disappeared, I suspect taking the secret of the

Eridanians with him. So it would follow that the Eridanians had a very good reason to eliminate him. That makes sense. But on the other hand, Rodgers, the man from MI5 who was with him at the time, believes this was not a murder committed by the Eridanians. He bases his argument on the fact that the Eridanians were still trying to find Bradbury after the murder. Once again, we find ourselves back on the track of the so-called Higher Authority. What was the big secret of the Eridanians that Bradbury discovered while he was with them?"

"God knows," sighed Peter Arvatel, "have you seen his family?"

"Yes; and they know nothing."

"What about his friends?"

"I've seen his girlfriend. She was able to give me my two leads, the Higher Authority and Carlton House Terrace. Which is why I'm here."

"You mean you are seeing everyone in Carlton House Terrace?"

"Yes," I said, "what about the old Crockford's Casino building?"

"I think it's empty," said Arvatel, "but go to No. 1. They'll tell you what's happening there."

As I was about to leave the Viser building, I saw two men sitting in a van parked just outside Lady Sarah's house. I turned back and entered the Viser building once again. There I asked the doorman to put on my Burberry trench coat and drive towards the Foreign Press Association and enter it fast. He followed my instructions. The two men got out of the car and followed him into the FPA. Then I entered the FPA. I had asked the doorman to walk into the first room on the left, which was empty, and there I found him.

"Quick, give me my trench coat and leave." He handed me my coat and disappeared, leaving me alone in the empty room, where I called Dorchester's pretty secretary from my mobile telephone.

"Gabriella, I need your help," I said.

"What can I do for you, Mr Akova?"

"The two men who came in just now, where are they?"

"In the conference room with Mr Dorchester," she told me excitedly.

"Could you get me in? I have to listen in. It's terribly important."

"I suppose I could get you in through the back door. I mean, though the balcony."

I held her hand as we squeezed through a narrow door with led to the balcony. From there, she pushed the door open and we stood behind the thick, royal blue curtain.

"He walked into your building just minutes ago," said one of the men. Dorchester kept quiet for a moment, and then spoke. I recognised his voice immediately.

"The Higher Authority wants him out of the way now." He said. It was me they were talking about. Dorchester's tone was jumpy: "He must never find out about the contact with the Greys."

Gabriella pressed her body against mine—it was virtually impossible to concentrate in this position. But I had to listen to this vital conversation. So now I had some idea of the nature of Bradbury's secret. He had probably witnessed a direct contact between the Eridanians and the Greys. But what had been the message?

I hesitated for a moment, and then whispered to Gabriella, "It's best if you go back to your office now." She left, and I walked into the room holding my gun.

"Now then, gentlemen, you had better sit down—all three of you." I pointed the gun at the two men.

"What is this, Mr Akova? You dare to come in here with a gun in your hand?" Dorchester protested.

"Don't bother, Dorchester. I heard your conversation. I know everything now about Bradbury's secret. He knew about the direct contact with the Greys, didn't he? And these two gentlemen are probably his murderers."

"Mr Akova, I will have to call the police. You have no right to break into my private office like this." He was desperate.

"By all means. Call the police. It'll make things easier for me. Of course, you will have to explain to them why you want to eliminate me as well."

"You have no proof of that," he said primly.

"Ah, but I do. A witness, in fact, who listened with me to your conversation with these two assholes."

With a lightning movement, one of the men pulled out his gun and aimed at me. I shot him first. Blood spurted out from the wound in his belly as he fell on the thick red carpet. The second man threw himself onto the floor behind an armchair and fired at me. I was lucky; the bullet whizzed past my right ear and hit the glass panel behind me. As he was about to try for a second shot, I hit him twice, first on the leg and then on the arm. His gun fell to the floor. Dorchester was shaking like a leaf. I called out to Gabriella immediately:

"Gabriella, call the police now."

Later, the two wounded men confessed to murdering James Bradbury, but claimed that the order for the execution had come from the Higher Authority. A barrage of angry questions from Major Blount revealed that they were secret agents working for the government. It seemed that the British government's role in the matter was little more than that of a helpless bystander. Both Dorchester and the two men who were treated at St Mary's hospital for about a week, were held for questioning for at least three days. But to my own and Major Blount's amazement, they were released on the fourth day.

Twenty-Six

Lord Fitzpatrick's residence was a thirty-eight room stately home near Purley in Surrey. I found all the information about the family and the residence, in the current Who's Who. Debrett's Peerage and Baronetage and Burke's Peerage listed all the complicated ramifications of the hierarchy of the British aristocracy. There are five main grades of nobility: in the following order of importance: dukes, marquesses, earls, viscounts and barons. The four lower peers are titled 'lord' and all are entitled to sit in the House of Lords. Lord Fitzpatrick's title was inherited; he had been married twice, and had three children from the first marriage and two from the second.

The grand house had its own history, dating back to the seventeenth century and in the middle of a six hundred acre estate, it looked like a castle. My appointment with Lord Fitzpatrick was at four in the afternoon, an awkward time for me as I always have a nap for a couple of hours at that time every day. It is always easier for well-known persons to meet members of the aristocracy—at least, that was my impression. After all, I was quite well known as a pianist/composer. But the widespread publicity over the arrival of the aliens had raised my profile to the level of other celebrities in the country.

I was met at the door by the butler, but the two tall men standing a few feet behind him looked more like the bodyguards of the type depicted in Hollywood films, guarding American tycoons.

"This way, sir," said the butler and directed me towards the two men. I was searched thoroughly and then ushered into a large room, which looked like a drawing room. I had anticipated such a search as this lord was somewhat different from the others. So I had left my gun in a special compartment in the car. As I gazed upon the room, I remembered the special advice of the Turkish Secret Service Chief, Salih Yatmaz, on how to spot secret cameras in a room. There were at least five of them in this room alone.

Lord Fitzpatrick was a man of medium height and build, with something of a pot belly. He had a perfectly trimmed beard. With a large cigar in one hand, he approached and shook my hand.

"Good afternoon, Mr Akova, I've heard much about you. Major Blount speaks very highly of you."

"Thank you, your lordship."

"Tea?" he rang the bell and the butler entered within half a minute, "tea, George," he said, and added, "do smoke if you wish. I'm a smoker myself, as you can see."

"I know why you are here. Major Blount filled me in about your investigations into the murder of James Bradbury. There were several high profile murders and Bradbury's was the last. Shocking business. But you see, Bradbury crossed into forbidden territory. He had himself murdered two of our own men and was virtually beyond the point of no return. True, while posing as a collaborator with the Eridanians, he managed to collect some vital information about alien technology. Just when we and the British government were trying to steer the secret project through a very critical phase, Bradbury was exposed by the aliens as a spy…The Eridanians let him go. But when he murdered the two men who were following him, the Higher Authority decided to eliminate him. It was a difficult decision but we had evidence that he would use this secret information against the Eridanians. He was too much of a risk. Britain is about to play a prominent role on the world stage, and we couldn't allow one man to destroy it all."

"I have two questions. Firstly, when you say Bradbury murdered two of your own men, what exactly do you mean? Two men from MI5 or from the Higher Authority?"

"From the Higher Authority, of course. Two distinguished members of that Authority," he replied immediately.

"My second question is this: are you with the Higher Authority?"

"Yes," he replied, inhaling the smoke from his cigar. "The British government, the MoD and MI5 decided to form a High Authority to deal with extraterrestrial presence. This was at the time when you and your UFO Research Centre was very much in the news."

"But, your lordship, you said Bradbury was murdered because you had evidence he would use this secret information against the Eridanians. I'm confused. Do you approve of Eridanian domination?"

"Good Lord, of course not! Thank God, the controversy over Bradbury's murder and the secret project have largely been shelved. I dare say this is the politics of energy and oil research. But the secret project, if it becomes operational, will end it all."

"End what?"

"The wars over energy and oil. There will be no need for oil or any other kind of energy."

"You said Britain will play an important role on the world stage. Is this what you meant?"

"Yes, exactly," said Lord Fitzpatrick. "You have now become one of us, so I can tell you about the secret project. You see, through Eridanian space technology, the Eridanians have contacted the Greys. The arrival of the Greys is imminent. Their centuries old fight for supremacy in the Milky Way Galaxy will end with an agreement between the Eridanians and the Greys."

"What about Earth and mankind?" I asked.

"We will survive and advance to a much higher plain."

I tried very hard to hide my disappointment.

"But surely Britain is fighting to avoid the integration of the country into the Eridanian-controlled EU. With this policy, Britain will also become the slave country of the Eridanians."

"No, no, Mr Akova," he argued, "an accord between the two extraterrestrial civilisations grew out of a realisation that British diplomacy could in fact succeed in creating an interaction that would bolster a union between the two extraterrestrial people and our own people on Earth."

The situation had become even more complex. Clearly the Higher Authority was under the control of the Eridanians. But what about Major Blount? The man I trusted most. Was he with them as well?

"What did you mean when you told me, 'You are one of us now'?" He lit a second cigar in half an hour and lent back in his armchair, obviously very pleased with himself.

"Mr Akova," he smiled, "there is no longer any need for you or the UFO Centre to search for UFOs and extraterrestrials. The aliens are here and we are about to create a cosmic triumvirate. Take my advice, Mr Akova, don't fight it. Don't challenge the power of the Eridanians. No one will believe your story of the Devil and his demons."

I had learned a great deal and there was nothing more to say here. Lord Fitzpatrick escorted me towards the foyer and stood by the door. George, the butler, was staring at me. His large black eyes slanted upwards. It seemed that even the residence of one of the most prominent personages in Britain was under the control of the aliens…

With an unforeseen suddenness, the Higher Authority had moved above the British Government and MI5 and 6 for that matter. Now the Higher Authority was providing most of the muscle, dictating its policy which was in fact the new order of the Eridanian aliens. Interestingly enough, one report from the investigators of our UFO Research Centre indicated that the aliens had already injected a new spirit of Christianity and Roman Catholicism in particular into the EU. There were in the process of implementing the same treatment in the United Kingdom. Globalisation was the basis for much of the strategy applied by the aliens. Naturally, the change had occurred much faster. The Devils tried everything. The religious angle was yet another game played out by the Eridanians. Nevertheless, this was a significant step towards the unification of all Europeans. They were now trying to flush out the remaining strugglers who were still challenging the demons. The anti-Christ promoting Christianity was unbelievable, but true. With the exception of Major Blount—and I was not even sure about him—I had not met a single member of the British government who was actively involved in the struggle against Eridanian domination. Our organisation, the UFO Research Centre in London was quite small; just over fifty people were engaged in research on the aliens. Continuing our investigations and research and verifying our initial findings would now become extremely difficult as the aliens would try to stop us in more ways than one.

The Eridanians has now placed European unification into a wider international context by highlighting the increased interdependence of states. But at the same time, the aliens' pluralistic platform would be more complex and more vulnerable. I wondered how the British government would respond to the increased activities of the Eridanians. The infiltration of the aliens into the British government and the Higher Authority had dashed the hopes of those would were still fighting for their cause—those who wanted to keep out the alien dominated EU. Despite the stated aims of different approaches and models, united to challenge the alien domination, there was no clear way to predict what would happen in the near future, nor how the British and Americans would devise answers to the current list of issues at hand. From the time of the advent of the aliens, the destiny of the EU had always been negotiable. In actual fact, the EU, as an organisation with over 27 member states united under one umbrella was a perfect platform for the Devils to work from, as their aim was eventually to bring all those states under their control.

The mass media in Britain should have been the sentinel of liberty, but somehow it had sold out to the aliens, with the exception of a few daily newspapers and one or two TV channels. I set my mind on one thing, as I drove to the office: we needed to set up an emergency meeting with the Americans, the British and the UFO Research Centre in London. I also decided to call all the 'Chosen 36' who had now became the 'Chosen 37'—though who the new addition was I had no idea. At the office, within an hour, Clayton had contacted them all. They would arrive in London within a day. Members of the British government seemed to be too slow in their deliberations. So we decided to hold a meeting of the Chosen 37 first, decide on a course of action and then submit our decision to the USA and Britain.

I was not at all convinced with the story of an accord between the Greys and the Eridanians. An agreement between these two extraterrestrial civilisations who had always been arch enemies, together with an agreement with our own Earth civilisation seemed too far-fetched to be believable. The only way to prove that it was a tactical move to divert attention would be to contact the Greys. Telepathic communication with the Greys had been scarce in the past, but a concerted effort by the Chosen 37 might make all the difference. We had to try. But how on earth were we going to explain to them our current world situation? The Eridanians had taken a bold step towards an agreement. By doing so, they had won the trust and support of the people in the UK.

Only the Greys could tell us whether this plan to sign an agreement with their arch enemies—the Eridanians—was true or not. The Eridanians had extended their influence tremendously and they held the upper hand. There was no doubt about that.

Our aim as the UFO Centre in London was to coordinate the establishment of a well-organised, active front. Experts on British politics were busy preparing a list of high ranging officials, MPs, member of the House of Lords, Ministers and civil servants in key positions who were indisputably against any sort of cooperation with the Eridanians. These were people who insisted on joint action between the US and British governments to stop the infiltration and the eventual Eridanian domination in the UK.

The US and Britain had to define arrangements for collaboration in security policy, defence and military procurement. A definite action plan had to be implemented without delay. But how? That was the big question. How would they determine the target areas for weakening Eridanian control? A move to check Eridanian infiltration did not necessarily herald a widespread involvement of the British government. However, in my opinion, the plan to hold back the aliens should not be temporary and limited. Bearing in mind the present phase of developments in Britain, an all-out war against the Eridanians was out of the question. All decisions should be honoured and bridged. Also the news of the arrival of the aliens on Earth was relatively fresh in people's minds. The evil plan of the Devil and his demons coming from Epsilon Eridani had been widely publicised during the first two months of the most important event in the history of mankind.

A clear cut way, a mechanism that would become operative within a short period was the only way out. What had been done so far as a challenge to stop Eridanian control in Britain was a mere drop in the ocean. The speed with which the devilish aliens moved was extraordinary. The British government had to deal with the collaborators and the Eridanians themselves, at the same time. New evidence of strange activities at the MoD was now emerging at top level talks. Another wave of infiltration was a frightening possibility. An extraterrestrial phenomenon that could not be controlled or understood. The advanced technology with which they operated made the digitised wonders of the age look like child's play. A multi-media project swept through Europe, aimed at Eridanian controlling multi-national companies. Chunks of money were being spent by individual members of the EU on research projects. This was a strategy to devour the economy of the EU. The aliens had succeeded in creating an entrepreneurial culture with huge amounts of money being spent aimlessly, leading up to a master-slave society. The worst part of all this complex strategy was that the European leaders had already given their blessing to the evil force which was now working incessantly to break down resistance throughout the British Isles.

Inept arguments were paralysing all the efforts to conceive a feasible plan at least to stop the Eridanian onslaught. I was devastated when I read the reports of economic and financial experts, analysing the swift process by which the aliens had destroyed the democratic system in the EU through monetary manipulations unknown to mankind. It was impossible to predict the devils' next move. They might be implementing a completely different approach in Britain. No single action could diminish the dangers of fragmentation within British society. No scientist, politician or economist had come up with an answer yet on how to stop Eridanian domination.

Cradle Hill near Warminster was the arranged meeting point of the Chosen 37. Many sightings had been reported in that area. Scientists were able to detect a high level of ethereal energy left behind on landing sights. Not the usual radioactive material, but an ethereal energy which builds up into subtle energies, good or evil. We had lunch in Warminster and then reached Cradle Hill at around 4.00pm. We had plenty of time to prepare for the night...

We reached a copse with thick undergrowth and trees at the centre of Cradle Hill, and waited for the arrival of the mystery number 37. All 36 of us were occupied with fastening ropes to the poles of the tents. Suddenly a tall figure arrived, dressed in black. It was a close-fitting garment which looked like leather. He was very tall, probably 7 foot 5 inches, taller than Draco himself. The lighting was strong enough for us all to see him. We all stood there, staring in horror. This was not an ordinary man. Some of the people trained their torches on him and in the glow, I could see his long face. He walked into the centre and lifted his hands as if to assure us that he meant no harm to anyone. Clayton had spoken to him a couple of days before on the phone, and had said the stranger had insisted on being present at the meeting of the Chosen 37.

"Please, sit down," he told us in a deep base voice, "I will introduce myself and tell you where I come from. I am from Planet Centaurus in the Alpha Centauri system. I am what you call a Grey. As you know, our race of beings are diminutive, but we can change into any form we want. I am here to help you. You can call me Tamor. I was sent here with a mission—to stop the Eridanian invasion."

"We are the Chosen 36," I said, "people who have succeeded in contacting the Greys through telepathic communication. In fact, we had decided to make a concerted effort to contact your people, but now that plan is redundant, since you are here. I have to ask you a very important question. The Eridanians claimed recently to have reached an accord with your people, an agreement that would elevate mankind onto another, much higher, plain. We know that the Eridanians want to create a slave society out of the entire human population of the Planet Earth. We've been told through telepathic communication with the Greys that you are arch-enemies of the Eridanian kind. So is it true about this agreement?"

"There is no such agreement," he announced, "this is just another ploy of the Devil. I know that the continent of Europe and what you call the European Union is under Eridanian control. The web of Eridanians is widening into some areas in Asia and the far east. I am also aware of the brave struggle of the people in Britain. The perplexities confronting you are immense; the Eridanian civilisation is highly advanced. The powers that we possess are almost the same as the powers they have. We need no food, water or sleep. Immortality is there inheritance. We are the same. But man is at a very crucial stage on this planet. The demonic powers of the Eridanians have advanced even further. They are now in a position to challenge what you call 'God', the spirit of creation itself. The Eridanian finger is now on the pulse of the Milky Way galaxy."

"Fear constitutes great danger for mankind. Humans face a great extraterrestrial war. This will be final and absolute. I am here to prevent this extraterrestrial war. I will give you help both spiritually and physically. Mankind has to learn about the forces of will and challenge. Once you learn to execute actions through these forces, you will survive. I realise you have an enormous task. People have joined the Eridanians in their thousands. We have been watching you very carefully for a long time. We are aware of your activities down to the smallest detail. You have to deal with the problems within. But the fluctuating changing patterns of behaviour of the Eridanians is a major problem."

"When did you arrive?" I asked, "Are you on your own?"

"I arrived a couple of days ago, and yes, I am alone," came the reply.

"But how can you challenge the power of the Eridanians on your own, just one man?"

"Mr Akova," he answered, aggrieved, "do not concern yourself with what I will do or how I will do it. No human can understand our ways."

"Tamor, the problems within, as you call them, are fundamental developments within British society. Through the media now under Eridanian control, we have become the object of general public derision. No one believes our story any longer. Some members of the British government still retain their integrity, but the tactics of the Eridanians are difficult to resist. Many have been persuaded into their camp. What I am saying is that we need help to tackle these problems from within. The British are desperate, and the people who are trying to resist the aliens have no idea how to continue."

"Trust me, Mr Akova," he said, "you have a mission with the UFO Research Centre. You are the man who found the Devil's feather in your country and brought it to the world. You are helping the British. We have given you special powers. The other 35 people here are also within the sphere of our influence. They are protected too. You still have unfinished business here. You must continue the struggle. The Eridanians cannot touch you, and, as I have said, all the people here are protected." Tamor waved his two hands at us and suddenly disappeared.

The arrival of this Grey was a momentous event. The Greys who had promised to save Earth and mankind from the devils had at last sent a representative to deal with the rapidly deteriorating situation. But what he had said during those brief moments with us at Cradle Hill was a big disappointment. As a super-advanced being from the Grey civilisation at Alpha Centauri, he appeared to offer little. First of all, he had given us no hint on how the Greys would deal with the Eridanians; and secondly, he had told us we had to deal with the problems within ourselves. What sort of help was that?

In my experience, there is no one more dangerous than someone who tells the truth. All 36 of us from different parts of the world, the Chosen 36, had one special mission. The UFO Research Centre and the Chosen 36 had been the first to tell the world that the aliens had arrived; first in Salzburg and then in London. Millions around the world had been enlightened about the most important event in the history of mankind. But despite our warnings, little had been done to check the Eridanian advance. Within two months, the EU had fallen and the whole continent was now under alien control. This was a significant conquest. But so far, for whatever unknown reason, Britain had remained intact.

I was puzzled and bothered. A disturbing thought was flickering through my mind. Tamor's address to the chosen 36 had hinted at an exceptionally powerful Eridanian force that could not be challenged by the Greys. On the other hand, I had witnessed Grey power when a Grey UFO had charged down on the Eridanian UFO in Cornwall. There, the Greys had practically routed the Eridanians and their UFO had fled within minutes of the assault.

These contradictory indications did not make sense. Furthermore, Tamor's secretive attitude bothered me. He had not said a word on how the Greys were planning to deal with the Eridanians. All this, plus the fact that he had called the UFO Research Centre in London and asked to be present at the meeting of the elite of contactees made me suspicious. But then again, the extraterrestrials that we had investigated were able to disappear and reappear at will. That was a mastering of a technology which was probably thousands of Earth years ahead of us.

"I think we ought to try and contact the Greys now," I said to Emma and Clayton, "I don't trust Tamor, and since we cannot investigate his activities, I think we should try and make contact with the Greys as we did in the past, and ask them about Tamor…"

"What's bothering you, Turan?" asked Emma.

I told her of my experience with the clash of the two extraterrestrials in West Loo, again emphasising the fact that the Greys had had the upper hand.

"Well, I don't know," she said doubtfully, "maybe they have technologies which are very similar in essence. Maybe they have no superiority over each other."

"Emma, listen! The help we've been hoping and waiting for finally arrives. A Grey appears, And what happens? He talks to us for a few minutes, and then disappears! We don't know how to contact him. We don't know where he is or what he is doing. All this is very strange. So I say we try to contact the Greys now."

Emma and Clayton came round to my idea of thinking, and for the next half an hour, we prepared for telepathic communication with the Greys. All 36 of us sat on the ground in a circle. The message to be sent to the Greys was simple and straightforward: WHO IS TAMOR? We all repeated this question in our minds for ten minutes. We hoped that the celestial chariots above Earth would somehow pick up this message, feel the power of this mental energy sending a message to Alpha Centauri. After the long ten minutes, we sat there observing the night sky. Occasionally we could all see a light, a star-like light moving across and then disappearing suddenly as if playing a game with us…We waited until dawn.

None of us up there on Cradle Hill received an answer. I tried everything possible to stimulate further my effort, praying for guidance from the sublime UFO beings, the masters of light and good, the kings of angels. The moment I closed my eyes, the evil forces of darkness showed the ugly face of Satan. I felt sure they were here somewhere on Cradle Hill, breaking and destroying the messages we had sent to the Greys.

I saw the sun rise behind the grey clouds. It was a bleak morning, cold and dreary. The smaller hills around us looked lifeless. The evil demons had wreaked havoc all night, and the aura which was supposed to energise the concerted messages from the chosen 36 was swept away unceremoniously with the greatest of ease. Cradle Hill and Warminster, the hub of UFO activity for many years, the centre of many a Grey UFO landing witnessed by thousands, had become the playground of the Devil. These were my thoughts that cold January morning. At this critical juncture in the life of Earth, love, truth, joy and happiness had somehow been replaced by evil, cruelty, deceit, horror and ruthless demonic power. Even an optimist such as I am could no longer avoid thinking about the swift disintegration of the zealously guarded wisdom and power of human kind.

The issue on the executive power in Britain had to be resolved. The Higher Authority led by Lord Fitzpatrick seemed to be at the helm, but recent interviews with the Premier, Foreign Minister and Defence Minister suggested otherwise. The power struggle was viciously manipulated by the Eridanians, and the Chancellor of the Exchequer was indicted in a massive corruption scandal. He claimed he was innocent, and I believed him as I knew the Eridanians had drained the capital from the Bank of England to the level of total bankruptcy. The Higher Authority, the British government and MI5 and 6 were in a state of confusion. There was no clear agenda. The British parliament resumed its debate on how to consolidate its position whilst dealing with the Eridanians, as previous measured aiming to stop alien infiltration into government departments had been rejected by the upper chamber through Lord Fitzpatrick's insistence on cooperation with the Eridanians.

Most MPs had a rather foggy idea of what was happening in the country. They were very split on issues such as the failsafe cure for cancer and AIDS, plus the highly advanced alien technology that would inevitably open the way to a new world first in our own Solar system and then in other star systems. But the major overriding concern of all MPs rested upon a policy which did not jeopardise the safety of the British people as a whole. They wanted to protect their system come what may, and I admired them for that. Their actions were now calibrated on devising a plan to maintain the well-being of the people. First things first, they pulled out all the reserves from the Treasury in order to restructure the finances of the country.

As Tamor had said, I had some unfinished business to attend to…About that he was right. I had no time to analyse the current Eridanian strategy. I had to take some extreme steps to disorientate the Higher Authority. I had various options in mind, but as always, I preferred to improvise, and challenge their unpredictable moves by some unpredictable moves of my own. As I approached Lord Fitzpatrick's residence in Hampstead, I saw police cordoning off the mansion while confronting an angry crowd. People were protesting against Fitzpatrick's large scale cooperation with the Eridanians. I pushed my way through the crowd and wormed my way to the large entrance to the building.

The door flew open and I saw Lord Fitzpatrick's face. He bounded from his chair, wringing his hands in anguish, and grabbed the phone. His two body guards took some steps towards me, and he called: "It's OK, let him come in!"

"You think the Higher Authority can deal with the masses?" I asked him. He looked quite frail and helpless.

"These people are crazy, Mr Akova. What do they want from me?"

"I don't know," I replied, "but I saw placards protesting against the Eridanians to the tune of 'Down with the Aliens!', 'Eridanians out!'. What do you think?"

"But how did they find out about me and the Higher Authority?"

"The whole country knows about the agreement Britain is supposed to sign with the Eridanians. You yourself spoke about it openly in the House of Lords. As for your involvement with the Higher Authority, well, there were several reports in the papers and your name was mentioned." I said.

Lord Fitzpatrick's wife was sitting comfortably on the sofa, glass of whisky in hand.

"I told you not to get involved with these aliens," she remarked calmly, "leave this Higher Authority or whatever it's called. Just resign."

Clearly, she had more sense than her husband.

"Leave me alone, Sybil," he whined hysterically.

"I'll do exactly that if you want me to. But for God's sake, leave them alone," she scolded him.

"It's too late now," he moaned.

"It's never too late. I can help you." There had to be someone else behind all this. Lord Fitzpatrick was definitely a member of the secret Higher Authority, but he seemed to be too weak a person to lead such an executive body, which was in fact above the government. I wanted to help this pathetic man.

"Your lordship, shall we adjourn into the study. Thye two of us alone there, perhaps we can find a way out of this mess."

As soon as he was behind his desk, he thumped his fists violently on the table in petulance. His conduct was hardly appropriate to a man of his background.

"They are all imbeciles," he groaned, "you don't know anything about it. At our last meeting, it became evident that the signing of such an agreement would have been against the interests of the country, and I pointed this out. But I was outvoted by the other members of the Higher Authority. I realise now that they take orders from someone. No one knows who this person is. Although I opposed signing this agreement, I was indicated as the member who wrote the final draft of it."

"Well, did you?"

"No, of course not, Mr Akova. But through the media which is, as you know, under Eridanian control, they put the finger on me. In the eyes of the public, I am the man who sold out his country to the enemy."

"You have to give me the names of all the other members of the Higher Authority," I told him.

Lord Fitzpatrick was very cooperative for the rest of the evening. He explained how all members of the Higher Authority had received large sums of money from this mysterious source. All these were startling disclosures. The Higher Authority consisted of seven members, including Lord Fitzpatrick, Not in order of importance, they were listed as follows: Deputy Premier David Stockton, Defence Minister Raymond Fawler, Undersecretary to the Defence Minister, Sally Harwick, Undersecretary to the Foreign Secretary Horace Durrell, Director of MI6 James Furner and Furner's deputy, George Madsen. Of course, the seventh member was Lord Fitzpatrick.

During the next three to four days, Major Blount of MI6 and I interviewed all the members of the Higher Authority. They all claimed they were taking orders from a mystery man whose identity was secret from them. They never saw him. Orders were sent to each member in separate envelopes. One member, Raymond Fawler, said that the mystery man's orders were very contradictory and he had in fact ended up giving a much freer arena to the Eridanians.

"The intensity of his hatred for the British government is very puzzling," he said, "everything he touches disintegrates into a grey area where the alien vision of a society of obedient slaves is almost realised. People are being drawn into a process where they are possessed by uncontrollable greed."

Nothing strange about that, I thought to myself, *for this was the way of the Devil.* It would be unthinkable for the British government to have conventional ideas about this most unusual, critical situation. Despite expert advice from American scientists and alien experts both in Britain and in the USA, the issue of alien control over most of the key positions in the government seemed unresolved. The seven members of the Higher Authority had no idea about the identity of the secret leader. They could not be sure whether he was on the side of the Eridanians. One day, he would raise questions as to the viability of an agreement with the aliens, and the next he would conclude that the highly advanced Eridanians would contribute tremendously to the life of the human civilisation on Planet Earth.

I asked Fawler how the members of the Higher Authority received their orders.

"A courier brings the envelopes to the meeting. First we would all be informed about the date, time and venue of the meeting, then a different courier would bring us the envelopes."

"When is your next meeting?"

"I don't know whether we will have another meeting. The premier is insisting on dismantling the Higher Authority altogether."

"He must not do that." I said, "I have to carry out an investigation first with the couriers and then with information from other sources as to the identity and whereabouts of the so-called mystery leader. This is not just my idea. The MI6 chief, Major Blount wants us to seek out this mystery man. Mr Fawler, please try to persuade the premier to wait until we find some leads on this case. Otherwise every attempt to find this secret leader will be rendered futile."

"You are right, Mr Akova," said Fawler dispiritedly. "But the demonstrations near Lord Fitzpatrick's home may hold him back. He may never call another meeting."

"But you have to try and contact this man and call a meeting yourself. Can you do that?"

"No, Mr Akova, that is the problem."

"OK. Now, here's what you do. Ask the premier to release a statement to the media to tell the world that the next meeting of the Higher Authority will determine the strategy of the British government."

"Right," said Fawler, and left meekly.

The British Premier, who had been in France for a meeting with the French Prime Minister, landed at Heathrow to a tumultuous welcome. He was the youngest Conservative premier in the history of British politics and he was very popular. Thousands greeting him, crying, "Down with the Higher Authority!" "keep the aliens out," "EU out, Britain in!" My request for another meeting of the Higher Authority before its dissolution was supported by Major Blount. The following day, Fawler said that the premier had agreed to comply with our request.

My mind was set on five extraordinary characters that I had met during this most extraordinary trial in the history of the world, that is the advent of the extraterrestrials. First had been the old count, whom everyone knew had lived in the Carpathian Mountains in his own castle. He was known as Prince Vlad. History tells us of his fights with the Turks, but most important of all, Bram Stoker's novel had made him world famous. Later, I found documented proof in the notes of Bram Stoker that this evil character was in fact an extraterrestrial who had arrived first in Transylvania and then in Yorkshire. Second and third were Lorenzo de Medici and Luigi Gonzaga. Their extraterrestrial origins were also established beyond dispute. The fourth character descended to Earth claiming he was from the star system Alpha Centauri, Tamor, of course. He had told us he was a Grey in human form and had promised to help us. The fifth was a mystery man who gave orders to the members of the Higher Authority.

Draco, Lorenzo de Medici and Gonzaga were almost invincible. Furthermore, they appeared, disappeared and then reappeared in different European and American cities. They were as elusive as ever. Tamor had arrived at Cradle Hill. He had talked to us—the Chosen 36—for fifteen minutes, and then disappeared into thin air without trace. The abilities of these extraterrestrials to appear and then disappear in different spots on Earth with a technology totally unknown to mankind, made it utterly impossible to investigate their activities. At least, for the time being. The only one left for me to investigate was the mystery leader who somehow managed to dictate political, social and economic dogmas to the British government and who was probably quite shaken by the growing opposition to his policies.…

Twenty-Seven

The road stretched into the forest as I followed the courier who was delivering the envelopes to the members of the Higher Authority in Carlton House Terrace. The courier parked his car in a cul de sac and walked towards the forest…I was in the town of Baldock in Hertfordshire. I parked the car about fifty metres from his car and walked slowly towards the man, As he stopped at the entrance to a house I could see under the porch light that he was of medium height. I stopped dead as I saw another man coming to the entrance from a side alley next to the house. I glanced at my watch. It was 9.00pm. The man handed over something to the courier and hurried back towards the alley into the darkness. I waited behind a tree for the man to enter the house, then moved towards the front door.

When I rang the bell, I knew of course that the man had every right not to allow me to enter his house. A clean-shaven blond man in his late thirties opened the door. He stared at me as if he had seen a ghost.

"I am the archangel who's come to save your soul from the devil," I said.

He relaxed into a smirk, "Come on, for Christ's sake," he retorted.

"I am working with the police and I'm here to ask you several questions."

He was distinctly worried at the mention of the police.

"What do you mean 'with' the police?"

"Well, I mean either you let me in to answer my questions or I'll call the police, they'll take you in and ask the questions at the police station. Of course, you'll have to stay the night there."

He thought for a moment, and then invited me in.

"Please come in. But I can assure you, I haven't done anything wrong or illegal."

"I know. But I'm hoping you will help me in my investigations. You see, I know you deliver certain envelopes to the Higher Authority at Carlton House Terrace in London. Now, the first obvious question: who gives you the envelopes?"

"Well, his name is Peter Campbell. I met him in a shop in Regent Street. I honestly don't know anything about him. But he seems to be at the shop all the time."

"Right. So far, so good. Now tell me, who was the man you met at the door before entering the house tonight?"

"I don't know him at all. He meets me here at the house and pays me."

"How much?" I asked.

"Five thousand pounds."

I could feel my eyebrows shoot up in surprise: "You mean you're paid five thousand pounds each time you deliver the envelopes?" I asked.

"Yes."

"Can you think of anything that might help me find the man who pays you?"

"Well, I've seen him on some occasions at the local pub in the evenings. He has a few drinks before he leaves for London."

"Fine. Now, let's go to the pub. Don't worry, he won't see you. Just point him out to me, that's all I want," I said, getting up.

The George J Hall pub was at walking distance from his house. As we approached the large window of the pub near the door, he stood behind me.

"You have to look inside," I whispered, "don't worry, he won't see you. Just show me which one he is."

A seedy old tramp walked past me and opened the door of the pub. That moment, the courier grabbed my arm tensely: "There! There!" he whispered urgently, "that's him, in the blue jacket, standing beside the blond in the red dress."

"OK, thanks," I said, "now you go home. Don't worry. I won't tell a soul about you."

"Thank you," said the courier, much relieved, and hurried back home.

Peter Campbell was a big man, probably in his early forties. When I ordered a beer at the bar, he glanced at me for a second. He had short hair, a round face and blue eyes. I decided to start a conversation with the barman in a louder than usual tone, to attract attention. I was almost sure the people next to me at the bar would join in.

"I saw some beautiful villas in Hertfordshire twenty years ago. I noticed there are many more nowadays, and bigger ones, too."

"Yes," said the barman, making an almost robotic movement towards the bar, "Baldock has become a fashionable residential area since the influx of people from Europe."

"That's very interesting," I said, thinking. Europeans coming to settle in a totally unknown small town in Hertfordshire? Very strange.

The barman glanced at Campbell, smiling apologetically as if for something he should not have said. Campbell spoke in a low voice: "Give me another shot of whisky, will you?" he ordered. He looked at me enquiringly, and continued in the same low voice, "Are you in the property business?"

"No. My name's Akova. I'm a pianist/composer."

"Where are you from, with a name like that?"

"I'm a Turkish Cypriot from North Cyprus. By the way, seen any UFOs lately?"

That fell like a bombshell amongst the crowd at the bar. An expression of shock and incredulity spread on all the faces almost simultaneously. At that moment, I felt like a stranger in a pub full of vampires closing in on me. I know it was a crazy thought, but all their eyes were blazing into mine. Campbell broke the spell: "No. Why? Are you interested in UFOs?"

"I'm also a UFO researcher," I told him, "I'm here to investigate two sightings which have been reported in the last few days."

Campbell brushed aside my remark on UFO sightings in the vicinity, but he was now more interested. I glanced around. The people at the bar kept quiet, staring at me. The other customers at the tables were also staring at me. Something was very strange here, I told myself, and decided to change the subject.

"Tell me about the Europeans who've settled here. Why Baldock of all places?"

"Don't take any notice of what the barman said," Campbell replied airily, "there are only a few who came as tourists and decided to stay. That's all."

But I remembered the barman's words: 'influx of people coming from Europe'. I could not think why people from European countries would want to settle in a totally unknown small town in Hertfordshire? As for the pub and the people inside it, there was a grey, ghostly and spine chilling component that seemed to hint at unearthly presences. I could feel it. After all, the Greys had bestowed those special powers on me. We were coming close to a gruesome discovery, I felt.

"So, you've come all this way just for UFO sightings, have you?" asked Campbell.

"Yes, and I'm looking for people who may be able to help me in my investigations."

"What sort of investigations?" he asked, insistently.

"Mr Campbell, all sorts of strange things have been happening in the world since the arrival of the aliens. I'm interested and I want to find out as much as I can about their activities."

The whole crowd was still; listening.

The questions kept coming:

"Who do you work for?"

"The UFO Research Centre in London," I said. I was doubtful that he believed my story about the UFO sightings, but the looks in the eyes of the people there were very unsettling indeed. Thank God, I had my shield on and my gun in the breast pocket. Campbell was most probably on the payroll of the mystery man at the head of the Higher Authority.

A furious thunderstorm hit Baldock at around a quarter to ten. The rain came down like a deluge. The stiff, robotic movement of the pub customers and their overall strangeness affected me like claustrophobia. They seemed to be closing in on me. Campbell spoke, and they stopped.

"Most people here converted to Catholicism, to purify their souls." That did not make any sense at all. He continued, "A powerhouse of unsurpassable fantastic realities that will shock and at the same time delight mankind. But the current situation hints at immeasurable consequences. Earthly concepts can't understand or accept this. A phenomenon of incalculable power intelligently directed towards humans. The London Man will rule over this country."

"What the hell are you talking about?"

"No power on hearth can break this stranglehold on humanity. No one can survive in the wake of extraterrestrial destruction. Terrifying, isn't it?"

"I don't understand."

Campbell buried his face in his hand with exasperation. Then he lifted his head, and snarled, gloating, "But you will understand."

"Tell me, Mr Campbell, who is this London Man?"

"You'll find out soon enough. I'll take you to him," he said, with a sinister smile. It occurred to me that he had been informed of my arrival in Baldock. A seamless cloak concealed by the insidious and sometimes vociferous acts of the evil supernatural seemed to fall in its place. I'd come to learn one of the basic tenets of Eridanian culture, if you can call it that. They were always unpredictable…

Campbell's short outburst of lunatic, dramatic mixture of completely unrelated topics was a revelation in itself. Somehow, his extraterrestrial brain clicked onto different subjects one after the other. From that moment on, I knew what I was dealing with. The Eridanians had entered the bodies of the local people of Baldock. Campbell seemed to control the rest of the crowd in the pub.

"Can I buy you a drink?" he asked suddenly.

"I'll have a lager, thank you," I replied, as alert as ever with my back against the wall. None of the people surrounding my end of the bar uttered a word in this disturbing atmosphere. Their relentlessly unnerving stares focused directly into my eyes. But I was protected. Then I noticed a pinkish-red smoke rising slowly from behind the bar. A pleasantly stimulating odour with small particles floated up into the room, and for a moment, I felt dizzy. And then I realised the danger of being taken by the extraterrestrials.

I was perilously close to becoming a prisoner of the demented Campbell and his band of men in the pub. Then it happened. The door of the pub opened and a young woman hurried in, calling out my name.

"Mr Akova, you are late. We were supposed to meet at nine," she called, and approached me, and took my arm. The brooding power of the evil one which had spread all over the room, creating a particularly deep sense of horror, ended abruptly as she pulled me towards the door. I had no idea who she was. But she had definitely arrived at the right time. I felt weak and dizzy as I walked out into the fresh air, hearing Campbell's rough voice faintly calling after me, "Remember, the London Man. Come tomorrow evening and I'll take you to him."

The rain had stopped. A gust of wind blew into my face and I was back to being a normal person. Nevertheless, the power of that pinkish smoke had been quite disturbing. Its smell and those particles seemed to render me unprotected, for the first time.

"Come with me," said the young woman, briskly pushing me into the front seat of a Jaguar.

"Thank you," I gasped, "but who are you?"

"First we go to the hotel," she told me, driving up the road away from the pub and into another leading out of town. Jennings Hotel stood on its own on a small hill, surrounded by a forest. It was fairly large, and the receptionist, a tall, bespectacled man, gave an especially warm smile to the girl.

"My fiancé," she explained briefly, as we walked up to the first floor to room number 7, which turned out to be a suite. As we sat down, she offered me a drink from the minibar next to the large double bed. After those chilling moments in the pub, I felt safe and glad to be there.

"Mr Akova, my name is Dorothy. I work with Major Blount. He asked me to follow you wherever you went."

"But we've never met," I commented.

"New recruit."

"Well, thank you again. You came just at the right time. That Campbell character is definitely deranged. It felt as if I was sliding into a nightmare. The pub was so oppressive. It was full of aliens, Dorothy, completely devoid of any redeeming human emotion. They looked like humans, but it was all a show. God! It was the first time I had felt so weak and vulnerable. Not even my powers could repulse the evil there and by the time you arrived, I had almost fallen victim to the satanic madness. But why was I unable to protect myself?" My relief at being safe had made me gabble, and she smiled at me kindly: "Well, I'm just glad that I arrived in time," she said, content with her performance. "Major Blount said you would try to find the mystery man at the head of the Higher Authority. He also said you were a Turkish Cypriot, a pianist/composer and that you worked with the UFO Research Centre in London. How did you get mixed up with these aliens?"

"It's a long story," I sighed, "It all started with the feather like object I found in the Karpaz Peninsula of North Cyprus, after a UFO had landed there." I explained briefly the events that had followed that fateful discovery.

"Unfortunately, no one believes the dramatic struggle going on between the forces of light and darkness. No one believes that the Devil is here with his army of demons. It sounds just like a science fiction story, doesn't it? The supernatural realm of Satan, the King of the devils, is permanently established here on Earth. We are trying to rid the world of the scourge of the evil aliens."

"I believe you," she said softly, but it was clear her knowledge was limited, and she admitted she had not had the time to study all the developments which had unfolded since the arrival of the aliens. "I'm sorry, Mr Akova, I know very little. But I'm sure I'll learn a lot from you."

We ordered sandwiches and coffee, and conversed till 3.30 in the morning. She did not bother to get a separate room and slept in the double bed, while I slept in the large armchair. During those few hours of sleep, I had a nightmare. A little demon squatted on my chest, and I could not move a muscle. I woke with a shout, and saw her sitting beside me on the armchair, trying to soothe me.

"I'm sorry I woke you up. I had a nightmare; I couldn't breathe or move..."

She held my hand, "It's OK now," she murmured gently. I felt myself nodding off in her kind presence, while a rain pounded against the windows and the wind whistled through the old wooden shutters. She returned to bed, and I slept like a baby until 8.45 the following day.

The next morning we breakfasted in the dining room of the hotel. When I told her the whole story, she looked a bit apprehensive. Her imagination was working.

"Dorothy, how can you investigate the inexplicable and non-existent. The evil extraterrestrials are there and then they disappear. It's as if they are flaunting their power. What we've found out so far is a daunting amount of information. We have seen that within a short period of time, they have taken control of the media in Europe and in the UK; that they get their extraordinary powers from their own UFOs which land at different locations in Europe and the UK. I have proof of this. But we have not been able to stop them."

"The bizarre convolutions of alien presence are as mysterious as ever. I have been jumping from solving one plot to solving another. Now you see these devils and now you don't. But one thing I have established, and that is that there are five main operators pulling the strings: Dracula, De Medici, Gonzaga and—during the last few weeks—Tamor, who claims to be a Grey extraterrestrial (which I don't believe), and of course the mystery man at the head of the infamous Higher Authority. But nothing adds up. There is something missing. On top of all this, the anti-scientific scientists both in the USA, in Europe and here in Britain have moved into their camp. We have a very complicated situation and Britain is the only EU member country struggling to keep them out."

"How can we stop them? Can't we eliminate them altogether?"

"Dorothy," I said urgently, for it was vital she understood the magnitude of the challenge ahead, "until now, neither scientists nor researchers have been able to find the source of the power of the Eridanians, and our aim—when we do find it—is to destroy it. It follows, then, that if we can't get at their power source, they will continue to have the upper hand."

"But you just said that you saw their UFOs landing and fuelling them up with some sort of power," she said.

"Yes, that's right. That was in France, and it was spine chilling. But what can we do? We have no way of telling when their UFOs arrive. Furthermore, there are some friendly Grey UFOs who visit us regularly and it is impossible to tell which is which, so shooting them down would be out of the question."

"But surely, with our present sophisticated technology, we could spot them just as they arrive," she objected, seeming not to have heard my last comment about the Greys.

"Not so. Not with UFOs. They appear and disappear. It's not possible to track their movements."

"Now I'm worried, Mr Akova," she said, her face clouding.

"Call me Turan, please."

"OK, so what happens now?" she asked.

"We were hoping for a Grey intervention. After all, the Greys—you know, the friendly aliens—promised to help us. I should tell you that they contacted me and told me that their power was superior, enough to drive out the Eridanian devils. But the so-called Grey Tamor who interrupted our telepathic communication seemed not at all confident about that."

"How strange," she whispered, her knee touching mine under the table.

It was clear that we had entered a complex psychological labyrinth. But what had disturbed me most, was Tamor's attitude. When I had seen the clash of the two different UFOs, it was no contest. The Greys seemed far superior and the evil ones had to leave in a hurry. But Tamor had been doubtful about the Greys winning a definite victory against the Eridanians. We were now facing duplicitous and dangerous gods and goddesses from the star system Epsilon Eridani. The evil ones temptingly evoked a dreamland with no death. People did not even question these promises. This was a frightening reminder of the extent of the Devil's influence. The physical, emotional and spiritual effects were disastrous. There were many who were being taken over by the Eridanians and we had no way of preventing it…

In the evening, after dinner, I decided to return to the same pub. After all, Campbell had promised to take me to this London Man. I was prepared to walk into a trap simply to find out more about the London Man and the Europeans who had settled in Baldock. I was dedicated to this mission. Dorothy opposed the idea vehemently, but seeing my mind was made up, she decided to accompany me there. This time, we entered a completely different world. The place was full of women, and Campbell was at the centre.

"Ah!" he shouted above the chatter, pointing at me, "here you are, ladies and gentlemen. This is the man you've been waiting for. This is Mr Turan Akova, the famous pianist/composer. Now gather round, girls, and entertain the genius."

"Campbell, what is this? Where did all these women come from?" I gasped.

"These are the Europeans," he said, offering drinks to me and Dorothy at the bar.

"This is my girlfriend, Dorothy," I said, "now tell me, what was the trick you tried to pull on me with that odd coloured smoke?"

"Oh, that. That was nothing. Just something to arouse pleasant feelings and change the atmosphere. You felt a little dizzy, didn't you? That's what happens the first time…nothing to worry about, though."

And then I saw her. She was probably the most bewitching, sexy girl I had seen in a long time. She had long blond hair and blue eyes, and a marvellously lithe body. I feared this was another of the devil's games. She approached me and stood tantalisingly close, gazing straight into my eyes. I could feel a challenge coming up; she was definitely a tyrannical, demonic seductress…

"I have always wanted to meet you," she told me softly. Flattery gets women everywhere with me. "You must come with me now,"—even orders sounded sweet coming from her, "and then afterwards, I'll take you to the London Man."

Dorothy grabbed my hand in alarm, "Don't go, Turan," she warned. But I had already made up my mind. Even though I was probably risking my life, the promise of sex lured me on.

"Don't worry," I whispered back, "just go back to the hotel and wait for me there. I'll call you."

She left, and the beautiful seductress closed in on me. She looked innocuous enough, I told myself. She took my hand and pulled me into a dark corner of the pub. She was mystery itself, a warm and sexy enigma. She slid her arms around my neck and pressed her lips against mine. Her body pulsated with hunger for sex, and I was ready to oblige. All of a sudden, the world became a dark place. I don't know why, but I suddenly thought of the fiend, Count Dracula. Something about her reminded me of Draco. How well these Eridanian controlled women played on the major weakness of men.

You could call it one of my more idyllic idiosyncrasies. No, no, this was much stronger than that, and it was not idyllic either. This was an addiction to showing my appreciation of the opposite sex. It was an extreme addiction, I am the first to admit, to beautiful women. You might say that all men love beautiful women, and yes, this is largely true. But there are those who talk about beautiful women and do nothing, and there are those who have to act when they encounter them. Passionate lovers and great performers command the respect of all females. So, there you have it: the difference between a true playboy and the paper tigers who enjoy the company of women but make love to them only in their dreams. I mean no disrespect to anyone, male or female. These are the facts of life in the heterosexual domain. The feminists may protest but whether they like it or not, gone are the days of the male chauvinist pigs. Now we live in a world of inspiring libidinous relationships and the so-called old-fashioned flirtations which flourish into great, stunningly delicious love affairs still exist. Thank God for that!

But coming back to the beautiful woman in my arms; this was no Harlequin romance. She was made for love, a real, human woman. Thoughts of Draco faded as we indulged in wave after wave of blissful sex—which could have furnished material for a scientific study of the inventiveness of human sexual behaviour— she led me through a secret door out into the street.

"Now we go to my place," she said breathless with excitement and excursion.

"Lead on," I said, and we started walking in the deserted avenue leading out of town…We turned into a darker side road and practically danced to the door of a large Victorian house. She opened the door with her key and threw herself on the large sofa with an exuberant, reckless laugh. I saw the large grand piano in the corner of the sitting room beside the glass door leading into the garden. Our foreplay intensified as we lay on the sofa. It was fairly dark inside, as she had not bothered to switch on the lights. With a sudden movement, she slipped from under my body and disappeared into the darkness of the room. A crescendo of extraordinary sounds resembling the cries of animals and birds filled the room, while I sat on the edge of the sofa, fumbling for my gun. It was most unsettling.

The shadows of the wind-tossed branches of the trees in the garden, illuminated by the street lamp, performed their own Dance Macabre. Then I saw the figure of a woman in black standing beside the piano. I was terrified for some reason. The noise stopped and the woman spoke hoarsely: "You naughty boy! Your mother tried to teach you to read music. But no. You did not want to learn. You were always composing and arranging music—but now, child, come. I will teach you to read it." And the lights flickered on and off for the following few minutes.

"But I have a psychological block," I protested, "which prevents me from learning to read it…" I stopped talking, questioning my sanity…The beautiful woman had gone and the figure of an old woman, probably in her eighties, stood there, arms outstretched, motioning me towards the piano. There was chill in the air, a vague unease. The wrinkled face of the old woman became visible under the light. I stood up, still holding the gun in my hand, and pointing it towards her.

Then the lights went off again. The old woman's voice changed once again as she spoke. This was in a much lower tone. The light from the garden caught the gleam of a lethal stiletto in her right hand. She jumped on me like a wild animal. I pulled the trigger three times, aiming at her chest. She fell—and seconds later, vanished. I was on my knees behind an armchair when the lights came on…There was no one in the room. Then I heard footsteps on the floor above. Someone was descending the stairs. Shortly afterwards, a man with long white hair stood just a few feet away from me.

"I am the London Man," he announced, "you can relax. Christine is my daughter and here she is." Christine came downstairs and stood beside her father. She was as beautiful as ever.

"But why?"

He sat heavily in an armchair, holding his daughter's hand. He was obviously depressed and he continued sadly, "Mr Akova, what you have been through here is not my daughter's doing. We have unfortunately become toys in the hands of the aliens. A tingle turns into a tremor within seconds. Sporadic supernatural activity is the game they play. These Eridanians have extraordinary powers. Vexing problems are solved with just a movement of the arm or with just a few words. They are indestructible. I'm glad you found me. Actually, I admire your courage. I was planning a press conference. Please take me under your protection and take me and my daughter to London. The Higher Authority no longer exists. I resisted as much as I could the negative influences of the Eridanian technology. But it wasn't just that. The power of animating people, possessing their minds and souls…it was horrific to see. This cosmic horror has come to our own planet. I honestly don't know how Britain can survive. As you know, they already control the EU."

"I apologise for my behaviour, Mr Akova," said Christine, "they made me do it."

"Don't mention it. But tell me, who is the Campbell character?"

"Oh, he's just a pawn used by the aliens," said Christine's father, and then introduced himself properly.

"My name's Roy Wright. I am a former Conservative MP." He told me he had been appointed undersecretary to the Prime Minister, but unwitting eagerness had led from one thing to another, until he had been appointed head of the Higher Authority. He said the bitterly dark slant on alien presence had been a challenge for him and reports in the media of the collaboration of the Higher Authority with the Eridanians had in actual fact been a diversion, a paradoxical dichotomy that would disrupt the alien plan. But apparently this was a meaningless struggle to defeat the Devil…The true nature of the peril was quite adamant in several encounters with the Eridanians.

In fact, the danger of Britain falling into the hands of the aliens had assumed such significance that the Higher Authority had had to divert its activities so as to appear in opposition to the government, giving full support to the aliens. At first, this had been dismayingly convincing, but the tactic had been trounced by the devil with nonchalant ease. With a lingering smile on his lips, Mr Wright confessed he was now ready to join the struggle against the Eridanians.

The Europeans in Baldock were in fact new recruits of the Eridanians in Britain. I found the willingness Roy Wright, aka the London Man, to disengage all activities of the Higher Authority and join the ranks of the government somewhat unexpected. In fact, I had expected a much tougher stand from the alien controlled leader of the Higher Authority. His behaviour the previous night had been quite out of character. After all, he was the man who had dictated a hard line policy which included pre-meditated murders and eventually the controversy surrounding the tightly coiled strategies had led to the break-up of the ring of men who ruled over Britain.

I thought that perhaps he had been too glib; his confession too easily given. The daughter Christine's explicit sexual teasing continued the next day. I did not encourage her—at least for the time being. Living with the aliens and not being able to tell who was who posed a continuous risk, as the aliens and their allies had no consistent, comprehensive pattern of behaviour. They had paranormal powers that could see the future, change it, create real images of people and then make them vanish. Evil was embedded in the ordinary. The Eridanians and the

Eridanian controlled humans were inclined to rely heavily on human weakness. Suddenly you would be faced with a plethora of new ideas and completely inexplicable conceptions. The menace came from the unfamiliar and cold-blooded manner. At times, cool, sensible relations with humans led you to believe that these aliens were in truth trying to help humankind. But a sudden swerve would show you the face of the devil with savagery and madness unparalleled even in horror fiction.

They played on human bewilderment, and no one could even begin to understand their actions. The horror was sometimes checked by the light and energy coming from the Greys' UFOs and by the special powers of the Chosen 36, but that was not enough to stop them finally. All the research on UFOs, all the efforts to stop the infiltration of the devils into our midst met with a remarkably lively intelligence. I remembered the old man walking up and down Oxford Street with placards hung about his person. The hand-written message on his placards read: The end is at hand…An image of the distant past when I had been a student in London. Well, now it seemed as if the ultimate triumph of evil was at hand. This was by no means the end of the world, but it was the beginning of a downright catastrophic period in the life of Planet Earth, when a world and its people would be drained of their goodness by the evil forces from another star system.

Unseen terror, horror, perversion, demonic intrigue, possession of humans so that they become like robots, unsettling, unpredictable supernatural power, corrupt strategies, grisly murders and above all, insurmountable devilish plans to dominate the whole world, all these coalesced to form the last phase of completion. It seemed that the fifty odd people at the UFO Research Centre in London, the Chosen 36, and an uncertain number of strong-minded people in government were the only ones left to keep up the fight against these enormously powerful aliens. Officialdom in Britain was not as effective as we had anticipated. There was no word of encouragement from the Americans either.

We returned to London with Roy Wright, the London Man, on the following day. Dorothy said she would follow me around wherever I went. She was a good, intelligent agent. I promised to visit her in her 'secret office' at Major Blount's headquarters. When I went home to my Mayfair flat, I thought about the evil which had confronted the mind and soul of humankind, and how it could not be comprehended. A horrific reality which changed faces at random. I called Emma and Clayton at the Centre. We had to have another meeting. We also had to have another meeting with the premier and the Defence Minister.

From the day I had found the feathers to this time, I had trailed the aliens from Europe to America and back, and I was still nowhere near solving the mystery. The hard evidence I had gathered so far proved beyond any doubt that the Eridanians were evil aliens. The fact that these were devils masquerading as humans was the most appalling twist to the affair. I had proof of that too. But no one believed it any longer. The arrival of their leaders in the persons of Count Dracula, Lorenzo de Medici and Luigi Gonzaga highlighted the whole unbelievable event into a terrifying reality—a reality which I had uncovered. That had been no mean feat. I had also found out that the power and energy they needed was pumped into these creatures from their UFOs which landed at different spots all over Europe. Worst of all, they had become permanent residents of Planet Earth. But what about Europe and the European Union?

The Eridanians had taken over the European Union, one of the most powerful economic organisations in the world. They had chosen Europe as their base, and no one knew why. How could we stop them from getting the energy they needed? That was the big question. But one thing was certain. Britain was a special 'area' for them. They were using weird methods for the takeover in Britain. How could anyone prevent the supply of energy when the location of the next UFO landing was unknown? Nevertheless, the Eridanian insistence and efforts to take over Britain puzzled me. After all, there were other countries on the borders of the EU, but alien presence in these countries was scarce.

They had established themselves in a power block in Europe, but Britain was still outside their sphere of influence. True, they had gained ground over the previous couple of months, but somehow Britain survived. This, to my mind, was also odd. The aliens had taken over the whole of the EU from Portugal to Greece, within a short period, while just one country—Britain—struggled to keep them out. But why was Britain so important for them? This was the big mystery. Perhaps the answers lay hidden somewhere in England. The aliens were trying to strip all authority from Britain. But they had not succeeded yet.

Twenty-Eight

The meeting with the Prime Minister and Defence Minister was held at the premier's offices in Whitehall. Emma, Clayton and I represented the London UFO Research Centre, while the under-secretaries of the Premier and the Defence Minister were present. A full report of our findings and proof of the evil plans of the Eridanians were submitted to the Premier. He was well aware of the result of our investigations as all the information was passed on regularly to his office. He looked at me enquiringly: "Well, Mr Akova? I'm open to suggestions. What do we do next?"

"Because the UFOs can't be detected by conventional radars, British and American scientists have been working on a device that will reveal them before they land. Once they have managed to do this, we can hit them on the spot, just as they land. If we succeed, then there is no way they can obtain the energy they need to survive on earth."

"But I remember you said in an earlier report that these aliens had become almost human and that they were living here permanently." His wary response alerted a possibility that was also at the back of my mind. The Eridanian and Grey UFOs were very similar in shape. They were both saucer shaped craft and one could not really distinguish one from the other.

"You are right, of course." I conceded, "These creatures do live on Earth now, and their numbers are growing by the minute. But I did see quite recently a landing of one of their UFOs and I actually saw them line up to receive their energy. The same thing happened in Whitby and in West Loo. But we have another problem, which is that of not being able to distinguish between the two types of craft. This is another aspect that demands examination. The Americans have films of both kinds of UFOs, so we are hoping that a careful study would show us the difference…"

"Tell me truthfully, Mr Akova, is there a danger of destroying one of our ally's UFOs?"

"I'm afraid so, at present, at any rate. But I think the Americans will be able to help us on that one with their pictures, and hopefully, we will be able to eliminate that risk."

"And what about our so-called allies? Is there any indication if or when or even how they will help us?"

"Alas, no," I replied. "There has been no word from Tamor, the Grey who briefly showed himself and then disappeared. And I have a certain feeling that there has been some kind of new development in the striking power of the Eridanians which has given them the upper hand. At least, this was the impression I got from the brief encounter with Tamor."

"Whatever gave you that idea?" asked the Defence Minister.

"Well, Tamor did not seem at all sure about the outcome of a possible clash with the Eridanians. He merely said they would 'try' to help."

"Hmmm…that's strange," commented the Premier thoughtfully, "I had interpreted your eye-witness accounts differently. Grey power actually had the Eridanians on the run on at least two occasions. This was what I read in one of your reports."

A surreptitious and delicate performance by Draco, De Medici and Gonzaga lad led to the downfall of the EU within a short period. We were now sliding inexorably into the world of the unknown. What lay in store for mankind on Earth? A world in which reality fused with fantasy and dream. These three main players were at work all the time, but no one knew of their whereabouts. I suspected they could well be the secret engine driving forward the Eridanian conquest. They were always shrouded in mystery. But as Britain was, in my opinion, a very special place for them, and since they were concentrating their efforts of a takeover in this country, they had to show up somewhere…but where?

The British Space Research Association was perhaps the place to start a new investigation. After all, it was one of their duties to pass on the technology of instantaneous contact with other star systems and their civilisations. The actions of Draco, De Medici and Gonzaga were disjointed and made no apparent sense. I remember seeing primordial images at a session with this organisation. A scientist at the association had talked about UFO landings on Cradle Hill and at Stonehenge over five thousand years ago. These could be the starting point of my investigation: whether there had been UFO landings at these sites. But it was impossible to explain. Was there a link between those landings so long ago and the special status of Britain for the Eridanians?

Frankly, I had no idea. That there had been UFO landings in England in that distant past was a tempting thought, but there was nothing in any investigations conducted so far to corroborate back this up. I discarded the possibility, as I was well aware that the devils were experts in producing images which had no relation with reality. Nevertheless, the Wiltshire area which encompassed Cradle Hill, Warminster and Stonehenge—all UFO landing sites—was crying out for a thorough investigation. The material I had collected in my archives clearly pointed to a flurry of UFOs and crop circles in the 1960s and early '70s at Cradle Hill. It is worth noting that during this time, there was a deliberate attempt by hoaxers to disprove these landings at Cradle Hill. They failed, of course.

Only about a year before, I had been invited to the Marlborough International Jazz Festival, to play avant-garde jazz solo on the piano. At any rate, in the four days I was staying there, I took the opportunity to examine the famous crop circles in the area. Crop circles of amazing complexity of shapes and sizes appeared in fields which had been empty the previous night. Scientists and other experts tried very hard to find a scientific or otherwise convincing explanation for the mystery, but could come up with none. There were many theories bandied about, regarding their significance: had they been a sign of the UFO presence? However, the arrival of the alien Eridanian extraterrestrials had pushed the crop circles mystery onto the back burner for the time being and this was why I decided to conduct a detailed investigation on them. Experts with highly sensitive, digitised equipment would be called in to conduct an on the spot examination of the circles. With the blessing of the British government, Emma and I decided to investigate first, the British Space Research Association and then, to embark on a much wider examination of the areas in question in Wiltshire: namely, Cradle Hill, Warminster, Marlborough and Stonehenge.

The British Space Research Association headquarters were about three miles to the west of Slough in an area not unlike Area 51 in the USA. This was like a base with the highest category of secrecy. Top security measures in an area of about ten square miles were in force. The Premier and the Defence Minister had obtained our security clearance, so we were allowed to enter and leave the premises at any time during the day. Emma made a list of all the people who were employed at the BSRA, from the director to the chauffeurs and truck drivers. The list was very useful, of course, and she had underlined the ones who were especially vulnerable to Eridanian influence, those who might be collaborating with the enemy. They were merely suspects; we had no certain proof that they were Eridanian controlled. We knew that they might well turn out to be ordinary employees.

The first man we visited in his office was Ralph Lorimer, a nuclear physicist who worked with the aliens when the space people's technology was installed at the base for direct and instantaneous contact with alien civilisations in star systems within a radius of fifty light years, within our own Milky Way galaxy. It was with this technology that the Eridanians had first infiltrated the European Space Agency and simultaneously spread their influence and control over all the EU. Now the BSRA was a new target for the aliens. The first contacts with Epsilon Eridani, Tau Ceti, Alpha Centauri and Zeta Reticuli had earned unstinting praise from the British scientists. But these scientists had no idea about the foul plans of the devil.

Ralph Lorimer was by no means a suspect. The aliens were careful enough not to attract attention by demonstrating a normal scientific activity, an outstanding technological feat was accomplished and the people at the British Space Research Association were led to believe that this was a wonderful gift from the great civilisation of Epsilon Eridani.

Much to Emma's disgust, Lorimer was completely oblivious and even indifferent to the condemnation of the Eridanians as an evil race. A fanatic scientist, he enthused about the Eridanian technology, "This is what we have been waiting for," he told us delightedly, "can you imagine? Now we are able to contact a civilisation in Zeta Reticuli, over thirty-seven light years away from Earth! This is unbelievable!"

"But that's beside the point," said Emma sternly, "Mr Lorimer, doesn't it mean anything to you that the aim of the Eridanian aliens is to dominate mankind?"

"Stuff and nonsense!" said the scientist, "as if anyone would believe that!" I told him that the investigation of the BSRA had been a government decision, and that he had to cooperate with us.

"We are looking for three aliens known as Draco, De Medici and Gonzaga. Have they been here recently, or do you know of anyone in the base who has any information about their whereabouts?"

"Mr Akova," he said expansively, "I will most certainly try to help you as much as I can. Those three were here during the first contacts we made. There were three more people with me during that historical occasion: Jameson, Keller and Hunt. I'll call them."

As they entered the room, Emma looked at the list in front of her on the table. "Nope," she said to me, "none of these three are underlined."

"What do you mean 'underlined'?" asked Hunt.

"It's not important," I said, "only that we underlined the people that we had to see here. Mr Lorimer, here, suggested we talk to you. Since you have met the three Eridanian leaders we were talking about, we thought perhaps you might be able to give us a clue about where we could find them."

Hunt mentioned that Draco had enticed a girl to join him for dinner; maybe she would know.

"Well, only if she succumbed to his enticement," Emma pointed out drily.

"I think she did, actually," he replied.

"Then let's talk to her," Emma said.

Lorimer picked up the phone and asked for Jenny. Emma showed me the list again; Jenny Simmons' name was underlined.

Jenny was a pretty girl, of about twenty-five. She looked extraordinarily pale, as if all her blood had been drained from her body. She looked around uneasily, as she stood in the doorway.

"Please, come in; come and sit down, Miss Simmons," coaxed Lorimer. She sat herself in a chair near Emma, the only other woman in the room.

"Emma and Mr Akova will ask you some questions. Just try to give them as much information as you can," said Lorimer gently. Jenny nodded obediently.

"Jenny, did you go out with Mr Draco?" asked Emma.

At the mere mention of that dark name, she started with alarm. Her hands entwined, she twisted her fingers anxiously, "Yes," she replied in a small voice. Then she gave herself an almost imperceptible shake and sat straighter, composing herself. Clearing her voice, she answered briskly, "He invited me to dinner. I must admit, I found him rather attractive, you know, in a classical way: tall, dark, handsome…"

"Were you aware that he was not a real human?" I asked her.

"Yes, but it didn't bother me at all, as he explained that he was in human form so it was almost the same. We had dinner somewhere in Soho in a lovely restaurant. Then he invited me home. I wasn't sure I should accept, but then I thought, why not? After all, he had acted like a true gentleman all evening."

"Where was his home?"

"I'm sorry," she bit her lip, looking a little embarrassed, "I really can't say. By the time we had finished dinner, I was feeling rather tipsy. He had a chauffeur driven Rolls. I rather thought we were heading towards the west country. Actually now that I think about it, we were in the car for at least two hours. And we had a few more drinks in the car as well. And he closed the curtains as well, so it was impossible for me to see where we were going. Then he kissed me. I let him, and he kissed me again and again. By the time we had reached his home, I was feeling quite dizzy. When I got out of the car, I saw a huge castle in front of me. I could hardly believe my eyes!"

"A castle?" I was intrigued.

"Yes, a castle. I'm quite sure about that."

"What happened next?"

"We went inside and sat down in the hall. He brought me another drink. When I'd finished drinking, I felt numb. I was unable to move. Then he carried me upstairs in his arms, into a bedroom. I realised now that he was going to take me. I felt so dizzy and helpless; that last drink had been terrible. I couldn't move or resist...yet..." her voice trailed off as she followed her thoughts.

"Yet what?" I asked.

She looked at me squarely in the eyes, "Yet there was this strange feeling of attraction." I shivered, despite myself, at the ease of this sinister seduction.

She continued: "He undressed me and I lay there too weak to move, and he made love to me. It was extraordinary; ghastly but mesmerising. I was absolutely shattered by the morning. Then he started to kiss me on the neck. It was more of a bite than a kiss. I was able to push him away by then but not before his strangely sharp teeth had pierced my skin. I didn't really have the strength to stop him. Then he told me his chauffeur would take me home. I never saw him after that."

"Clearly, vampire habits die hard," Emma commented with a wry smile, "but Jenny, when did all this happen?"

"Two weeks ago," she said, looking worried.

"Well, my dear, I think you will have to go for treatment now," said Emma gently.

I explained to Jenny that she would become a normal person after special medication. Two weeks was too short a time for her to become a full vampire. The spreading of the plague of vampirism in England was the last thing we wanted. But Draco had chosen Jenny to initiate the contagion. Thank God, there was a definite cure for cases such as this in today's world.

"I think we had better make a list of all the castles in the west country," I told Emma. "This is the only clue we have. But I have a feeling that this place is somewhere in Wiltshire."

The rest of the day was spent interviewing more people who were considered vulnerable, but they turned out to be untouched by the evil which had possessed others.

I chose Marlborough as a base for our stay in Wiltshire, in a large house just outside the town. Once we were settled in, I examined the list of castles in the county. None of them fitted Jenny's description. We visited a couple during the day, only to find that Draco had been neither seen nor heard of in those parts. I knew, of course, that he had the power to create images and then make them disappear within seconds. The castle Jenny had described was probably just such as image, created for that particular occasion. Such was the way of the devil. The growing number of pseudo humans was a clear and open danger to all. And I knew we would encounter some of them here in Marlborough. We had our shields on all the time. The first place to visit was the Green Dragon, a large pub in the High Street, at lunch time.

Marlborough is a small town. But even in a small town we had to look in all the pubs and restaurants. I had a picture of Draco taken during my few days in Whitby. Indeed, it wouldn't be very difficult for anyone to identify this tall, good looking mystery man. Suddenly, it occurred to me that Draco was capable of changing his persona, his identity and physical body instantaneously. Furthermore, we had no idea if he would be alone or with his two deputies, De Medici and Gonzaga. We had to look for strangers who had bought or rented houses somewhere in Wiltshire. This was a daunting task, as Wiltshire is the fourteenth largest county in England.

Emma and I sat glumly planning our strategy: "I suppose the best place to start would be the estate agencies. We could ask them to tell us which houses have been sold or rented during the past month or so."

"Good thinking," said Emma.

The first estate agency was the largest in Marlborough in the High Street. Lumberts specialised in houses mostly in and around Marlborough, but the Director, Mr Pawson was very cooperative.

"Of course we do have some properties outside Marlborough," he told us, "say, within a radius of ten miles. Some gentlemen were interested in one of them about eight miles to the west," he smiled astutely, "in fact, I think we have three gentlemen there you'd be interested in interviewing."

"You say they are dangerous people, Mr Akova, shady characters who would jeopardise the security of the country. So," he concluded with a smirk: "I regard it as my duty to help you in your investigations."

He rose abruptly, "Come with me," he ordered, and glanced in Emma's direction, "you, too, young lady," and Emma obediently rose, walking ahead of me. Mr Pawson led the way into another room behind his office. We entered and the old door slammed behind him, the chains rattling. This was quite extraordinary. For a moment, I thought we had entered another dimension. Or perhaps we had moved a hundred years or so back into a Victorian past. The room looked ancient.

At first, it made no sense, but then Mr Pawson explained: "There were some people in the street, whom I wanted to avoid. I did not want them to see you."

"Why?"

"Mr Akova, these people have been asking question."

"About what?"

"About strangers such as you asking questions," he said. "They said they were from the local police."

"So, all the better." I said, "Perhaps they can help us in our investigations as well."

"Well, I don't know," said Pawson doubtfully, "I don't think they are from the local police."

"Why not?" asked Emma.

"Well, this is a small town and I've never seen them here before. They look like complete strangers."

"Or they may just be new here," I suggested. "One way to find out is to call the police and ask someone you now to come here. He will be able to identify them if they really are from the police."

"I think I'll do just that," he said, looking into the shop from a hole in the wall. "There, you see? They are talking to my assistant."

Mr Pawson telephoned the local police and asked for a Mr Trender. He spoke to someone and then hung up.

"Mr Trender will be here shortly."

"Mr Pawson, this room…"

"I know, I know…" he interrupted, "you are wondering why the Victorian décor. Well, it's not imitation—it's the real thing. These are original pieces of furniture from that period. Our company is over a hundred years old. We decided to keep this room as it was originally back in the 19th century in memory of our founder. Mr Jack Lumbert."

He looked out again through the spy hole in the wall. "OK. Mr Trender is here. Now we can go out," he said.

As we approached Mr Trender, the two men were still talking to Mr Pawson's assistant. They had not seen us and apparently, they did not know Mr Trender who confirmed that they were not from the local police.

"Why do you claim to be from the local police?" asked Trender of the two men, who were standing near the counter.

Suddenly, all hell broke loose as the two men pushed Trender to the floor. They took advantage of the few minutes' panic in the shop to flee. They jumped into a royal blue jeep parked just outside and drove out of the High Street. Mr Trender had not expected that kind of response. He got up immediately and called the station, giving descriptions of the car and of the men. It was our first day in Marlborough, our first visit and already we had witnessed something of an incident. It flashed through my mind that these men had known of our arrival beforehand, and had followed us into Lumbert's. But I discarded the idea. Mr Pawson invited us into his office to dispel the unease created by the incident. He was assiduously polite.

"Mr Trender, Mr Akova, madam, please, let me order you some coffee."

We all sat in his office. Mr Trender seemed a congenial man, and Emma explained to him our reasons for being there.

"Well, I can tell you, there have been some strange characters in our town lately. Complete strangers. I met some of them through some friends in social gatherings. They are not the normal tourists we usually get. We have plenty of those coming from London during the festival season. I've read a lot about aliens, but I can't be sure. Tell me, Mr Akova, could these strangers really be aliens?"

"They could well be. We know for a fact that there are many amongst us in human form."

"Another think I can't understand is this. How could a vast organisation like the EU fall into the hands of these aliens?"

"Well, research tells us that there has already been an alien presence in Europe for a much longer period than we realised."

Just then, a very attractive young woman walked into the office. Mr Pawson got up immediately to greet her. He introduced us and offered her his chair. Mrs Collins told him she had come for the mansion in Marlborough. At first, I had thought she was a customer, but Pawson corrected my assumption: "Mrs Collins has an estate agency as well," he told us, handing her the leaflet about the mansion.

She was standing beside me, her scent lingering in the room.

"Are you looking for a place in Marlborough?" she asked me.

"Yes and no," I replied cryptically.

"That's interesting. You must come up and see me some time," she said, handing me her card…Minutes later she left.

Mr Pawson was simple and unpretentious, neither pompous nor ostentatious. He was a modest man.

"You should go and see her as well," he told us, "she is divorced and now lives alone. Quite young, in her early thirties, I think—a very independent woman."

We said goodbye to Mr Pawson and left Lumbert's. Mr Trender accompanied us to our rented car. Our next stop would definitely be Mrs Collins's estate agency. We drove around Marlborough looking for it, and I had to ask for directions from a pedestrian.

"Take the first right turning, and then the second turning on the left. This is a long road with a forest towards the end of it. That's where you'll find Goreham's Lodge."

Goreham's Lodge was a large mansion standing on its own on a hill surrounded by a forest. I got out of the car and rang the bell at the gate.

"Mr Akova," a woman's voice which must have been Mrs Collins's was heard under the small screen pointed straight at us, "what a surprise. I didn't expect you so soon."

"Well, here we are," I smiled—for the benefit of the camera.

The gate opened automatically and I drove the car into the estate. When I parked the car outside the large building, two men in black approached.

"Please, come in," said one of them politely and we entered the mansion. The shadowy interior of the building struck me a somewhat strange. This was a sunny day, but it was dark inside.

Mrs Maureen Collins was a beguiling redhead and very much aware of her attractions.

"Why so dark in here?" I asked.

"Oh, I've just moved in, believe it or not. I only bought the place a couple of days ago. I decided to move my offices here as well. In fact, the cleaning women are coming today, so I've drawn the curtains across for them to steam clean them. Please follow me," she told us, and led us into another room off the hall, which was much lighter. "This is better," she said, turning to us with a smile, "there's lots of sun in this room."

"Oh, this is very pleasant," I agreed.

"Well now, Mr Akova, when I asked where you were looking for a place, you replied 'Yes and no'. What did you mean by that?"

"Simply this. We have already rented a house in Marlborough. We want a list of the strangers who have bought houses in the vicinity. We want to interview them."

She looked as us both suspiciously. "You are not with the police, are you?"

"No. In fact, we are with the UFO Research Centre in London. Emma here is the director. I am a researcher. I am sure you know about alien presence in England."

"Yes, indeed I do. I think that's most exciting. I have read a lot about them in the papers. Is it true they have cures for cancer and AIDS?"

"Yes, they do—but these aliens, these Eridanians, have only one aim: to dominate the world and turn mankind into slaves. Britain is now fighting for its life. The EU has fallen. It's under their control. This has had a crippling impact on the rest of the world. We are, I suppose, also agents of the British government. The findings of our research tell us that the leaders of the Eridanians are somewhere in Wiltshire. In fact, Wiltshire is for some unknown reason very important to them. We are trying to find out why."

"Well, I must admit there has been rather an influx of strangers enquiring about property in this vicinity. I'll give you a list of those who applied to my agency. Perhaps that will be of some help."

"Definitely," I said gratefully, "In the meantime, try not to get involved with any of these strangers. They are nasty pieces of work who use methods beyond any rational comprehension—they are dangerous."

She frowned, "Now I'm worried. How do I keep them away? How should I tackle this problem?"

"Just tell them you have nothing for sale at the moment. We'll think of something more specific later on." I told her.

We had to wait for Mrs Collins to print out a list of the buyers from her computer as her secretary had not yet moved into the new premises. I explained to Mrs Collins how Wiltshire had become the centre of UFO activity during the last few months. Accumulated evidence all pointed to an undeniable presence of extraterrestrials in Wiltshire.

There were seven more estate agencies in Marlborough, and over the following three days we visited all seven of them, and discovered four sales in Marlborough. The first two were not local residents, but lived on the outskirts. These were normal customers merely buying new homes there. But the other two were large mansions bought by a Mr Tom Ormond. The two homes were just a hundred metres from each other in a secluded area in Marlborough. The director of one of the agencies, Milton & Co, told us that Mr Ormond had paid something like 2.6 million pounds in cash for them. We took her address and drove to the property. The first house was empty, and we walked to the other and rang the bell. These two mansions were vast; I had had no idea that there were so many of them in Marlborough. A man in his thirties opened the door.

"Mr Tom Ormond?" I asked.

"Yes, how can I help you?"

"We are government agents. We would like to ask you some questions." I said.

"What is this about?"

"We won't take too much of your time," said Emma.

"Please come in," he said reluctantly, obviously uncomfortable with our presence in the house.

"We are investigating extraterrestrial presence in Wiltshire, and Marlborough is our first stop." I said.

When he said he knew nothing about extraterrestrials, his face became strained. The outright denial of any knowledge of aliens did not convince me at all. So I asked the next question.

"You have bought these two large mansions. Are you going to live here alone? Why did you buy both these houses? One can surely accommodate a family or even more than one family."

"Wait a minute," he said, reddening in protest. "I don't have to answer all these questions."

"Oh, I'm afraid you do," I said softly, "you see, we are not ordinary government agents. We have been chosen as special agents to investigate this extremely important matter; chosen by the Prime Ministry and the MoD. So you can safely assume that we have special powers. We can, in fact, take you to the police for questioning. We can also search the house without a warrant. So, I'm afraid you have to answer our questions now."

"OK, OK," he sighed, "I'll tell you what I know. I was given the money and instructed by a man named Draco in London."

Now we were getting somewhere, I thought.

"Where, in London?" I asked.

"In a house in Carlton House Terrace."

"Which one?"

"No. 1."

"Wait a second! That's where an FPA man in uniform is on duty around the clock to give the key of the Foreign Press Association to members."

"Well, I don't know about that. It was just the place I met Mr Draco. He gave me an open cheque, plus two hundred thousand pounds for my trouble."

"Did he say he was coming to live here?"

"No," said Ormond, "but he did ask me to have both houses cleaned and ready for guests who would be arriving here in the coming weeks."

"Have you been contacted by anyone else while you were here?"

"No."

"OK. Let me tell you this. You will be watched 24 hours a day. You will contact us the minute someone walks in through that door. If you don't do what I tell you, you will be in great trouble. Now, do you understand that."

"Yes," he said meekly.

I left Tom Ormond my address and telephone number in Marlborough and we left. The next day, I sent a specialist to both houses when Ormond was not in and put a tap on the telephone lines in each house. Draco, De Medici and Gonzaga did not need to act in secrecy. In fact, they were openly campaigning for a take-over in Britain. But the elusiveness of the three men was the bulwark against their enemies. They could appear and then disappear at will. UFO activity heightened in Wiltshire, and especially in Cradle Hill, Warminster, Marlborough and Stonehenge and it left its indelible impression on the area as a whole. There was something which drew the Eridanians to this area in particular.

Perhaps Cradle Hill or even Marlborough—or both—held the primary key that would unlock the mystery behind the Eridanian choice of Wiltshire. Where was that key, though, and what was the mystery? The Eridanians made it clear that the old order must be swept away. Their new order was full of promises of immortality. I felt that a physical and forceful invasion of Britain was imminent. Scientists who had done research in Wiltshire for a long time insisted there were energies there that could be defined as evil. These dark forces wreaked havoc with the whole system of individuals. These evil energies were in the soil of Wiltshire. It made sense. Otherwise, why would the Eridanians use the Wiltshire landmarks? What was so vital about their landing places there? The scientists claimed all these places must have been energised or else they had been brought back into operation by a complex plan.

It was true that all activity revolved around various centres in Wiltshire. Namely, Marlborough, Cradle Hill, Warminster and Stonehenge. But what did this evil force mean? Was this the power they needed on Earth? But no scientific application, no new scientific findings could untangle the web. The only clue we had to finding this invisible evil lay in the soil of Wiltshire itself, which could well have been contaminated by the Eridanians centuries ago. The scientists were working on that.

So, Draco had bought two large mansions on the outskirts of Marlborough. Why would he have done that? Was Wiltshire the base of the Eridanians that I had been seeking? Did they really need the energy that was stored in the soil? The scientists had found this energy in these four centres. I telephoned the MoD and asked them to keep a 24 hour watch on these centres. Not just UFOs but any unusual activity would be reported back to me.

I wondered how Draco and his armies would react to such a close watch on these four sites. I knew, however, that even though we may take the most stringent measures, they were capable of removing their energy sources elsewhere—unless they knew something that I did not, a secret that would keep them in Wiltshire. One thing I had observed about the Eridanians was that they never followed me around during my investigations. I could always hide and listen. This was perhaps the oldest game in the book, but I had to try. We had already left our contact details with Ormond. This meant that Draco would know where we were. We could expect a surprise visit at any time. Like good boy scouts, we had to be prepared...

We not only had to fight the Eridanians but the vociferous, critical and acid attacks from the intellectual elite. The public was stupefied by the magical yet diabolical wonders of the alien civilisation. They could not believe the impossible achievements the Eridanians had already accomplished. A cure for cancer and AIDS and the promise of immortality: these appealed to them most of all. On the one hand, the British government and the UFO Research Centre in London were warning them of the ultimate domination over mankind, of enslavement, and on the other were the Eridanian-controlled organisations and the British population was overwhelmed with enthusiasm. This triggered a crisis in which at its height the future of mankind was held in the balance.

It would be a calamity if the tide was to turn in the Eridanians' favour. While we sat in our rented house in Marlborough, Emma looked through the latest results of the scientific findings.

"The energy from the soil covers a wide area. By the way, there have been no reports of UFO landings in those areas during the last week or so. I wonder why there is a lull in their activity…"

"I don't know, Emma. But I've made up my mind. I'm going to go to the houses Draco bought, to try and find out more."

The narrow lane leading to the rear of the houses was an ideal spot to park the car. I found a turning into a field and parked the car behind the trees. The first house was about a hundred metres from the car. I remembered a similar occasion when I had been attacked by a Doberman and had to escape by climbing a wall to safety. So I had to be wary about the possibility of dogs guarding the house. No dogs, thank God…I pulled at the old fence enough to provide room for me to enter the garden. Then I hid behind a tree and watched the house. It was a cloudy, cool spring evening.

This was the house Emma and I had visited earlier on during the day when we first met Ormond. There was no movement and it was dark inside. The wind whispered through the bushes near a window as I crawled on the lawn towards the large building. Suddenly, I heard the sound of a chopper. The light from the helicopter illuminated the lawn. I had enough time to throw myself behind a tree very near the wall and the bright light from the chopper missed me by a few seconds. The devils had arrived. I could not see who they were, but the towering figure of Draco was unmistakable. Four people, including Draco, entered the old building through the back door. Almost immediately, the lights went on and I could see the inside of the house. I had to get in somehow.

I tried a small door to the left. It was unlocked. When I opened it, I could see stairs going down to the basement. As I descended them, I could hear a heavy thumping noise coming from above. I stopped and then I edged as far as I could into the dark room. What was that noise? It was impossible to tell. I don't know what it was used for, but in the pitch darkness the room seemed to me to be empty. I pulled out my small torch and walked around the room trying to find a way out. I was confronted before long by the stairs again, and when I climbed them, a thin line of light appeared in my vision coming from under the door. I listened and waited just to make sure three was no one anywhere near the other side of the door.

As I had been in the house during the day, I guessed that this door would open up to the left side of the large hall. I was right. I squeezed past another door which led into a long corridor. I heard people talking in the hall. I crept through the doorway and on to the end of the corridor. I saw the windows with their drawn curtains on the left. Slowly, I slipped behind the curtains. Luck was once again on my side. As I moved to the right, I saw a large glazed door and I moved behind the curtains there. The curtains were long enough to cover my whole body down to my feet. The place where I stood was fairly dark which suited me just fine. I could see the four men seated in the hall. Instinctively, I parted the curtains a little, just enough to see them all.

"What the hell is this?" Draco was fuming, "this man Akova had the audacity to come into my home? Why? Do you think he knows our secret in Wiltshire? Why can't we get rid of him? He's been causing problems throughout our mission on Earth. And now he's in Wiltshire because he suspects something."

"They think we get our energy and power from the soil here and at Stonehenge, Warminster and Cradle Hill. Their scientists found something in the soil…an energy…and—"

Draco interrupted Gonzaga full flow: "Let them think that. They are on the wrong track. Ormond, make sure Akova is at home and blast him to pieces. That's the only way. We must finish him off now."

"Yes, sir," said Ormond obediently, and got up to go.

"No, no…Wait a second. Not yet. I want to play with him for a little while longer," said Draco.

"But you said he was dangerous. Would it be wise to let him live?" asked De Medici.

"I want to find out more about his power. He seems to be invincible. Clearly he has Grey power. You see, I encountered him once in Whitby. He knew how to attack and defend. This is very unusual in humankind. Mankind is normally helpless against the extraterrestrials. Humans are an insignificant race. But this man Akova appears to be an exception."

I wondered how he would 'play' with us. But whatever he planned, it was bound to be nasty. Extraterrestrials in human form always spoke in English. The conversation which lasted about half an hour ended suddenly when De Medici, Gonzaga and Ormond retired. Draco sat for a while and then walked into another room. This was probably the study. The door was open and I could see him through the thick curtains. He grabbed a bottle on the bar, and started drinking. He emptied it in a few seconds. That was quite unusual. Minutes later, he left the study and went upstairs. Then the lights were turned out. I waited behind the curtains for another twenty minutes, just to make sure there was no movement in the house. Then I peeped into the study. The fire was still burning in the grate. I looked at the empty bottle in the firelight. It was an ordinary whisky bottle. Then I saw identical bottles in the bar. I took one and left.

At home, Emma was waiting for me, and I told her of my secret mission into one of Draco's houses.

"What's the bottle?"

"Draco drank it in one go. He finished the bottle in ten seconds. That's interesting, don't you think?"

"Why?" asked Emma.

"He seemed pepped up afterwards."

"So you think there is some sort of energy in that drink?"

"Maybe. I think we should have it examined."

"I thought energy from the soil in the three sites made sense and that's where they sucked their energy from," she remarked.

"Apparently not. This is the find of the night. It's important. Draco was talking to De Medici and the others, and he said we were on the wrong track. So this means their energy comes from somewhere else. Perhaps the drink?"

"Yes…maybe…" Emma seemed rather disappointed. "But we are back to square one. We still don't know why they are here in Wiltshire."

She was right. Why were they here? Was this a secret invasion of the country? An alien incursion? Surely, UFO activity in Wiltshire had something to do with alien presence here. But what? Or did Eridanian presence have something to do with the Grey UFOs landing in Wiltshire? Did the Eridanians really need some sort of energy to survive on earth? What I had witnessed in Chateau Villeneuve suggested they had gathered around once in a while to get energy from their UFOs. But nothing was certain. The more I investigated, the more I realised there was nothing to stop them.

Emma seemed desperately unhappy. Although the British government supported our efforts to continue the investigations, there was little they could do with the current technology in Britain. The USA, on the other hand, with the most powerful technology available to them, did not intervene. They just watched the events in Europe and Britain and waited. But for how long?

"You know what, Emma?"

"What?"

"I think the US government should be warned. If Britain falls, the whole European continent will be under the control of the aliens."

"You say if Britain falls. What chance do we have against them? None whatsoever. The Americans? Yes, let's warn them. But do you think they'll finally decide what to do?"

"I think they will." I said firmly.

We had to make sure that the report we sent reached the President himself. So we sent it by hand to the CIA chief whom we'd met some time ago. I also asked the British Premier and Defence Minister to appeal to the President.

"Let's go and meet the three devils, Emma," I suggested.

"Why not?"

I telephoned Draco's hose. I asked Ormond whether we could visit Draco in the evening. Ormond said he would call back in five minutes. He did and said, "Mr Draco will be expecting you at around 9.30 tonight."

I put a shield on Emma too and we drove up to Draco's house at the stated time. This would be an opportunity to talk to Satan. After the fight in Whitby when he fled, this would be our second meeting, but this time we would sit down and talk like civilised men. Quite frankly, I had not expected him to accept my offer of a meeting. But he had. What could I possibly hope to achieve from it. Nothing. But meeting the devil in person would be the experience of a lifetime. I had no intention of pleading for mercy. The Greys' advice had always been to challenge the devil. That was what I wanted to do. There had been no sign of any movement from the Greys yet, and Tamor had disappeared quite without trace.

The possibility of an Eridanian/Grey extraterrestrial war on planet Earth was a colossal menace. Such a war would probably destroy earth civilisation. But there had been no word from the Greys as yet. No sign of any presence at all. Efforts to contact them had proved fruitless in the recent past. They had promised to help mankind in the past. At this critical stage in the history of the world, I simply did not understand what they were waiting for. Whatever…I was still confident enough to challenge the might of the devil. I was equipped with Grey power!

This was my third visit to Draco's house. But it struck me as rather odd that we would find him so easily. After all, we had just started our investigations in Wiltshire. Maureen Collins was the estate agent who had sold two houses to Draco. Was she really an estate agent? Or had she been collaborating with Draco? I suspected everyone. After all, there were so many Eridanians or Eridanian controlled humans nowadays in every part of Britain.

If she were a collaborator, why would she want us to find Draco? Perhaps Draco had been informed of our arrival and wanted to meet us and had instructed Mrs Collins to give us his address. If that had been the case, then why would he have wanted to meet us? After all, he was still in a precarious position in Britain. He knew the British government wanted to keep them out. Therefore he tried to keep a low profile and no one had any information about his whereabouts. So why the sudden change? Was he now ready for the final move in Britain? Was there a new development giving him the upper hand in this country? Why had he chosen Wiltshire and Marlborough in particular as his headquarters?

We were met at the door by Ormond. Inside the house, De Medici and Gonzaga greeted us with extreme politeness. We followed Draco's two deputies into the hall. Surprise, surprise…there was Maureen Collins with Draco. They both got up and walked towards us. Draco stood tall as always. He looked quite relaxed and smiled. "At last, we meet again, Mr Akova," he said, shaking my hand, "Miss Fitzgerald, I have heard so much about you. Welcome."

Emma was perplexed and did not say a word. We all sat down near the fireplace.

"Mrs Collins, I did not expect to see you here," I said.

"Well, Mr Draco is a client and I have to make sure that everything is in order. We have to sign some documents. Mr Draco was kind enough to invite me here," she said, "what about your investigations? Any new strangers buying homes in Marlborough?"

What kind of question was that? She probably had no idea who she was dealing with. Draco simply smiled. There was complete silence for at least a minute. Realising she had said something she should not have said, Mrs Collins slowly raised herself from the armchair next to Draco and prepared to leave.

"I am sure you have private matters to discuss. So I had better go," she said, "see you soon, I hope. Don't hesitate to call if there's anything I can do for you." She walked quickly to the door and left.

"Now we can talk," I said.

"Would you like some coffee?" Asked Draco, "I must say, it's a wonderful drink. My favourite hot drink here on Earth." He ordered Ormond to bring some.

"Now, ask away, Mr Akova."

"Why do you want to do this?" was my first question.

"Why do I want to do what?"

"To take over Britain." I answered.

"'Take over' is the wrong expression. We want to bring forth a much higher level of life to humankind. We are one of the most advanced, what you call 'extraterrestrial' civilisations in the Milky Way Galaxy. We are one of the Galactic masters and we want to transform mankind into a civilisation of peace and tranquillity."

"What you really mean is transform mankind into a subservient people," I said.

"Wherever did you get that idea, Mr Akova?"

"Your people rule over the whole of the European Union. Why Europe?"

"Europe is the cradle of Earth civilisation. The region where scientific research began. Of course, other continents have their points, but Europe is way ahead in scientific research."

"Surely you know that the USA is the superpower in the world. Their technology is far more advanced than any of the technologies in Europe."

"It's not just the space technology that we are interested in. The most powerful country in the world…that they are. That is exactly the reason why we decided Europe would be the very best place to start. The Americans would have reacted violently to our presence. Whereas the Europeans are much more flexible. I'm sure you observed how they embraced our civilisation in a short period of time."

"Embraced? Surely you mean they were forced to accept. By the time they realised who you were, it was too late."

"And who am I, Mr Akova?"

"Everyone knows who you are and why you are here."

Draco thought for a moment. He made a small whistling sound through his lips and answered: "You mean I am Satan. And we, from Epsilon Eridani are the

Devil's civilisation. Man has feared the devil so much over the centuries. The devil is an extraterrestrial being, and Satan's armies are here on Earth to conquer and rule," he said, with a devilish smile on his long face. "Mr Akova, no one believes that story anymore."

"The Greys know it. They will arrive soon."

"Mr Akova, I doubt that very much. Even if they did come here to Earth, they don't have the power to defeat us."

"How can you say that! The last time I saw a clash between your people and the Greys, you fled."

"On that particular occasion, our UFO was not fully equipped to take the kind of action that would take the Greys by surprise. That's why we fled…" he paused for a moment and continued: "You are waiting for the sons of light to come and save you from us. They will never come. Your deficient human minds have already been weakened by the magic of our power."

"You say you'll help mankind advance to a higher plain. How do you propose to do that?" asked Emma.

"Miss Fitzgerald, thousands of people have already been cured of cancer and AIDS. This is just the beginning. Mankind will have immortality, just as we do. The new system will guarantee very high incomes for everyone. There will be no talk of the economy. One currency will circulate throughout the world."

"And you will be in charge, naturally," I chipped in.

"Naturally. We are the only ones who can stop a nuclear holocaust on Earth. We are offering you the Golden Age with Eridanian extraterrestrial civilisation."

"No. You are offering us nothing but slavery to the devil."

"Mr Akova," Draco sighed, exasperated, "we are a vastly superior civilisation. You don't have either the power or the technology to challenge us. So, it goes without saying that we rule over inferior beings. Man has to look within himself to find the truth. With us, the human race will achieve mental and spiritual abilities unheard of until now. They will come to understand cosmic and universal intelligence."

"I found your 'feathers' in North Cyprus. And now, look what has happened!"

"I know," he said with some sympathy, "you feel guilty about it all. That you have brought all this upon the world. You don't have to feel like that. We would have come anyway."

"But what about the Americans? They will probably strike soon."

"If they do, the whole American continent, north and south, will be destroyed. They stand no chance against our superior weapons."

"But what about the Grey power and technology that the Americans acquired after the 1947 UFO crash in New Mexico?"

"Yes," he said, "we know they have developed on that very technology, but we are dealing with that threat. If you can call it that. Our people in America are working on it."

"So you also have people in the USA?"

"Of course, we do, Mr Akova. When we are ready, we'll take America as well. Then Asia, Africa, Australia and all the rest of them."

"What about Turkey and North Cyprus?"

"Oh, yes, they are both outside our influence at the moment. But their time will come."

Draco's plans for the world seemed far-fetched. Nevertheless, the Eridanians had proved they were capable of transforming the whole European continent. This they had done with a lively physical and spiritual energy and skill. True, the European leaders had not offered much of a challenge and the Eridanian intrigue and complicated evil strategies simply carried them through with the greatest of ease. Interestingly enough, there had been very few violent incidents throughout the domination of the EU.

When we left the mansion, I could not help wondering why Draco had let himself be found so easily. After all, despite his over-confidence regarding Eridanian power as opposed to that of the Greys, he knew full well that I and the Chosen 36 as a whole formed the nucleus of the resistance against them. We had the power to stop them and gain time. I had to find out why Wiltshire had become the all-important centre for the Eridanians. This was the reason that had prompted me to start a new investigation. At first, they destroyed the political establishments, then the whole of the EU member states suffered a sudden collapse of their social structures.

Those humans who had been transformed by the evil Eridanians were now wicked. They would abide by the rules of the Devil. These evil beings would control those humans in the same city or country and their lives would change radically. Now there were devils lurking in the shadows all over Britain. The evil ones worked in harmonious dedication to lead the masses to doom and damnation. People lived in stark terror. The devil was here in this country—or city or town or village, or in one's home—and there was nothing that could be done to stop it.

A combination of the fear of the devil and expectations of a life with none of the familiar problems of mankind was very attractive indeed, and most of the people were mesmerised by the possibilities offered by such a future. A fear-filled obedience to the devil—that's what it was all about. Surrounded by unbridled wickedness, people were helpless against such enormous evil powers.

There was a sudden upsurge of abductions in Wiltshire. The people who were kidnapped by strangers were eventually returned. But there had been no reports of UFOs during that period. In almost every abduction case, none of those abducted remembered what had happened to them. They were all in a state of trance. This was not like the possession that many people have experienced all over the world. This was a full transformation. But the transformation did not turn them into some obnoxious form. They remained as normal-looking as any other person in the street. None of them could resist or fight the abominable, infernal devil.

The meeting with the great Satan and his two deputies should have been the most important event of the whole episode. Instead, it was an anti-climax. He had made himself available to us shortly after our arrival in Marlborough. It was all arranged. Obviously he had had us followed all the way from London. At any rate, the meeting was quite ordinary. But the human forms of Draco, De Medici and Gonzaga were extraordinary. It was amazing, unbelievable. No one would suspect that underneath the skin of the human form was the devil himself.

Draco cranked out the same argument of humankind advancing to a much higher plane with the extraterrestrial Eridanian civilisation. We all knew, of course, that this would be the end of human civilisation on Earth and mankind would become the devil's slaves. Eridanian controlled people in Britain appeared to get on with their normal lives as before and the Eridanians had succeeded in erasing the robotic behaviour of the transformed. The current strategy of the devil was creating something far more disturbing than mere slaves under Eridanian control. Now there were reports of products of alien insemination. The dismaying vividness of such a development kept creeping into the corners of my mind.

Clearly, our investigations needed a much deeper analysis. But most important of all, our lives were in constant danger. Major Blount made sure our house was under 24-hour surveillance. We had full protection. I also had protection with the aid of the shields. The Wiltshire mystery triggered off another possibility. These creatures must have chosen Wiltshire for a special reason. I remembered my Chateau Villeneuve experience. Draco and all the others had in fact stored energy from the UFO which had landed there. Perhaps there were regular landings by Eridanian UFOs for that purpose, to fill their bodies with fresh energy.

Seven more scientists joined the three who were already in Marlborough. They inspected the grounds for radiation and foreign cosmic energies at all the suspect sites. How do you trace the unknown? These four Wiltshire sites were unquestionably areas where many UFOs had landed. Although we were now able to distinguish between the UFOs of the Greys and those of the Eridanians, who could tell which one was arriving at these special spots, out of the cruel vastness of outer space? One could detect a complete inversion in the findings of the scientists. Lack of transparency was one thing, but second by second, mass changes, physical impossibilities, conversion of DNA to RNA and God knows what else was another. We were up against a universal force. An evil monstrosity…

Twenty-Nine

Mist hovered on the cold, late November evening, while Emma and I walked slowly uphill into a narrow road. Roberto's Bar and Restaurant was about three hundred metres from the house. The dapper Roberto himself and his wife greeted us at the door. I remembered him well from my last trip to Marlborough a year earlier, when I had been performing at the jazz festival. The three hours I had spent at the restaurant then had been quite memorable, as I had been practically manhandled onto the stool of a white grand piano in the corner to play some popular tunes. The musical orgy ended with 'tenor' Roberto singing two arias from *La Traviata*. It had been a smashing evening, with delicious pasta and wine.

On this evening, the place was packed, but Roberto had arranged a table for us near the bar.

"Welcome, Mr Akova," he said delightedly, "It's good to see you again. It's been over a year now, eh?"

I introduced Emma and we sat down. Our neighbours at the next table were three young women—or maybe two young women and a man; it was difficult to tell. Luigi Tenco's *O capito che ti amo*—a beautiful Italian song from the '60s—was playing, and the atmosphere was warm and relaxing. Tenco had committed suicide over an unhappy love affair, but his song lived on to work its magic.

"You will play for us later, perhaps...?" asked Rosalina, Roberto's wife, taking our order.

"Of course, I will," I said, the smiling woman—or was she really a man?—at the table nearest to us catching my eye.

As we were finishing our dinner, Emma's mobile phone rang.

"Yes?"

Then she listened. She mouthed to me that it was Clayton. After four yes's and five 'I see's', the conversation continued for another long five minutes. She replaced the mobile phone in her bag. There was an uncomfortable feeling between us and then she spoke, "Clayton says I must go back to London," she announced finally, "three officials have arrived from the USA. Apparently they have some new findings. The Premier called for a meeting and I have to be there. He didn't want to discuss the matter in any detail over the phone. So I must leave tomorrow." There was regret in her voice.

"Pity. Just when we were beginning to enjoy ourselves."

"We still have some time tonight," she smiled, a little sadly.

But I was truly disappointed. I grabbed her hand and squeezed it passionately.

She responded with a harder squeeze.

"I'm sorry, darling, but I have to be there. You know how it is."

"Yes, well…" I sighed, and then bucked myself up. After all, she was not to blame, "Let's enjoy this evening, anyway. But call me after the meeting and let me know what's happening there," I said.

The person of indeterminate gender at the next table was about to say something, when I got in first.

"Yes, I remember now. We met here, didn't we?" I said. He—for he was a male—looked conspicuous in his pink blouse/shirt and thin white trousers.

"I'm glad you remembered," he said, clearly demonstrating his homosexual tendencies with feminine gestures…I looked enquiringly towards Roberto behind the bar as the man in the pink shirt introduced us to his two lovely companions.

"We can join our tables, if you like…" suggested David. I remembered him as David Cobham and the two young women introduced themselves as Tina and Christine.

"Why not?" I replied easily, and gave a nod of affirmation to Roberto who came forward to join our tables. "What would you like to drink?" I asked.

Emma looked uncomfortable and rather put out, but made an effort to smile.

"Oh, how nice. Thank you. We were drinking white wine."

I ordered a bottle of white wine for them and one of red for us. David who had been sitting opposite me suddenly leaped to his feet and squeezed a chair between Emma and myself. What's this? I thought.

"Dear Emma, you don't mind if I sit next to Mr Akova, do you?" he said ingratiatingly.

"Sure," she replied shortly and moved her chair away to make room for him.

"I know about your investigations," said David with a sinister smile.

"How did you learn about them?" I asked.

"Turan, come on. This is a small town. Maureen Collins told me. She's a close friend. It's very exciting, isn't it? I really admire your courage, you know. Somebody has to discover the facts and reveal the truth, don't you think so, Emma?" he turned to Emma, who was gazing at her wine glass disconsolately. His words were as effusive and admiring as a woman's might have been, his long blond hair fell sleekly at the sides. He looked as meticulously groomed as a winner in a beauty contest, and could have easily been mistaken for a woman.

"Are you really interested?" asked Emma, slightly cynically, betraying her chagrin at having her final evening with me interrupted, "most people don't seem to care one way or another."

"I am more than interested, my dear. I am a researcher myself. And so are these two." He indicated his two companions.

"So now we are five researchers sitting at the same table," I said to David, "do tell me about your experiences."

"Well, the people have many uncertainties about what is happening. So there's still hope. When a person has been taken over by the aliens, he or she is well aware of what is happening. They actually want to rid themselves of this extraterrestrial control over their body, mind and soul. Does that make sense to you, Turan?"

"Yes, it does, and it's a valid point. But mankind is trapped now in an evil web. The Devil is cunning and frighteningly clever. This is much more than super-intelligence. They go back in time, travel into the future, devour the present at will. It's been some time since they took over the media giants of the world. Controlling the internet is one way of controlling people's minds. The search engines of these internet companies have now been re-equipped with extraterrestrial technology. Colossal internet companies are now under the control of the Eridanians. Their declared mission is to make all the information in the world available to everyone. They say they are truly committed to the idea of innovation. But the knowledge they spread throughout the world has changed within days. They are spreading the evil ways of the Devil. I'm talking about a vast, a huge scale infiltration into people's minds. This is what they call global communications. In actual fact, these are the Devil's' laws and they will dominate the whole world. It's a very disturbing and deadly trend. The Devil is everywhere."

"Do you really believe that the origin of these Eridanian extraterrestrials is the Devil himself?" asked David.

"No, I don't. Belief doesn't come into it. I know this is what is happening. I have seen the arrival of the Devil on Earth. There are much bigger storms brewing on the horizon, David. Britain has survived so far, but if we don't find and destroy the power by which they continue to live on our planet, human misery and devastation which is waiting on our doorstep will enter our lives. Their strategy is something of a paradox. One day they appear to be helping mankind, the next, they destroy all values within societies all round the world. But don't be mistaken about their goal. It is the domination of the whole world. The quick stream of information is poisoning the brains of all men. When you go online, what you get is not just information, but evidence, evidence of the power of the devil. Sites are available to anyone. So you can imagine the size of the monstrosity spreading outward like a contagious disease, and infecting the whole world. The so-called internet democracy has become the internet dictatorship…"

David was confused. His two companions looked perplexed. They looked at me with wide eyes. Christine spoke first:

"Is there any hope of finding this power you're talking about and destroying it?"

"There's always hope. The scientists are working on it," said Emma, by now hooked into the subject, her disappointment forgotten. "We may have a breakthrough soon."

"But the problem does not end there. The movements and strategies of these evil extraterrestrials change every time they encounter a challenge. For example, an inexplicable and unprecedented crisis cripples Earth technology. Their tactics are well beyond human understanding." I said.

"What is their weakness?" asked Tina.

"From my personal experience, I can say that, if you challenge them—if you can show them you are not afraid—then you have a chance." I replied.

"But surely, if they are such an indestructible power, they can eliminate any human whether he or she challenges them or not."

"You are right. But they don't seem to be doing that. It's very puzzling. There have been very few deaths and all of these were under mysterious circumstances. Furthermore, the humans who were murdered were immediately reincarnated and re-animated under Eridanian control."

"That's very strange, isn't it, Tina love?" David remarked, still unconvinced about the Devil aspect of it all. Emma looked at me and I knew she had had enough. She wanted to leave.

"OK. Forgive us, but we have to leave." I said, rising from my chair. "Where do you live, David?"

"Just up the road, here. You'll see the sign 'Nightlife' on the gate. It's a large house about half a mile from here." He looked at me questioningly, "Drop in any time, do," he said. We said our goodbyes and Emma and I took our leave.

When we entered the house, I told Emma I had to go out again to try and find out more about this David Cobham and his two associates. As Major Blount had promised, there were four men keeping our house under surveillance. I left the house and walked up hill. I found David's 'Nightlife' and decided to wait behind a tree just opposite the house. I had to wait for half an hour before I heard some noises coming from the direction of Roberto's restaurant. Looking down, I saw David and the girls. I waited for them to enter the house and after fifteen minutes, I moved towards the gate. I was surprised by the absence of guard dogs in the garden.

I reached the back door, and peeped in. There was a blind over the door window, but I had a limited view from the chinks around its edge. To my astonishment, I saw Draco's disreputable form hovering over the three of them. They had appeared to be normal back in the restaurant, but now my suspicions were aroused. I sensed some sort of danger looming over this beautiful Wiltshire town. So far, the evil Eridanian plan had emerged with two striking features. Control of the EU and the whole of Europe, with the exception of Britain, and the creation of an Eridanian/human race by crossbreeding with humans. These features incorporated an extraterrestrial dimension which transcended the earlier visitations, abductions and encounters with UFOs. This was a permanent settlement of an evil, dark force on Earth.

I moved in closer to a rear window. The black clouds this Marlborough night were ideal for my mission. Draco touched David and the two girls one after the other, with both hands on their heads, like a blessing. It seemed like an initiation ceremony. How on earth had they got mixed up with Draco, I have no idea. Or was this their first meeting with the evil monarch of hell? Another thing: I had watched David and the girls enter the house, but I hadn't seen Draco go in. I could not think how he had entered. He must have used his appearing/disappearing facility. I was perilously close to being caught, when

Draco appeared on the porch. He was not instinctively hostile to anyone; in fact, he rather enjoyed toying playfully with we primitive humans. But he was cunning, and how! A super intelligence compared to mankind. I almost buried myself into the ground as the count walked slowly through the garden and then out into the road. I waited for fifteen minutes, and then rang the doorbell.

David opened the door. "Turan Akova! Goodness! What a surprise! Please come it."

"David, I'm so sorry to trouble you at this late hour, but this is urgent." It was indeed late, 1.30 in the morning. And Tina and Christine were in the sitting room. I noticed the reflection of the sitting room in the window pane and the black night beyond, and snapped curtly, "The curtains. We must not be seen from outside!"

"OK, OK, Turan. Relax, for God's sake." He drew the curtains across the windows, "Would you like a drink?"

"A shot of whisky would be nice," I said.

He poured the drink and came back, promptly sitting himself opposite me.

As usual, I thought that honesty was the best policy, and so I started to speak.

"I saw the whole thing. I wanted to come and talk to you about our meeting at the restaurant. You see, I wasn't sure about you. For all I knew, you could be one of them."

"But darling, I am one of them, if you get my drift," he laughed, but his laugh had a hysteric edge to it.

"David, be serious. I'm here to help you."

"How can you help us?"

"Well, in the first place, what did he do to you. He touched your heads. It looked like an initiation ceremony."

"No, no, nothing like that," replied David excitedly, "he said he was measuring the energies in our bodies."

"Where did you first meet him?"

"At Roberto's. He is a good looking, sensitive man and he has a nice sense of humour. He is fun. After you left this evening, he called me on my mobile and asked whether he could pay me a visit, so I said yes."

"David, do you know who he is?"

"I have no idea. Just someone I met…"

"David, he is the Devil. He is Satan, the leader of the Eridanians."

There was a shocked silence and then he threw back his head and shrieked with laughter, "Oh, come on, Turan! The Devil? Satan?" Then he stopped suddenly in his tracks. I assumed he was remembering what I had told them at the restaurant. "I'm sorry, Turan, but the idea of the Eridanian extraterrestrials being a race of demons seems too unbelievable…"

"Unbelievable it may seem, but it is true." I forbore to tell them that Draco was in fact Count Dracula who had arrived in Transylvania almost five hundred years before. Neither did I want to mention De Medici and Gonzaga, also aliens on Earth from centuries earlier. Anyone, not only David, would find such a story ridiculous.

I could no longer differentiate between an Eridanian controlled human and a normal human. This momentarily worried me. But slight peculiarities in a man's behaviour would give him away. There was nothing strange in David's behaviour. As for his companions, they just sat there drinking and listening with awe.

"Are you OK, David?" I asked, "Tina, Christina? You don't have any strange feelings, do you? If so, you must let me know while there is still time to erase them."

"No, no, nothing…" said Christine, getting up and walking towards me with a gleam in her eye.

"I think she likes you," giggled David.

"So do I!" shouted Tina.

"Oooh! Let's have an orgy!" David clapped his hands with delight.

"I have to go now," I said, "I will see you later."

"Promise?" he asked.

"Promise," I said, and left.

The next morning, I drove with Emma to Great Bedwyn station where she caught the train to Paddington. When I returned to the house, I thought a lot about David, Tina and Christine. David with his coquettish mannerisms and quick wit had a great sense of humour. The girls had seemed awkward at first, but David's congenial and extrovert personality seemed to encourage them to abandon their prosaic lifestyle and stuffy morality.

The following day, I had luncheon with Sir Jack Pritchard and his wife. They too I had met a year earlier at the jazz festival. They suggested that membership of the old Conservative Club in Marlborough would introduce me to people who had been long-time residents of the town. The Pritchards had arranged a meeting and the Conservative Club had asked me to give a lecture on alien presence and the potential dangers that lay ahead. Among the topics to be discussed were: the advent of the evil extraterrestrial Eridanians, the fall of the EU, the major economic and political events that were now beyond the control of the EU member states, and the struggle of Britain against the aliens. I wanted to meet as many people as possible.

The lecture was quite unexpected, but with a topic like extraterrestrial presence and the current state of affairs with regard to Britain's complicated and diverse efforts to keep the Eridanians out, there was tremendous interest and I spoke to a packed hall. One thing I noticed during my conversations with members of the Conservative Club after the lecture was that the majority of people living in Marlborough were unaware of the dangers surrounding their beautiful town. I thought it was too early to review any sort of information on the apparent concentration of aliens in Marlborough and in Wiltshire as a whole. This would undoubtedly lead to panic.

"The current situation is best understood by considering the interaction of the players," said the club chairman, a Mr Henry Dankworth. "I take it these aliens have evil plans? How on earth can we challenge them, when we know how superior they are to us in weaponry, intelligence and technology generally? It's a really hopeless situation, isn't it, Mr Akova?" He certainly had a gloomy outlook.

"Not quite," I replied emphatically, "they are, of course, in control of the EU. A further expansion to include Britain and other countries would place into question the fundamental assumptions concerning the common interest and the defence of mankind as we know it. The scientists are working day and night to try and determine the power or energy these aliens need to survive on earth. So far, the findings tell us that they cannot survive on earth for long periods. We still do not know how to deal with this problem. Once we pinpoint their energy source, we can stop them."

The three ladies standing beside the chairman nodded in agreement. Any mention of the Devil was bound to be misconstrued as pure fantasy. Most of these people were of noble descent and were used to glamour and excitement, a kind of razzamatazz and although genuinely interested in what was happening, they would brush aside Satan and his army of demons invading Earth as an absurd suggestion.

"Well," said the lady on my right, "my husband tells me the crunch will come at the end of the month. He says the Americans will intervene."

"May I ask, who is your husband?"

"Sir Adrian Illingworth. He was with the MoD, but is retired now. But he is very much involved and I think he is well informed," she replied with a smile. I made a point of remembering his name. After all, one acquires information when one least expects it. The whole argument of a US military strike was based on the unfounded perception that the scientists working at the secret base Area 51 in Arizona desert had been able to decipher Grey extraterrestrial technology. But I was bothered by another small detail. Maureen Collins, David, Tina, Christina, the chairman of the Conservative Club Mr Henry Dankworth, Sir Jack Pritchard and his wife. These were the people I had met so far in Marlborough, not forgetting Roberto and his wife. I had met Sir Jack and Roberto a year before, so they were exempt from suspicion, for the time being. I wondered whether there was any link between these people. Did they have something in common? With the exception of Henry Dankworth, who had been introduced to me by Sir Jack, it appeared as though my meetings with the others were not exactly arranged, but it was difficult to suppose that they were chance meetings. What could a homosexual, two girls with little knowledge of aliens, and a former MP—now Chairman of the Conservative Club—have in common. Nothing, except perhaps the fact that they live in Marlborough and frequent the same restaurants and pubs. Maureen Collins, on the other hand, should be treated separately, I thought.

Sir Adrian Illingworth's wife invited us all to a party in her house the next day. After the cocktail party at the Conservative Club, I returned home and checked my e-mail. Nothing. I had asked Emma to send me important messages by hand. The Eridanians controlled the internet and they could read all messages. The telephones were probably bugged. I found an envelope which must have been slipped under the door when I was not at home. The message was from Emma. The note read as follows:

Turan,

Scientists here and in Wiltshire have come up with a theory. Actually, I think this is no longer a theory but fact. An Eridanian was seriously injured during clashes with the police. After a week of treatment at the hospital, he was interviewed by the police and gave them information which could be vital. He said the Eridanians cannot survive Earth's atmospheric pressure and density for long periods. They have to leave in their UFOs and join the mothership orbiting Earth. They have to be fully energised n their mothership before they return back to Earth. This does not apply to humans who are under the control of the aliens. Products of cross-breeding are also immune. The American and British governments will decide on a course of action soon. Let me know what you think.

Be good, lots of love, Emma

This was probably the most important development in months. At long last, the scientists had found a weakness in the Eridanians which could be used against them. I did not know how, nor did I have any idea what kind of action the American and British Governments were planning. A military strike on UFOs landing in Wiltshire might spark off an extraterrestrial war on Earth. But both the USA and Britain had the technology to contain their military actions to specific area. A military strike on Eridanian UFOs was one way of dealing with the aliens. The Devil's strategies were always reinforced by their superior technology and unbelievably remarkable appearances and disappearances. One should not lose sight of the continuing elusiveness of the demons. There was always a check on the possibility of a military strike. The imperious behaviour of the aliens and their army of Eridanian controlled men were already permanently entrenched not only in the EU which was now under the control, of the Eridanians, but also in Britain. A major force of evil was now predisposing Britain towards continuing in the direction of the aliens…

Adrian Illingworth and his wife Lorna greeted the guests at the door of the large house in West Marlborough. Actually, the house was a couple of miles from mine. Sir Adrian had said eight thirty. I arrived at eight forty. A couple arrived, while Lorna, who was probably in her early forties, stood at the door welcoming the guests.

"Good evening, Mr Akova. How nice to see you again," she smiled, shaking my hand and pulling me gently inside. She let go as the couple at the door walked in. There were about twenty people in the pleasantly decorated hall. David approached with his inimitable style: "Turan, I enjoyed your lecture," he said.

"I didn't see you at the club," I replied.

"Naughty boy; you were too busy with the ladies!" he smirked.

I looked around. Tina, Christine, Maureen Collins, Sir Jack and Lady Pritchard and Roberto and his wife were all there. Nothing unusual about that, I kept telling myself. After all, Marlborough was a small town and the residents met regularly, I pondered about the possibility of a conspiracy by the five people I had seen with Draco, Maureen, David, Tina and Christina, with the fifth person being Henry Dankworth although I had no reason to suspect him. Perhaps it was his robot-like movements which struck me as rather strange. The mystery was beginning to unravel in my head when a young girl approached me extending her hand.

"Mr Turan Akova, I was at your last concert. What a performance! The fire-breathing intensity of your technique on the piano is amazing. You transformed the audience into another world. I am Linda Evans," she said.

"You spoke like a music critic," I said, taking her hand.

"I am a music critic," she laughed, her hand still resting in mine.

"Pleasant, warm and strong electricity flowing from my body into yours. Can you feel it?" I squeezed her hand.

"My God! It's so strong! Yes, I can feel it. No, no, don't laugh. I'm serious. Who are you? Do you have special powers?" She said all this with fervour and enthusiasm.

"We can leave this party together when everybody's gone. Is that a date?" I asked her.

She nodded, colour flooding her cheeks.

Sir Adrian's party continued until 1.00am and I met at least thirty people. At one point, I got a glimpse of the five talking to each other in a corner of the hall. I looked again, concentrating on the movement of Maureen's lips. I am not exactly an expert in lip reading, but I could read just two words issuing from her mouth: "Tomorrow evening." What were they planning for tomorrow evening? There were several artists in the crowd and we talked about music, films and theatre. It was odd. People did not seem to care. The seriousness of the situation had not yet dawned on them. Their nonchalance seemed abnormal. Such calmness and composure were not completely out of character of the British aristocracy—and there were quite a few of them at the party—but I sensed something much more sinister and cynical about their attitude. I realised that their interest in the subject after my lecture at the Conservative Club was purely for its entertainment value. How could they be so relaxed and jolly with such extraordinary horrific dangers on their doorsteps. Their attitude made my spine creep.

Linda Evans's sexual dimension was blatant from the moment I had met her. She was full of charming sexual suggestiveness. When we went back to her home, which was not far from the church, we had a few more drinks. Her erotic qualities reached a climax when she donned her short white nightdress. The seducing, the kisses, the sureness of her titillating touches were undeniably delicate and delightfully soothing. She was a very beautiful young woman, and we had a wonderful night of sex until the morning. We had breakfast in a pleasantly sunny kitchen. I asked her about my five suspects.

"Do you know any of them well?"

"Maureen is a good friend," she said, "I met David and his two friends recently at the pub. I think David has been in Marlborough for a long time. But the two girls with him seem kind of weird."

"What do you mean?"

"Well, I don't know," she grimaced, "they are total strangers."

"So? What's wrong with that?" I asked.

"Nothing, except that I have a bad feeling about them. They don't say much. One more thing. I have actually seen them exerting strong persuasive power luring two young boys into coming with them to David's house."

"Perhaps David is using them to attract boys for his own sexual gratification." I suggested.

"Perhaps. But I think there's more. Something happened the other day which is utterly impossible to explain. I saw David, Tina and Christina in the pub. They were having lunch. I left and drove straight home. My home is, as you know, minutes away from the Lion's Den pub. There on my doorstep when I looked in the direction of Rockford's Hotel, I saw Tina walking into the Hotel. How could she be in two different places at the same time? Surely this is impossible to explain."

"Perhaps she left right after you and drove to the hotel."

"Turan, it took just five minutes to get home and park the car," she insisted.

"Well, it is very strange, I agree. But you must remember these aliens can disappear and reappear in different places within seconds."

"I'm not an expert like you. But I have read a lot about the aliens since their arrival on Earth. In fact, I've been following recent developments in Britain and I know about you, Emma and the UFO Research Centre in London."

Linda explained that because of her recent investigations into the alien mystery, she had been assigned to interview me and Emma, and find out more about the UFO activity in Wiltshire. She had not been able to attend the lecture at the Conservative Club. But she had been able to follow the increased activism of the Eridanians in Wiltshire. She was here to help as much as she could. She further added that despite the avowed goals of the British government to block the advance of the aliens, the patterns dominating the movements and activities of the Eridanians did not provide us with a clear prediction of what would happen in the near future. I asked her about Maureen Collins.

"I found out that Maureen and the other four are going to do something tonight. I don't know what. Can you help? Could you perhaps ask to meet Maureen this evening? Or could you try and find out what they are doing this evening? Maybe she will confide in you."

"I will try," she said.

"It seems as though Maureen and Dankworth are not Eridanian controlled. Maybe they are unaware of David and his friends' involvement with the aliens. If indeed that is the case."

"You mean you're not sure about the girls? Not even after what I observed?"

"Linda, you're probably right. You can't imagine the kind of trick these devils play on the human mind. When I visited David's house the other evening, Tina and Christine appeared just like any other normal person, despite Draco's visit to the house. Satan and his demons can make you believe some people are fully under their control—whereas they are not."

At any rate, we decided on a strategy for the evening. Linda would go to Maureen's house, and I would follow David and the two girls. Later, I went home and sent a message to Emma by hand with one of the men on duty at my house. I asked her to follow the developments that could lead to a military strike in Wiltshire. A military strike decision would harden the position of the British government. But they had to try and halt the aliens' supply of energy from their UFOs. The whole issue revolved around a number of fundamental questions. The answers would help us evolve a much clearer picture about the nature of the Eridanian reaction should the US and Britain instigate a military strike. Would they retaliate with counter attacks with their superior weapons, or would their infiltration and control over people in Britain abound.

First of all, the basic direction of the Eridanians was in question. Would they become masters of a world which was already hopelessly engaged in averting a final defeat? Would millions of humans become slaves of the Devil and his armies of demons from Epsilon Eridani? Or would they continue on an extremely unpredictable, completely inexplicable strategy of confusion and change?

Secondly, the character of the Eridanians and their aim as an extraterrestrial civilisation was, of course, still a mystery to mankind. Was slavery of mankind an overblown fantasy? Or would their strategy for the future include other unknown components?

The third point was this: would the role of the European-level institutions change drastically? They controlled the EU as a whole. The Euro continued to be the major currency of EU member states. But the finances of the EU were once again controlled by the Eridanians. The aliens had no interest in the politics of the EU. Would they deliberately allow the Commission to shift gradually into an executive body linked to the will of the European Parliament? In other words, would they appear to be helping the EU to become much more powerful, while the Eridanians held the true power in their own hands?

My next question, the fourth, involved the balance between the European institutions. Would decision-making powers remain balanced between the Council of Ministers and the European Parliament? Would national parliaments be brought into deliberations of European-level policies? What would the Commission's future role be?

The EU countries had no available choices. Dominated by the aliens, they simply obeyed Eridanian orders. But they were not given in a dictatorial way. The Eridanians wanted the world to believe that they were here on earth to help mankind move into another, much more advanced phase of development. But the most interesting and unexpected issue of the alien domination was Britain's resistance to it. Applying similar methods, the aliens would have probably eliminated every single barrier to secure full control of the British Isles. But no. The British had survived. This was the biggest mystery of all. The UFO Research Centre in London, Emma, Clayton and all the other expert researchers and myself, we were able to challenge the aliens right from the start. No one could overlook the contributions we had made to repulse the onslaught of the Devil. But things had gone from bad to worse, and Britain and the USA now felt they had no other option but to strike.

But our role as the UFO Research Centre in London was probably a mere detail. I think Britain was a special area for the aliens, and Wiltshire an even more special region. All their efforts were now embodied in that one county. The Eridanian numbers were multiplying alarmingly. There was very little time left before the USA and Britain turned their most sophisticated weapons to the UFOs landing in Wiltshire. Britain had not yet lost or compromised its sovereignty. Nevertheless, the recent upsurge of violence—especially in the London area—dashed the hopes of even those members of the public who had optimistically believed the false promises of Satan. Those who had shown the courage to rise against the Eridanians were being eliminated one by one. A wave of money laundering, fraud, murder, looting and extreme vandalism was sweeping all over the country, and the authorities were unable to hold it back.

That evening, as I headed towards David's house, I noticed there was no moon. Minutes later, I saw about twelve lights appear in the sky moving slowly in formation. Then it started to rain, but the rain was black—I could see it by the light of the street lamp. I took out my torch and examined this black liquid on the asphalt. There were several people running about the street. When I touched and smelled the stuff on the ground, I could not believe what I had found. The twelve bright lights let drop more black rain. They were now only about five hundred metres from the ground. This black rain was petrol and diesel. The whole town was being drenched with petrol and diesel. Balls of fire were now falling from the twelve bright lights, igniting on contact a huge conflagration in Marlborough High Street, spreading from one house to the next. Fire engines appeared, fire fighters were dashing this way and that, and people were pressing themselves into escape routes through narrow paths between buildings as yet free from fire.

Within the hour, the entire Town Hall had been destroyed. The eastern side of the town especially was razed, almost to the ground. The fires raged for at least another two hours before the fire fighters, with the help of military units from the base near Salisbury Plain, brought them under control. There was nothing much I could do, except help people out of the debris. I telephoned Linda to ask whether she had been able to find Maureen. We arranged to meet at around 11.00pm at her house. Yes, she was with Maureen who had invited Linda to join her for dinner at the Rockford Hotel restaurant.

"I may join you there, later." I said, and she hung up.

David opened the door. He looked very shaken. His face was strained, and he stammered something incomprehensible as he pulled me inside. Tina and Christine were both sitting in the living room. Their faces were expressionless.

"Turan!" David exclaimed, "what's happening? This is madness! I went out for a few minutes…it's terrible! Where did all the petrol and diesel come from? Why, for God's sake?"

"The petrol and diesel came from the Eridanian UFOs flying over Marlborough. Petrol and diesel in the form of black rain. I don't understand it either. But David, tell me honestly, what were you planning to do this evening with Maureen Collins?"

"How did you know about that?" was his first response, "we were planning to dine together at the Rockford Hotel. I suppose it will be a late dinner after all this mayhem."

Minutes later, he had recovered his equilibrium and was his old self, desperately trying to push me into the arms of the two girls. Then, all of a sudden, the lights went out. It was most likely a power cut, caused by fire damage.

"Golly," shouted David, "now we move back several hundred years. Love by candlelight…how does that grab you, sexy boy?" It seemed as if he had completely forgotten the terror and confusion outside.

"David, this is no time for play."

Christine approached me and pressing her body against mine, murmured, "But you promised…" and kissed me full on the mouth. I thought it would be best to keep an eye on them for the rest of the evening.

"Come on," I said, "we're going to the Rockford Hotel."

A chubby, middle-aged woman with a big smile led us through into the large restaurant at the rear of the hotel, where we found Linda and Maureen. Linda was a jazz enthusiast and asked the lady to put on some jazz. She brought some CDs to the table. Linda chose the Dave Brubeck Quartet, one of the last recordings with the original musicians with Paul Desmond on alto saxophone, Eugene Wright on bass and Joe Morello on drums. It has been recorded just a year before Paul Desmond's untimely death. Everything seemed normal. Dinner was pleasant. Linda became a bit tipsy.

"Listen to this, Turan. I think you'll like it. Do you know Pushkin?"

"Not very well," I said.

Drink in hand, she recited Pushkin's words: *"Listen, Turan. Here we go. I was born when she kissed me, I died when she left me, I lived for a few weeks when she loved me…"* She stopped, gulping down her whisky, "What can you say about that?" She was now more than just tipsy.

"Nice. Except that if a woman leaves you, you don't die. You simply move on."

"There!" said David triumphantly, "I told you he was special." He moved closer to me, "Stop it...I like it." And he shrieked with laughter. Then he murmured into my ear, "Admit it. Your knee touched mine."

"David, stop this nonsense. I'm not into men."

"Then come to me," invited Tina.

The sexual dares were getting out of hand with each double whisky served at the table.

"So what's happening, Maureen?" I caught her off guard with this sudden question. "What were you planning to do tonight? I mean you, David and the girls?"

"Who, me? Nothing...just dinner. I'm glad you managed to join us." Her response was forced, and I knew she was lying. She was fidgeting nervously. I had drunk four beers and was now on my fifth. I have always been a beer drinker. I excused myself to go to the men's room, down the end of a long corridor. When I returned, Linda, Tina and Christine had gone.

"What's happened? Where are the girls?"

"Linda was drunk, so the girls decided to take her home," said David, bored, and then changed the subject, "but where the hell did all that petrol and diesel come from?"

"From our flying enemies," I said, and turned to Maureen who seemed quite uncomfortable for some reason.

"What's the matter, Maureen? Something seems to be bothering you. Perhaps I can help..."

"I'm worried. I'd better go and make sure Linda's OK," she said.

"She's a close friend, isn't she?"

"Yes, she is."

As we left the hotel, Tina and Christine came running towards us. Christine grabbed me by the arm, crying, "They took Linda. Quick! Call the police!"

I called the police. The girls gave a description of the kidnappers, adding, "The car was a black Jaguar."

"First the petrol and diesel rain, and now Linda is abducted," said Maureen, stunned.

"You had better go home, Maureen," I said. "You too, David. All of you, just go home and stay there."

"Turan, I want to stay. Linda is my friend," pleaded Maureen. I did not have time to argue. David and the two girls left. I wanted to find out about her involvement in this affair, together with David, and the girls. If indeed they had any involvement in it.

"You'd better come with me back to the house," I said, while we walked through the back streets. The fire had been contained. The military were helping the council workers to clean up the High Street and the rest of the town which had been completely spattered with petrol and diesel. Apart from the Town Hall which was in total ruins, only a few houses had been burnt down. What was the meaning of all this? Why would they want to start a fire in Marlborough?

When we sat down back in the house, I had a dozen questions to ask, but I kept quiet for a moment or two, to give her space to frame her thoughts. She spoke first:

"I know you suspect me of having something to do with Linda's abduction. But why would I? Why would I collaborate with people who wanted to kidnap a close friend of mine? I don't understand why it happened." She looked noticeably better after the shock of the incident.

"Maureen, there is no sensible reason behind the actions of the aliens. But I wonder, does this have anything to do with Draco, do you think?"

"Oh, yes," she said without any hesitation, "he said he wanted to see me at David's house. I said OK, and then I called David to see whether he had been informed of my visit. David told me Draco had rung him to say he would be coming to his house."

"Didn't you think of asking him why he wanted to see you all?"

"No," she said, "why should I? After all, I had met the man on several occasions, and I had no reason to suspect him of intending any foul play. He is the most important customer I have ever had. He is buying up a lot of property in Marlborough and in other places in Wiltshire."

"Maureen, have you any idea who he really is?"

"Well, of course I have some idea. But quite frankly, I find it very hard to believe he is actually Satan."

"Maureen, take my word for it: he is. At any rate, the Eridanian extraterrestrial aliens are evil, and their plan is to dominate the entire world. We have documented proof. But let's not go into that now. Just tell me what happened."

"We sat at David's house for at least half an hour. Then Draco left. But I cannot remember what happened during that half hour. Except—now, wait a second—yes…yes…I remember Draco mentioning Linda! But that's all. David, the girls and I, we seemed to be in a trance. It must have been some kind of hypnotic power shrouded in mystical distortions of reality coupled with directions slowly entering my brain and suppressing the rest of my thoughts. I can't remember what happened then. But the end result was that we all agreed that we should go to Rockford's Hotel for dinner. Then you came to the hotel…and, well, you know the rest."

"Why would Draco want to abduct Linda? And why involve Maureen, David and the two girls when he could so easily abduct her from her home?"

Once again, the unfathomable ways of the Devil. I left Maureen and drove straight to Draco's house. By the time I reached it, it was past midnight. The gates were open and I drove straight in. Two men approached.

"I want to see Mr Draco," I said.

"Wait here, please, sir," said one of the guards, while the other went into the house. Minutes later, Draco came to the door.

"What a surprise, Mr Akova. To what do we owe the pleasure?"

"Cut the crap and give me Linda, Draco!" I said.

He winced delicately, "Dear me, such vulgar language…is it really necessary? Who is Linda, anyway?"

"You know who she is. Your men abducted her this evening."

"You are mistaken, Mr Akova. My men have been here at the house all evening, and quite frankly, I have no idea who you are talking about." He stepped back into the hall, opening the door wider, and said: "Here, come in and search the place, if you want to."

There was no point in arguing. I left in a rage, driving as fast as I could towards Linda's house. Maureen, David and the two girls were already there. A police car was parked outside.

"It's OK, Mr Akova," an inspector said, it was Inspector Trender whom I had met earlier when I first arrived in Marlborough. "Miss Linda is safe and at home."

"Thank you," I said gratefully, and hurried inside. Linda threw her arms around my neck and I held her very close. I realised that I had become extremely fond of her in a very short time.

"What happened, Linda? Who were those people?"

"I don't know, Turan. They wore masks."

"But why would they want to abduct you? What did they want from you?"

"I don't know. They took me into a room behind the church. They asked me to keep away from you. They also asked me to stop writing about the extraterrestrials."

"Have you published any articles on UFOs and extraterrestrials in the recent past?"

Linda confessed that she had written two articles on the subject, one published in the magazine *UFOs & Extraterrestrials* and the last one in the *Daily Express*.

"But these articles were based purely on some research I'd done in London. I did visit your UFO Research Centre in London and Emma handed over some valuable information on extraterrestrial presence."

"I see. It's the first time they've threatened someone from the media. And believe me, there are very few left who are outside their control. You are a free-lance journalist and quite well-known, I take it. From now on, you stay with me. When you return to London, contact Emma. I will, of course, organise two bodyguards protecting you at all times. You don't have to worry about anything. I'll make sure no one can touch you. But I want copies of those two articles. Also, try and think back. Might there be any other reason why you were abducted?"

Of course, it was quite impossible to cocoon Linda in security at all times. But she would be safe with me here and with our people in London. This was definitely a Draco operation. He had people working for him everywhere. Indeed, a strange incident. No matter how well-known a journalist she was, I doubted wither her articles on the subject or her research on UFOs would constitute any danger to the Eridanian cause. About an hour later, we went to my house. I had been lucky. My street was unpolluted by the petrol and diesel.

"You can have the bedroom next door to mine," I told her, and tried to coax her into going to bed. She had to rest. But she wanted to talk and have coffee instead.

"How long did they keep you, Linda?"

"Almost two hours."

"English, were they?"

"Well, they spoke perfect English," she said.

"Why did they let you go?"

"They said it was just a warning…"

I refrained from asking any more questions except for one final one.

"Linda, did you feel any change in your physical or mental condition? Did they perform anything like a ritual? Did they touch your head or any part of your body?"

"No, nothing like that," she said. I kissed her and she retired into her bedroom. Although she had enough information about extraterrestrial presence. I sensed she had doubts about the existence of Satan. That was no problem, as I could prove that with bona fide documents. It would be impossible for her not to believe it. I had witnessed the endemic magic of the devil, beguiling people into credulity. The Eridanians could also indulge in mesmeric tactics, but there was no trace that this had happened to Linda.

I must say, I was totally baffled by her abduction. Then again, the peculiar behaviour of the aliens was sufficient in itself to explain their action. After all, the overarching ambition of their plot was the domination of mankind. One might infer from the activities of the Eridanians in England that they had moved on from gradual infiltration into society, to extreme violence, murder and abductions. The main reason behind this change in strategy was probably the knowledge that both the USA and Britain were preparing themselves to attach the enemy wherever they landed. Another new and important development was the eye witness accounts of astronauts who had actually observed a whirling massive UFO fleet ready to descend to Earth. This was definitely a frightening possibility.

In all the institutions of the EU and in some of the British government departments, deception had already been institutionalised. This type of deception surfaced as a result of the Pluralists, who were under the full control of the aliens, having the upper hand in a new European society were globalisation was and would be the basis for much of 'business' in the coming decades. In a seething ocean of extraterrestrial civilisations in the Milky Way galaxy and in other galaxies, the Eridanian devils' arrival was the fate of Planet Earth. And all this time, there was still no word from the Greys.

Thirty

Even if the USA and the UK blasted off several Eridanian UFOs at different landing points, how on earth would they be able to cope with a whole fleet of UFOs now threatening to retaliate? If the Greys arrived to save humankind and Planet Earth, what would be left of this world in the wake of an extraterrestrial war? Detecting UFOs landing in Europe, Britain and in the USA was a daring project and it was not yet fully operational.

The gradual leaking of the myth of immortality preached by the Eridanians made its mark in Britain and many hundreds of normal people had defected to the Eridanian side with the promise of everlasting life. Furthermore, social, political and cultural differences were embodied in the culture and ethos of the Eridanian devils. Their aim to create a closely interrelated pluralistic platform controlling international politics and economics was hugely successful. The whole economic, financial and political structure was now under the control of the Eridanians. But the whole thing was a farce; a pack of lies. The aliens were dominant in every department of the EU. With their extremely powerful technological and military capabilities, the Eridanians dictated their own policies. A mammoth web of deception and disguise gave the masses the impression that the EU was functioning as it had done before the advent of the aliens.

It is interesting to note that the whole of the American continent—north and south—had, over the past sixty years, been the main area of UFO visitations. This was due to the fact that the Van Allen Radiation Belts over South America where there was much less atmospheric pressure were the ideal entry points for all UFOs. And yet the Eridanian aliens had chosen the continent of Europe as the first great chunk of land to capture and bring under their dominion. But this was not an ordinary invasion. It was executed by gradual infiltration by the unspeakably devious tactics of the Devil. In Britain, alien presence had been challenged from the start, and one could argue in favour of the British government and people and complex interdependence. No one could deny the density, the level and strength of interactions between citizens, members of the government, UFO groups and organisations throughout the country, different regions and companies. The role of the UFO Research Centre in London was indisputable as it had publicised the facts of this colossal and most important event in the history of mankind, describing the rapidity of the effects of the evil force in all the countries of Europe.

The vulnerability of humankind was another problem. But the evil extraterrestrial Eridanians' issue based politics comprised of managing natural resources, global inequality (poverty, famine, disease), environment (CO_2 emissions causing global warming and melting icecaps), together with population growth and transnational matters (drugs trafficking, AIDS, nuclear proliferation and pollution). The aliens had adapted themselves to human ways so seamlessly and in such a short time that it was now quite impossible to differentiate them from humans. But I suspected a certain confusion on the part of the Eridanians at the behaviour of the British. The competition and squabbling between several British ministries and other government departments created a complex situation for the aliens. The British attitude and the implementation of various strategies became essentially problematic for the evil forces of Satan. The notion of a separate domestic and international environment disappeared, to be replaced with a cross-cutting view of a world engaged in space politics and extraterrestrial technologies. It is strange, but the island people had somehow disrupted the plans of the Eridanians who had taken over the whole of the EU within three weeks, but who were still struggling to get a foothold in Britain after six months! On paper, the aliens had reached the peak of economic integration and complex interdependence, and coupled with the full control of the media, they seemed to be moving fast towards a final victory over Britain. But in reality, the situation was quite different.

Not just the British government but the scientific community, MI5, MI6, the London UFO Research Centre and many other organisations which did not trust the aliens, provided an all-encompassing focus on the outcomes of the various strategies which had dumbfounded the Eridanians more than once and forced them to resort to violence—not the way of the Devil as far as I could tell from previous experience. The plot of the aliens was simple: bringing humans into their camp and taking them over. But there was much more, a cynical twist: a

307

magic wish granted to man: unending prosperity and an immortal life of pleasure...

At home, I found a letter from London delivered by hand. The two agents watching the house would inspect each and every item sent to my Marlborough address. I went inside, thanking the two men for their excellent work, and opened the letter. It was from Emma.

Dear Turan,

I have been instructed by the Premier to ask you to attend an Extraordinary Meeting to be held in two days. Present at the meeting will be the US Secretary of State for Defence, the CIA and FBI chiefs, the British Defence Minister and of course, the Prime Minister. We have to be there, both of us.

Naturally, the big debate will be on how to distinguish between Eridanian and Grey UFOs. But it also focuses on strikes that will not endanger life in populated areas. Of course, as you suggested earlier, there is another option, which is to postpone the strikes indefinitely and continue the search for an ultimate and effective weapon that will halt the Eridanian domination. At any rate, let me know when you arrive in London.

Love, Emma.

Already, one could hear the tolling of bells warning of a catastrophic extraterrestrial war on earth. The danger was there for all to see. Once the strikes began, the Eridanians would not sit back and watch. They would most definitely strike back. And who would tell where the rapacious demands of alien vanity would lead us? With their unbridled power, the Eridanians could destroy Earth as we knew it.

Emma and I were in the conference room at the MoD, before the others had arrived. To help me out, Emma had written a report, suggesting a postponement of the strikes. First of all, it was still quite impossible to distinguish between Eridanian UFOs and Grey UFOs. Of course, this was a major obstacle. The spacecraft of the two extraterrestrials were similar in shape. My argument was based on this crucial problem.

The others arrived and the meeting started. The American Secretary for Defence talked almost incessantly and a trifle wistfully, but his argument in favour of strikes was shallow and unconvincing.

"We have the technology to wipe them from the face of the Earth," he urged.

The whole debate about the strikes became pointless. The fact that the aliens had not been able to take Britain over in the last six months indicated that there was a substantial obstacle obstructing them from their goal. This invisible and mysterious obstacle was rooted in Britain alone. The British Premier openly supported my idea to postpone any strike indefinitely.

"Mr Secretary, do I take it that the Americans have a new technology superior to that of the aliens?" asked the Premier.

The Secretary replied, "Yes, and no."

In a rare fit of candour, the Premier's response was sharp: "Then why do you keep such vital knowledge under wraps?"

"It's not under wraps. We are still at the experimental stage," was the secretary's answer.

The British Defence Minister punctured the tension with a new proposal: "Why don't you try the new technology in America, while we in Britain wait for a definite result?" The Defence Minister was wearing a crumpled shirt beneath a dark pinstripe suit, and looked pale and gaunt. Nevertheless, he was smiling albeit a little bitterly. He also directed the meeting's attention to Emma and myself: "I suggest we listen to Mr Akova and Miss Fitzgerald here. They know more about the aliens that the whole lot of us put together."

The flamboyant and outspoken American Secretary for Defence sat there, giving me a jaundiced eye.

I started my speech: "We need more time. I can challenge the leaders of the aliens in person. The power which the Greys have given me seems to deter these other aliens in a strange way. This power seems to work on the aliens and checks their movement to take over Britain. It also helps others who want to resist the aliens. So you see, we pose a challenge, and they seem to be confused by the intricate policies of the British government. That is another reason why we should wait. They do not seem to be moving in any particular direction. Our actions are simply holding them at bay. This may appear to be a risible solution for now, but it has worked so far."

Emma's eyes twinkled with vigour, "I have a report here of all our findings and experiences with the Eridanians," she said, "they operate quietly and strictly in the shadows. They enjoy performing their tricks on humans. True, their dark evil is unleashed on humans every once in a while, but when challenged, they back off and resort to other kinds of tricks and strategies. The petrol and diesel rain which started fires in Marlborough is just one of those examples," said Emma.

I chipped in: "The aliens have no intention of starting a war—I am sure about this. They are obsessed with finding their way through the confusion, and I am sure they will resort to other peculiar tactics. I also think that Britain holds a special importance for them for some unknown reason, and I intend to find out why."

After about an hour or so, the Americans continue to express different opinions, but our argument, together with the support of the Prime Minister and his Defence Minister prevailed. The strikes were postponed, but the Americans reserved the right to strike at Eridanian UFOs in the USA. This would be just one or two strikes to see the Eridanian reaction. Personally, I would not take such a risk. After all, the aliens could strike back with all their might. The British were not able to prevent the American decision. It was a controversial issue. But no one could deny that England was definitely especially important for them, and that Wiltshire was the centre of their activity. The few TV stations and newspapers which were still outside the control of the Eridanians were already revelling in the headlines, announcing: STRIKES IMMINENT, and ANGLO-AMERICAN ONSLAUGHT ON UFOs.

My aim was to seek the reason behind alien concentration in Wiltshire. When I got home to Charles Street, something made me remember the information handed to me by a strange character just before I moved to Marlborough. Searching through my files, I found his essay written about the research which he had conducted in Wiltshire. The report said he had found a source of energy unseen and unheard of anywhere in the world. He named these energies the Sama Rays and claimed the Eridanians' source of power lay beneath the ground and on the stones at Stonehenge. Since the arrival of the Eridanians he had been trying to prove his case with on the spot investigations on the grounds of Stonehenge. In pursuit of that goal, he had even dug into the ground at the centre of the world's most famous prehistoric monument.

His name was Brian Haskey. He was a strange scientist and his unorthodox methods of investigations and experiments had kept him out of the scientific community. Nevertheless, his research rested on a theory of extraterrestrial energies which has been stored at Stonehenge thousands of years earlier. I parked the car and walked among broken branches and bushes in a long clearing, in front of his home. He met me at the door.

"Mr Akova, at long last, we meet again," he said. The fifty acres which surrounded us had been inherited from his father. "Come in and sit down. We have lots to talk about." There was a large sitting room off the hall, with at least six armchairs. We sat in two of them.

"Mr Akova, I have the secret of the Eridanians. And believe me, you cannot brush it aside like a pinch of salt. It's all there," he said, and continued excitedly, "I saw it on several occasions at Stonehenge. Their energy has been stored in the stones. There is some energy on the ground also, but the main source comes from the stones."

"I'm all ears."

"Well, Mr Akova, you know there have been reports of landings at Stonehenge. I camped there for a few days and then I managed to get into the forbidden zone and hid behind the stones. It was then that I saw two UFOs land nearby. They emitted very bright, white rays which seemed to pierce the stones, and moments later, yellow and red rays—which I call Sama rays—went from the stones straight up into the rear of the spacecrafts. This continued for at least five minutes. By the time the military came, it was done. The UFOs became invisible but the coloured rays continued for another two minutes at least. Then the whole process stopped."

"All this happened when you were hiding in the forbidden zone?"

"Yes, Mr Akova. I was lucky no one saw me. Then I slipped off into the night after they had left."

"So you're saying that the aliens get their energy to survive on earth from the stones at Stonehenge?"

"Yes, Mr Akova."

"This is a very interesting find, Mr Haskey." "You see, I, too, saw the alien leaders and their devils consuming the energies—the bright white rays—coming from the UFOs. It is certainly possible that they obtain their energy from Stonehenge and then distribute it to all their kind throughout the world. In other words, the UFOs 'fill up' from Stonehenge, and then distribute it to the alien population wherever they may be. So if we stopped them from getting the energy at the primary source, Stonehenge, then they wouldn't be able to pass it on to the aliens."

This presented an opportunity to test whether the Eridanians would be forced to leave Earth because of the lack of this essential energy. I asked Haskey about his experiments.

"The experiment on the destruction of the coloured rays is almost full proof. But we need to try it out on the spot when a UFO lands at Stonehenge to refuel. Oh, and one more thing," he said, "just to be on the safe side, I have deposited all the documents about the experiment in a bank in the West End."

"Good," I said, "now, I think we have to ask the government to close off the Stonehenge area for about a week while we camp out there and wait for a UFO landing." Then I had an idea: "What about a steel cover over the stones at Stonehenge."

"With respect, I don't think so, Mr Akova. Those rays will go through anything."

"I suppose you're right. So when is the best time for you to leave for Wiltshire?"

"Tomorrow would be OK for me."

"Right, I'll get onto the MoD and ask them to close off Stonehenge from the public for about a week. I'll arrange for two men to pick you up from your home and bring you to mine in Marlborough. Bring all your equipment."

Why had I not given serious consideration to Haskey's experiment before now? It was certainly worth trying. But the other British scientists were of the opinion that any project thought up by Hasky was not worth taking up. One scientist I knew well had said: "All his projects have failed so far. His intelligence is off the wall and what's more, he would try anything to succeed."

I had not taken everything Haskey had told me at face value. The man exuded confidence and energy, but there was a bitter rift between him and the other scientists, and his reputation had suffered in Britain because of their gossip. But despite this controversy, to me, he seemed no phoney.

This time, I was alone in a desolate place. The only media giant left in England tried to present the current situation on UFOs and the Eridanians emphasising optimism for the future. Clearly, this media organisation with its three daily newspapers and a TV channel was dedicated to accessing all the information available on the aliens and how they could be stopped. But the dismal advance of the aliens was too blatant. So far, Cradle Hill was unquestionably the favourite landing site for the Grey UFOs. But there had been no reports of sightings at Cradle Hill for weeks. The Grey extraterrestrials, who were supposed to stop the Eridanians and who had arrived from Alpha Centauri, the nearest star system to Earth, were no longer there. Their behaviour had no logical progression; there was no explanation for what they did.

There were many questions which raced through my head as I sat alone in the big house in Marlborough. A whirlpool of confusion prevailed. There were many people in England who were panicking to the point of hysteria. No one knew what was happening. The controversy over the Eridanian claim that the world would become a beautiful planet to live on with no serious illnesses and immortality stirred up arguments for and against the aliens. But those who were for them increased each day. The sturdy common sense which showed the evil of the Eridanian plan for mankind seemed to have dissolved completely. It was only through the work of the government and of course our own UFO Research Centre in London that had created a profusion of unanswered questions. And those questions were impossible to avoid.

Haskey arrived at the house in the late afternoon. When we went up to Stonehenge, everything had been prepared for him. Three men had to carry his heavy rectangular machine into the middle of Stonehenge. Of course, there was no guarantee that a UFO would land at Stonehenge on our first night. We had to be patient. Within an hour, Haskey's machine was ready. We had coffee and sandwiches, enough to last till morning. It was a cold night. There was no one for miles. I saw shadows in the darkness but when I shone my torch at them, there was nothing there. Then minutes later I saw it: a very tall, dark figure moving slowly towards us. Haskey was asleep. The approaching figure was all in black, his cloak fluttering in the breeze. His face looked satanic in the dim light.

"Haskey, wake up and put on your shield; we have visitors!" I said, and nudged him on the shoulder. He jumped up in panic. The UFO made a loud whoosh as it landed just fifty feet away from us. Then five more tall figures, white figures, appeared near the centre. The whole place was lit up by the pulsating, blindingly bright, white energy rays. The UFO's rays hit the stones, as Haskey had told me. Haskey was all thumbs as he tried to put on his shield. I helped him. "Quick! Start the machine!"

At the push of the button, Haskey's machine started to shoot out white rays which looked much like laser beams, hitting the red and yellow rays emanating from the stones. It worked. The coloured rays were destroyed before they could reach the UFO. The tall black figure and the five white figures started to shoot rays towards us. We ducked for cover behind a stone. The alien's rays hit the machine and it exploded into a thousand pieces. The red and yellow rays kept issuing from the stones and entering the UFO. Seconds later, the aliens disappeared, and the UFO zoomed silently across the sky…

So, the UFO had landed at Stonehenge on our very first night. That was a piece of luck. And Haskey's experiment had worked, though unluckily, his machine had been destroyed in the process. But the six tall figures had come along before the UFO had landed. How could they possibly have known of Haskey's experiment? We had probably been followed. Someone in London must have informed Draco about Haskey's machine. Although it had been too dark to see his face, the tall black figure had most probably been Draco. As someone once said, "The operation was successful, but the patient died…"

"Well, what happens now, Haskey? Can you build another machine?"

"I don't know, Mr Akova," he replied sadly, "It took me years to complete this one."

I realised that despite the success of the experiment, it would be impossible to stop the Eridanians getting their energy from their UFOs anywhere in the world. I could ask the government to build a steel cover over Stonehenge, but that would not stop them either as I had witnessed the alien rays penetrating the steel.

Haskey left the next morning, and I returned to the Marlborough house. I telephoned Emma and told her what had happened at Stonehenge.

"So what should we do now, Turan?" she asked.

"Nothing, for the moment."

"What about the shield you are wearing? That works. The aliens' rays can't get through that shield, surely."

"Yes, you're right. But even if we did have a large shield covering the whole area of Stonehenge, that won't stop them either. It's true there's a certain amount of energy stored in the stones, but they will always be able to get their energy from their UFOs wherever they land."

"So what was the point of Haskey's project and his experiment?" she asked.

"Well, we now know that one of the reasons for choosing Wiltshire as their base is in fact Stonehenge. We also have proof that the yellow and red rays are absolutely vital for them to survive here on earth."

"But you said they can get that energy from the coloured rays from the UFOs. So Stonehenge or not, they can get their energy from their own UFOs."

She was right, of course. But the Wiltshire mystery was by no means solved. Through Haskey, we had found out about the energies in the Stonehenge stones.

That alone was an important find. God knows what other secrets lay hidden in Wiltshire. Draco, the leader of the aliens, had moved to Marlborough and it seemed he now had his headquarters in the town. Why? I had no answer to that question. Except that there were more UFO sightings and landings in Wiltshire than anywhere else in Britain.

I decided to stay in Marlborough to investigate. First of all, I had to try and get into Draco's two mansions when he was not there. If he had decided to establish his HQ in Marlborough, that meant his operations were being conducted from there. No matter how different from us, and no matter how advanced, a super-intelligent civilisation like the Eridanians should have a strategy and conduct their affairs on Earth from a base. Their intergalactic crusade and their plan to colonise the defenceless civilisation of mankind on Planet Earth had been a success so far. They simply could not be bothered with Africa, Asia, SE Asia, Australia or the Middle East. The only two areas they wanted were Britain and the whole of the American continent—both north and south were the two areas they wanted most, after the completion of their take over in the European continent.

People well versed in examining the behaviour of the devils had already given up. The behaviour pattern of the Eridanian was totally inexplicable and unpredictable. Of course, there were still some scientists filled with a sense of concern and fascination. They were in Marlborough and offered to help me in any way they could. I was convinced that the special, mysterious and unknown reason why there was such an immense concentration of Eridanians in Britain held the keys to a full understanding of their motives. And now there were reports of humans transformed into Eridanian-controlled beings who had had surgically implanted mind-control devices in their skulls.

There were people in Marlborough whose faces were as haggard as those of skeletons, but they denied any contact with the aliens. I was astonished to see many people in Marlborough who had become disabled and were moving around in this small town on quad bikes. They also denied any contact with the Eridanians. The tacit complicity of this strange class of disabled people who were now in their hundreds was mind-boggling. I burrowed through the files of at least five doctors who dealt with such cases, but could not find one in which there was any proof of illness. There was no explanation why or how these people had become disabled. There were no clues at all, said the doctor, who confessed himself utterly bewildered at the large number of disabled people in Marlborough.

One doctor who was considerably interested in alien presence in Wiltshire was shrewder and more guarded, and had a most compelling argument. He had extrapolated the numbers, adding, "My calculations have reached around a thousand people in the last three months. I'm sure it has something to do with the aliens." When I finished my investigations into the case of disabled people in Marlborough, my heart was pounding with anxiety over another Eridanian mystery. This was another strange case which confounded all investigators. As I sat in a restaurant not far from the High Street and ordered my English breakfast, I saw a middle-aged woman wearing large glasses come in on her quad bike. I had an impression of evil the moment I laid eyes on her. She was accompanied by a man. A strange, malign influence settled over my whole body.

The inexorable development of strange happenings in Marlborough had a cumulative effect on normal people. Within days, they witnessed a great increase in the number of those in league with the Devil. Some had panicked, sold their houses and left the town. There was an oddness that I had never seen since my arrival in the town. Something beyond the boundaries of the known was happening here. There were no murders, no violence, but horror and the supernatural reigned triumphant in this law-abiding community. For example, the sudden appearance on the street of a mysterious army of more than a thousand disabled people could not be explained.

A gust of wind swept through the street as I drove towards Draco's mansions. I parked the car in a small side road which led nowhere, about two hundred metres from the mansions, I surveyed the two residences through my binoculars. I got out of the car and moved to a higher spot to get a better view. The strong wind had lessened into a light breeze from the west. I shivered in the cold winter evening. I looked again. The landscape appeared to be rapidly changing. The hauntingly dark stretches of the small forest beyond where I was standing, revealed an irrational monstrosity and a multiplicity of nightmares. With renewed vigour and determination, I shrugged off yet another example of the Devil's horror, deceit, such as landscape transformation. Then a deadly spell overcame me with accelerating horror. The soulless and sadistic tricks of Draco were at work once again. The mise-en-scène resembled a view in Dracula's castle. Changing the landscape was not a new trick, apparently. Unbelievable as it seemed, the surroundings of the two identical mansions and the mansions themselves had changed dramatically. Was he really aware of my presence in the vicinity? Weird and wizardly, and with enormous powers, Draco was now raised to his most influential and catalytic alien apotheosis. Even my telepathic vision and the special powers I possessed through the Greys seemed to diminish under this demonic force. But somehow I had to get through this blatant show of terrors.

Did he really possess powers that would tell him every move I made? No, I did not really think so, but still, I decided to wait a little longer…Half an hour elapsed as I walked to the two mansions. In the moonlit evening, I could see that the landscape had once again changed to normal. An otherworldly exhilaration came over me in a maze of thoughts of the impossible. How cold those two mansions and their surroundings change completely into a centuries old castle and then back again, to normal? Why would this dramatic change occur on the instant I arrived near the mansion? Or was this some kind of alarm system to keep out people who wanted to enter the mansion grounds.

Slowly I moved nearer, much nearer, to the mansions. There was no light or movement inside. This was no ordinary mansion with guard dogs and bodyguards. I climbed in through an open window at the back. Earlier I had asked two agents of Major Blount to keep an eye on the mansions. They told me Draco had left an hour earlier. He went out almost every evening and returned after midnight. I made my way half way across the great hall with torch in hand. I had been here once before with Maureen and Emma and had been impressed by all the appurtenances of wealth. There was an uneasy atmosphere in the great hall. My mind was preoccupied with the thought of finding something, some sort of clue that would lead me to uncover Draco's secret. The secret of the energies that enabled the evil leader of the devils and all the other Eridanians to live on Planet Earth.

First, I went down to the basement. This was a large room with office equipment and computers lined up against the wall. I closed the door and switched on the light. There were no windows in this basement room and no one could see the light from outside. I searched every single desk and drawer. Nothing…nothing…Then I saw it. A large feather-like object in a rectangular transparent box stuck to the ceiling. I stood there staring at it in great astonishment. This was identical to the feather-like object I had found in North Cyprus right at the start of this long episode, which heralded the arrival of the evil Eridanians from the star system Epsilon Eridani. I was transfixed with terror for a moment or two. There were many wires stuck on the ceiling. First time lucky, I thought.

I pulled up a chair, raised my hands to the ceiling, pulling the transparent box with the large feather-like object with all my strength. I managed to get it unstuck. It was almost a metre long. Quickly, I ran to the door of the basement and switched off the light. The object under my arm, I climbed out of the same window and moved slowly towards my car. It had been too easy…

It was around 11.30 when I drove back home. My nerves were somewhat strained as I placed the wretched alien object in the small room behind the study. The smaller version of it, which I had found in North Cyprus almost eight months earlier, had brought with it so much trouble to the world that I dreaded to think what would happen if I pressed the large button on the Devil's Feather—as I called it. Was this strange feather-like object the provider of the source of power for the devil? One thing was certain. The blinding white rays enabled the Eridanians to survive on Earth. If indeed this alien object emanated the vital energy for them to survive on Earth, then this meant that I had achieved something. It meant that I had found the main source of their power. Well and good. But if it sent out a signal for more Eridanians to come and land on Earth, then God help us all. That was a chilling thought. I had to decide. Either I would destroy it or rather try to destroy it completely, or I would press the button and see what happened. There was always the possibility that either way it would not make much difference. Finally, I decided to call Major Blount.

Two MoD officials, the Prime Minister's under-secretary and two space research scientists were informed of the situation and would arrive in Marlborough the next day. I could not reach Major Blount at first. A devastating clap of thunder resounded over Marlborough as I sat waiting for a call from Major Blount. It was very difficult to anticipate Draco's next move when he discovered his 'precious' object was missing. He and his two deputies, De Medici and Gonzaga, would probably pay me a visit as I was most likely first on the list of suspects. I had become one of their prime targets, if not their most important adversary.

I stretched my legs and closed my eyes for a few seconds. Later I was awoken by the antique clock striking midnight and at the same instant, the telephone rang. I had been asleep in my comfortable armchair for at least forty minutes. I picked up the phone.

"What's happening, Turan?" Major Blount's distinct baritone voice sounded anxious.

"We may have a breakthrough," I told him, "I have Draco's large feather-like instrument here at my house in Marlborough. It is identical to the small one we have…"

"How did you get it?"

"Breaking and entering," I said.

"Then I should have you arrested."

"Two MoD officials, the Prime minister's under-secretary and two space research scientists are going to arrive for a meeting tomorrow. I hope you'll be able to make it too."

"I'll be there…"

I had had too many sleepless nights, and was hoping this one would be an exception. I took off the shield and put the gun on the table. Minutes later, I fell asleep once again.

Thirty-One

Every precaution had been taken by the authorities to conduct the operation secretly and discreetly. A field a couple of miles north of Marlborough and very near the largest crop circles in the area was chosen. We were all attired in space suits and protected with the shields in case of radioactivity spreading into the air from the strange Eridanian object. Traffic had been diverted into other roads leading in and out of Marlborough. We were now ready for the 'big' moment. Would it be possible to control and destroy the energies the Eridanians needed to carry on living on Earth? Indeed, was this object instrumental in supplying their main power source?

It was 11.15 in the morning, a sunny, winter morning when the two scientists pressed the button on the object. While we waited, a recurrence of the same sizzling, deafeningly loud noise which I had heard almost a year ago in Salzburg lacerated the air around us. About a minute later, it stopped abruptly. I was half expecting something like a laser beam of blinding white lights to come out of the instrument. The scientists repeatedly pressed the button about seven times. Each time, the sound decreased, and with the last attempt, it ended.

The two scientists who had been studying the original 'Devil's Feather' from North Cyprus looked up in astonishment at us all lined up in spacesuits and with protective equipment. The instrument lay on the table and was simply inoperable. There was no question of anyone providing an explanation. When he had found out the feather-like object had been removed from his house, Draco and his men had probably cut off all links to it by using some kind of remote control device. My expectations of finally discovering the source of the Eridanians' power and energy were dashed once more. It was a major disappointment for all of us.

"I suppose the Space Research Agency should take over from here onwards," said the Defence Minister, almost murmuring the words into my ear, cool and composed. "I mean, the instrument. Perhaps they can work on it."

"Yes," I said, "they ought to work on it. But I think this instrument should eventually be destroyed. At the moment, the Eridanian leaders are based here in Marlborough. As you know, they are in human form with false identities and nationalities. They are all EU citizens. At the same time, they do not deny the fact that they are aliens. I'm afraid many people here in Britain nowadays have a highly idealistic view of alien presence. Ever since they arrived in Britain, they have managed to take over control of most of the media. Through the media, people have been led to believe that the aliens promote purity, truth and everlasting life. But on the other hand, many are thoroughly tormented by their presence. How this is possible in Britain, we do not know yet. Bearing in mind that millions of people in Europe and the EU as a whole have fallen victim to their enigmatic and evil power, I cannot understand how half the population here have managed to ward off their power of control over humans. This is another mystery. I think we should destroy the instrument and see what happens."

"Yes, quite. Well, Mr Akova, Major Blount will inform you about our plan B. Personally, I think we ought to plan our next move together with the Americans," said the Minister and then, noting the worried look on my fact, added, "I know you don't care for the proposed American action plan of striking down and destroying some of the UFOs, but don't worry. We won't act without your recommendations. We trust you people. After all, you are the experts."

"Thank you," I said, shaking his extended hand.

The Defence Minister left in his chauffeur driven Rolls while Major Blount and I stood near the scientists from the Space Research Agency who were packing up their gear. They then left in their white van. I gazed upon the endless fields, wondering about the crop circles. We were standing about a hundred feet away from the largest in Wiltshire. I felt sure they were in some mysterious way linked to the Eridanian aliens or the Greys.

The more I searched the truth, the more I seemed to be led away from it. My recent investigations with the UFO Research Centre in London had met with ridicule from people supporting integration with the Eridanian extraterrestrials. The aliens had successfully instigated a global conspiracy to cover up their evil ways. But as I had told the Defence Minister earlier, despite the massive, super intelligent propaganda coupled with extraterrestrial technology and powers of transformation beyond human understanding, there were still many millions of people in Britain who were struggling desperately against alien domination. How and why? I did not know yet. The extraterrestrial Eridanians were able to take over the whole of the EU, the European continent, and yet Britain and its people—perhaps more than seventy percent of the population—had somehow survived intact. How and why? It was a mystery.

It would be totally illogical and nonsensical to suggest that the will and character of the British people was not the sort which would surrender easily to extraterrestrial power. The British public were divided into two camps. Those who had been transformed by the Eridanians and served them without question, and those who somehow and quite mysteriously found an extra-special strength to challenge them and try to keep them out of Britain. How did that happen? It seemed as though a secret hand had touched and protected them from the Devil. But whatever their beliefs about the aliens who came from the star system Epsilon Eridani, these people rejected them, challenged them and fought against these despicable, vile creatures. How did those who survived stand up to such powerful extraterrestrial technology? I decided to carry out a thorough investigation in Marlborough and Wiltshire as a whole, with a team of investigators from the UFO Research Centre in London. Wiltshire was the centre of UFO activity and a lot of abductions.

There had been many reports of human encounters with aliens. According to the first reports that we had received from abductees at the Centre, there had been more than one hundred and fifty cases of alien abduction and all these cases were remarkably consistent accounts of abductions by Grey aliens. Emma sent me the full list and I was astounded by the fact that almost ninety percent of these had occurred in Wiltshire. Warminster, in the west of the country, had become known globally as the epicentre of UFO phenomena between 1964 and 1978. But there had been very few cases of abduction over those years. Now it was a completely different story. Abductions by Grey aliens had increased to such an extent that within a period of eight weeks, the figure had reached one hundred and fifty. This was the fruit of investigations conducted by our own team from the UFO Centre in London. The first question that sprang to mind was this: why would the Grey aliens abduct so many people in Wiltshire?

Despite the efforts of the chosen 36 to contact the Greys for help and guidance against the evil Eridanians, the appearance of Tamor who did not look at all like a Grey alien was hardly what we had expected, and might even have been taken as an imposter. The Eridanian aliens had no need to abduct humans. They had already settled into the community of mankind in Europe and Britain. There transformative and traumatic technology added millions of humans to the

Devil's rang. That in itself was a frightening fact. But these facts could not be determined by counting the numbers of Eridanians in Europe, Britain or in any other country. Extensive research in Europe, Britain and the USA proved to some extent that the numbers announced by official sources were not exaggerated. These numbers included the transformed humans.

The gleeful insanity of the Devil was fatal. Their powers of instantaneous infiltration into the minds of humans were miraculous and unstoppable. I realised this made the struggle of the British even more remarkable. Wiltshire had become, once again, as in the sixties and seventies, the most important centre of UFO activity. But this time round, we knew that the Eridanian leader and his deputies had established their headquarters in Marlborough. I had to investigate the Grey aliens' abductions in Wiltshire. This was a completely new angle. Perhaps the Greys were trying to reach us through the abductees in Wiltshire.

The strategy of Draco, De Medici and Gonzaga was outrageous but it worked. They simply transformed the devil image of the Eridanians into an extremely superior extraterrestrial presence on Earth. People in Europe now believed the accord between the EU and the Eridanians would place them on top of the world as the number one superpower. In actual fact, the Eridanian aliens were in control of every single institution within the EU. Now was the time to start a new mission. It was just a matter of time before the British government, together with the Americans would meet and determine a new course.

My mission was twofold. First I had to try and persuade the British and Americans not to wage war against the UFOs. Secondly, I would try to establish Grey presence in Wiltshire and possibly convince the officials that the Grey aliens would eventually help mankind to end the domination of the world by the Eridanians. I talk about 'my' mission. But this was really the mission of not only the UFO Research Centre in London but also of all the experts on UFOs and extraterrestrial civilisations. One extraterrestrial civilisation—the worst possible one—had arrived on Earth and already succeeded in taking over power in one of the most important economic organisations in the world: the EU.

I had several telepathic communications with the Greys and so did the others included in that special category of the Chosen 36. But the appearance of Tamor, the extraterrestrial from the star system Alpha Centauri, almost a month ago at Cradle Hill, was the only real, face to face encounter of the third kind for a long time. Tamor had not said much when he had appeared, and disappeared as quickly as he had arrived. He did not tell us anything about a possible Grey intervention to get rid of the Devil and restore the human status quo in countries all over Europe. Furthermore, there was no evidence of Grey alien presence in Wiltshire. How could anyone understand such highly superior intellect and technology?

First on my list of abductees was an 87 year old pioneer of UFO studies. John Woodcock, a journalist and writer, was instrumental in presenting a very strong case of alien visitations in and around Warminster. He also claimed to have been visited in his own home by two extraterrestrials. A report of this recent abduction by aliens had become national news in the media. Woodcock now lived in Marlborough with his wife. He was now on his last legs, but seemed to be plateauing for the moment. At least, that is what Mrs Woodcock told me when I rang for an appointment: afternoon tea at exactly four thirty in a typical English home. John Woodcock's affinity with space people was quite legendary. He said he had a special relationship with UFO beings which had arrived at Warminster and Cradle Hill. His home had always been, for over forty years, in a gloriously isolated small forest a couple of miles west of Marlborough.

"I'm so glad you are here, Mr Akova. Actually, I wanted to meet you and I would have called, but you beat me to it." He remained sitting back in his armchair as he spoke.

"I have read your books," I told him, "and I must say, your accounts of alien presence in Wiltshire were always very inspiring for us all. We have a thick file on your UFO research material at the London Centre."

"Thank you," he said, smiling and did not look or sound like a man of ill health who had retired from active life. "Mr Akova, I am well informed about every single development since your first encounter with the devilish Eridanians in Salzburg. Throughout my long years as a ufologist, I have never encountered any kind of demonic forces. Nevertheless, you people have proved to the authorities their arrival and their plans for colonising Earth. But from what I've gathered, Earth technology cannot challenge their superiority. At any rate, I am sure mankind will triumph in the end."

He paused for a few seconds as he sipped his tea, "Well, and what is it I can do for you?"

"There has been a sudden surge of abductions in England in recent weeks. Research by the experts and the UFO Research Centre in London shows that ninety out of about a hundred alien abduction cases have occurred here in Wiltshire. I examined the list of abductees. They are mostly in and around

Marlborough and Avebury, also in Salisbury. A team of experts are interviewing all the abductees. Here, at this point, I must emphasise our investigations revealed all of these alien abductions took place within a short period of just one month. It is also interesting to note that ever since the arrival of the Eridanian extraterrestrials, there have been very few reports of alien abduction in the country and none in Wiltshire."

"Furthermore, Draco, the leader of the Eridanians and his deputies suddenly decided to move into Wiltshire and now have their headquarters here, in Marlborough. Sudden, dramatic and very strange things are happening all around us. It has been virtually impossible to even begin to understand how they have managed it, but the devils' domain so to speak, the EU, and yet they are here all the time and appear to be concentrating on a massive onslaught to secure full control in Britain. But most important of all, Wiltshire is the centre of all this activity. We are in the midst of a highly convoluted mysterious phase of our investigations. You are on the list of abductees, and I would very much appreciate it if you could tell me exactly what happened."

"Well, now, Mr Akova…" he waved his right hand as if he wanted to divert the conversation towards a highly important topic, "you have said it all. I have absolutely no regret about the whole affair. This last encounter—I do not call it an abduction, though for others that is obviously what it was, but not for me—was by no means my first experience. As you probably know, I have been visited by them twice in my own home. My third contact was at Cradle Hill. All three encounters where almost thirty-five years ago. My guest—here in this very room—was the same alien in human form during those first two visitation. The third alien was a different character, but once again in human form. On all three occasions, I was warned of the dangers lying ahead for Earth. They talked of evil forces within every single society all over the world."

"What happened?" I asked him, "were you taken into the alien spacecraft?"

"Oh, yes," he said, "and I went willingly. I wasn't forced. I was simply transported into the UFO. One minute I was in this room, the next, I found myself in the alien spacecraft."

"What about your wife? Did she see your encounter with the UFO being?"

"No, she was asleep. It was 3 o'clock in the morning, and I woke up when I heard a whooshing sound coming from the garden. Then I saw the very bright white lights of the UFO. Seconds later, I was in the UFO itself and was greeted by a lanky fellow."

"How did you communicate with him?"

"Mr Akova, it's amazing and truly unbelievable, but he spoke perfect English. You realise, of course, that these extraterrestrials possess superpowers. He said he was a representative of the civilisation we call Greys. My reaction to that was exactly the same as it was in my three previous encounters years ago. I told him there had been many visitations by Grey aliens since the Rosewell case back in 1947, and it was a well-known fact that their physical features were as follows: humanoid, about four feet tall with a disproportionate head, large, very dark, almond shaped eyes and a thin line resembling a mouth, with elephantine ears and long arms almost dragging on the ground. He said the Greys could transform themselves into human form." Woodcock was speaking excitedly, "I asked his name. I asked him what he wanted."

"Well? Did he give you a name?"

"Yes. He said his name was Tamor." I sighed with satisfaction. *Now we were getting somewhere,* I thought to myself. This was the very same alien I had met at Cradle Hill. Woodcock insisted that he had been entrusted with a coherent message. "Tamor said he wanted me to deliver a message to the people of earth. 'Why me, and what was the message', I asked him. He said only the people who had been in contact with them were best equipped to help mankind."

"Mr Woodcock, did he tell you about the dangers facing humankind? When he mentioned devil forces, did he tell you anything about Eridanian extraterrestrial presence? And most importantly, did he tell you how they would help mankind? Did he tell you that mankind's only adversary was the Eridanian extraterrestrials? Did he tell you anything about the secret of the Eridanians and how they managed to take control of Europe in such a short time? How are we supposed to fight the devils and get rid of them? Did he tell you anything about that? Would the Greys save mankind from this devilish alien presence?" I was bombarding this man with so many questions, and yet he remained calm, clasped his hands and looked at me gravely.

"I am sorry," I said, "I got carried away. You see, Mr Woodcock, Tamor is the alien I met briefly when he appeared at Cradle Hill only a few weeks ago. We are trying desperately to find the answers to all these questions."

"It's all right. I understand, Mr Akova. But I'm afraid I don't have all the answers. There have been many contactees over the years."

He said only those humans whose research on UFOs span long period of Earth time were chosen to spread the message. Only those Earth people who believed in the supreme beings from outer space had reached the highest cosmic level of universal intelligence. They may not be fully aware of the powers they possess, but they would eventually lead mankind out of the evil looming over the world. The message was simple. He said we had proof of their civilisation's visitations to Earth. Those who did not believe suffered, and their bodies and souls were taken over by evil forces. But they could be saved too. Those who believed must spread the message all around the world. He said the message should be heard loud and clear in every single corner of the world.

"Mr Woodcock, did Tamor say anything, anything at all about Eridanian presence here in Britain or elsewhere in the world?"

"No. He just mentioned evil forces. I'm sure by that, he meant Eridanians. Of course, I did mention the Eridanian extraterrestrial presence. He simply replied by saying 'You must spread the word, spread the message. Believe and challenge them'." Once again, that word 'challenge' had come up.

In every single encounter with the Greys, whether through telepathic communication or physical contact, 'challenge' had been the word pronounced over and over again. I had never met Woodcock before, although he was quite well-known as a UFO researcher in Britain. He had become one of the top UFO experts in the world. We had met the same extraterrestrial—Tamor—, the Grey in human form, and we were both delivered the same message: Challenge! This was my first interview for a long time with an abductee. Here, I was feeling a little closer to solving the mystery of a very large concentration of extraterrestrial presence in and around the towns of Wiltshire.

While he spoke, the same irritating and slightly disquieting question propped up in my mind once again. Since their aim was to help to free mankind from the terrorising Eridanian threat, why didn't the Greys organise an all-out assault against them? But I realised that ever since my first physical contact and during my numerous telepathic communications with these gloriously supernatural beings, their conduct, short conversations during encounters and their messages, were completely foreign to man's reasoning. One could not understand the hidden meaning of their messages except for their face value and it was virtually impossible to reach a rational explanation through their behavioural patterns.

After Woodcock's account of his contact and my own experiences, the word 'challenge' or the command 'Challenge them and you will have the power to keep them out!' were the only clues to how we were supposed to, in some mysterious way, end Eridanian supremacy over mankind. But I for one, as a primary witness to the Devil's inconceivably superior faculties and comprehensively evil, weird ways, remained powerless and the magic word 'challenge' was hardly enough to dislodge the alien presence on a massive scale. An ultimate weapon or a Grey extraterrestrial strategy to banish the evil ones from the face of the Earth, that is what the world needed.

Woodcock cocked an eyebrow at his wife standing near the door as he lit a cigarette. She was looking very indignant at her husband's bad habit.

"Mr Akova...I asked him why Wiltshire was the centre of so many extraterrestrial visitations. Why Wiltshire? What was so special about it? He repeated his earlier statement. It was odd. He sounded like a robot programmed to repeat the same sentence. Believe in us. Spread the word and challenge them, he said. Oh, yes, I remember now. He also said something which was really puzzling. He said, 'Explore Wiltshire and you'll have the power to see your miracle. I honestly don't know what that means. What miracle?"

"Perhaps he was referring to Stonehenge, or the crop circles, or Silbury Hill. Stonehenge we've already examined. There is definitely some kind of extraterrestrial energy stored in the stones. But the experiment conducted in my presence at Stonehenge by a scientist was a total failure. Crop circles? Well, there is no proof that these were made by visitors from outer space."

Silbury Hill is I think the only other strange sight which has not been thoroughly investigated. Maybe Tamor was referring to one of these strange phenomena. Perhaps there is a miracle hidden somewhere in Wiltshire. But what did he mean by 'your miracle'? A man-made miracle? "I honestly don't know, Mr Woodcock. The Eridanian extraterrestrials in human form also speak English and they don't sound like robots. The Greys on the other hand, do not speak much, do they?"

"No," said Woodcock thoughtfully, "well, after all, they are two different species. Tell me about these Eridanians. You say you've spoken to them?"

"They speak just like any other human. I have met Draco, their leader. By the way, Draco is short from Dracula. Count Dracula."

"Yes. Oh, yes, of course," Woodcock exclaimed, "I remember the stories in the papers. You were interviewed on TV as well."

"To tell you the truth, no one really believed my story about Dracula. It was a fantastic find for me. I mean, the secret notes of Bram Stoker referring to the arrival of the extraterrestrial Dracula. At any rate, Draco is now a fully-fledged human. He is able to manipulate everyone and everything with unbelievably fantastic powers. He is the immortal Satan. He is at the helm of the evil forces Tamor was telling you about. But coming back to the 'miracle'…now we have to search for a human miracle in Wiltshire. Honestly, I don't know why the Greys do this. They seem to be doing it all the time…They never give us a straight answer, just clues. And believe me, we have nothing much to go on. How do you go about looking for a miracle in Wiltshire, for God's sake?"

"Well, I think your obvious choices should be Stonehenge, the crop circles and Silbury Hill…"

The interview with Woodcock opened a new page as far as my investigations were concerned. First of all, we had more or less established the Grey extraterrestrial's presence in Wiltshire. Secondly, Tamor's mention of a 'miracle'—although vague and with no clues as to what it was and where it was, could perhaps lead us to the truth we were searching for. Why was Wiltshire so susceptible to all these mysterious phenomena? Some explained it by suggesting that this beautiful British county's history of human occupation was the main reason. It was a well-known fact that Wiltshire was littered with ancient monuments, pathways, burial grounds and stone circles. But the UFO sightings and continuing alien presence and the crop circles meant there was some 'thing' far beyond the imagination of mankind.

Woodcock had met Tamor as I had. This was another important development in this long and mysterious saga of the Eridanian and Grey extraterrestrial presence in Wiltshire. Tamor, the extraterrestrial Grey in human form was probably the leader of the Alpha Centaurian civilisation. I left Woodcock and promised to keep him posted about our latest findings. At home in Marlborough, I called Emma and asked her to organise a meeting with the investigators who had interviewed the abductees in Wiltshire. Around fifty of our investigators who had interviewed eighty-five people in and around Marlborough, Warminster, Avebury and other towns in Wiltshire.

Most of those abductees referred to complex processes and simultaneous thoughts transplanted into their brains, and there was a striking similarity between almost all the cases. They were all exposed to a very bright white light. None of them mentioned any sort of experiments on their sexual organs, which had been quite common in abductions during the last twenty-five to thirty years. It took over five days to examine most of the reports of the investigators who had interviewed the abductees. Through telepathic communication, they were told of the fate of Earth. Once again, the same message was delivered:

"Challenge the evil forces." Through strenuous and extensive research, we were able to single out those who claimed to have developed their paranormal and telepathic abilities. Only five of the abductees were told of a miracle. "Search for the miracle in Wiltshire," was the message. All abductees said they felt much stronger after their experience in alien spacecraft. The conclusion drawn from the reports suggested almost a reverberation of the same pattern. In other words, it seemed as though all of them were now ready to challenge the evil with an extraordinary psychological and spiritual power. Maybe this was the Grey way to fight the Eridanian aliens. I most certainly hoped it was.

During my investigations in Wiltshire, for some unknown reason, I had never set foot anywhere near Silbury Hill except when we tried to operate Draco's large instrument near a crop circle. On a cool January morning, I drove up to a mound with Emma. Silbury Hill, in the Marlborough Downs, was a strange place, not at all in harmony with the surrounding features. It was the tallest manmade mound in Europe estimated to have been built in 2,500 BC, approximately 4,600 years ago. It was a really incredible sight and its base covered least six acres. No one could explain why it was built and who built it. One of the investigators of our Centre in London was an astrophysicist, and he had interviewed several of the abductees. He was also an expert on extraterrestrial, celestial energies. It was a foregone conclusion that Wiltshire was abundant with extraterrestrial material probably lying unseen or undetected on the ground. His team of ten men and women arrived at the location.

We had obtained permission from the authorities to dig up the mound. After forty-eight hours of arduous excavation, we were able to find a metal door on the southern side which led to four layers of stone about three metres inside the mound. Climbing up the stones we reached the walls on both sides which sloped inwards into a narrow passage way. Torch in hand, Emma, the expert and I walked through the pitch-dark corridor and suddenly reached a flight of steps. The steps, seven to be exact, carried us up into a fairly small room. What struck me at first glance under the torchlight was that the layers of stone, the walls, the steps and the room looked as if they had been built quite recently. This was definitely not a prehistoric secret chamber of some sort. There was nothing unusual about this room except that it was painted in white.

My torchlight moved around the room and we spotted at least a dozen circular holes in the walls. It was getting more interesting every inch of the way. Then at the other end of the room, I saw stairs. We climbed up and entered another room. This room was larger than the first and it was no longer pitch dark. I could see some light coming in from the holes in the wall. Soon afterwards we climbed up another set of stairs into the third and probably the highest enclosure.

"Any radioactivity?" I asked the expert.

He checked the floor and the walls with his instrument.

"Only alpha radiation made up of helium atoms and a very small amount of beta with some fast moving electrons. No gamma radiation so far, and that's the harmful stuff…"

"What are we looking for, Turan?" asked Emma, clearly very tired on the morning of the second day.

"A miracle," I said, "remember what the alien Tamor told Woodcock? He said, 'Look for your miracle in Wiltshire'. Now let's go in."

When I opened the door of this secret chamber, I was almost blinded by the extremely bright light covering a very large room from one wall to the other. There was also a thick ray of even brighter light pouring in from the large circular hole in the ceiling. Both Emma and the expert stepped inside with me.

Our first glance at the white light filled us with awe.

"God Almighty! What's happening here?" I asked the expert.

"This is it," he said, overwhelmed by the light, "this room is full of celestial extraterrestrial energies." He touched the walls at the entrance on both sides with his other instrument.

"Amazing!" he gasped, trying to protect his eyes from the light…

Suddenly, a tall dark figure appeared at the other end of the room. I could scarcely see it at first. Then it approached us with the delicate movements of a ballet dancer. The bright light was dimmed by a stroke of his right hand, and Draco stood there, smiling.

"The light was too bright for you, anyway…" he said. "Mr Akova, how resourceful of you. You are always the first to seek for the improbable or even the impossible."

"What do you want, Draco?" Emma and the expert stood frozen with fear. I stepped forward facing him. His hair was abnormally long and his bushy eyebrows were joined together. His general appearance did not evoke the Devil. There was no hint of the vampire either. He looked like an ordinary human being.

"Mr Akova, do you know where the energies are coming from?"

"Yes," I said, assuming that the 'miracle' Tamor had mentioned to Woodcock was in fact the energies somehow penetrating the mound at Silbury

Hill. The message of 'challenge' which I had received umpteen times from the Greys was ever present in the corner of my mind, like a dramatic opening to a defence mechanism.

"Well, I ought to congratulate you for your perseverance. Your effort in search of the truth is admirable. But as you can see, I have neutralised the energies."

All of a sudden, a man from the team of experts rushed in and stood very close to me, whispering in my ear: "There's a crowd outside, waiting to come in," he said. "They say they've come for the miracle."

Obviously, these were abductees who had been told of this 'miracle' by their Grey alien abductors.

"Tell them to wait," I told the man and sent him out. Draco put a hand on my shoulder in a friendly gesture.

"I take it the man who just whispered to you was referring to the crowd outside who has come for the miracle? Mr Akova, I ask you, is it really necessary to trouble these people further with false hopes? You know of the terrorising methods of abduction by the Grey aliens as you call them. The extraterrestrial biological entities from which they developed over a period of almost five thousand earth years is so feeble and inferior compared to the powers we possess. They do no harm, but they are inadequate. And you are absolutely wrong to believe that they will eventually become the saviours of mankind."

"You still haven't told me what you want," I said.

"I want us to sit down and talk," he replied promptly. "You've been a primary figure in the search for the truth right from the start. I suggest a meeting between just the two of us." He paused for a moment, his large dark eyes focused on mine.

"Now it's the human in you talking, isn't it?" I guessed.

"That's what I like about you, Mr Akova," he smiled, "you have an extraordinary talent, to divine, appreciate and understand the mind and soul of the person before you. Yes, we are all human now. You have a wonderful world and we share it with you. All for the benefit of mankind."

I realised that the whole gamut of my worst fears were about to be realised. The Eridanian leader had made short shrift of the Grey extraterrestrial power, light and miracle with a wave of his hand. It was a dreadful thought and I did not want to believe it. He continued:

"I know the British trust you implicitly. The British government can send in their representatives, but they'll have to wait in another room while we talk. This is my only condition for the task that will ensue after our meeting."

"So you want to start negotiations with the British government. Is that it?"

"Well…perhaps…But first of all, we must get together and talk." He stepped back and was now getting ready to leave. "I will expect you at around ten tomorrow evening at my twin mansions. Mr Akova, people are ignorant of the structure and meaning of our presence. You have the will and the power to understand."

"Right. I'll be there at ten tomorrow evening." I confirmed as Draco performed his vanishing act once again. Seconds later, the dimmed light in the secret chamber became as bright as it was when we first saw it.

During the next couple of hours, the abductees who had gathered outside the mound were let in one by one and were fully reinforced by the light. But at the same time, they seemed to be tormented by a mysterious and powerful force.

I knew it the moment I met one abductee, a middle-aged woman from Avebury. She told me: "I don't know whether this is the only way to end the evil spell. Mr Akova, is this bright light the miracle that will deliver us from all evil?"

"I'm sure you will have enough strength to challenge the evil forces, the evil extraterrestrials. I know this sounds like science fiction but rest assured, you've been sent here with a purpose. You were abducted by the Greys; you were told of the miracle; and now you have been cleansed by the bright light from above."

She gave a half-smile, thanked me and left.

At the end of the day, I realised they were all hopelessly entangled in a complex situation of not knowing what to do next. Alien presence had now become truly endemic in Wiltshire. The Grey extraterrestrial 'miracle' was obviously the light in the mound. During my encounter with the UFOs in Cornwall months before, the Eridanian UFO soared off into the night sky when confronted by the Grey extraterrestrial spacecraft. At the time, it seemed as though the Greys had the upper hand and were in fact superior to the power of the Eridanians. But after the Silbury Hill 'miracle' when Draco had simply shrugged off the Greys as an inferior alien race, I had begun to doubt Grey promises and wondered about the possibility of the Greys repulsing and eventually terminating the presence of the Eridanians on Earth. The devil had penetrated every level of society in human form and as such, they seemed as human as the next man. No one could tell the difference. Now our mission to get rid of them was an almost impossible task.

Reports from our own investigators in Europe were full of squalid stories of greed and corruption. The EU had become a playground for the Eridanian extraterrestrials. Britain hung on just by a thread. Despite the grim and depressing state of affairs, both Emma and I felt stronger and more resolute after the 'mound miracle' at Silbury Hill. For the first time, she insisted that the planned meeting with Draco would somehow yield new insights for a new strategy. We were the first two persons to consume the white, bright light at Silbury Hill.

"Turan, I don't know how to explain this, but it's as if a new learning process materialised instantly, erasing all fear of the aliens. It happened seconds after the light hit me from head to toe."

"I know that feeling, Emma," I said, "I've had it all along. But now I feel stronger, too."

The expert and his team stayed near the mound until the arrival of officials from the MoD. A small British Army contingent was stationed at Silbury Hill immediately afterwards. I drove back to my house in Marlborough with Emma. I contacted Major Blount who was constantly liaising between us and the British government, and explained to him what had happened at Silbury Hill.

"The meeting with Draco is set up for tomorrow evening. It's to be private, just him and me, at his request. Government representatives will sit and wait in another room. It's an unusual request, but I think he wants to negotiate some sort of agreement."

"Well, I have news for you, too," the Major told me, "some cabinet ministers are putting pressure on the Premier and the Defence Minister to start negotiations with the Eridanians. I dare say this is an attempt to launch a new initiative to end all the confusion and distress caused by alien presence in Britain." Major Blount was very close to the Premier. "But what about the Grey power at Silbury Hill?" he asked, "do you think it'll work this time?"

"I honestly don't know. Emma and I have doubled our energies under this light." I said, and then pondered on how I was feeling. It was like having the capacity to run the mile in under two minutes, or to predict or more or less read the thoughts of others, or to understand the most complex situation instantaneously, and with extraordinary precision, better than even the most intelligent human beings.

"I hope to be able to arrange for the Premier's under-secretary and his aides to arrive at your home in Marlborough tomorrow afternoon," said Major Blount.

"Who is he?"

"I think you met him briefly during a meeting with the Premier. A Mr Edward Houston; a nice chap and well-versed in extraterrestrial activity in Britain." Major Blount had a terrific track record not only as Chief of MI6's operations section, but also as the man who organised government strategy to combat the widespread positive response against the ruthless, devilish plans of the Eridanians in all the ranks of officialdom.

"You are coming, of course."

"Turan," he said, "I wouldn't miss this for anything." And hung up.

The Premier's under-secretary, his three aides and Major Blount arrived at about four, tea-time. After tea and coffee at the newly built Bridges Hotel, Major Blount joined me at the house for a short briefing. The British government's policy had not changed. While the Premier and Defence Minister still believed Britain would be capable of resisting any offers from the Eridanian aliens for a comprehensive agreement, an oppressive influence within the cabinet was pulling opinion in the opposite direction, in the form of demanding negotiations at top level. Major Blount said that Houston, the under-secretary, was the young, strong man in the Conservative party, designated as a potential successor to the Premier. However, Houston's father, a Conservative back-bencher, had apparently plunged into dissipation, wasting his money foolishly, and this compromised the young man's position as under-secretary to the Premier. Nevertheless, much to the visible annoyance of several other ministers, the Premier supported this brilliant young politician.

The Major said the current situation within the government was a minor cabinet crisis: "There are those who want an agreement and those who reject such a move. But the worst of all is that we don't know who wants what. I think the Eridanians have infiltrated the government, but it's impossible to say who and where."

We had dinner at the hotel restaurant with the London party. Houston was cordial, quite chatty and turned his attention to the girl sitting next to him quite flirtatiously. She was one of his aides. He was determined to carry through the Premier's policy despite the renewed pressure of some cabinet ministers for a negotiated settlement with the Eridanians. He recalled our meeting, adding, "Mr Akova, why do you think this Draco fellow wants to speak to you alone?"

"Well, the devil moves in unpredictable and very strange ways." I ventured, "But he did insist that I had a much firmer grasp of the extraterrestrial mentality."

"And do you?" he asked hopefully.

"I have had several experiences with both the Greys and the Eridanians. Yes, I think I can handle it."

"I've come up with certain ideas, or rather, questions," said Houston, enumerating on his fingers the points he wanted to put to me. "Firstly, how on earth were the European Commission, the Council of Europe and all the major European governments taken over by the aliens within such a short space of time? I fail to understand how or why the EU gave in, while Britain continues to resist. Secondly, we don't know what sort of agreement they'll offer, if indeed this is their true intention. My third question is this: since they seem to be more powerful and much more advanced than the Grey extraterrestrials, and since they know the Grey aliens can't help us stop them, why bother to negotiate with the British government for an accord? I mean, they can surely just take Britain over as well."

"Let me begin with your last question, and answer them in reverse order," I said. "The innumerable irregularities of the Eridanian alien pattern of behaviour are extremely puzzling. One cannot make any sense of it. We cannot even begin to understand their complex attitudes or actions in the process of trying to take over Britain. Swift, instantaneous and ever changing strategies conducted with audacity and verve, and, of course, supernatural powers together with their advanced technology seem to be the trademark of the Eridanians. We do not even know whether Draco will actually decide to go for an accord with Britain. An accord similar to the one signed with the EU. I think this answers your second question. As for your first question, well, I have a theory. I think the Eridanians penetrated all the institutions of the EU long before I found the 'Devil's Feather' and before their official arrival on Earth in Salzburg. Evidence of the past lives and presences of Draco, De Medici and Gonzaga and the fact that their origins and arrival on Earth go back to Romania and Italy supports this theory. I think they planned and executed the European section of the grand scale invasion perhaps during the last 10—15 years. There is also supporting evidence which clearly indicates alien strategy on EU enlargement…"

"Very interesting," replied Houston, "but it's only a theory. I mean the enlargement policy and strategy of the EU eventually shaping up solely through orders dictated to them by the Eridanians and through their presence in Europe."

"Yes," I said, "as for Britain's agonising effort to maintain its integrity, well, I base that on a high concentration of alien presence in here and in particular, in Wiltshire."

Houston rose from his chair swiftly, "Would you excuse me," he mumbled, and left the table. He returned ten minutes later with a briefcase. Soon we were ready to go. He joined Major Blount and Emma in my car and the other three aides followed us in their own rented car. I did not know what to expect. Draco seemed different and was by no means hostile. He had been downright friendly at Silbury Hill. I knew, of course, that he possessed enormous powers. He was tirelessly industrious, and one never knew what to expect. His originality was tremendously challenging, and he also had a dynamism and intense masculinity. He definitely had a sexual magnetism where women were concerned. I wondered why he had chosen me for a one-to-one special meeting.

Just as a precaution, we had all been provided with shields in case of a nasty surprise. I drove into the side road which branched off to the twin mansions. Two girls approached as I parked my Daimler very near the large door. As we were ushered into the mansion, a butler and another young woman took our coats. Then I saw our host Draco coming towards us in the hall. He greeted us one by one, and led the way into the large hall. I could hear soft, rather romantic music caressing the air. All very charming and pleasant.

"I think we should all have a drink before we begin our meeting with Mr Akova," said Draco. Two more young women appeared behind a long bar on the left. Three more young women walked in through a side door. One of the women behind the bar stood like a statue, not moving a muscle, but when Draco looked into her eyes, a hint of a smile came to her lips. Minutes later, there were at least ten girls and three to four men in the hall. Draco was perhaps planning to entertain his guests.

"Mr Akova, Major Blount, Mr Houston and the charming and beautiful Emma Fitzgerald," he introduced us to the men, looking last at Emma with a smile. He stood beside the others, "I don't know your names, but I'm sure we'll get acquainted soon enough."

Houston sat on a stool at the bar, but raised himself on his elbow when Draco put a friendly hand on his shoulder.

"I hope you don't mind me having a private meeting with Mr Akova, first."

"No, not at all," replied Houston calmly, "but my government is anxious to hear your terms for an agreement."

"Rest assured, Mr Houston, I will do my utmost to reach an agreement," said Draco.

Emma seemed to have assumed a sulky, capricious air while she sat at our table with two of Draco's young women. Their unabashed flirting eventually humoured her out of her mood as Draco joined us at the table.

"Your hospitality is overwhelming, Mr Draco," said Emma, holding out her hand to him. He kissed it lingeringly and suggestively, and pursued her implacably to the other end of the bar.

"She's your girlfriend, isn't she?" asked the blonde sitting beside me, "and you love her very much, don't you?"

"Yes," I said, my eyes following Emma and Draco who were now moving around the room conversing like old friends. I wondered whether we would ever be able to get rid of this fearsome phantom.

"You're Mr Draco's guests, I presume?" I asked.

"Yes," she replied, "Mr Draco pays handsomely for our services. We are not prostitutes."

There was a minute's silence after that comment. A roll of thunder broke it, as I simultaneously felt a strange fascination drawing me closer to my companion.

"Why don't I show you round the castle?" she suggested suddenly.

Castle? I thought, that's odd.

"Sorry, I meant mansion, of course." She seemed to be enjoying the stillness of the atmosphere in the hall, as she walked towards the stairs and I followed.

"Upstairs is particularly beautiful. I hear there are weird stories of ghosts in this mansion."

"Where are you from, Judy?"

"From here, Marlborough," she replied as she walked in front of me, tossing her long blonde hair as she moved. She was wearing a white silk dress. On the first floor, she opened the door on the left.

"Let's go in," she whispered, and switched on the light. She had a beautiful body and I could see the fine features of her lovely face. She shut the door gently and stood dangerously close to me, took my hand in hers, and squeezed it. Seconds later, her lips were on mine in a long kiss. Then she moved away from me.

The room was beautifully decorated with drawn royal blue curtains. There were flowers on the floor. Judy opened the balcony door, and I looked up. The clouds were scattering slowly, and I could see some stars. We blended with the silence, the ever present sexual attraction, the passing wind and the slightly damp smell which rose from the ground below. With a heightened poetic imagination, I observed a high spirited and adventurous young girl stimulating me all over. She could not have been more than twenty-two, perhaps twenty-three. Seconds later, her mobile rang, and the spell was broken. She answered the phone: "Yes?" and then, turned to face me with cool indifference: "Duty calls…"

She closed the balcony door. I heard a scratching on the window panes.

"One of the ghosts has been watching us," I put my arms around her waist from behind, and kissed her on the neck.

"We must go down," she said, and we left the room and paused in the corridor.

"Perhaps we will meet another day," I said.

"Yes, I'll find you."

"Is that a promise?"

"Yes, but now, please go." She said and left me, hurrying down the stairs.

She went down before I did. Looking down the corridor, I saw a door ajar on the right. The light was on. I could not control my curiosity and peeped inside. A few feet inside, a man lay crumpled up on the floor.

"What the hell? What happened to you? Do you need any help?" I tried to give him a helping hand.

He snapped at me: "I'll be all right!" but he could barely raise his right arm to stop me, "you're here for the experiment, are you?"

I had no idea what he was talking about, but I said I was.

"What you see here is supernatural come-uppance. You're not a priest, are you?"

I laughed at that, and told him I was far from it, and then asked him about the experiment. He had a bald head, pointed ears, and large mouth and his face was full of fear. "You see, I've been a priest all my working life. My belief in Christ was so great that Mr Draco said I would have to go through a test to erase the biblical claptrap from my brain and soul. So what you see here is a rare display of contrition. He said I had sinned against the most powerful God of the universe. He also told me that my repentance would be rewarded in the end."

"Do you believe him?"

"Yes, of course. He proved it to me. I am now paralysed. But this is temporary. Soon, when the experiment is complete, I'll be a new man. I beg of you, don't tell anyone you've seen me here, and please close the door when you leave."

I had seen many examples of Eridanian manifestations during the last six months, and this 'experiment' was just another devil's game. The man was actually savouring his torture; a priest allowing himself to be cleansed of the Christian faith and reanimated by the devil. I was not seen by anyone when I slipped back into the hall. Emma and Draco were still at the bar. I was wondering about the whole raft of offers which would no doubt be forthcoming from Draco. I was more or less preparing myself for the worst kind of truth. There was not even a wisp of positive, tangible evidence to suggest that our challenge to survive against the might of the aliens would be sufficient to stop their advance.

Draco greeted me with his usual charm, while Emma, Major Blount, Houston and the others were escorted into another room together with the girls. I followed him into another room at the other end of the great hall. Inside, I shivered, for the room had a damp chill to it. The curtains were drawn across, and the large study was distinctly gloomy and unwelcoming.

Draco did not sit behind the large desk near the windows in the spacious room. Instead he pointed to a smaller desk in the centre.

"*Sic itur ad astra*," he said. "I suppose that's the best way possible to start our talks. I'm sure you know that's the way to immortality. The destiny of man and Earth and the destiny of our own extraterrestrial civilisation lies in the heavens. We have to merge with mankind, and as you know, we've done that already in Europe."

"Very impressive," I commented.

"Thank you," he smiled, and continued. "Now, let me start with Europe. As you know, there was a clash between those in the EU who saw this organisation as an intergovernmental association of nation states, and those who viewed it as a step on the way towards the 'United States of Europe'. In terms of this polarity, one can say that the initial acceptance of a plan to go ahead with the second choice and the whole package was a clear victory for the pan-Europeans. But the plan has not yet been fully realised. If these policies of uniting the peoples of Europe under a federation had been fully implemented, they would have acted as a major force, predisposing Europe towards continuing in the direction of the pan-Europeans. But the plan was not fully implemented, largely because of the Commission's overtly interventionist approach to liberalisation."

I was truly surprised to hear Draco talk like a professor of European politics. Of course, I always knew these aliens were capable of learning anything in an instant. This was the strategic mastermind of Draco bringing the EU under full control of the Eridanians with the pretence of a United States of Europe. But they had already concluded their European takeover successfully. The last round of enlargement to the east and south had also been completed, leaving Turkey out as always.

"I'm anxious to hear your offer for an agreement," I said.

"Well, Britain is a unique case. They'll never hand over their sovereignty to Brussels. They reject the Euro, they have very long standing, close relationships with Commonwealth countries. Britain's alignment with the Americans is a very special case. These are some of the points to be discussed at a later date, in the context of European unity. Unity of mankind under one roof, that's our aim. But for us, the problem of extraterrestrial challenges within Britain itself and in Wiltshire in particular poses a threat to this unity."

"What do you mean by extraterrestrial challenges? To what are you referring, Mr Draco?"

"We have completed the last round of EU enlargement through following plans devised over the last fifteen years For us, Britain is vital in the United States of Europe. But more importantly, the extraterrestrial presence in Wiltshire is of paramount interest. By mentioning extraterrestrial challenges in Britain, I am referring to the secret war between the Greys and the Eridanians. Their claim that they will save mankind from the evil of the Eridanians is ludicrous."

Draco continued fervently, "What you call the Grey extraterrestrials started a ferocious campaign against us as soon as we arrived here on Earth. Mr Akova, there have been many visitations here on Earth during ancient times, in Egypt and of course, during the period when Jesus Christ was alive. But let us talk about modern times, as you say. I admit the Greys arrived here before we did, but their egotistic quest for power and to rule over the whole world has always been their primary aim. They want to expand their relative power positions. But their action plan denigrated this tendency as reflective of the baser Grey instincts that lead them to commit acts of aggression and to attempt to strengthen themselves in ways that are likely to provoke counter-measures on the part of not only the human civilisation but our own civilisation too."

"Wait a second. I have not seen any act of aggression on the part of the Greys yet."

"They work secretly with robots in human form," he told me. Perhaps there was some truth in what he was saying. But I could never be sure about the possibility of Greys using robots for contacts with humans.

"Let me ask you this, Mr Draco, what's preventing you from taking over Britain?"

"I'll give you a straight answer, Mr Akova. The Greys in Britain and many millions of British people who are now processed into becoming Grey-controlled humans."

"So what do you suggest? What is the agreement you want?"

"Simply this. An agreement with Britain to merge with us. In other words, a stage by stage integration of humans and Eridanians into a much higher level of live. Handing over power to a joint authority independent of the EU. With this agreement, Britain will become part of an integrated economic system. The British will have our technology; there will be a sort of technological interdependence between us and Britain. Naturally, once we sign this agreement, the Greys' power of humans in Britain will be eroded."

"First you say a joint authority of Britain and the Eridanians and then you talk about Britain becoming part of an integrated economic system. I find this contradictory since you refer to a joint authority independent of the EU."

"You are right. But think about the present situation. The British have always opted for an independent policy with regard to international political forces. But you must admit, it is widely accepted that the globalisation of the world economy has been established. Britain is one of the few examples of a nation state in the world. Human civilisation of Planet Earth is so backward that they are still talking about the nation-state in crisis. The nation state is threatened from above by globalisation and the supranatural structures of the EU, the development of which is itself linked to the globalisation of the economy, and threatened from below by the fragmentary forces of ethnic nationalism. Nationalism is another primitive part of your political existence which has not yet been totally emasculated by globalisation. So, in actual fact, Britain's position in the world will not change much as far as EU politics is concerned. But she will have our technology, provided she accepts a joint authority."

Draco's offer was no different from what they had already given to the EU. And it was obvious that the joint authority was the first step towards Eridanian dominance in Britain. Draco tried to camouflage their real intentions by a greater emphasis on a 'no change' situation in Britain, and added that their central proposition was advanced space technology coupled with the acquisition of medical 'miracles' and other possibilities bordering on 'everlasting life'. He avoided mentioning the economic and monetary areas of Britain.

"What about Britain's economy?"

"We won't bother with that," he said, "Britain will manage her own economic and monetary matters. Of course, we will organise financial contributions for the well-being of British society at every level. There is no need for complicated economic plans. There will be an economic order benefitting all mankind."

"But that's a general overview," I challenged. "How will mankind benefit through this new economic order?"

"Mr Akova, the income of ordinary people in EU member states has quadrupled since our official takeover of their organisation. There will be less work and more income. But our plan goes far beyond a purely economic vision. The whole structure of society will change, with a reawakening of humans in a new dimension transcending the earlier, primitive methods."

I could almost believe him. Draco's offer for Britain was simple, but at the same time cunning, in that it seemed to offer much more than it demanded in return. The man was now much more sympathetic. Suddenly a strange feeling took over my whole body and soul. I tried to resist it but it was there with all the power of the creature in front of me. Draco moved closer.

"Mr Akova," he purred, with a sinister smile, "I'm sure you'll agree that this is the way for Britain."

"Yes, you're right," I said, hardly able to believe the words issuing from my mouth.

"Let's go out for a bit of fresh air," he suggested, and I obeyed. We walked out of the room into a very large garden behind the mansion. When I looked back, I could not believe my eyes. Draco was at it again. The landscape and the whole building had been transformed into a castle; a castle with all the features of a quintessentially gothic structure. Draco's demonic laugh shredded the air, and I shivered in the cold, trying desperately to regain my normal faculties. But there was no change. Another figure appeared, emerging slowly from the dark side of the garden. She was bewitchingly beautiful. I looked at her again. It was the girl I had accompanied into the room upstairs. Was she a female demon? She held my hand. There was a feeling of impending evil. Draco's pernicious influence created a gnawing distress and torment within me, but at the same time, I desired the young girl in front of me, pulling me towards her.

"I enjoy doing this, Mr Akova," he said, still laughing, "you can see she wants you." There was something evil lurking in the depths of my unconscious.

"Now you will compose for me," he said, and I realised I had surrendered all my will to this evil monarch. I had no strength to challenge him. Together with Draco and the girl, we entered the room once again.

"You go in," commanded Draco, "you will compose for me. You are a musical genius, Mr Akova." He was trying to make me compose music redolent with horror, fear and torture; music that depicted all the characteristics of the Devil…But why? I had become a slave of the powers of Satan…I could not understand how or why I was in such a position. On the one hand, I was really my normal self, but I was unable to challenge Draco.

Inside the hall, Emma watched me with fear and dismay. She sensed immediately that something was wrong. I obeyed Draco and had neither the will nor the power to neutralise his spell. Even though I knew deep down that Draco's plan had always been one of colonising Earth, and that this agreement would bring about the downfall of the British government, thus breaking up the resistance of the people against the Eridanians, I was now ready to advise Houston that signing this agreement would be in Britain's best interests.

"Ladies and gentlemen," Draco raised his resonant and rich voice, while I was getting ready to play. There were probably between one hundred and fifty to two hundred people in the hall. Where had they come from? I had no idea.

"Turan Akova is the great improviser and a daring innovator. He is unequalled as a pianist and his success in phenomenal. Wherever he performs, his new techniques, inimitable style, brilliant improvisations, great compositions and magnetism as a pianist-composer moves audiences to wild, uncontrollable, hysterical adulation…Now he will compose for us. I give you…Turan Akova!"

There was total silence in the hall for about thirty seconds. My fingers moved with great agility and the first passage was a ringing mass cry with violent overtones and fearful climaxes resounding in the great hall, like a barrage of musical thunder. Although my avant-garde new music was inspired by my excessive interest in space and extraterrestrial civilisations, and I categorised this type of music as 'Space Music', what I played that evening was not just extraordinary but horrifying. During the performance I developed a strange compliance with something evil, something compelling me to obey Draco. I was transfixed with terror in a wave of supernatural activity which paralysed my normal senses and yet pushed me into sporadic nuances of mysterious energies streaming down through my fingers onto the keyboard.

This new composition together with my improvisation lasted for about twenty minutes. I was applauded with violent enthusiasm. What a performance. I was well aware of the fact that Draco would delight in destroying the human species, first by making them slaves of the Eridanians and then he would create a new type of human. Calm down, I told myself, and concentrate. The thought of challenging Draco was there. I walked through the crowd of people who were trying to embrace, kiss and hug me, showering me with accolades for my compositions and performance. When I reached the bar, Emma furtively took my hand.

"I'll tell you later," I said.

Houston grabbed my hand and congratulated me.

"I had no idea you had a musical career. I must say, what you played was exciting stuff, but very frightening indeed." He gulped down his whisky and stood in front of me. "So, tell me, old chap, how did it go? Is there any hope of a settlement with the Eridanians?"

"Yes," I said, turning to Emma, who was trying to hide her anxiety, "let's ask for some coffee."

"Mr Houston," I said, "Draco will send the terms of the agreement he is offering to your office tomorrow. I think they are being very generous, and frankly, I would personally advise the government to sign it."

Draco's powerful concentration, his mysterious spell which was making me say things I did not want to say was becoming more intense, and the cumulative effect was dragging me deeper into desperation. This was some kind of mental aberration. I was obeying his irresistible, powerful demands. All my perceptions, my ability to discriminate between good and evil, to understand and reject his plans were benumbed. I had somehow to get out of this unaccountable state. I was being reduced to a puppet of the Devil. I had been stripped of all my powers and my struggle to regain them was held in check.

When Draco joined us at the bar, Emma made her move.

"Darling, with all this excitement, I've developed something of a headache. I think I must have had too much to drink. Would you give me a lift home?" she asked.

"But Miss Fitzgerald," Draco intercepted, "you don't want to leave us so early. The party's just beginning to warm up."

"You'll excuse me, Mr Draco, but I think I'll have an early night. But I promise I'll send Turan back to you."

I took comfort in the knowledge that Emma wanted me out of Draco's residence, at least for an hour or so. She knew me so well. An uncertain, vague and strange cold thrill of a sensation prevailed while Emma made her goodbyes and we left the mansion. Efforts to regain my former self had shrunk to their lowest ebb as I stood by the car. But within seconds the fresh air injected a kind of vitality into my body. Emma drove me home.

As soon as we stepped inside the house, she took my hand with curiosity.

"I've never seen you like this before."

"Well, and what is it that you see, for God's sake?" I asked her impatiently.

"You look pale. You may not realise it, but you acted very strangely back at Draco's mansion. Your behaviour was quite out of character."

Thirty-Two

"Oh, God! Emma, I'm definitely under his spell. Thank God, I'm aware of it! And thank God, though I'm powerless to get rid of it, I am still in possession of my faculties. Come, hold my hand. We must try to communicate with Tamor, the Alpha Centaurian. I think I can dispose of this evil monstrosity with his help." Clearly, I had yielded to the temptation of the Devil.

"Quick! Emma, hold my hand and repeat this sentence in your thoughts. 'Great Tamor, please help me to erase this evil Eridanian spell'."

We must have repeated this telepathic call at least twenty times when quite suddenly Tamor appeared in the room. He was dressed in white and his eyes radiated a brilliant light.

"The evil spell will soon disappear and never will it bother you again," he said. Immediately afterwards I was struck by a magical, frighteningly bright, white light which seemed to have cleansed my brain, body and soul. It was impossible to describe the strength of the power. The moment the light struck my body, I knew Draco's magic had evaporated into thin air. Tamor raised his head towards the stars, the moonlight streamed in through the curtains and I was reborn. He looked taller, his hands clasped, his eyes turned towards the heavens.

"Tamor," I called out to him. I had so many questions to ask him, but he had disappeared in a split second and my questions were left unanswered. Nevertheless, I was thankful for his timely intervention which had cast away the evil spirit and returned me to my normal self.

I decided to return to Draco's mansion. Emma objected, as she was very much concerned about the possibility of a stronger, perhaps fatal, evil implantation by Draco in my brain, that could cause a permanent loss of memory and strip me of all my powers.

"But Emma," I insisted, "remember what Tamor said. Draco's magic can't touch me anymore."

"Yes, I know he promised you that. But at the same time, don't forget the Eridanian has the upper hand at the moment. He proved his powers were superior to that of the Greys—he proved it at Silbury Hill. So anything can happen and I can't help worrying."

"Well, don't worry, my darling." I said, "Come with me if you like."

"No, I'll pass on that one, thank you! But how on earth did he get you to agree to the settlement he offered. It's beyond me!"

"Oh, he plays all sorts of games. It's his nature."

By the time I went back to the mansion, Houston and his people had already left. Draco greeted me at the entrance.

"I knew you'd return," he gloated, "you've come back for the girl, haven't you, you devil…" he chuckled.

"It's ironic you use that name for me…"

"Come on, Mr Akova, the Devil is an abomination you Earth people have been creating over the centuries. Advanced civilisations in the universe possess supernatural powers. Some are far more advanced than others. It's as simple as that. We cannot expect mankind to understand the complexities of cosmic development and the configurations of intricate astral interstellar networks in relation to astonishingly advanced intelligent galactic life, and the creation of other species, whose life-span covers mostly a period of over 5,000 years earth time."

"Mr Draco, you should lecture humans on extraterrestrial civilisations."

"That's a very good idea," he exclaimed enthusiastically.

"But tell me, how are the Eridanians placed among the extraterrestrial civilisations in the Milky Way Galaxy?"

"No need to boast about it, but we are among the top," he said smugly, without a moment's hesitation.

"What about Houston and his friends?" I asked him, "they left early, didn't they?"

"Mr Houston said he had to deliver our message to the government immediately."

That meant I had to hurry and contact Houston and stop a possible signing of an agreement with the Eridanians. If the Eridanians had not been of the Satanic race and if they had not planned to turn mankind into their slaves, their offer would have had enormous potential. In actual fact, what Draco was offering was incredibly tempting. First of all, mankind would possess a mine of amazing scientific data which would be tailored especially for human society. However, thousands of people in Britain were already suspecting a catch and were beginning to see through the grand deception.

The French scientist, UFO researcher and author's best-selling 'Alien Contact' trilogy—'Dimensions, Confrontations and Revelations', and his last book, 'Forbidden Science', had sold millions in many languages. In these books, he suggested a new political organisation—Peripherism—to challenge the aliens in control of the EU. He urged mankind to put an end to the consortium of nations under one roof. His theory rested upon a network of independent sovereign states. In other words, the EU breaking up and its constituent countries returning to their original states before the European Community was first established. He held that a group of discrete, independent nation states would be able to challenge alien domination.

The deliberate attempt on the part of the Eridanians to create a complicated and yet closely interwoven society of humans merging with the aliens was by no means based on the single and individual personality of Draco. To us, at the UFO Research Centre in London, there was a sharp contradiction between the first hand evidence we had gathered so far of the Devil's methods, which made all fake and sham and this generous offer of the agreement which was to be signed by the British government. This was a case of serious abuse. But the Eridanians wrapped this up in such a beautifully presented package that it was quite impossible for any human to extrapolate the facts. But the British government was able to keep abreast of developments. The highly skilled art of several American UFO researchers in determining the patterns of alien behaviour was also quite extraordinary. Through the unyielding, dynamic challenge of the Chosen 36, our Centre and the efforts of these ufologists, the Eridanian tide was turning. Even rumours of an agreement with the aliens aroused antagonism amongst normal people who detested them. There was even talk of a violent protest, coming from various religious extremist groups who demanded the implementation of the American strike plan, an all-out war against the aliens. Nevertheless, the British government pressed forward vigorously with their tactics of prevarication and continued to create a certain confusion which the aliens could not see through.

The creation of a world of passionate emotion was another tactic of the Eridanians. This worked with people who were enmeshed in power politics. The shadow Defence Minister demanded an emergency meeting with the government in a fit of disillusioned rage. Throwing the onus of a possible permanent solution to the problem on the Premier and his government, the bumptious attitude of this politician was well-supported in Parliament. In London, I expected stinging official government rebuke, but no official statement was forthcoming.

The Eridanians were quick to sense the danger of a rejection of their offer, and tried to crush any rise of a liberal, anti-alien tendency throughout the country. This was done through the media they controlled. Now we were faced with the possibility of a great eruption which would be extremely difficult to suppress. Thank God, the Premier's policy was unobtrusive, deeply probing and intense. A good example of solidity and terseness. The man was infallible and extremely courageous.

I called Houston's office. His secretary said he'd gone. For at least a month, there were no striking news stories about the Eridanians in the printed media, and the scarcity of alien news led to the reporting of stories of secondary interest. But now some papers featured forceful, apt and catchy headlines followed by stories about the possibility of the signing of an agreement with the Eridanians. One report said the government was planning an emergency meeting to reach a final decision. The Premier was on an official visit to France and the report said he was due to return the following day. I called Houston's home. Mrs Houston said he had just left and had not said where he was going.

"He seemed to be in a hurry." She explained, "It wasn't at all like him. Normally, he tells me his whereabouts. At any rate, I should try his mobile, if I were you, Mr Akova."

I did. The phone kept ringing, but there was no answer. As the Defence Minister was also in Europe with the Premier, Houston was the only official I cold contact. I had to find him immediately and explain to him why he should not advise the government to sign any accord with the aliens. Major Blount told me that he often frequented the men's club, Turner's, in Waterloo Place, just off Carlton House Terrace. When I made enquiries, I was told they had not seen him for days.

I began to worry when Houston did not return home that evening. Mrs Houston called at around midnight to ask whether I had been able to find him. I decided to pay her a visit. Their home was off Piccadilly, in Dover Street. They lived in an old Victorian house, with modern buildings surrounding it everywhere you looked. When I parked the Daimler about fifty metres from the house, the street was almost empty, apart from a few indistinct scurrying figures.

The three-storey building was half-hidden in a pall of smoke. It was difficult to tell where it was coming from; it was strange. But minutes later, I could hear the siren of a fire-engine. There was a fire in the adjacent street.

Mrs Houston was a pretty young woman in her early thirties.

"I'm sorry to disturb you at this late hour, Mrs Houston, but I just wanted to ask you a few questions." She was a pleasant, polite woman, whose family dated back eight hundred years. Her father, Lord Robins, was a life peer. Major Blount had given me all the low-down about the family just before Houston had arrived in Marlborough. Houston himself was the son of the (feckless) Earl of Blanford. So the Houstons were in the aristocratic milieu.

"Do come in, Mr Akova," she smiled as I entered. "I have heard so much about you. I must say I'm fascinated by this alien presence, and of course, I know about your prodigious musical career. I listen to your music quite often."

"Thank you. It's a pleasure to meet you."

"Do come in," she said, walking sedately into a large living room on the left. She was wearing a tight blue dress and looked as if she had just returned home, still wearing a fashionable high-heeled shoes.

"Please, sit down. Would you like a drink? I'm having whisky."

"Whisky's fine," I said.

She took a whisky bottle from the small table in the corner and poured some into two glasses, and then sat in an armchair opposite me.

"Mrs Houston—" I began.

"Call me Mary."

"OK. Mary, I must find your husband now. I don't want to go into great detail but he was with me in Marlborough. False information was given to him there, and it would be fatal to the British people as a whole if he acted on it and it became official. While I was looking for him, in between following up my leads, I was able to attend a conference on the subject—which is a possible signing of an agreement with the aliens. Some cabinet ministers who support this were present there. You appreciate that one has to have considerate skill to separate the facts from the official rhetoric. Even in the leaflets they had out, the message is generally empty rhetoric, what they want the media to publish. But the information I need is different. At any rate, most of the cabinet ministers are on the wrong path. The Premier and the Defence Minister are unfortunately away in France. From what I have gathered so far, the supporters of an agreement seem to have become a majority and can now outvote the Premier and his Defence

Minister, and all the others who oppose it. So I have to find your husband, you see, and ask him to see these people to convince them that it must not be signed. Don't worry. I don't think he is in any danger. But I have to find him now. Can you help me? Perhaps you could give me the contact details of his closest friends? He might be with one of them."

"That's easy. But he would have called if he was going to be late or detained somewhere for the night."

"Did you see him when he arrived from Marlborough?"

"Yes, but only for half an hour or so. And the next morning he left in a rush."

"Did you speak to him?"

"Yes, but only for a few minutes," she said.

"Did you notice anything strange about his behaviour?"

"I don't think so," she said slowly. By now, she was looking worried. "Mr Akova, you said he was not in any danger, yet you are asking me these odd questions."

"I'm sorry. There really is no reason for you to be unduly worried. Perhaps you will find this difficult to believe, but the aliens may have put a temporary spell on him. Your husband is a key figure in the government and the aliens want him to believe that their agreement is desirable. You see, I was under their spell for a time, but I managed to get out of it. I must find him and make sure he is OK."

"Aliens? Spell? Good heavens, Mr Akova. How on earth can people put spells on other people?"

"These are not people. They are aliens and they have extraordinary, supernatural powers." I did not want to mention the Devil, but she did so herself.

"I have read a great deal about them. I wonder, are you referring to this Devil-talk?"

"Yes," I said, "they are wild, wilfully ugly, hideous and coldly cerebral creatures. But they are in human form and you can't tell the difference between an Eridanian in human form and an ordinary human. We are dealing with a super-intelligent, highly advanced civilisation. I'm afraid this 'devil-talk', as you put it, is true."

"God!" she gasped, "what are we going to do?"

"We have a chance of repelling this evil presence with help from the Greys—the other extraterrestrial civilisation, who are the good guys. But we'll talk about that some other time. Now, please give me the names and addresses of your husband's friends."

Houston had three close friends who were all from well-respected families. I made an appointment with the first one—a George Cutler, who was the managing director of a multi-national company based in London, manufacturing and exporting woven and machine-knitted articles. A good looking young man, probably in his mid-thirties. He was wearing a black pinstriped suit with a red tie. When I entered his office, there was a young woman standing beside his desk.

"Mr Akova. Mary called and told me about Edward's disappearance. What the devil is he up to now?" He looked up and the woman standing there, smiling at us. "Excuse me. This is my sister Ann. Mr Akova. Ann knows him better than I do, don't you, Ann?" he said and his sister responded immediately.

"Well, I suppose that's true." She embodied the sort of icy beauty perceptible only to those who admired animal warmth, "We always meet at the Club, that is the Cavendish Club in Mayfair."

I had been to this club once or twice with friends. It was one of the most prestigious clubs in London. It was a membership only club which boasted one of the best restaurants in town. It did not have a casino, but some members played poker occasionally. The Cavendish Club was in Berkeley Square. I remember meeting Omar Sharif, the Egyptian actor, there once. He was a keen backgammon player.

"The last time I saw Eddie was about a week ago. He was with someone I know. A girl from the club. Many temptations beset the path of a good looking young man, Mr Akova. Especially one who moves in high places in the government. Girls like to flirt with him."

I sensed a note of jealousy in her voice. "What about this girl?" I asked. "Could you give me her name and address. Perhaps I should start looking for him there."

"I think that would be a good idea," Ann looked at her brother, who seemed completely uninterested in the affair.

"What about you, Mr Cutler? Do you have any ideas about where he may be?" I enquired.

"No, I'm afraid not. Not now anyway. But he's always been a playboy of sorts. He likes his girls."

"Let me give you her name and address," said Ann. "Jane Latimer is the name and her address is no. 18, Heron Quays, London E14. It's in Canada Water, on the Jubilee line."

Heron Quays was a small street sandwiched between tall office buildings. There were a few houses there which looked like homes. I found number 18 somewhere in the middle. The walls outside were painted red. I rang the bell. A beautiful young girl opened the door. I must be quite sincere about my thought at that moment: so many beautiful girls grace this land of Britain. They must rate among the most beautiful in the world.

"Yes? Can I help you?" she had red hair and red lips and she was wearing a long, yellow nightgown. All of a sudden, I felt chilled.

"My name's Akova. I'm looking for someone by the name of Edward Houston." There was something about this young woman which didn't agree with me. My brain was almost blanked out. I wondered whether Tamor had given me some other special powers which detected Eridanians in human form who had supernatural abilities as yet unheard of in today's scientific milieu. Perhaps she was one of them.

"You've found him," she said, pulsating with a strange energy which entered painfully into my body. But Tamor's powers worked wonders. The cold horror of her evil powers shattered within seconds and she focussed her very bright green eyes on mine, a viciously exasperated great awakening of her alien self. From just one stare from those beautiful, yet terrifying, eyes, I could clearly sense and detect a display of satanic supernatural grit. The entire weird encounter diminished as Houston appeared at the other end of the hall.

"Mr Akova!" he exclaimed, "what a surprise! How on earth did you find me?"

"Just luck, I suppose. Your wife suggested I look for you at George Cutler's office, and his sister Ann directed me here."

"Well, she would, wouldn't she, the bitch..." Jane Latimer spat out.

"You must come with me, now, Mr Houston. It is of the utmost importance."

"Sure," he replied, "but first of all, I must keep my promise to Jane. We are going to visit friends in Hampstead. You're welcome to join us. I'm sure Jane won't mind."

"It'll be a pleasure to have you with us," said Jane, back to her normal human self. "I'm sure you'll enjoy the party."

"What party?" I asked.

"It's a luncheon. A lunchtime party, if you like. The birthday party of a friend of Jane's." Houston explained.

The birthday party was at a large house not far from the pub Jack Straw's Castle, up on the hill. There were at least fifty—sixty people in the hall. Extraterrestrials mingling with humans? Was this at all possible? The people inside the hall were warm, generous and jovial and once again, the place was filled with stunning women. The music of Stravinsky, Schonberg and Berg mingled with the blinking lights. It was a rainy day and it was dark inside. While drinking my beer, I looked around—and then I saw her. Judy, the blond girl from Draco's mansion was standing at the other end of the bar. Jane approached me and in an aggressive, almost threatening manner, she asked me to dance. Dancing to Stravinsky was altogether a new experience.

"You want her?" she pointed to Judy.

"Yes, desperately," I joked.

"She wants you too, you know." She said, leading me to the other end of the bar.

"Why, it's Mr Akova," cried Judy with delight, "so, we meet again…"

I had always cultivated a certain equanimity of temper, not taking life too seriously and taking whatever it offered in my stride. Suddenly, I heard new music start up: the composition Draco had forced me to write. It had such terrifying vehemence, that I loathed myself for it.

As the music got louder, Judy pulled me into a corner right behind the bar. I kissed her, our bodies vibrating incessantly against each other, our excitement climaxing into ecstatic pleasure. In the meantime, I followed Houston's every movement. He was dancing in the middle of the hall with another girl. Then quite suddenly, I heard three shots. People screamed with terror and ran towards the door. Houston fell to the floor. I saw a man dressed in black moving towards him with a gun in his hand. He was wearing a black leather coat. Houston was struggling to get up. I pulled out my gun and fired at the legs of his attacker.

The whole incident lasted for about half a minute. I helped Houston into a chair and called an ambulance. He had been lucky. Two bullets had hit him on the right shoulder and the third had missed him completely. I also telephoned the police. They police arrived and the ambulance took Houston to the hospital soon afterwards. The assassin was also taken into the ambulance accompanied by three police officers from Scotland Yard. Major Blount was also there. He handed me a card with my name printed on it, to make things easier with my dealings with the police. Although I was known and had the confidence of Scotland Yard, an MI6 card would indeed speed up my investigations and would no longer entail much painstaking interviewing of often reluctant or even sometimes positively hostile police officers who did not understand how or why a Turkish Cypriot with the strange name of Turan Akova was meddling in their affairs. Police sometimes have their reasons for withholding information.

In the first instance, this shooting of a high-ranking member of the government was treated as a political assassination attempt. As always, there were scores of reporters investigating the attempted murder. One of them, a senior reporter, recognised Major Blount and the Chief of MI6 and asked him whether there were other unknown reasons for this incident to be hushed up by the police and other officials.

"We are investigating other possibilities. But a political motive may prove to be the real reason behind it," said Major Blount. This reporter recognised me, too.

"Mr Akova, apparently this is not a run of the mill case. We know you are involved with alien presence. The government is in the middle of a crisis regarding the Eridanians. There were reports in some papers about a possible signing of an agreement with the Eridanians. You were a journalist once. Can you give me a story along those lines? Is there a new development? What about Under-Secretary Houston? Was he involved in the drafting of the agreement?" He was using his imagination as well as his ingenuity, and I knew he was with one of the major dailies outside Eridanian control.

"Yes. A final cabinet meeting is scheduled for tomorrow, when the Premier and Defence Minister arrive from France. The government will decide whether to sign an agreement with the Eridanians or not. Naturally, Mr Houston is the key figure in this affair, as he delivered the alien offer to the cabinet members. But this attempt on his life was totally unexpected. I honestly don't know who is behind this. That's all I can tell you now."

Mrs Houston was already at the hospital beside her husband. Jane and Ann Cutler sat opposite each other in the corridor. I knew about Jane's affair with Houston and it looked as though Ann had been involved with him earlier. Major Blount and I went into Houston's room and assured him that he would be protected at all times. Then we left and visited the criminal at St Mary's Hospital. The manner in which the crime was committed had been strange. The two police officers in the room had little to say.

"We are working along certain lines, but we are not yet in a position to give a statement," said one of them. I did ask Houston whether he had submitted the official offer of the Eridanians to the Premier. He said he had left the document in the safe hands of the Premier's secretary, Margaret Holstein, as the Premier was in France. Houston's shooting did not make any sense. After all, he had delivered a document—with my blessing, of course, which supported the signing of an agreement. So why would Draco have him shot when everything was running smoothly in his favour? I had been too late to prevent the document from reaching the Premier's office. I told Houston what had happened and that my recommendations in favour of an agreement were in fact the result of that terrifying spell.

"I've prepared a new report advising the government not to sign an agreement with the Eridanians under any circumstances," I told him. The cabinet ministers had to wait for the Premier and the Defence Minister before a final meeting could be held. This was perhaps an over-hasty decision, but it would most certainly keep the ministers supporting the signing of an agreement at bay.

The criminal, a Roger Arlington, said he had been paid £50,000 to do the job.

"I was approached by two men. I don't know who they were. That's the plain truth. I have no idea either who the man Houston is. We followed him to a house and then I was told where he would be tonight. They paid me cash and told me they'd have me followed to make sure the job was done properly."

Jane and Houston were, as far as I could gather, the only two people who knew where we were going. But how did the mysterious two men find out about that? Jane was definitely a suspect. On the other hand, we could have been follo0wed to the 'Castle' in Hampstead by the men who had approached Arlington. Either way, I had nothing much to go on. Later, I asked Jane to join me for dinner. We went to a small restaurant in Fleet Street. She was quite shaken by the incident, but was already beginning to ask questions:

"Mr Akova, why would anyone want to kill Edward?" she asked.

"I don't know. But let me ask you this. You and Edward were the only two people who knew where we were going. Did you talk to anyone before we left the house? Did someone call you before I arrived at your home?"

"No. No one called. We were in bed, anyway," she said. "But Mr Akova, I think you should question Ann and her brother too."

"Why? OK, so she told me Houston could be with you. Now tell me the truth. Was Ann involved with Edward?"

"Yes, she was. And she didn't like it at all when Edward left her for me."

"For God's sake, Jane. He's a married man!"

"Mr Akova, Edward is a well-known figure both in the government and in the Conservative Party. He's been tipped as the next leader of the party and the next premier. His work involves many vital issues that have to be tackled by him alone. As for the fact that he's married, I'm probably more intimate with him than his wife! I know him inside out and I can tell you he is a mere pawn in the global game of power politics, despite his important position. But this incident makes you wonder. Perhaps he is a threat to someone. So could this be a political assassination attempt? On the other hand, the signing of the agreement with the aliens cannot be kept outside politics since it involves the future of Britain as a whole," she said.

"You are a political commentator, aren't you?" I quipped, "So you think the Eridanians have a hand in this? But why should they? The draft agreement with favourable recommendations by me is now in the hands of the Premier's secretary. You see, I was tricked into supporting the alien offer. But already another report has been sent to the Premier's office, explaining why the first report is null and void. I think a particular combination of circumstances have brought about this incident. It seems to me you and Ann are in the centre of things."

"I will be very open with you, Mr Akova. Ann is jealous. She is also in love with Edward, and would do anything to get him back," she explained darkly.

"You don't expect me to believe for one moment that Ann hired two men, paid them £50,000 to have the man she loves so much shot dead?"

"No, but others may be involved."

"When you say others, who do you mean?"

"I don't know, maybe his brother," she suggested.

"Why him? What do you know about him?"

"Well, he has some strange friends who are members of the Cosmic Life Society, a newly established thing preaching the betterment of humans together with the extraterrestrial civilisations. In actual fact, many people have been led down the primrose path. I was there once with a friend and I saw him. I think you should investigate him also."

358

This Cosmic Life Society stretched beyond the bounds of credulity. Nevertheless, she was right. Ann's brother and his strange friends presented another angle.

"OK, so let's see. We've checked the most probable explanations. First on the list are the Eridanians. For some unknown reason, they may want Houston out of the way."

"Well, I know for a fact that he's always opposed an agreement with the aliens," she told me.

"I was not aware of that," I had only just met the man.

"Oh, yes. He told me. You ask Edward."

"I will…"

It was quite obvious that apart from the normal investigations, I had to analyse far out into the framework of the government's recent policy towards the aliens. I had no doubt in my mind that the Eridanians had infiltrated the government itself. Perhaps Draco was playing another game with stupendous powers unleashed over the people who supported an agreement with him. A couple of days later, I visited Houston at his home, where he was resting. We had a chance to talk alone when his wife was in the kitchen. I asked him about Jane and also concentrated in particular on Ann.

"Do you think Ann could have been involved in some way?" I asked him. He strenuously denied any kind of relationship with her in recent months.

"But you did have an affair with her," I insisted.

"Yes, but that was over a year ago. No, Mr Akova, I don't think she is involved in this dreadful business."

"I talked to her," I said, "she was shocked by the news. She told me she hated Jane and said she was not worthy of you. But quite frankly, I am not getting anywhere with either of these two girls in your life. What about Ann's brother? I'm told he's a member of the Cosmic Life Society. Some of his friends there have been described as cold and mechanical, which suggests alien presence."

"George has always been a funny sort of character. But he's still a friend."

"I think I will interview some of the cabinet ministers—those who support an agreement with the aliens."

"Good idea," he said.

Through my contacts in the Conservative government, I was introduced to a senior member of the party. Timothy Walton said I should talk to a Mr John Davidson, who was one of the candidates for the leadership of the party. Walton described him as too decadent to be a leader of the party and too timorous and half-hearted to fight against the signing of the agreement. Another member of the party said Davidson had clarity, good leadership qualities and a vision of a new Britain!

Assessing the current situation, it seemed to me that the old competition that used to exist between the USA and the old Soviet republics had now been replaced by a new competition between the Eridanian controlled E?U and the USA. Britain and Turkey were the only two allies the US could rely on in a crisis. The power struggle was at its peak between the politicians in Britain who supported the Eridanians and the other camp which was determined to reject alien domination. The murder attempt on Houston, the under-secretary to the Premier and one of the strongest contenders for the leadership of the Conservative Party was part of this scenario. It was apparent that the focus had shifted towards the opposition now established within the cabinet itself and supporters of an agreement with the Eridanians had acquired a dangerous momentum.

With the exception of a minority group within the party, Labour also insisted on the signing of an agreement. It was really absurd that the tail of the Eridanian supporters was allowed to wag the EU dog on an issue of such importance. Most of these politicians were unaware of the dangers involved in a decision to allow the establishment of an Eridanian controlled Britain. They felt Britain should not be left out, and were blind to all the extraterrestrial technological know-how and enormous financial gains in an enlarged EU.

The British government would have to stand up to these pressures and make it clear that their threats would not be allowed to precipitate a major crisis between the two factions. The Premier and the Defence Minister, the two strong men in the government, were determined to pursue what they perceived to be Britain's national interests both at home and abroad, without fear or favour. Those who supported an agreement with the Eridanians had already disabled the government to the extent that it was virtually impossible to reach a decision without first dealing with their threat.

The European Commission was also pressing for an agreement between Britain and the aliens. But the Premier had shown independence by breaking away from the moribund EU process and taking a new initiative. Houston was an important figure in the implementation of this initiative. My appointment with Davidson, the other Conservative leadership candidate, was on a Friday in

February. He suggested dinner at the restaurant at Crockford's Casino. We settled down for dinner, and he started off by expressing his admiration for my research on UFOs and my inimitable compositions. His conversation was circumspect and diffuse, but he had a brilliant mind and his reasoning behind the support of an agreement contained ideas like rose blossoms on a straggling and ill-pruned bush.

Some sounded like extemporisations which could not be substantiated. "The whole course of current political strategies, including that of the Premier, is destined to flow into a new channel—that of a joint human/extraterrestrial cooperation." He was fastidious in temper, perhaps a little spoiled by unbroken adulation and prosperity and he was a complete master of his medium. One particular belief of a united human/Eridanian world he never seemed able to cast off, not so much because of his stubbornness or weakness, as because of a decided, settled state of mind. He was determined to carry out this policy.

Clearly there was something about Davidson that bothered me. He was definitely not an Eridanian controlled person, however, that I had determined. Yet he insisted that Britain would be able to negotiate an agreement far more advantageous that that of the agreement between the Eridanians and the EU. Although his style was glitter and tinsel, he would scatter his political arguments which were at times elaborate and incongruous far and wide, and claim unchallenged supremacy over others who opposed his ideas.

"What can you tell me about the murder attempt on Edward Houston?" I asked him.

"Mr Akova, you are without question or cavil, the chief perpetrator—no, no that's not the right world—the central figure who claims the Eridanians aliens are evil. I beg to differ with you on this point. They are highly advanced not only with their technology, but also in mind and spirit. They could have taken over Britain as they did the EU. Instead, they offer us a separate agreement. Why? Houston is against it. Sometimes he is too blunt and straightforward. He is paying no heed at all to the conflicts within the government and within the party, for that matter. He is a wit and a bon viveur, extremely fond of social intercourse and extremely fond of his girlfriends. I admire him for his serene and unruffled confidence. What can I tell you about the murder attempt? Nothing, really. I don't see why anyone should want to eliminate him."

At that point, I did not want to mention the possibility that he was conspiring to eliminate his most important rival in the race for the Conservative party leadership. Was Davidson such a ruthless man? His determination to win was unfaltering. There were no obvious episodes of wavering tendencies in his political and personal life. No digressions. He did not hide behind the veil of politics.

"I wish I could help you more, Mr Akova," he intoned mournfully, stroking back a wisp of his long hair.

"If I find anything, I will contact you, Mr Davidson." I said.

"Please do." He nodded in affirmation.

I had already made up my mind. Davidson was a brilliant politician with a cultivated mind, but because of his admiration for the aliens, he was still not able to judge the magnitude of the nefarious effects of an Eridanian dominated Britain, once an agreement had been signed. Draco and his men had moved into a new area—that of earth politics—and were completely intrigued and enamoured by British diplomacy. They had succeeded in dissolving the public fear of the Devil and the unknown through their own media. Davidson left the restaurant at around ten fifteen. I said I wanted to stay on and gamble at the roulette table for a while. His home address had already been given to me by Major Blount, and I intended to pay a clandestine visit.

The large estate of the Davidson family was a few miles to the west of Sevenoaks. The Tristar—as it was called—was a yellow stone building. I parked my Daimler about five hundred metres from the large gate. Then I jumped onto the roof of the car and climbed the ten-foot wall. It was a moonlit evening. Scanning the view, I could see the distant grey hills. The estate seemed endless. There were many flowerless plants with feathery leaves all over the place. I watched out for any dogs, but there were none. I walked along a mossy garden path. Right in front of me there was a small lake with three swans drifting on the water. Pine trees in the surrounding park rose high into the sky and the whole place looked like a scene from a romantic fairy tale. Further to the left, I could see an area covered with grass the size of about two tennis courts.

I looked up. The heavens were completely clear of clouds. Then all of a sudden, I saw a dazzling light in the night sky coming towards the very large mansion. Within seconds, it was about fifty metres above the ground. After several zig-zagging movements, it hovered downwards and landed on the grass. By that time, I was hiding behind a pine tree approximately ten metres from the UFO. This was totally unexpected. A flurry of UFO activity had been reported in the papers and on TV in recent weeks, in almost every corner of England. I looked at my watch. It was twenty past eleven. Three figures jumped on the ground and headed towards the back door of the mansion. There at the door stood a woman who was probably one of the housemaids. The entire household was alerted by her screams.

The tall figure in the centre looked like Draco. The lack of an around-the-clock surveillance of a central figure like Davidson in the Conservative Party was indeed a strange omission. The responsibility of maintaining the efficiency and total commitment of MI6 was in the hands of Major Blount. We all knew how the pattern was generated as far as the MI6 was concerned, but it was quite apparent that Major Blount, with considerable variety in his tactics, had completely alienated his operations from the rest of the intelligence agencies. He had no intention of giving way to violence or violent extremism. He was capable of quick decisions and welded his operatives into a single instrument for the furthering of his aims. Because of the power he wielded, he was upright, a fair-minded man, a leader who took a line of his own. As Draco and the two men with him entered the house, the screaming stopped.

The operations of MI6 could never be adventitious. But on this cold February evening, I was on my own. I was used to working alone with confidence and unerring audacity. I passed the back door, trying to avoid the screaming housemaid and climbed in through a window. It was extremely difficult to hide with the bright lights in the large hall, but I managed to throw myself behind a curtain and peep through for a time. As far as I could see, there was no one in the hall. There was a beautifully designed large fireplace at the other end with a blazing fire, which let out enormous heat. Then I heard noises coming from the door to the right of the fireplace. I crept around for a while and then finally tiptoed towards the adjacent room.

I opened the door slowly and looked inside. The light was on, but there was no one there. Quickly, I slipped in, and closed the door behind me. There was another door which opened onto a room from which voices could be heard. Just in case, I switched off the light and moved towards that door. I pressed my ear to it and I heard Draco's sonorous laugh. I could hear clearly what they were saying.

"I think the attempt on Houston's life was very well performed and served its purpose. We had no intention of killing him, of course," said Draco, "but I think now he will withdraw from the leadership competition."

Obviously, the murder attempt had been planned and executed by Draco and Davidson. Why had they not killed him, though? Was this warning enough to keep him out of the race? Was Houston really such a coward that he would end a brilliant political career and make no effort to challenge his adversaries? I had just met him, so I did not really know him that well.

"Chaos in both political parties when details of economic ruin are announced," I could hear Draco and imagine the red glint in his eyes while he continued, "no more confusion for the people of Britain. We take over, and save Britain from economic ruin."

I shuddered at the thought when I remembered I had not locked the door. So I did, and this time put an eye to the keyhole. I could just see Davidson sitting in an armchair, sipping his drink and smoking his cigar. I had developed an amazing way of smelling out a fib, and I knew that Davidson had lied to me during our conversation at dinner. He was a conspirator and a major one at that.

"The Premier and the Defence Minister cannot survive much longer. He will probably remain at the helm when he finds out Houston, his prodigal son, is no longer a candidate for the party leadership. And that's where we want him."

"My men are ready to move in." Draco was stern and cold, "But the General must take over first."

God Almighty! What was this? Were they really planning a military take-over?

Suddenly, I heard the creak of a hinge, and turned back to the door. I felt a vague sort of fear and seconds later, my heart swelled. I saw a shadowy figure at first, and then with light falling onto the body, I realised it was a woman. Already, I had gun in hand. She closed the door and switched on the light…There she was, the blond girl with the flue eyes that I had met at Draco's mansion back in Marlborough the night we had our meeting. She was wearing a pink dress and she looked exquisitely beautiful. She awakened in me a million desires.

"Put the gun down. I'm here to help you." She whispered.

"How did you know I was here?"

"I'd just come out of my room upstairs and saw you come in."

"Judy,…who are you? How can I trust you? I met you at Draco's place, and how you are back with him again."

"True. You can't know whether you can trust me. But I have to be with Draco for a time."

"Why?" I asked her.

"I'll explain later. This is the time for love. Come with me," she pulled my hand.

"Make sure your mobile is shut this time," I warned her, "they will see us."

"The housemaids are gone. The butler and his family have retired for the night."

"But I have to listen to what they have to say. It's extremely important."

"I'll tell you all about it," she said, smiling.

We walked out of the room hand in hand, like lovers. We climbed the stairs to the upper floor and moved slowly towards the end of a long corridor. There she opened a door, pulled me inside and locked the door behind her.

Perhaps it was wise to put a little more distance between me and Draco. Now I was in a private room upstairs with one of the most beautiful girls I have ever seen. How lucky can you get?

"Your music is extraordinarily brilliant and verging on the bombastic. What is love? Is it an attraction both spiritual and sexual? Is it an evanescent joy and sometimes tears which dominate your soul. You have very high vibrational qualities. Electricity just flows through your body and enters mine. Your charm is unsurpassed," she said all of a sudden.

"You should be a writer," I said, still bemusedly contemplating whether this was really the right time and place for love. But how could any man in his right mind resist temptation of such beauty. This time, I asked her a straight question.

"Who are you, Judy? Are you one of us or one of them?"

"I am human, Turan. As I said, when we first met, Draco employed me and some other girls to entertain his guests. One thing led to another and he really paid us all handsomely. But forget about that and let's talk about your music. Let me tell you something. I was always enthralled by it. Your compositions are not predicated on familiarity. They are original. You are the idol of millions. Did you know that? Are you aware of the fact that you are the most monumental figure in twenty-first century music? Your compositions speak with such intensity and sweep, imponderable, limitless immensities that many are transformed into an everlasting excitement and climaxes of infinite force."

She started undressing and I must confess, I relished every bit of her body and her movements. An hour of bliss and yet I wanted to continue. She was the kind of girl you did not want to stop making love to. It was almost like an addiction. While we smoked, I wondered whether Draco would look for her.

"No," she said, "I was about to leave when I saw you and came down. I can give you all the information you need. Now you have a spy in Draco's kingdom!"

"But I don't want you to be in any danger. You mustn't take any risks."

She tossed off my concern as nonchalantly as sipping a drink.

"Why do you want to help me, Judy?"

"Well, I believe in what you've been saying about the Devil. A deep, very dangerous, horrific and weird drama is unfolding and you and your people are fighting against enormous odds. Nothing is left except for weak and trivial opposition coming from the Premier and his Defence Minister. Distinct from all other developments, your struggle against evil is overshadowing them all. Today a cosmic network embraces the world. In it, you find the most powerful extraterrestrial race. That of the Devil and his people. But there is hope. The Greys will come in great numbers. Despite humankind's isolation in the universe, the struggle against evil will eventually prevail upon the greys to act swiftly and come up with a sound plan to get rid of the Devil."

"Bravo! You are very well informed. But tell me what you know that I don't know. I heard them speak."

"They say Houston will withdraw. The premier will stay on at the head of government and run again for party leadership. But why did they bother with Houston in the first place? It doesn't make sense. Surely there were easier ways to end his political career than to appear to attempt, deliberately, to kill him. I say appear, because it was obviously just a frightener; they never meant to kill him."

"You're right," she said, "but you know better than I how the Eridanians operate. Let me tell you this. The next step is to contact the general."

"What general, Judy? Don't tell me they are planning an army takeover?"

"I don't know. The man we are talking about is General Harris. I don't know who he is."

"Well, is he a British General in the British Army?"

"I don't know, Turan. All I have is a name."

It was four o'clock in the morning when we left Davidson's residence. Judy had no place to stay in London, so I arranged for her to stay at my pied-á-terre in South Kensington. Not even Emma knew anything about this small cottage which I kept for guests such as Judy. Then I went home to Charles Street. I slept for about six hours and got up at 11.30 am. The General Harris Judy had mentioned was first on my agenda. It would be unnecessary to dig any deeper into Davidson's activities. He was being used by Draco. Emma had been visiting her parents and she was not in the office. But the two secretaries had been gathering information on Davidson.

"There's no need for that now. I know he is with the Eridanians. But I have something for you. Please try to locate William Harris. A General William Harris."

The girls worked for at least two hours. They found on the internet only one William Harris. He was a retired general in the British Army. He had retired quite early at 50, and was now living in London. His biography was short. He had been in Europe and then in Iraq, and there was nothing to link him to the Eridanians.

He was the only General William Harris on the internet. I telephoned another former general in the British Army—a General Charles Pickford—and asked him about Harris.

"He has a reputation for trustworthiness and integrity. He lives a quiet life."

When I told him about the possibility of General Harris being involved with the aliens, he chuckled and his reaction was one I did not expect.

"Harris and aliens? No way!" he said, "I really can't see him involved in such dangerous and complex matters. He is a solider of the old school. It's amazing how he managed to keep those qualities, but he is like that. No. I don't think so, Turan. Harris is a perfect gentleman and he has always kept himself out of the limelight."

"Well, I have to see him anyway. Because his name came up in an investigation involving the aliens."

"He is almost always at home. Just go to him, and you'll see for yourself."

General Harris's house was a modern building just next to a shopping centre. While I was waiting for him to answer the door, I remembered the other general's last comment, "He has always been an effective person as his career shows. He leaped into major new stories when he advised the British government and the Americans to withdraw their forces from Iraq. But no one would listen to him. I think that's the main reason for his early retirement."

A small, thin, neat man appeared at the door. I could tell from the description the other general had given me, that this was the man I was seeking.

"General William Harris?"

"Yes?" he replied enquiringly, "how can I help you?"

"My name is Turan Akova. I have been investigating alien activity in Britain. May I please have a few minutes of your time?" I asked politely. When he smiled, I thought he had already recognised me.

"By all means, Mr Akova." He made me feel more than welcome as he stepped back to let me in. "Please come in. I recognised you immediately from your concerts on TV. You are well known as a pianist/composer."

A good looking, well-dressed woman, probably in her forties, approached us, extending her hand.

"Rose, darling, we have a celebrity in our home. This is Mr Akova, a Turkish Cypriot pianist composer. My wife, Rose."

"Pleased to meet you. I'm sorry I did not ring for an appointment," I said apologetically.

"Oh, don't worry about that," he said, "please sit down."

The room was a nicely decorated living room with four large white armchairs and a large dining room table with eight chairs around it. There were two large paintings on the wall behind where Harris was sitting. Surrealist works by the English painter, William Wallis, who had created a new style with extremely bright colours, complex shapes and shadows, merging with exquisitely penetrated depths. Visions in the subconscious mind and abstract figures converging with bizarre surroundings.

The General stood in front of me in his royal blue velvet smoking jacket and white corduroy trousers. There had been many reports and articles in the papers about the murder attempt on Houston and Davidson's activities. Thoughts chased each other in my mind, placing Harris right in the middle of a controversial puzzle about aliens, Draco and the political struggle within the Conservative party. Suddenly, two very large Alsatians rushed into the room, baying and snarling.

"There, there...sit," ordered the General and they both sat obedient as lambs at his feet. "Do excuse me, Mr Akova, but they seem to be doing this all the time." Then I returned to my thoughts. Among the same newspaper reports there was a stinging official rebuke from the Premier denouncing scandalously untrue claims which pointed to a serious crack in the Conservative Party, and utter confusion within the ranks of the government to reach a final decision on an agreement with the aliens...

"During my investigations into alien activity, I found out that someone with the name General William Harris would play a major role in some secret action, in collaboration with the Eridanians. Please forgive me. This is an extremely important matter and I want to make sure. I've examined the list of all British generals and you are the only William Harris on the list."

He blinked, and did not hide his astonishment.

"I can assure you, I have no contacts with any of these aliens or people who are connected with them. Nor, for that matter, with the government." He seemed highly sensitive, "Surely, there must be some mistake. You say you've checked the list and I am the only William Harris?"

"Yes, definitely. I've checked and double-checked not only through official channels, but also in person at the British Army HQ in London."

"What about American, Australian and New Zealand generals?" he asked.

"I checked those too. There's no William Harris on their list." I said, "I am faced with insoluble puzzles and I cannot understand how or why anyone would want to use your name. An army takeover could be a possibility."

"Well, I'm extremely concerned about this," he said thoughtfully.

"General Harris, I've asked New Scotland Yard and MI6—I'm sure you know Major Blount—to look into the matter," I said, "In the meantime, please think back. Have you been contacted by anyone during the past week? Did you speak to anyone about the aliens?"

He looked at his wife. Mrs Harris crossed her legs and regarded her husband quietly. Then she spoke.

"No. As far as I can remember, there were no visitors during the past week with the exception of our son, Peter."

"Your son?"

"He is an executive Director in an engineering firm."

"Does he have any special interest in what's been happening in Britain? I mean with alien presence and the possibility of an agreement with them?" I asked.

"No, nothing like that. Naturally, we are all very concerned about the latest situation. And we follow the news. But that's all."

I left General Harris's house with only one thought in mind. To find a clue that would lead me to this mysterious General William Harris, who was up till now non-existent. Despite ingenious, inexplicable tactics on the part of Draco and his aliens, I was almost always able to detect certain weaknesses of the Eridanians. A confusion, something which bothered them. Fumbling that revealed themselves. The mystery behind General Harris's identity was in my opinion no senseless misunderstanding. I could not for one moment feel less full of hate for the Eridanians. Were they really planning a military take-over in Britain, one of the most democratic countries in the world? But why would they resort to such a tactic when they held all the cards? The theory of an army takeover would appear to be viable at first, but the way of the devil was not a well-trodden path. When I left General Harris's home, I decided to try the Ministry of Defence as well. My telepathic impulses urged me to go there. I was receptive to any thoughts that might come in from the Greys or from others who were able to practise telepathy. The Ministry was at its old address and was now like a museum. Nevertheless, it was there as always. The receptionist directed me to the second floor Archives Department. A middle-aged lady with spectacles stood behind a desk.

"Yes, sir?" she said, placing a file on the counter.

"I was wondering whether you could help me. I would like some information about a General William Harris, a British Army General who served during the Second World War."

I did not realise the whole system at the Ministry had been computerised. Within ten minutes, she handed me a printout of the list of generals who had served during World War II.

"Here you are, Sir," she said. Apparently, she had also gone through the two pages and underlined a General William Harris on the list:

General William Harris, born 1905, died 2003 at the age of ninety-eight. He was with the Royal Welsh Fusiliers at first, but later reached the rank of general in 1939 at the age of 34.

He was probably the youngest general in British military history. Somebody said this was not possible, but it was there in the records of the Ministry. He was stationed at Folkstone with the Third Army and landed in Normandy, France, on D-Day. Harris was decorated with the Victoria Cross and was on the Queen's list in 1959, when he received his OBE. He retired at the age of eighty-one.

He retired in 1970 but he had taught at a military academy until the age of eighty-one. I asked the lady to give me the address of his family. I also asked where he was buried. She told me he had been buried at St George's Cemetery near Chelsea. She looked at me enquiringly.

"May I ask why such an interest in a general long gone? After all, he's been dead for four years now."

"Well, his name was mentioned in an investigation. MI6 is involved and I'm sort of helping them."

"You're not the only one who has been asking about the general," she said, this time smiling reflectively, apparently remembering something.

"That's interesting," I said, "you gave him the info on the general as well?"

"Yes, the address of the family and the cemetery."

I left the Ministry and drove straight to Neasden, to the home of General Harris's grandson. Clive Harris greeted me at the door. He was the only grandson of the famous General. I had rung him earlier.

"Mr Akova, please come in," Clive Harris was about sixty but quite young-looking, with fairly long hair and a whitish beard.

"Thanks for receiving me on such short notice, Mr Harris," I said, shaking his hand. We walked into his study and the tall figure of a butler appeared at the door immediately.

"Can I get you anything, sir?" he asked.

"Yes, Henry. Mr Akova, I'm having whisky. What about you?"

"Yes, whisky will be fine."

When we settled down with our drinks, he told me he had already been visited by a man who had asked about his grandfather.

"I can guess why you are here. You see, I've been following the developments in Britain right after the arrival of the aliens. I know what you are up against. But I have to tell you exactly what's been happening and then we can go on from there." He seemed eager to come to the point without further ado.

"You see, I do not think we have a choice. I have been a lawyer for a long time. But now I am an empiricist. These aliens—I mean, the Eridanians—they are so powerful and so advanced that it would be futile to try to stop them."

"You may be right up to a point," I replied carefully, "but there is something which bothers them here in Britain. I haven't been able to put a finger on it yet, but there is definitely a certain kind of power or situation—or even it may be the presence of the Grey extraterrestrials—which blocks their advance when they are on the verge of dominating the whole of Britain. Otherwise they would indeed gain control of the country within days."

"Yes, but let me tell you this. When I encountered a UFO just over a month ago at my uncle's estate near Leicester, I have had this vibrational aura widening the horizon of my psychic equilibrium."

371

Harris told me that the place in Leicester had been aglow with bright light, and that he faced the aliens without the slightest fear.

"Ever since my encounter with the Eridanians, I've been on the path to perfection. The UFO parked on the lawn for over fifteen minutes. Then two more, smaller spacecraft landed on either side. But the UFO in the centre maintained the white, bright shafts of light."

"I was really very excited about the whole affair. I do want to help you. But first, let me explain what happened. The UFOs left and I returned home the same day. Now, the man who visited me said he represented the Eridanians. No secrecy at all. I knew he was an alien in human form. He looked like a heavenly figure."

"Interesting euphemism," I commented drily. He continued.

"He said he had come to ask me to give them permission to exhume my grandfather's body from the cemetery. What he told me was unbelievable. He said my grandfather had been contacted by the Eridanians during the Second World War in France. From that moment on, he had special powers. He said Grandpa was instrumental in the success of both the British and American armies during the last two years of the war." He paused for a moment, drinking his whisky. "I gave them permission, of course."

"But why did they want to exhume his body from the cemetery?"

"He said they would re-animate him. Can you imagine it? They intended to bring him back to life?"

"But why? For what purpose?"

Suddenly, he excused himself and left the room on the pretext that he had to give me something. Minutes later, he returned.

"They said my grandfather would be entrusted with the great task of delivering mankind onto a much higher level."

"An army takeover?" I asked.

"No, no. Nothing as primitive as that."

"Then what?"

"They didn't tell me," he paused, and then resumed, "Mr Akova, I have heavenly and cosmic powers. Good and evil are universal. We must embrace the Eridanians with love and affection."

The man was a nutcase. And yet what he had told me was very interesting to say the least. Especially the claim he had made about his grandfather and his

Eridanian contact. He was obviously overjoyed that he would see his grandfather alive again.

"Now let me help you. I honestly would like to help you as much as I can. This strange man did not realise it, but while I was writing out my permission for them to exhume the body, I saw a document that he had forgotten on the table."

Now I am writing it out on a piece of paper. I'm sure it will come in useful in your investigations. Here it goes.

Place: The island of Ibiza.

Town: Santa Eulalia del Rio.

Meeting place: Puig de Missa.

Operations: The human egg cell the size of a grain of dust. Mass of long-chain molecules. Molecules coded to construct a human being.

Date: 10 March 2007

Subject for re-animation: General William Harris.

"This is fantastic," I said. "This means, I suppose, that they will take your grandfather's body to Ibiza. God knows why, but there must be a reason for it. Well, Mr Harris, thank you so much. This is valuable information. In fact, it could be vital."

The girls at the office had prepared an information pack on the island and especially on the town of Santa Eulalia del Rio. The Carthaginians had founded the town in 650BC; the Arabs had ruled from 901 to 1235AD. The island was reconquered by Guillermo De Mongri 'Sacristi' of Gerona. Petro, Prince of Portugal and Nuño Sans, Count of Roselló, divided the island for themselves. The reconquest occurred in 1235. The characteristic feature of the last phase of six centuries was marked by isolation. The basic concern of the people living on the island was the defence of lives and property against constant attacks by pirates. Reading this material on the flight to Barcelona, I came across a very interesting visit by General William Harris to the island and in particular to the town of Santa Eulalia de Rio. Now we are getting somewhere, I thought. There was no mention of any UFO sightings in Ibiza, however. But the time of his visit coincided with the beginnings of his tremendous success during the last year of the war.

I was just in time for the last ferry boat to the islands. This was Don Carlos, a first class ferry boat going first to Mallorca and then to Ibiza. It was around a twelve hour journey.

We started off from Barcelona at around midnight. The ferry boat had a restaurant, a bar, an all-night bar, an all-night snack bar and a disco. I had been to Ibiza once before, a long time ago when a Belgian girlfriend had invited me to stay with her. Three weeks in a beautiful town. The island of pines had other very pretty spots, but Santa Eulalia de Rio seemed a special place. Many famous actors, musicians and writers had their holiday homes there. On that occasion, I remember meeting the late famous British actor, Terry Thomas, in a pub. There I also met the Turkish twin sisters, daughters of one of the richest businessmen in Turkey.

It had been the end of October when one day, we decided to take a walk and ended up on the top of a hill. It was raining on the way up, and there I saw the most interesting mausoleum ever. We were almost soaked by the rain when we reached the entrance. This was indeed very strange. There were seven layers in a large and long corridor. On each layer stood glass coffins, in which were wooden coffins, which in turn contained the corpses of the dead. The caretaker told me all the bodies had been mummified Egyptian style. When I asked why, he replied in broken English, "They don't like to be under the ground. They want to be up there, Signor. It don't make no difference when you're dead, eh!"

At any rate, this was the Puig de Missa. This was the place where General William Harris's body would be re-animated in two days' time on 10 March. After a very late diner at about 1.00am, I went down to the disco where I met an American man with two girls, also Americans. They were going to Mallorca. I stayed with them for an hour or so, then I went up on deck. The off season ferry boat was unusually crowded. While I sat at the all night bar, a young Spanish couple sat on two stools beside me and we started conversing until the early hours of the morning. It so happened that they were also going to Santa Eulalia de Rio. They were the owners of the famous restaurant el Naranjo.

"I had dinner there once with a girlfriend some years ago," I told them.

"So," the wife replied, "It is off season now, so why are you going this time? Is it another girlfriend?"

"No, no...I wish it were," I trailed off, not wanting to go into any detail about the reasons for my visit. "I am interested in your glass cemetery up on the hill, the Puig de Missa. I am on the heels of some strange aliens who will be visiting the cemetery soon. So now you know!"

"Go on with you!" said the husband, laughing, "you're pulling our legs."

"No, I'm quite serious."

"Ah, now I recognise you!" cried the woman, "you're the pianist/composer. I saw you on TV."

"I didn't think I was so famous…When did you take over the restaurant?" I asked them.

"Only last year," she said.

"We have a piano there. Perhaps you can come and visit us one evening," said the man.

"I'd love to," I replied.

Why would Draco want to bring a general from the Second World War back to life? And why would the re-animation operation take place in the small holiday village of Santa Eulalia del Rio on Ibiza. Why did General Harris visit this town during the World War II? Had he been contacted by the Eridanians all those years ago, for the first time? Most important of all, what would the general's mission be in Britain, and why had he been chosen, of all people. It was obvious that the struggle within the Conservative Party had put a severe strain on the British Premier and the Defence Minister. Their control over the government hung in the balance. Why would Draco turn his full attention on the political scene in Britain? The obvious answer lay in the fact that Draco needed desperately a British government which would sign the agreement without further delay. But there was still a tremendous opposition both within and outside the government to such an agreement. It seemed that maintaining complete control over the British government and equal control over the population had clearly become untenable.

I believe there was some thing or force preventing the aliens from delivering the final blow. The signing of an agreement would not be enough to gain control over Britain. Perhaps the presence of Grey aliens in Britain was the reason behind the Eridanians' reluctance to strike for complete domination of the British Isles. But the Greys had barely make their presence felt and when one day, all those years ago, I walked into the mysterious world of the paranormal and the supernatural, I had hoped for a much more direct and effective intervention from the 'good' extraterrestrials. True, within a few years, and especially after the advent of the devil and his armies, Grey alien visitations had increased tremendously. Britain had become the most concentrated area. Even the Americas were now second on the list.

Now everyone saw through the impenetrable bureaucracy both in the USA and in Britain which had served to cover up the truth about the UFOs, together with the enormous campaign of the sceptics to ridicule the visitations of the extraterrestrials as pure fantasy, and the opposition of the debunkers had simply been rendered null and void. But coming back to the Greys, their power and technology seemed inferior to that of the Eridanians. I had witnessed Draco's open challenge to Grey power in Wiltshire. And this is why I suspected a certain kind of earth power or a natural phenomenon in Britain was holding the Eridanians back and prolonging the struggle in Britain. But I had no idea what this special force was.

Draco's intrigues which had disfigured the whole of the European Union within a short period of time were somehow being held in check in Britain. Long months of anxiety passed in relative quiet. But the tension was always there. What kept them out? Why was Britain such a special place?

"Did you hear of any UFO sightings or landings in Santa Eulalia? After all, this is your own town…" I asked the Spanish couple.

"Well, no…" said the man thoughtfully, and then sat up suddenly, "actually, now I come to think of it, there was one, I think. It is only hearsay, but an elderly Spanish gentleman who lives in town was interviewed by the local press three months ago after he had claimed there were regular UFO visits in the vicinity of the town. I think he's about eighty-five now, and quite a famous painter; a very energetic man. He comes to our restaurant quite often. You can see him if you like. His name is Ronaldo Alfonso Delantes."

"Yes," I replied, "I think I will do just that."

It was about ten in the morning when the ferry boat reached Ibiza harbour. I shared a taxi with the restaurateur couple and we arrived at Santa Eulalia at around ten past eleven. I went straight into the hotel. For the first time, in complete secrecy, there would be a re-animation of a dead person, General Harris. I was the only person who knew about the operation, apart from Harris's grandson. It suddenly occurred to me that Draco, De Medici and Gonzaga were all figures of the past, but now they were here as leaders of the Eridanians in the 21st century. So why not bring back someone like General Harris of the recent past? Why? What was so special about General Harris?

I had to find a way to hide in the Glass Cemetery and observe the process of reanimation. I had to find out what his mission would be in Britain. I slept for a couple of hours and then went up the hill. It had been drizzling for at least an hour. Black clouds gathered on the horizon and right above the hill. My brain was working overtime over the possibility of a nation being transformed into the world of wicked extraterrestrials. The support for the Eridanian aliens had become so strong that many people now openly talked of their allegiance to the Gods who came from Epsilon Eridani. The threat of becoming slaves of the devil did not bother them at all. The UFO Research Centre in London, all the scientists who had been involved right from the start, the UFO researchers who witnessed the evil conglomerate of Satan at work fought tooth and nail to show the true facts to the public, but to no avail. The promise of immortality and remarkable financial gains made everyone glow with passionate and unswerving loyalty for the Eridanians. Our argument of the dramatic infiltration of demonic supernatural evil in society was now a feeble effort and could in no way stop the avalanche of people converted into the Eridanian camp. Draco and his demons were blazing a trail, and thousands were following it.

Thirty-Three

It was around two in the afternoon when I reached the entrance to the Glass cemetery. The guard had not yet arrived, so I sat on a bench near the door. The drizzle had turned into heavy rain. I moved towards the entrance and stood under the ledge coming out of the wall above the large door. Soon afterwards, a car stopped near the door and a tall man in a distinctive blue uniform and cap walked to the entrance. He mumbled something in Spanish and I replied in English.

"May I have a word with you, please?" I asked.

"Yes, of course," he replied and lead the way into a small room inside.

"Do you speak English?"

"Yes. A little."

Major Blount had contacted the Spanish police in Madrid and asked them to help me in my enquiries. My police contact and facilitator there was Eduardo Fabrizio de la Contes. In case, I ran into difficulties with any of the officials, this was the man I would turn to for help. But there was no need for that now. I explained to the caretaker that this was an official investigation with the cooperation of the Spanish police and that I had to hide in the cemetery to observe what was happening there. He was most willing to help.

"Come! Come!" he told me, "I show you place. No one see you there. OK?" I asked him if there was to be a burial that day.

"Yes," he said, "they are coming from London."

The interior of the Glass cemetery was a hollow place, which looked like a cave in the side of a cliff.

"One thousand and two hundred and twenty-five," he said, suddenly pointing at some stone steps which lead up into a small cave in the upper layer. "Very old stone."

"You mean stones from 1225."

"Yes!" he said firmly.

The small cave of a room was above the glass coffins and I could see almost all of them. But just to make sure, I asked him to show me the burial place of the people coming from London. We went down again, and he showed me an empty glass coffin on the third layer. This was perfect. It was just under the small room which was to be my hiding place. I paid the man a thousand US dollars for his services, and asked him whether he had any knowledge of the time of arrival of the hearse.

"Three thirty. After one hour, yes?" he told me.

Now was the time to come to grips with the unfolding drama. Why would they re-animate General Harris's body here in this small Spanish village on the island of Ibiza? There was still time to see Ronaldo Alfonso Delantes, the elderly gentleman whose name had been given to me by the Spanish couple form the boat. The man was well-known by everyone, and the guard directed me to his house about a mile from the Glass Cemetery, and ended up driving me there himself. The old man opened the door and eyed me suspiciously.

He was wearing an old white Montgomery and dark blue velvet trousers; a clean-shaven medium height man with spectacles. I explained to him why I was there. In fact, I told him the whole story. He asked me inside and we sat on two chairs near a small table.

"Mr Akova, I'm surprised you don't know about the hill in the village. You've been a UFO researcher most of your life, and you've never heard of it?"

"I'm ashamed to say I haven't. But maybe you can tell me what's so special about this place."

"There have been many visitations here on this hill. I am lucky that my home is so near. I saw a lot of bright lights coming from the UFOs and piercing through the glass coffins. Add to that the belief about the dead coming back to life with the energies deposited on this hill by visiting UFOs, and you will understand why they are bringing this man all the way from London to re-animate him here."

"Did you yourself see any of the dead here coming back to life?" I asked him.

"On one occasion, I saw a man whom I had known walking out of the cemetery. But I'm not absolutely sure whether it was him. He had been dead for about a year."

Perhaps this was an Eridanian re-animation centre. But why on a small island in the Mediterranean? Could this be the place where the true significance of Eridanian power and technology regarding immortality was revealed? Was the

379

hill yet another extraterrestrial energy store? Delantes had in fact done some research going back to what the Spanish called *la reconquista*—the reconquest— in 1235. Had there been an Eridanian presence here on the hill going back all those centuries? But I could not yet link General William Harris and the hill, the Glass cemetery, to the re-animation process. After all, this could have been done anywhere else in the world, as far as I knew. Or even in Britain where the aliens were present in great numbers. There was nothing to connect General Harris to the hill except his brief visit right after the end of World War II. There was something missing…

I could not help but admire the inscrutable wisdom of the Eridanians which engendered instantaneous reactions and moves that could not be traced to any particular place and time. Their healthy vigour had wrung words of praise even from those scientists who were working incessantly to end the violent outburst of the abuse of all human nature, the black evil which ruthlessly slashed away human civilisation with fearful precision. The whole Eridanian plan was so complex and yet so simple and no one involved in the fight against these aliens could afford to be hasty in their conclusions. I was not entirely oblivious of what was happening, but the sudden, totally unpredictable tactics of the Eridanians were so intractable that I had to investigate their every move, disregarding the prevalent belief of those transformed into their camp. Draco had strenuously denied their evil intentions but we were going through a phase never before experienced by humankind.

I returned to the hill and minutes later, the man in charge of the Glass Cemetery arrived. As I walked with him through the entrance, it was twenty minutes past three. I had a small video camera in my bag and I was determined to film the whole event. As I rushed in, I saw a young man in woolly knickerbockers standing outside the door. There was a cheerfulness and distinct amiability about him, not at all the air of a man about to attend a funeral or enter a cemetery. I waited in the small room with video camera at the ready for the party from London to arrive. The uniformed caretaker had disappeared and the young man, smoking a cigarette, moved slowly towards the centre. There was something likeably flippant about him. I peered at him once again from my eyrie and all of a sudden was gripped by the most painful pang of nostalgia. It was my Belgian girlfriend, Denise who was standing below me in this very same glass cemetery.

At long last, they arrived. Two very large, tall and muscular men carried the wooden coffin inside and placed it in the empty glass shelf. Right behind the coffin, I could see De Medici and Gonzaga. The young man who had entered the cemetery earlier was already hiding in the corner at the end of the corridor. As the two big men opened the coffin, I started filming, focussing on the decomposing face and body of General Harris who had been dead for four years. De Medici and Gonzaga both held twelve inch 'instruments' in their hands. Within seconds, bright lights converging into one circular white light hit the General's body. It was like a very strong torch light bobbing towards the coffin. I was fascinated. The light entered the body which was rocking from side to side, and the instruments of De Medici and Gonzaga were like a conjurer's hands moving swiftly to invoke an exceedingly fantastic magic. I braced myself. The video camera rolled. After approximately five minutes, the General was lying in his coffin like someone sleeping. There was no trace of the decomposition. But there was also no movement. Then De Medici plucked anxiously at his instrument and the very bright light switched on once again. The General's right arm jerked as if in spasm, and his eyes opened. It was like Count Dracula rising from his grave. Then the arms and the legs followed by the torso trembled with such force that the wooden coffin itself rocked sideways.

General William Harris rose from the dead, and climbed out of his coffin.

"Jolly good show," he exclaimed, jovially patting De Medici on the shoulder.

This re-animation had in fact outdistanced all the other scientific, technological marvels of the Eridanians. Perhaps this was the everlasting life the aliens had promised their followers. Now I had everything on film.

"Believe me, it was a long, long six years," remarked the General, "I feel perfect, absolutely A1. But what happened? Why didn't you bring me back right after my death?"

Gonzaga smiled winningly, "This is the right time for you," he said.

"We have to return to London immediately," said De Medici with undisguised excitement. So they prepared to leave, I looked for the strange young man with the knickerbockers. He was gone. I kept low, still hiding in the small room above as they left. I then crept downstairs wondering about the General's mission. Approaching the entrance, I saw a blue Mercedes pull up near the gate. They all climbed in and the car moved slowly downhill towards the town. I searched for the mystery man who had been hiding in a corner somewhere, but he was definitely gone.

381

I waited for at least half an hour. The attendant came back to the cemetery just before I left.

"Where were you?" I asked.

"I went to my mother, she is very old," he said, "I think better for you to be alone, yes?" Then he took out a piece of paper from his top jacket pocket.

"This is for you. A young man left it."

I thanked him and walked away from the Glass Cemetery. I looked at the message which appeared to be written hurriedly, but it was perfectly readable in capital letters:

EVIL MEN WILL ALWAYS CONTACT THE EVILBEINGS OF THE PLANET ERIDANUS IN THE EPSILON ERIDANI STAR STYEM THE MINISTRY OF DEFENCE IN LONDON SHOULD BE YOUR NEXT STOP.

How Could he have known the next move of the Eridanians and General William Harris? Who was this young man with the funny knickerbockers? Where had he got his information? I thought for a moment. Well, perhaps it would be more accurate to say that common sense was struggling for supremacy in the corners of my brain. Where else could he have got this information but from the Eridanians themselves whose business it was to conceal such vital and secret information. Intelligence concerning the resources and actions of a possible Eridanian attempt to neutralise the powers of the government and force them into signing the accord fell into Major Blount's department at MI6. What was their plan? Obviously, they would not bother to bring back to life an old General unless it was a highly important mission. If this mission was not an army takeover, what else could it be?

The road leading to the old painter Delantes's house was lined with pine trees. I decided to see him once more before I left the island. He did not seem at all surprised to see me.

"I was expecting you," he said, "just tell me what happened at the cemetery. I must know."

"De Medici and Gonzaga re-animated the General with two instruments. When he was up and about, he asked why they had not brought him back from the dead the day he died. So I suppose that means he had been in collaboration with the Eridanians for a long time and he was expecting the re-animation operation. But why, I don't know. They left for London. Something very interesting occurred at the same time." I told him about the young man and his note, and we read it together.

"You're right in assuming that this young man must have obtained the information about the MoD from the Eridanians. So he must be close to them."

"Now the question is, why would he give me the information about the MoD if he is indeed working for the aliens? That doesn't make sense."

"Right again," he murmured, "now let me think. It's possible that the landing of the UFO I saw on this hill coincided with General Harris's visit which was in 1945, just after the end of the war. Maybe there is a connection there. Let me go through my notes and diaries of those years. In the meantime, try and find out the exact date of the General's arrival in Ibiza."

"OK, but this may take a couple of hours."

"I have all the time in the world."

"Later, we can have dinner at El Naranjo restaurant." I suggested.

I telephoned Emma and asked her to find the arrival date of the General in Ibiza. It was a very difficult task. I asked her to contact Major Blount, the British Army Records Office, the MoD and the War Office. In the meantime, he made coffee and we conversed for at least two hours, by the end of which we had heard nothing from Emma.

"Mr Akova, this is a mysterious island. And the town of Santa Eulalia del Rio looms out of the sacred mists of a measureless past. This was a meeting place not only of pirates but of savage races and exquisitely civilised people, too. I don't claim to be an expert on UFOs but I have had an opportunity to observe and study in detail the visitations on the hill. A resonating electro-magnetic field, that's what we have here. A scientist friend from Madrid University confirmed this while he was here on holiday last summer. He said the energies which he had detected were not of this world. He took samples of rocks and stones and at the same time succeeded in diverting the energies into a glass bottle by some strange scientific experiment. I know this sounds rather bizarre and unlikely, but the contents of the bottle were examined by the Spanish Space Research Agency in Madrid. The results? An unknown energy."

He spoke perfect English and the account of his experiences was indeed very illuminating. His suggestion that General Harris's visit may have coincided with a UFO landing here made sense. I glanced at my watch. It was 7.30pm.

"Wait a second!" I sat up, with a sudden new thought, "glass. You said your friend had filled a glass bottle with this mysterious energy. Now I have been asking myself, why a glass cemetery? Could it be that glass is a special material for the aliens? Tell me, how long has it been since people started using glass coffins?"

"Well, as far back as I can remember, this has been the custom. But I don't know when the glass cemetery was built. We can find out about that from the historians. I have contacts. Your point may prove to be valid," he added.

There had still been no word from Emma. It was now after eight o'clock, and we strolled down the mini golf course and into Casa de la Inglesia and then into Ayuntamiento. El Naranjo was in Casa San Jose. It was 10 March and a Saturday evening. The place was almost full. The Spanish couple I had met on the boat greeted us with delight at the door.

"How lovely to see you, Mr Delantes, Mr Akova." Said the woman who was dressed in a red flamenco-style dress. Paco de Santiago was playing his guitar on a platform. He was a supreme artist, performing and improvising caprices in all modes; his music was timeless. He was brilliant.

My mobile rang as we were ordering our meals. It was Emma.

"Turan, sorry, but it took ages to get the information on General William Harris. Thank God, the British Army Headquarters still keep records of the comings and goings of all the British Generals. General Harris visited Ibiza on 5 November 1945, right after the war. They have all the details. He flew into Madrid with the British Air Force plane, and then took a train from Madrid to Barcelona. Like you, he boarded a ferry boat from Barcelona to the Balearic Islands. He arrived in Ibiza on 6 November 1945."

"Is there any record or information about the purpose of this visit?"

"No, nothing," she said.

"Well, this gives us something to work on, at any rate. Emma, you're wonderful! Thank you." And I hung up.

"He was here in Santa Eulalia del Rio on 6 November 1945. Could you check your diary and find out if that was the date of the UFO landing?"

Delantes had brought his 1945 diary with him. He put it near the table lamp and turned the pages carefully.

"Ah, yes, here we are. The UFO landed near the hill on 7 November 1945!" he announced triumphantly.

"The next day! Of course, he must have stayed the night…"

"I must say, I admire your robust optimism," he remarked smilingly, "now, let's see. So the landing of the UFO coincided with the General's visit to the town. And his first reaction after coming back to life was: "Why didn't you bring me back right after my death?"...This indicates that he must have been transformed by the Eridanians sometime during the war. I think you must take the young man's message seriously and go back to London now. Obviously, they are planning something."

"You're right. I'll take the first plane out to Madrid tomorrow morning."

"Call the airline now and make a reservation," Delantes stopped for a moment, and then added, "let me have your phone number. If I come across any more information, I'll be able to contact you."

Sunday, 11 March was full of sunshine. As the plane flew over the islands, I wondered about the Eridanian plan. What could it be? His presence had all of a sudden protruded upon us from the dead. I was perhaps deluded into thinking that this was yet another trick on the Devil's part. No, I didn't think so. This time round, I was the only person who had found out about their plan, whatever that might be. I started from the beginning: the General was an old Eridanian-controlled human. They had brought him back for a reason. But what was it, this reason? Did the General possess special powers that would bring about the downfall of all resistance to other Eridanians in Britain? How?

I could understand how General Harris had become an Eridanian controlled human all those years ago, but why had he been chosen by the Eridanians and what was his mission. That mystery was shrouded in darkness. I suspected Draco was now getting ready for the final assault. I could see and feel the menacing omens. I continued undeterred. Whatever his mission, General William Harris had to be stopped. His return reflected the plain truth about Eridanian presence on Earth. The contacts with humans had begun a long time ago. The major flurries of UFO activity in the USA and Britain started more or less during the same period between 1943 and 1947.

Another interesting fact was that both the Greys and the Eridanians had arrived on Earth during this period. That could easily be viewed as perhaps rivalry between them, culminating in the exploitation and domination of Earth. Explanations which purported this reasoning were quite accurate in the records of the US Air Force. One thing was certain. Both Greys and Eridanians were super intelligent beings from two separate extraterrestrial civilisations from different star systems. They were both intelligent beings of the highest order. These two extraterrestrial civilisations had both counteracted gravitation and had used interstellar magnetic fields to travel at the speed of light. Years of research at Area 51 in the USA revealed that this system was part of their technology.

I took a taxi from Heathrow and went straight home. It was around 2.30 by the time I had finished my lunch at the Porthole, restaurant in Market Place in Mayfair. I slept for at least two and a half hours. The phone rang. It was Emma. I told her about the mysterious young man and his message.

"So you're going to the MoD tomorrow?" she said, excitedly.

"Yes, I am," I replied, "the note says General Harris will be there. Of course, I will inform Major Blount about the whole affair."

"But how would they cope with General Harris returning from the grave found years after he has been dead?"

"I have no idea, but I don't think he will hide the fact that he was brought to life by the Eridanians."

"Have you any notion about what they're up to?" she asked.

"Absolutely none!" I replied.

Draco was a character of a thousand shades, each overlapping the other, and becoming indistinguishable in the process. I told Major Blount I would be going to the MoD and he assigned me several men to keep the place under surveillance. When I entered the ministry building in Whitehall, two men met me at reception.

"Major Blount asked us to escort you to the Minister's office," said the tall, thin one. We took the lift to the top floor. There, they waited outside in the corridor while I walked into the Minister's office. A young woman of about thirty whom I had met twice before, raised herself from her chair behind her desk and extended a beautifully manicured hand.

"Mr Akova, how nice to see you again."

"Thank you. Likewise," I said, "how are you?"

"I'm well," she smiled.

"I would like to see the Minister, if possible."

"I'm sorry. The Minister is indisposed. A virus, his wife said today. But his newly appointed under-secretary is here. Would you like to see him?" she asked.

"Newly appointed? What happened to Mr Davies?" I had met the previous under-secretary on several occasions during the past few months.

"He's been appointed to a new post at the British Army Headquarters," she told me.

This was quite unusual and I felt uneasy at the news.

"That's strange," I commented, "he seemed quite happy here."

"Well, you know how it is in ministries." She came closer and her strong perfume made my head spin and the back of my neck tingle.

"Well, I'll see the new under-secretary, if I may?"

"Certainly," she said. As she moved past me, I held her arm gently.

"Before you go in, can I ask you something?"

"Anything. What can I do for you?"

"Have you heard of a General William Harris coming here either today or yesterday?"

"General William Harris?" she thought for a moment, her hand on her chin, "no," she said, "but I'll just ask the other departments to make sure. I'll see you when you are finished in there."

"What's his name?"

"Mr Terry Ives," she said.

She entered the under-secretary's office, closing the door behind her. Minutes later, she came out smiling: "Mr Ives will see you now, Mr Akova."

I walked in, hearing the click of the closing door behind me. Behind the desk stood a man in his forties, bespectacled, with a nose like a plum. He did not move a muscle, and his expressionless face seemed to bode ill.

"Yes," he said coldly, "how can I help you?"

"My name is Turan Akova," I said, and he interrupted me immediately.

"Yes, I know. I am also well-informed about your stories, Mr Akova. The Devil and the evil Eridanians. Quite frankly, I don't believe a word of it. I'm not going to mince my words, when I tell you that these theories of yours are quite ridiculous. We have a golden opportunity before us, an opportunity to raise ourselves to unprecedented heights of spiritual and technological advancement. Your UFO people are trying to stop us. Another thing. I don't understand how this government cold let a Turkish Cypriot meddle in such important matters. No disrespect, but it is highly irregular."

He was still standing in the same spot. I could feel his anger and resentment from the iciness of his speech.

"Mr Ives, I work with the government. Whether you believe it or not, the Devil and his demons are no long the stuff of legends which we have heard since time immemorial. They are real, and they are extraterrestrials, and they are here, trying desperately to take over Britain. We at the UFO Centre, the scientists both here and in the USA, are absolutely convinced of their devilish activities and plans. There is no question about it. Frankly, I'm surprised you don't subscribe to these facts. But that's beside the point. I've come here to ask you about

General William Harris. Is he here at the ministry? If he is, I have to see him. It's important."

"Who?"

I repeated his name: "General William Harris."

"There is no such person here," he said menacingly.

It was difficult to work out the kind of man he was. Had his new authority gone to his head? Was he putting on airs to deny his rather common background? Who was he? What was he? Was he another recruit, an Eridanian controlled human? He was extremely irritating, that much I did know, and there was no point in wasting any more time with him.

"Thank you," I said curtly, and left his office. The secretary was no longer smiling. She had probably heard our conversation. She was disdainful and indifferent. I left my telephone numbers with her and she said she would call. I left the building at a loss to know what to do next. Finally, I decided to call on Major Blount to assess the latest situation. For the first time, he was looking worried.

I told him what had happened in Santa Eulalia del Rio and all about General William Harris.

"Mr Davies called and said he wanted to see you," he told me, "he said you should go to his home which is actually in Bruton Street, very near yours. He did say it was important."

"OK, I'll go now. Could you please make some enquiries about this General Harris? We have to find him and find out what they are planning with him."

"Don't worry. We are already putting out feelers," he said. I left in a hurry but arranged to meet him for dinner later on.

I rang the bell in Bruton Street. It was early evening but quite dark. There was no movement in the house. I waited for a few minutes and then pushed open the door. The small hall led into a large living room connected by glass doors. The light in the living room reflected still shadows on the glass. There was an oppressive silence in the house: a dead silence. I pulled out my gun just in case, and opened the glass doors. There, in front of me, was Mr Davies, sitting in a large armchair about ten feet from where I stood. His eyes stared at me, unseeing. There was a reddish black bullet hole in his forehead. His hands hung down on either side, his head tilted slightly to the left. There was no sign of a fight.

As I pulled his head forward, I saw a blood stain the size of my hand on the light blue velvet armchair where his head had rested. Blood spurted out of a hole at the back of his head. Then I saw her sitting in a chair in the corner. She was motionless, her eyes wide open, dazed. In mingled fear and shock, she looked from her dead husband to me. Her yellow skirt was torn at the sides, and her white blouse ripped open to the waistline. Suddenly, she started screaming. I hit her twice on both cheeks. Under the strong light, I saw a bruise on her left temple, the size of a fifty pence piece.

I telephoned Major Blount. The ambulance, police and he arrived within twenty minutes. After about an hour, Mrs Davies's shock had subsided, her fear had left her and she looked quite sane again. Still, I thought it best to come and see her the following day. Now we had murder on our hands once again. Who had murdered Davies, and why? Was there a link between this crime and the arrival of General William Harris on the scene? Had Davies been the recipient of vital information about the General's mission? All these questions hung in the air for the time being. I hoped that Mrs Davies would be able to give me a clue about what had happened in the days leading up to her husband's murder.

"Where the hell is he?" I asked nervously while seated at Stone's restaurant in the Haymarket with Major Blount.

"You mean the General?"

"Yes," I said, gulping down the Spanish red wine.

"Draco and his men are probably hiding him somewhere in London. I have our people following them, but so far, we have no clue to go on," he said.

"What about Davies, though? Why was he murdered?"

"I don't know, Turan. But I have a sneaking suspicion that somehow he found out about the General's mission."

"What about the Defence Minister? Suddenly he is indisposed. And what about Ives—he's his new under-secretary? He's definitely Eridanian controlled." I said.

"Most likely so. I think they have taken over the MoD. I mean, just look at the situation. The Minister is apparently ill. Davies has been removed from office ending up in an obscure job at the British Army HQ. Then he is murdered at his home. It all adds up to one thing. The aliens are now in charge at the MoD."

The head waiter stood near our table.

"Would you like some coffee, sir," he asked solicitously.

"An espresso, please," I said.

"One for me, too," said the major. He drank it and left soon afterwards. I decided to walk home. I telephoned Emma at around 10.30; I suddenly had a terrific urge to see her. Every parting from her was like a little eternity. I said I was walking home and asked her if she was free to join me there. She replied that she would be there at around 11.00.

It was bitterly cold on this March evening in London, and there were no nightingales singing in Berkeley Square tonight! A feeling of weariness and exhaustion was stealing over my body. As I walked into Charles Street, a man dressed in a white trench coat appeared in front of me. My hand on my gun, I stopped.

"Forgive me, Mr Akova. I followed you from the restaurant. I have some information for you," he said politely.

"Who are you?" I asked.

"My name is Michael Stevens. I am a private detective. You see, I have been doing my own investigating."

I was actually surprised and a bit annoyed. I don't like strangers suddenly appearing out of nowhere, trying to hand over information. I scanned his face. There was a resemblance to someone I had seen recently. But who? I could not remember. He must have sensed my displeasure, and apologised again.

"I'm sorry, Mr Akova. But bear with me for a few minutes, please," he asked me firmly. His voice was soft and even. I sensed a change in his demeanour.

"OK," I said, "go ahead."

"I have been investigating the Premier's office. Through a relative close to him, I found out that two EU commissioners from Brussels had secret talks with him. My relative—a cousin actually—she is one of the premier's secretaries, was able to listen in. She said there was something very odd about the whole meeting. A strange newcomer was present. An elderly Englishman. Susan—that's my cousin—says he has convinced the Prime Minister than an accord with the Eridanians would be in the best interests of Britain. As you know, the premier is opposed to signing such an agreement with the aliens, but now he has agreed to sign it. That's odd." Then he added with fervour: "I can assure you this is very reliable information coming from my cousin. She also opposes any agreement with the aliens."

I checked with my informants at the Prime Minister's office. The information was correct. I called the major and told him about the private eye. He said MI6 had been following him for days.

"He's after a story, a big story to sell to one of the Sunday newspapers," he said, and then added, "just forget about him, Turan."

"But I have to speak to the Premier. Let's go to see him tomorrow."

Major Blount said he would try to arrange an appointment and hung up. I went home and poured myself a whisky. Minutes later, Emma arrived. After a few drinks, we decided to retire early—11.35 is early for me. She placed her pretty arms around my neck and pressed her body to mine. Her gentle, warm kisses glowed upon my lips. There is only one word to describe that evening: bliss.

The meeting with the Premier was in his office in the Commons. The Premier seemed extremely agitated by the news.

"The Spanish and Portuguese Commissioners said they needed help from Britain. They have organised a resistance group against the Eridanians. How on earth did they make up such a story?"

"Prime Minister, apart from these commissioners, was there anyone else at the meeting?"

"Yes," he said, "an elderly man. He seemed to be advising the two men."

I showed him the photo of General Harris, "Was it him?"

He examined the photo carefully for a few seconds. "No," he said.

"How old do you think he was?"

"Ah, yes, that was another thing…rather odd, I thought. He seemed too old for the job. He must have been in his nineties."

"What about the two men from the EU? The Commissioners? Did you have any reason to suspect them of being Eridanian controlled spies?"

"Quite frankly, Mr Akova, I'm not sure," said the Premier, clearly unable to give me a straight answer.

"What kind of help did they ask from you?"

"They want to 'commaunitairise' EU policy bringing it under the sway of the commission. They could well be mollified by the Franco-German idea of 'constructive abstention'—a new formula to encourage majority voting. I mean. The aliens control them anyway. You see, they are trying to outflank stubborn resistance within the EU against them."

"But there is definitely some resistance in the EU against the aliens?"

"Oh, yes, definitely," said the premier.

"Will you support them?" asked the major.

"Well, my government is going to discuss the matter at length. Gentlemen, you know my government has no intention of signing any agreement with the aliens. But we are going through a period of violent controversy within the

Conservative Party." He looked my way: "What's happening with your research?"

I told him exactly what had happened in Ibiza and about General Harris.

"Unfortunately, we have not been able to locate him yet. I suspect the elderly man at your meeting was him."

"But this is a different man from the picture you showed me," he protested.

"True, but as you know, Draco has all sorts of tricks up his sleeve. We have no idea why he took the trouble to re-animate this man, and on the island of Ibiza of all places. I think Draco and his men have a plan."

When we left the commons, Major Blount spoke his thoughts: "I wonder what the plan is…"

"Go on, Major, give me some ideas. You're the expert on counter-intelligence after all." I urged him eagerly.

"This isn't counter-intelligence. My dear chap, we are dealing with super-intelligence; evil, extraterrestrial and devil-sponsored activities with strokes of indefinable alien, other worldly, deadly, dark surprises. I mean, look at the situation now. You say the elderly man at the meeting with the Premier could be General Harris, and yet this man bears no resemblance to Harris. Maybe they put a new face on him. But why?" I am confounded. Turan, sometimes I have this notion, "Let's arrest the bastards, all three of them, Draco, De Medici and Gonzaga and send them to the hell they came from!" The major shook his head in bewilderment.

"How terribly austere you are," I complained reproachfully. "Believe it or not, I got used to their inexplicable strategies. That is why I venture into totally unexpected tactics to confuse them. You're right, of course. Something's cooking and we have no way of finding out what it is, unless…"

"Unless what?" asked Blount curiously.

"Unless I track down the General and stop him."

I asked Major Blount to dig out as much information as possible about the General. Maybe he had a living relative somewhere. With Emma, we continued the search for a relative on the internet at the UFO Research Centre. Finally the major was able to find a lady, Eliza Francisco, who was the general's sister. She lived in London, in a flat in D'Arblay Street, in Soho. I was quite familiar with this street. The Turkish Cypriot Association had been there for ages, and in my student days, we used to go to the Association frequently for food and dinner when we longed for our own local food. D'Arblay Street had quite a few striptease joints and many flats with red or pink door bells with cards, announcing 'Model', the ubiquitous euphemism for prostitute. It was about three o'clock in the afternoon when I pushed open the red-painted iron gate and marched up to the second floor, to Mrs Eliza Francisco's door, No, 7. The corridor was littered with cigarette butts and empty beer bottles. The door opened and there, standing and staring at me was a young woman with drab hair and eyelashes matted with mascara.

"Is Mrs Eliza Francisco in?" I asked.

"Yes, please," she replied with a heavy accent, Spanish or Italian.

"If you would be so kind as to tell her that I would like to see her. My name is Akova." I said.

"Yes, please," repeated the young woman as if those were the only two words of English she knew.

I sat on a large, blue armchair, the only one in the hall. Minutes later, Mrs Francisco walked in. She had an elegant figure, a remarkably well-preserved body for someone of ninety-eight. Her face looked old, but her make-up was carefully applied to her mouth and cheeks.

"Yes?" she enquired, standing near the entrance to another room, "can I help you?"

"My name's Turan Akova. I want to ask you a few questions about your late brother, General William Harris."

"Come in," she said politely. I took in a whiff of brandy as I walked past her into the room. She shook her head, perplexed.

"This is rather strange. He's been gone over four years now. But tell me, you are not English, are you?"

"No, I'm Turkish Cypriot. Mrs Francisco, please tell me, have you heard anything, anything at all about your brother recently?"

"Not unless I hear voices of the dead from the other side! Wait a bit—who are you?"

"I work with the government. We are conducting an investigation into your brother's activities during the last years of World War II. We are desperately looking for clues that will head us to find out more about the aliens' involvement in the current disturbing situation." I said.

"But my brother is dead and gone!" she pointed out somewhat dismally, "what do his activities at the end of the war have to do with the aliens? After all those years, how could any information about him give you a clue?"

"Well, I'm here to tell you the truth. And I hope you can help me."

She was speechless, and moved nervously in her armchair.

"Bring us some brandy," she ordered her maid, sizing me up from head to toe. It seemed as though my presence held all the fascination of a thrilling mystery story for her.

"Go on...!" she urged, "don't keep me in suspense. What is this truth you want to tell me?"

"Your brother, General William Harris, was brought back to life on the island of Ibiza by the Eridanians. We believe he is being used by the aliens. They want to take over Britain and your brother is a key figure in this final mission." I said.

She was horror-struck. "Brought back to life? How is that possible? Are you mad?" she protested with such spirited objection that I had to force myself to remain calm and explain to her what had happened at Santa Eulalia del Rio.

"Yes, Mrs Francisco. It happened. And I watched it happen." I told her.

There was a pause as she took this in, and then she shook her head vehemently. "No, I don't believe it." Then she looked up at me with a start, "Did you say Santa Eulalia del Rio?"

"Yes, why? Do you remember anything about this town? Have you been there?"

She was suddenly confused and seemed not to be able to articulate her feelings. "Yes, I was there, in the early fifties with my first husband, a boxer. He died twenty years ago. Peter Walters was his name. You see, my first marriage was a *mésallience*. Bill stayed in that town for quite some time. He was always talking about sublime beings visiting him at night. He said he had seen these little men coming out of a UFO which landed in a nearby forest. Now I remember. Yes, I remember..." The news I had given her had evidently transported her into the past, and she was now thoroughly absorbed in trying to remember those times.

"What else did he say about the UFO and the sublime beings visiting him?"

"Wait. I'm trying to remember." After a pause, she spoke again: "Yes, it was like this. He told me about an axis. He said he controlled this axis. I honestly don't know what he meant by that. The only reason why I remember this, is that he repeated the same story every single day and night. Personally, I thought he was going crazy..."

"Mrs Francisco,—"

"Oh, call me Eliza, for heaven's sake!"

"I understand that Francisco is the surname of your second husband?"

"Yes. He was Spanish. A well-known author. He died ten years ago."

"I'm sorry." I said.

"I'm sorry, too," she replied curtly.

"Well, Eliza, it's of the utmost importance for you to remember anything at all about this so-called axis."

"Peter, my first husband, asked him about it. But I remember Bill saying he was not allowed to talk about it."

"But are you quite sure he said nothing about it?" I persisted.

"Oh, I can't remember!" she replied impatiently, "It was such a long time ago. I really can't remember."

"You and Peter spent some time with him in Ibiza. Was there anyone else staying there with you?"

Now she looked as if in a dream, reliving what she had seen all those years ago.

"No. But we had visitors coming to that beautiful house near the forest," she said.

"Eliza, was this beautiful house that you speak of anywhere near the Glass Cemetery on top of a hill?"

"Yes!" she cried triumphantly, "I remember now. Yes! The Glass Cemetery…"

"But tell me about the visitors. Was there anyone close to your brother? Perhaps he had a girlfriend?"

"Too many people visited the house. I can't remember. Let me see now. There was a young girl who was extremely fond of my brother. But I can't recall her name."

"What about the painter, Delantes? Did he visit the house? His full name is Ronaldo Alfonso Delantes."

She turned her cool gaze on me, and said scathingly: "Mr Akova, we are talking about events which happened fifty to sixty years ago. Surely you can't be expecting me to remember an occasional visitor to the house?"

"I wish you could remember. He is in his late eighties, and still lives not far from the hill, about a mile from the Glass Cemetery. I met him on my visit to Santa Eulalia del Rio a few days ago. He did not mention your brother's house. I think that's odd, because they were neighbours, after all. The chances are that they met during your brother's stay in the town."

Eliza was a remarkable woman with character. Before I left, I asked her to try to remember three things: firstly, what was this axis? Secondly, was there any link between Delantes the painter and her brother; if I could establish that Delantes had been a regular visitor to the house and was a personal friend, why would he not have mentioned this to me? Finally, the girl Eliza had mentioned as being fond of her brother, could be a very important lead. Eliza promised to call me if she remembered anything at all along these lines.

This was the first time the word 'axis' had cropped up in our investigations. When I returned to the Centre, I asked Emma and ten other people who work for the UFO Centre to seek out every single detail about the concept of 'axis' in relation to the activities of the Eridanians. They in turn contacted three British scientists who prepared a report on the regular scientific explanation of 'axis'. The scientists' explanation was simple enough. The report said, *The rotation of the sky is due to the actual rotation of the Earth on its axis. Working from the Celestial sphere theory, we can say that the celestial equator is the projection of the Earth's equator onto the celestial sphere. The poles are indicated by the direction of the axis of rotation.*

The British astrophysicist Christopher Newbury had written a book about the movement of the stars in the Milky Way. He could explain to us not only the axis of the planet Earth and its rotation with emphasis on the solar system and the sun, but he could also illustrate the facts relating to the movement of the nearest star systems to the Milky Way.

We sat in the large room at the Centre, taking notes while he more or less gave us a lecture on the star systems, their axes within their own constellations and in particular what he called 'angular momentum'.

Newbury said, "The angular momentum of a body can be defined as a measure of the total rotational motion that body happens to possess. When we talk about axes, we have to explain why and how an axis of several star systems in our own Milky Way can in fact form a meaningful combination with lines that depict inter-stellar travel and cosmic time sequences. For axes to have any meaning in outer space, we have to revert to the celebrated Doppler Shift. When a body in outer space moves close to us, an apparent change or shift takes place in the frequency of that body emitting radiation."

"Naturally, we have concentrated on the star system Epsilon Eridani, the home of the Eridanians, and its relation to Earth as far as the axis in outer space is concerned."

I put a question forward: "So what is your assessment of the axis of star systems in the Milky Way in relation to our Solar System?"

Newbury adjusted his glasses, looked at me with some interest, and answered my question.

"Mr Akova, the Epsilon Eridani star system is only 10.8 light years' distance from the solar system. This system is similar to our own sun. It is slightly smaller and cooler—spectral type J—and it has a system of planets. Now, the proper motion of the star systems nearest to us is so slight that it is not noticeable with the naked eye even over periods of centuries. This is where we have to revert to cosmic time sequences in outer space. There are different time sequences in different parts of the galaxy. In other words, a year earth time is 365 days, but a year in a distant planet orbiting another star system can be 3,650 days earth time." Newbury walked to the blackboard and drew some diagrams. "For example, the seven stars of the Great Bear were in this position 100,000 years ago earth time. This second diagram," he placed the seven spots at a slightly different angel, "shows the Great Bear as it appears today in the heavens." Then he put the seven stars in a distinctly different position, "This third diagram shows how the seven stars will appear 100,000 years into the future. The same system applies to the star system nearest to Earth in our own Milky Way galaxy."

"Now let us consider only our closest stellar neighbours, stars up to 5 parsecs (16.3) from the Sun. These are Alpha Centauri (4.3 light years). Barnard's Star (6 light years), Sirius (8.7 light years), Epsilon Eridani (10.5 light years), 61 Cygni (11 light years), Procyon (10.4 light years), Epsilon Indi (11.4 light years), Tau Ceti (11.6 light years), Omicron Eridani (16.2 light years), Altair (16.3 light years)."

Newbury's lecture was extremely interesting. He looked at me again, "Now, Mr Akova, coming back to your question on the axis of all these star systems that I mention in relation to our Solar System. Conventional space is curved. In other words, travel between Epsilon Eridani and Earth, although to our senses a straight line is in fact a curve. If we somehow puncture the 'bubble' of curved space and take the path I show you in this diagram," he drew a straight line between Epsilon Eridani and Earth, "this straight line would represent a short cut. This is travel through another dimension. So space travel between Epsilon Eridani and Earth could become ludicrously short, or even instantaneous. This means that with this straight line, we have a straight axis. It is interesting to note that the same theory of a straight line axis applies to all the other star systems that I mentioned earlier. So this means a straight line axis from all these star systems could in fact make possible instantaneous space travel from them to planet Earth."

"Are you saying that all these star systems have straight line axes to earth and their civilisations can reach earth instantaneously?" I asked.

"Yes, it seems that is a possibility. How the Eridanians plan to use this axis and why is a total mystery." Newbury said finally, "If indeed this is the case."

I asked Newbury to print a map of that part of the Milky Way showing the sun and all the other nearest star systems that he had mentioned at the beginning of his short but extremely intriguing theory.

A straight line axis from Epsilon Eridani, the home of the Devil and from other 'close neighbours' star systems to Earth. A short cut, or rather instantaneous space travel. What was the meaning of all this? And what could a theory, involving our nearest neighbours in the Milky Way have anything to do with General William Harris? From the information we had gathered so far, the Eridanian extraterrestrials had solved the problem of inter-stellar travel. So there was really no need for such instantaneous space travel for the Eridanians. It did not make sense. Why straight lines from all these star system? Of course, this theory was just one possibility. Newbury explained to us the meaning of axis in relation to straight lines from all those star systems.

A link between this grand astronomical plan with instantaneous space travel and General William Harris who was supposed to use the axis—whatever that meant—was simply non-existent and almost impossible to explain. How could anyone establish a link between these two? The other possibility could be earth-based. An earth based axis from where and for what purpose?

We developed photos I had taken at the Glass Cemetery. The photo of General Harris and all the rest of the information was computerised and sent immediately to all the intelligence services in European countries and in the USA. But all the efforts to locate the mystery man General Harris would be in vain as the Eridanians could change his face, his physic and even his age. Finding this man seemed like an impossible task. Nevertheless, I, as always, had at least one lead. Eliza Francisco, the General's sister. She could try to contact her brother. Or vice versa. She would most probably not be able to recognise him with a new face and appearance. But if he decided to contact her, she would know he was her brother. But would he contact her? Would he risk being seen with her?

I had to investigate, I had to go to her again. I had to find this man and find the link between him and the 'axis' that he mentioned. Eliza said her brother had told her that he controlled the 'axis'. What was the meaning of this? What was the axis? I sensed something profoundly important at work. Were these the first signs of a final cataclysm? And what about the Grey extraterrestrials who promised to save the Earth and humankind? Where were they? I had so far understood that their reasoning and actions indicated higher super-intelligent planes. It was quite possible that they had mastered time travel and were coming to us from the future. If Newbury's theory proved to be correct and the Eridanians were indeed planning to permeate their enormous powers through the axis from the other star systems, why 10 star systems? Surely they would not want to meddle with the Grey extraterrestrial domains of Alpha Centauri and Tau Ceti. These two star systems which were supposed to be the home of the Greys. Why would the Eridanians include the Grey star systems in this grand plan?

Obviously, the Greys and the Eridanians were the two pre-eminent extraterrestrial civilisations in the Milky Way. Well, at least one part of the galaxy. The two extraterrestrial civilisations had different methods, both of which were totally beyond human understanding. Many people would scoff at the stubborn policies of the government and insisted an accord should be signed with the Eridanians. I decided to walk home from the Centre at Marylebone High Street, to my home in Charles Street, knowing full well that the shadow-lurking demons of Draco were following me all round London. I wanted to wait for at least a couple of days before I visited Eliza Francisco again. At home, I practised on my Bosendorfer grand. My next piano recital was in a month's time at the Purcell Room. I included some new works in my 'new music' programme.

Thirty-Four

After a couple of hours' practice on the piano, I went into the study and sat behind the computer. Emma and one of our computer experts had worked out a special program for me to keep abreast with the latest developments on alien activity, not only in Britain but in the rest of the world. At the press of a button, I could log in to this program and read all the news. One report from UFO researchers in Marlborough said there had been a sharp increase in Grey activity in different locations in Wiltshire. Nothing unusual about that, I thought. It was a well-known fact that there was a massive Grey presence in Wiltshire. One famous British UFO researcher, a Mrs Fiona Richardson, whom I met on several occasions, claimed she had held a conversation with one of the Greys at a spot not far from Stonehenge. She said the Grey extraterrestrial had told her the Eridanian plan to take over Britain would be foiled and the evil ones would leave planet Earth. No one could verify or disprove her claims.

There was still a great element of mystery surrounding Grey activity in Britain. At the end of the second day, the quiet stillness of the atmosphere in London unsettled me. The lively variety of cultural activities, the shows, the cinemas in the West End were all unusually quiet. Darkness reigned in the streets and the few figures I saw walking past me were probably disciples of Satan. Draco, De Medici and Gonzaga disappeared without trace. Agents in Marlborough reported back a scene of desolate, grim, painful and unhappy existence. The people were in a state of indecision and they waited in anticipation for the surrender of Britain to the Eridanians.

Agents in Marlborough reported no movement in Draco's twin mansions. The place looked deserted, they wrote. No word on General Harris either. With this uncertainty, many devout Christians awaited the second coming of Christ to save them from the evil. The fact that there had been no communication with the Greys made things much worse, as people who knew of their pledge to save mankind simply gave up hope. I would never give up hope. Clearly, there was something holding them back from the final thrust. It has been almost two years since the arrival of the Devil on Earth. But no sooner had I a thread placed in my hand, than it was taken away again, and I was left with nothing but the knowledge that I had acquired about the peculiar ways of the Devil.

Most of the Eridanians' actions were vehemently advocated, but their unthinking, clairvoyant behaviour complicated matters beyond any sort of limit. There was no balance or proportion. Their multi-dimensional and extremely persuasive dialogue held such vigour. A power eliminating all challenges to their supremacy almost always rising into great thunderous variations and yet occasionally filled with a serene and unfathomable beauty attracting mankind into a deep, devilish cluster of non-committal attitudes.

The devil's games were working. They promised sheer delight, and many thousands joined them. There were all passing through a stage of a remarkable dawn of a new era and were completely unaware of the dark side. A shallow, desperate world of humans who would eventually become slaves of the Devil. Suddenly, I realised I had learned a great deal about the ways of the Eridanians. But the Greys with whom I had communicated on many occasions and who had endowed my body and soul with so much power and invincibility were still a mystery and I had little knowledge about their activities.

While greatly optimistic about the future, I was always able to accept the bleak facts. It was a gloomy, overcast day when I set forth on my mission to find General Harris. My only lead was Eliza, his sister. I rang her doorbell. It was eleven in the morning. Not a sound. I waited for a few minutes, ringing the bell again and again. After about five minutes, I forced the lock with a knife-like piece of metal I always carry with me. The door opened and I entered. Quickly, I searched the rooms. There was no one in the apartment. At first, I looked in the bedrooms. I search both thoroughly. Nothing. On the kitchen table, I found a piece of paper. On it was a well-drawn map of Europe. The black dots on it clearly marked the locations of ten of the main cities and towns: London and Marlborough in England; Paris in France; Madrid in Spain; Santa Eulalia del Rio again in Spain; Florence in Italy; Zurich in Switzerland; Berlin in Germany; Istanbul in Turkey. New York was also shown on this map, although it is not in Europe. There were straight lines from each centre to the other. The paper on which the map was drawn was quite large, about three feet wide. The most distinctive part of it was that all the straight lines eventually ended up in Marlborough. As I examined the map once again, I heard the front door open. I pulled out my gun and remained seated at the kitchen table. A beautiful young woman walked into the kitchen.

"Mr Akova!" she cried. I did not recognise her at first.

"Who are you?" I asked.

"I can hardly blame you for not recognising me," she said, while I put the gun back in the holster, "I am now almost sixty years younger. Isn't that wonderful? I have a full life ahead of me."

"Eliza? Is it really you?"

"It sure is, Mr Akova! I had no idea my brother has such unbelievable powers. It's remarkable, isn't it?"

"Yes, remarkable. Except that eventually, you will become a slave of the Devil."

"Oh, pooh! Don't you want to live forever?" she asked enthusiastically.

"Let me answer your question with another," I said, "do you want to live as one of the Devil's slaves forever?"

"Oh, come on, Mr Akova. Don't tell me you believe in that Devil stuff!"

"I don't have to believe in it. I know it to be true." I said, "Anyway, the Grey extraterrestrials can do it for you. With the Greys, you can live your life again and again as a young person and you don't have to become a slave!"

"Well, then, you must introduce me to them." Eliza was so happy with her transformation that she did not realise the seriousness of the situation/ She was jumping from her alien identity to her human self and was completely mesmerised by her second life as a young woman.

"Where did you get this map, Eliza?"

"My brother left it."

"Did you tell him about me?"

"I would have told him, but somehow we didn't have enough time to talk. At first, I didn't recognise him as he had become a young man in his thirties. When he walked in, I thought he was a stranger, but the main features of the face were the same. So I recognised him immediately afterwards. It's amazing, Mr Akova, he has the power to make you young again! Isn't it incredible?"

"Eliza, are you sure you didn't mention my visit?"

"No. No, I didn't. My transformation was complete within five minutes. He said he'd visit me again and left in a hurry," she said.

"How come he forgot the map?"

"I don't know."

"Why did he show it to you in the first place? Did he tell you anything about it?"

"Yes, he said he wanted to show me how he controlled the axis."

"What else did he say about it? Anything about what he planned to do next?"

"No, Mr Akova. Nothing."

"Eliza, how could he forget such an important piece of evidence? A map showing how he controls the 'axis'—whatever that means?"

"I don't know, Mr Akova. He put the map on the kitchen table and then he went into my bedroom where he performed the transformation process on me. I was so excited! Can you imagine the feeling? I was becoming a young woman once again. I forgot all about the map. And he was in such a hurry to leave, I'm sure he forgot the thing as well."

Maybe she was telling the truth. But I doubted very much that the General would have left behind such an important item by accident. But why else would he have left it behind? Had he known of my visit to his sister? Had the map been left for me to see? Was this just another trick to confuse and complicate matters? Or perhaps it was a red herring?

"Eliza, do you have any photos of your brother as a young man?"

"Let me look at my old photo albums," she said, clearly eager to cooperate. She brought in a large album and sat beside me.

"Here we are. Now let's see." She turned the pages one by one. Then she stopped, "Here is a photo." She pointed to a photograph the size of a postcard. "There he is. I am on the left and his girlfriend is on the right. There, do you see him? Good looking man, my brother."

It was not a very good photograph, but I could see the face. There was a resemblance to Eliza.

"Eliza, I am trying to save you and your brother from the clutches of the Devil—in this case, the Eridanian extraterrestrials—but I need your help. You have to make an effort to rid the spell of the evil ones. Your brother must do the same."

"What do you mean? I don't want to be old again. Please, Mr Akova, don't ask this of me." She gripped my arm hysterically.

"Don't worry. You will remain as you are now. But you must help me. First of all, you must not tell your brother of my visits here. Now let me take a photocopy of the map and bring back the original. I'll be back in ten minutes."

I found a stationery shop just around the corner, took a photocopy and returned to find Eliza preening herself in the mirror.

"Yes, I must admit, you are a stunner," I said, "the diamonds are gorgeous, too."

She looked at me under her lashes, undeniably flirtatious.

"Would you like to have a drink with me before you leave?" she asked, full of the confidence of her new appearance.

"Why not?"

She poured brandy into two empty glasses and sat beside me.

"Eliza, are you quite sure you did not mention my visit to your flat?" I asked her again.

"Yes, I'm sure. Why would I lie to you, for heaven's sake?" she protested.

"For one thing: to protect your brother."

"No. I did not tell of your visit," she repeated in the same protesting tone.

"I must have the truth!" I said relentlessly, "I promise I will help you. But don't worry, you will remain as the young woman you are now. You must promise not to tell your brother about my visit, and not a word about the map."

"OK." She said with conviction.

"Eliza, I'll do everything I can for you and your brother. Trust me."

"Do you really have the power to keep me young just the way I am now?" she enquired ingenuously.

"Look, I'm not a magician. Of course, I have some powers which the Greys endowed me with. At any rate, those who are cleansed from the spell of the Eridanians remain as they are." I assured her, with a quick glance in the direction of the front door where the bell had just been rung.

"Quick! Tell me where I can hide!"

She pulled me by my hand towards the balcony door.

"Go down the fire escape to the corridor on the lower floor and stay there until I come and get you," she whispered.

I hurried towards the balcony as she walked towards the front door. I peeped through the curtains before descending the fire escape. I wanted to see the General's face.

"Bill!" she cried. I suppose she wanted me to know the identity of the caller, "I know what you've come for. You left your map behind, didn't you?"

"Yes, dear," he said, heading for the kitchen. She followed him. I stood motionless on the balcony.

"What's it for, this map?" she asked.

"Top secret, I'm afraid, old girl. Don't concern yourself about such matters. Just enjoy your new life as a young woman."

With a slight change of position behind the curtain, I could just manage to see them.

General Harris took out a bundle of money from the inside pocket of his royal blue jacket and handed it over to Eliza.

"Here you are. Take it. It's about thirty thousand pounds. There's plenty more where that came from. I'll give you some more on my next visit."

"How can I contact you," asked Eliza.

"You can't," he said firmly, "I'll come back, I promise." And with that, he left.

Down on the lower floor, I called Major Blount immediately, giving him the description of the General and asked him to have his men follow him.

"Please, Major, no arrest yet. I have to find out what they plan to do. Please let me know the location as soon as he enters a house, and I'll take it from there. Of course, I'll need your men to follow me from then on."

I thanked Eliza and hurried downstairs. The General has just turned into Oxford Street. There, a black Rolls Royce stopped and he got in. I ran to my Daimler parked about fifty metres from the Rolls and caught up with them at the next traffic lights.

There were two cars between my Daimler and the black Rolls. I was a trifle nervous for no reason at all. Was it just a coincidence that the General had forgotten the map at his sister's place? Or maybe it was a stroke of luck for me. As the black Rolls turned into Queensway, it dawned on me that Newbury's map of the ten nearest star systems might have some connection with the map of Europe with ten centres clearly marked on it…ten and ten…Ten star systems and ten cities and towns in Europe. Was that another coincidence? Now I was getting very excited about the maps and could not wait to return to the Centre and compare them.

The Rolls swerved sharply towards Paddington Station and stopped near a curve at the large entrance. I parked my car three cars away from the Rolls on the same side of the street. The General got out and walked into the station. At that moment, Major Blount's two men caught up with me.

"Mr Akova," said one, "can we help?"

"Yes, please. Just ask the man in the ticket office where the gentlemen in the blue jacket is going. Tell them it's police business, and show them proof of your identity."

"OK," he said, and walked towards the ticket office. The fast train gong west to Bristol would leave in five minutes at four forty-five. The plain clothes man came back and whispered into my ear the word, Maidenhead.

I bought a first class ticket to Maidenhead and boarded the train. The General's seat was right next to the sliding door which led from one compartment to the other. I sat at the other end. The whole affair concerning the General had been pretty shoddily handled by Draco and his men, I felt. This was rather intriguing. It was a freak condition, a strange situation, and seemed quite amateur. But Draco, De Medici and Gonzaga had no idea I had found the General's sister and that I was the only person who knew what he looked like.

I tried to remember the lines on the map while the train whizzed past Reading. There was a convergence of the straight lines from different spots in Europe, and the place they converged was Marlborough. Before leaving, Newbury had told me how the Eridanians' position the anti-gravity inertia field, making it intense in several directions. This was in actual fact property of matter by which it remained in a state of rest. But if in motion it continued moving in a straight line unless acted upon by an external force. Newbury had said that the straight lines would carry horizontally placed energies and meet up in one specific place—which was, of course, Marlborough.

It was too complicated. These electromagnetic energies had both electrical and magnetic properties. Perhaps the 'axis' was all the lines on the map joining together and all the star systems having the same straight lines joining together, ending up on Earth. What was 'axis'? Was it an imaginary line going through the centre of a rotating object? Or was it a line dividing a regular figure into two symmetrical parts? I did not have a clue. But we had to organise a sturdy resistance to their plan, whatever that might be.

The train stopped at Maidenhead. The General rushed off. There were three other passengers who disembarked there plus, of course, the Major's two men who were following me. General Harris walked into an avenue under the bridge. It was dark and windy. At that moment, I saw an extremely bright light in the sky. It looked like a UFO. Come on, I said to myself, it's probably Mars or Jupiter. But the light became larger and larger, and moved in the sky, descending like a leaf fluttering from a large tree. Then the bright light zoomed upwards and to the west, and disappeared within two seconds. I looked up to the street sign: Dawson Street. The General walked half way up the street and turned into a house on the left hand side of the street. Suddenly it all looked very familiar. My amazement grew by the minute. What the hell was happening here, I asked myself. Now I remembered. This semi-detached house was the home of Gabriella Miller, a girl I had met at the Foreign Press Association some years ago. I had not seen her for at least three years. We had gone out for a month or so and then she had to go to Australia. I wondered now if she had kept the house and whether she had returned. I had visited Gabriella in her house three years ago. It had been an unforgettable evening for both of us. What were the chances of ending up in this very same house? A million to one? It was like winning the Lottery. Or could it be that Draco and his demons had investigated the full history of my life in London during the past ten years? If this was the case, I was in for a nasty surprise.

I rang the bell after waiting for about fifteen minutes. Blount's two men walked up and down separately, keeping an eye on me and on the house. The door opened and there she was! By Golly, it was Gabriella. She stared at me in the dim light, and then almost threw herself into my arms.

"Turan," she spoke in a soft whisper, her index finger on her shapely lips and nose. "Where have you been all this time? What a surprise! Why are you here?"

"It's a long story, Gabriella. Let's have a private chat before we go in." I explained what had been happening over the last 12 months or so. Draco, the Eridanians, De Medici, Gonzaga, the Greys, the UFO Research Centre in London, the Chosen 36…the lot.

"Do you know the man who just walked into your house? Why is he here?"

She walked with me towards the garden gate.

"Turan, I married a year ago. My husband is Felix Leyton, an aerospace scientist. Since the arrival of the aliens, he was contacted by this man Draco and asked to prepare reports about the British Space Research Centre. Although well-known in scientific circles, he had—for one reason or another—shifted into the background. At any rate, I don't know who our guest is. He is an ex-general, I believe—though he looks remarkably young to have come so far in his career, and to be an ex-anything—and I have absolutely no idea why he's here. The reason I hushed you is because all three of them are down on their knees in the hall shaking their heads and waving their arms in a rather peculiar manner. I guess it must be some kind of prayer meeting or something. Turan, the whole thing is quite bizarre to me."

"Are you involved with the Eridanians in any way?"

"No, not at all. On the contrary, I'm just an innocent bystander."

"Gabriella, this meeting in your house cannot possibly be a coincidence. I think they know everything about my private life in London."

For some reason, one of my ex-girlfriends had been chosen. But why her?

"I think they wanted me to make contact with you and probably with your husband. Let me tell you this much. They are evil and they are on the verge of taking over Britain. The strange man who arrived just before me is General Harris—he was a general during the second world war. He's involved, and he is, I'm sure, an important part of their plan. By the way, I should let you know that he died four years ago, and they brought him back to life again. Indeed, he has been rejuvenated, which accounts for his youthful appearance."

"Turan! You're not serious."

"I'm deadly serious. I watched it happen. Gabriella, can I trust you? I have a mission. I have to stop them. Something catastrophic will happen if I don't. I don't know what exactly, but I have a feeling of impending and irreversible disaster…so we have to trust one another."

"Turan, I'll do anything to help you."

"Well, don't worry. No harm will come to you or your husband," I reassured her.

When we walked into the house, I wondered aloud who the third man might be.

"His name is Timothy Gallagher. Apparently an acquaintance of my husband. He is a civil servant at the MoD. I don't know him. It's the first time he's ever come here."

We walked into another room and sat on a couch. After a long five minutes, the door opened and in came the General. He looked me straight in the eye, and I could almost feel the fervour pulsing in his evil soul.

"Mr Turan Akova," said Gabriella, "General William Harris." We shook hands. He looked in his early forties.

"Let's go and sit somewhere more comfortable," suggested Gabriella.

She led the way and I followed the General and the MoD man.

"Would you like a drink, or something softer; tea or coffee?" she asked. I was sitting opposite Harris, the better to observe him.

"Do you have any beer, Gabriella?"

"That's a good idea. Shall we all have beer? What do you say, Timothy?" Timothy nodded. He was mute.

When Gabriella was out of the room, the General spoke:

"There are many questions to be answered, but first things first. You're an intelligent man, Mr Akova. By now, you will have concluded that this is not a coincidence: Santa Eulalia del Rio, my being brought back to life…But I can hear you questioning, why Gabriella of all the people in your private life in London? Well, I can tell you. She is not fully aware of it yet, but she is one of your famous Chosen 36. She was abducted at the age of seven by the Greys," he paused, while he lit a cigarette, "Draco and his men have still not been able to neutralise the power the Greys gave her. Interesting, isn't it, Mr Akova?"

"Yes, very." I said.

"So now we have two of the Chosen 36 with us."

"What are you getting at, General?"

"Nothing, except this. She has more power than any of the other 34 or 35 people in this famously elite group. I know we are not able to force our will on any one of them, but that is of no consequence. Earlier, I told you that you were very intelligent. But you are also very stubborn and very silly indeed."

"How so?"

"Mr Akova, you are a Turkish Cypriot who has come all the way from an isolated island in the eastern Mediterranean and you are leading—more or less— the British government into a war they cannot win. The mind reels when it attempts to understand the reasoning behind your actions."

Gabriella walked into the room with the beers. Her face paled at the General's next words: "You may be a musical genius, Mr Akova, but I can't understand how the mighty British government would let a Turkish Cypriot dictate their plans against such invincible powers as those the Eridanians possess. You are simply stupid and irrelevant. The Eridanians will take over Britain and you cannot stop them!"

There was no way I could respond politely to these harsh and critical words. But I reminded myself, the General was not being himself—it was the Eridanian in him which was speaking. I wanted to listen to what else he would say, and so I kept quiet. The General was now about to lecture me about the Eridanians.

"The iridescence of the Eridanians cannot be matched with any other extraterrestrial civilisation, including the Greys. I admit there have been startling developments in Britain ever since the arrival of the Eridanians, but your efforts are entirely tenable. The immensity of the enigma of the mighty Eridanians has fallen upon Earth. The highly advanced Eridanians cannot be challenged. Not even the Greys can save you now. Grey power is like a yawn on the face of the infinite."

He raised his voice and poor Gabriella almost spilled her beer on the floor which was covered with thick rugs.

"You are a playboy. But that's no reason why you should have affairs with twelve women at the same time." Something had definitely cracked up in his brain. He started to make completely senseless remarks.

He did not mention Eliza, though. That meant he had no knowledge that I possessed a copy of his map. There were two or three cases of Eridanian controlled humans who had gone completely haywire. Suddenly, the General stopped talking. He drank his beer, but before I could get a word in, he started up again.

"Gabriella, my dear. Don't worry. You and Mr Akova are now united and will have a wonderful time together. You—both of you—are coming with us," he said, pointing a finger at us.

Before we could respond, three men with automatic weapons walked into the sitting room.

"What is this?" I got up, protesting.

"Just shut up and do as we say, Mr Akova," snarled the General viciously, "you are coming with us. All good things come to an end. I don't mess around with people. Either I kill them or I kill them." He let out a cynical bark of a laugh.

"Mr Akova, you came here by your own accord and soon you'll be gone into kingdom come."

"Listen, General, you don't have to take Gabriella. She is not involved really. Just leave her alone," I pleaded with him.

"I'm afraid that's not possible. I have to destroy all the evidence, as they say. Plus, don't forget that she has become one of the Chosen 36. She has the power of your little Grey friends," he said maliciously.

"Is there anything I can do to make you change your mind about all this? I mean, killing us won't help matters." I was trying to gain time, and somehow I had to contact Major Blount and his men.

He shrugged his shoulders, as if snagged by the thought that he had got it wrong. I'm sure something clicked back in his brain. This could happen in

Eridanian controlled humans. It was a complex situation when a 'mix-up' of alien and human identities produced some kind of chain reaction in the brain, causing the subject to lose all consciousness of his or her current personality. The result was a complete waywardness in a normal conversation, leading into maddeningly senseless, insane dialogue. It happened as I thought it would, and I played along, hoping to take advantage of the situation and confuse him even further.

"A melody of haunting splendour travelling and exploring human nature," I said, and continued without a pause, saying whatever came into my mind: "The universally loved masterpiece of all time. Thoughts that are always pure and expressive."

He looked at me and seconds later, got up from the armchair, his arms outstretched. His movements seemed to lack vigour and energy.

"Lay down your arms!" he shouted to the three men with the automatic weapons.

"But sir..." one of them objected.

"You dare to disobey your General?" he roared. "The prisoners will have tea now. Gabriella, would you be so kind? I mean the fact that our sun is a G2 star and has a stable life expectancy of 11 billion years doesn't mean we have to isolate ourselves from evolution. What is the purpose of controlling something you don't even understand? Liszt's daughter moved in with Wagner, didn't she? The Magic Mountain is still there. Controversy still surrounds the share-out of power between you and me. Foreign and security policy must be improved. A musical Europe and the Air Force." His voice trembled and he stopped talking. I seized my opportunity and grabbed Gabriella by the hand.

"General, do I have your permission to make tea with Gabriella in the kitchen?"

"You rascal! You rogue! Your reputation precedes you, not only as a pianist/composer but also as a playboy. Don't be too long, children," he said.

I realised we had very little time. The last part of our conversation had somehow rekindled his confidence and he started to talk again in a manner which was bringing him back to his former self.

As soon as we moved into the kitchen, I closed the door behind us.

"Quick! Get into my Daimler and wait for me there! Turn right as you go out. You'll see it, a white car, parked about fifty metres from the house."

She slipped out quietly and went out of the front door. I returned to the sitting room with gun in hand.

"Don't move." I said to the three men who had actually put their automatic weapons on the table. But wait a minute, the General, Gabriella's husband, and two men were all seated around the room. One man was missing. Just then, I saw a shadow behind the glass door and I had just enough time to dive behind the desk near the window. The automatic weapons rattled down the side of the desk. As one of the men in the room grabbed his weapon and was about to shoot, I hit him twice in the belly. He fell on his face. He was very dead. The second man in the room was behind an armchair. Shots echoed in the house as the General lay on the floor. Fury surged through his whole body as he shouted: "Shoot them! Shoot them both—now!" Then in a jerky movement full of stops and starts, he raised himself from the floor.

I grabbed the collar of his shirt and pulled him towards me. His body shielded me from the shots coming both from the door and from inside the room, but he was struggling to get loose. I tightened my hold, but the man was much stronger than I had anticipated. He finally tore loose and threw himself behind the armchair. Now the shots came from both sides. Death tolled a bell in my ear and I could almost see Azrael in his long black robe getting ready to part my soul from my body. As the third man rushed in firing in my direction, I ducked and then shot him in the belly.

Another ten or twelve shots cracked from the automatic weapon held by the last man behind the armchair. I fired another five shots and then jumped through the glass of the window behind me. I ran like a sprinter towards the car. I heard shots fired after me and then I saw Blount's two men standing beside their car, shooting, shooting at the last man who was now in the garden with the General. This end of the street was shadowy and dark, cluttered with black figures moving, darting in all directions.

Gabriella stood by my car, spellbound. She was shaking with fear.

"Quick! Get in!" I shouted, and I almost had to pull her in. I started the car and drove straight into the main road under the bridge. I looked at the rear view mirror, keeping an eye on what was happening behind me. Nothing. I parked the car on a side street and called the two MI6 men.

"We are right behind you," said one of them.

"What happened to the General and the other man?" I asked him.

"They disappeared at the back of the house. I'm sorry, Mr Akova, but I don't understand it. We searched the house and garden in the back, but there was no trace of them. I honestly don't know how they escaped."

"Anyway, thanks…" I said. "Perhaps it would be a good idea to keep the house under surveillance. Report back to Major Blount, please. I'll call him myself.…"

It had been almost a year since the advent of the Eridanian extraterrestrials. During that period, all the data gathered was extensively written in every report with every single detail. I felt the need to look at these reports and study them thoroughly. But first I had to find accommodation for Gabriella. She said she didn't want to go back to the house in Maidenhead, and I did not blame her for that. Luckily, my neighbour next door in Charles Street had a flat for rent. I assured her that she was being protected twenty-four hours and there was no need to worry. This was a luxury flat and it also had a private telephone.

"Turan, I don't want to go back. It was an unhappy marriage anyway. I'm going to call Felix and tell him I am starting divorce proceedings. I'm sure he'll agree."

"Do that, Gabriella. You don't want to be mixed up with anyone in collaboration with Draco."

"Will you come and see me later?" she asked, clinging on to my hand.

"Yes, I'll come late this evening. I'll telephone you before I come."

The report on Eridanian behaviour was as follows:

They are not semi-embodied. The human brain and soul can be taken over completely. The transformed humans combine with the super intelligence biologically also. They are very advanced in the art and science of creating significant forms of technological patterns which can penetrate the brain and the soul…

'Go as you please and say whatever comes into your head'. It was a total mystery why the Eridanians chose this doctrine and implanted it into the brains of transformed humans. But this strategy overlaid the truth—the creative impulse of the human brain. That is why serious complications occurred of a dangerous mix-up of human and alien brainstorms resulting in confusion and mental aberration.

This is exactly what happened to the General. A full understanding of alien behaviour was quite unattainable. But the knowledge gathered so far pointed to a strange obliquity of a vision compatible with self-destruction followed by a massive recreation much more powerful than their previous structure.

Emma, Clayton, Newbury and two of his colleagues were present at our next meeting at the UFO Centre. We compared Newbury's map of the nearest star systems with the General's map of Europe clearly showing the ten centres: London, Marlborough, Brussels, Paris, Berlin, Zurich, Florence, Madrid, Santa Eulalia del Rio and Istanbul. A configuration of those then locations on Earth matched perfectly with the current position of the star systems in Newbury's star map. The lines going from one to another and finally joining up at Marlborough. That was already established. But why? What did it all mean?

Newbury had a new theory. He said that the planets of the ten star systems shown on the map were reasonably close to the star. Energies sent from these planets to Earth would normally be swamped by the relative flood of light and other energies emanating from the star itself. But if the energy wavelength travelling on an axis and lines with protective bands, escaped the atmosphere of each respective planet, and the atmosphere of the star, then the energy beam would produce a bright line doubling its energy output with the addition of all the other lines and reach Earth in no time.

So Newbury's theory suggested that a massive energy from the ten star systems would join together and converge in Marlborough. He said the position of the lines would almost certainly tend to alter due to the movement of the different planets. But despite axial and orbital rotation and the difficulty arising from the movement of the planets, the energy lights could remain in a constant position and hit the targets shown on the General's map of Europe.

"How long will the ten star systems remain in the same position?" I asked him.

"Perhaps two weeks. Our calculations show that there will be a slight movement of some of the ten," he said.

"So does this mean that the Eridanians will have to start their operations within two weeks?"

"Yes."

"You mean a massive energy will arrive in Marlborough?"

"That's correct."

"Can you tell us what sort of effect it will have on the town?"

"I'm afraid not. You see, we have no idea what kind of energies will be used."

"Can it be tracked down before it enters Earth's atmosphere?" asked Emma.

"Yes, that we can do. But I don't think we can stop them," he said.

"The unseen presence of a massive energy. But what is it for? Is it for their own survival on Earth?"

"Or is it a new power and technology to eliminate all resistance?" asked Clayton, deep in thought.

"Probably both." I said, but quite frankly I doubted very much whether Draco and his demons would embark on such a grandiose plan. Of course, it was interesting, and the fact that Newbury's map of the ten star systems matched perfectly the ten locations in Europe on the General's map was a compelling reason to search for a link between them. But there were two reasons why the whole idea did not click in my mind. First of all, Newbury's map included three star systems which were allegedly the home of the Grey extraterrestrials—Alpha Centauri, Tau Ceti and Zeta Reticuli. All contacts with Greys contained sufficient information about their homes bases and all three star systems were mentioned during physical contact and through telepathic communication. If this was the case, how could the Eridanians include in their plan the three star systems of the Greys? Furthermore, Zeta Reticuli was 37 light years away from the solar system and much further out and outside the radius of 16.3 light years.

Secondly, the perfect match between the maps could be sheer coincidence. Newbury was not one of our scientists. Anyone not associated with the UFO Centre was always suspect in my book. Was Newbury on the Eridanians' side? Perhaps he was on Draco's payroll. Maybe the whole story about the two maps was a plot to mislead us. Maybe the map was left behind for me to see, and later, Newbury would collaborate with them and prepare a map of the star systems to match the locations in Europe in the General's map. What didn't fit this theory was that I was pretty sure the map at Eliza's flat was not left behind for me to see.

"I wonder," said Emma in a distant tone, "I wonder if there is something in common with all the ten locations on that map of Europe…"

"Good idea, Emma," I said, "let's examine it. Let's start with nationalities and languages: Two English locations, Marl borough and London; two French speaking locations: Paris, Brussels; two Spanish, Madrid and Santa Eulalia del Rio; two German, Berlin and Zurich; one Italian, Florence; and one Turkish,

Istanbul. Of these eight countries, only two—Switzerland and Turkey—are outside the EU."

"Right," she said, and her face barely concealed her anxiety. "Turan, I have a feeling that some sort of operation is already underway. Don't ask me why; I just feel it very strongly."

"Emma, we know the logic of the Devil and the Eridanian demons inherent in their brains is light years away and is very different from our own. You may be right."

We had no convincing explanation.

"Boys and girls," I said to the five woman and four men in the large office, "we have much work. First let's find out if there have been any UFO sightings or landings in any of these ten locations. Then let us determine if the 'axis' is visible."

Thirty-Five

"If they're visible, we have to locate their starting point in all the locations. We have to put the full machinery of science to work. We can only do this with the help of the British Space Centre. There is no time to ponder about the lines. We have to break them somehow. Let us call it a probe. If the Eridanians are putting out a probe of negative energies to undermine all resistance, then we have to break it. But how? I don't know. We simply don't know what they are planning. Their behaviour patterns embody features beyond planning. They may be using unknown dimensions that we cannot conceive of. The Eridanians are infinitely superior cosmic people. Who would have thought that Eridanus, the largest planet of Epsilon Eridani, was in fact the home of the Devil? We cannot afford to make any mistakes. I know what I say doesn't really make sense. How can we hope not to make mistakes when we don't even know what we're dealing with? OK, you're right. But I'm right, too in thinking that the best way out of the current situation is to strike at every location on the map. Believe me, they don't know I have the General's map. So that's our only advantage…"

OK, so they did not know we had Harris's secret map. He had said he controlled the axis, whatever that meant. What did the 10 locations on the map have in common? The search to find the common denominator of all these locations kept us confined to the centre for hours. Nine of them formed three inverted triangles. The first, Marlborough, London and Brussels; the second, Paris, Berlin and Zurich and the third, Madrid, Florence and Santa Eulalia del Rio. Istanbul was kept out of this configuration. It seemed logical that all ten locations would form a pattern. But even if I could find a pattern, I still would not know what it meant. Each city or town on the map differed entirely from the other. But I could scarcely be put off because of this. There was not a single shred of evidence to suggest that all ten locations would have some mysterious feature in common.

My telepathic communications with the Greys had been slightly distorted of late, but I could not give up and write them off, not for one moment. They seemed, despite complete silence and total inactivity, our one and only trump card. But before final contact with them, I had to try to find the General and Draco. The night before, I had visited Gabriella in her new flat. We snuggled up together for more than four hours, and I left her flat at three in the morning. The following day, today, we had worked from nine in the morning until seven when we had a break for dinner. At around nine that evening, one of our researchers—Graham Rice—stood up and called out excitedly.

"Mr Akova, I think I have something. It may be nothing, but then on the other hand, it could be something." He was grinning sheepishly.

"Could somebody translate that for me?" I chuckled, "Well, something or nothing, let's have it, Graham." I walked over to his desk, while he went briskly through his papers. He produced a sheet on which he had jotted down a few notes.

"Well? What is it? Tell me what you've found?"

"It's all verified," declared Graham, "all ten locations have had UFO Research Centres established only during the last three days. It strikes me as odd that these centres became operational at more or less the same time. They are all new. But there is one exception—one location—Santa Eulalia del Rio does not have one."

"I think it's Something," remarked Emma approvingly.

"I do, too," I said. "Now, please get their contact details and so on. We'll have to check them all out."

"Do you suppose they have a secret Eridanian base at each location? Surely, it's a possibility…" suggested Emma, moistening her lips.

"Of course it is. But how are we supposed to find them, if they are there?"

"Tell me, Turan. There are still some people in Europe who managed to escape from Eridanian transformation, aren't there?" Emma wondered.

"Certainly, there are," I said. "Every city has a pocket of resistance, though they are not large."

Emma insisted on this theory of secret bases. It made sense as any alien energies coming from outer space would be stored in these bases on Earth.

"Well, I'm sure we have a list of people who can perhaps conduct an investigation for us. We can only try." I said, hoping these people would give us their unstinting support.

Emma observed my reaction with cheerless, bleak satisfaction. Within half an hour, the information on how to look for these secret bases had been communicated to at least fifty appropriate people in all the locations shown on the map. I was not very hopeful, but we had to try.

Suddenly, the femme de ménage appeared at the door.

"Dinner's ready," she said, "well, you've got to eat."

I don't know how she managed it, but Mrs Flagstaff could cater for twenty people, serving immaculate and delicious food. We had dinner at around nine that evening. After the meal, Mrs Flagstaff approached my table.

"I must speak to you in private," she murmured into my ear. She was blushing as she fidgeted around the table impatiently.

"OK. Give me my rice pudding first," I joked. "When are you going to let me take you out on the town and show you a good time, Mrs Flagstaff?" She was a loyal and contented woman in her mid-sixties not above responding in kind to my mild flirtatious joking.

"That's enough, you rogue!" she snapped back humorously. But as soon as we walked towards the door, she stopped, looking extremely concerned.

"What's up, darling?" I asked, never one to begrudge her a tête á tête.

"Mr Akova, there's a man on the terrace, a strange-looking man. I saw him when I went to get some bottles of beer. He didn't see me. He was standing there, looking into the sky, not moving at all. Like a statue he was. I don't know how he got into the building, honestly I don't. But he gave me the shivers."

"OK, Terri, just go back to the restaurant. I'll look into it."

I had my shield on and my gun was in its holster. I walked up the steps with a torch in my hand and opened the door leading onto the terrace. I switched the torch onto him and pulled out my gun. He turned slowly and looked at me. The face was familiar…Then I recognised him. It was Tamor, the Grey extraterrestrial from Alpha Centauri.

"Turn off the torch, Mr Akova," he said in impeccable English.

"Tamor, at long last you are back. We need your help. They have a plan and I have a feeling this will be the final blow to all our hopes for saving mankind. I suppose you know about the two maps?" I enquired. I could almost see the expression of approval in his human face. He was, as at our last meeting near Warminster, in human form. He waved a hand and started talking in a low voice.

"The Greys, as you call us, have miraculous gifts. Their mental, spiritual and technological advance has finally surpassed the powers of the Eridanians. When

I first met you, we were not ready to intervene. Now we are ready. We are now able to match the cosmic supremacy of the Eridanians…Yes, I know about the maps. The ten star systems on Newbury's map is quite accurate. But don't trust him. He works for the Eridanians. The star map can be interpreted as an application of the same system on Earth on your map of Europe. The two maps match perfectly. The Eridanians plan to strike and overcome all resistance on Earth and in particular in Britain by directing energies from the ten star systems to the ten locations in Europe. This is a massive and unavoidable time and distance combination. Now, we have the power to divert these energies back to their own star system. Don't try to understand this. At the same time, you are right in thinking that the ten locations on the European map must have some common denominator. This is a matter for Earth people. For you. You have to find out what is it and deal with it. If you find the connection, you will solve the problem."

"But how? Can't you help us find out what it is?"

"No," he replied, waving his hand dismissively, "I have told you, this is a problem for the Earth people. You have to solve it yourself. I will contact you again in the near future." He disappeared into the black night once again, as he had done at Cradle Hill, and I was left with many unanswered questions. I was really astounded by Tamor's sudden appearance. The good news was that the Greys would finally intervene and divert Eridanian energies emanating from the ten star systems bound for earth back to where they had come from. The bad news was that we had to find out the secret of the ten locations in Europe. I shuddered to think what would happen if we were unable to solve this problem. Once again, we were in the dark, with no idea of what to look for.

Back in the restaurant, I told Emma and Clayton of my meeting with Tamor on the terrace. It seemed unbelievable to them. Emma's eyes widened with disbelief.

"So what does it all mean, Turan?"

"It means that despite Tamor's reassurance that the Greys would divert the Eridanian energies directed at Earth, we still have to find the common denominator of the ten European locations. He said it was a problem for Earth people to solve. It's up to us to solve it."

Clayton coughed behind his hand.

"How could the Greys develop their technology to match that of the Eridanians in such a short period of time? Another question: Alpha Centauri and

Tau Ceti. These two star systems are known to be the domain of the Greys. How come they are included in the star map? How can the Eridanians suck out energies from the two star systems of their arch-enemies?" he growled, and continued, "By the way, the British Space Research Centre in monitoring the immediate vicinity of Earth and so far has recorded no alien energies or vibrations."

"Shouldn't we seek the support of the British government in this matter?" asked Emma thoughtfully.

"The unanimous attitude of the government is to give us a free hand in all related activities," I said. "The British Space Research Centre have already co-ordinated their various skills and technologies in detecting alien energies. Newbury is suspected, and Major Blount is investigating his actions. There are a number of other trails concerning several people who are collaborating with the Eridanians. But the curious inconsistency of the Eridanians' actions always point to a distortion of logic."

An avalanche of disquietingly irrelevant assumptions piled up in reports reaching the centre from the government—the MoD in particular. Speculation over the possibility of an agreement signed between the British and the Eridanians had withered away quite suddenly. While we worked incessantly to discover a common factor linking the ten locations in Europe, I could not help feeling that this was a race that could end in disaster.

This was no time for theoretical and experimental endeavours. We had to assemble a complete documentation on all ten locations in Europe. Personally, I thought we had very little time to do it. The same questions popped up every now and again in my mind. What do they have in common? Six of the ten were big cities, capital cities, but that was about all, unless they were all secret centres for Eridanian activity. But what kind of activity? The other four: Zurich, Florence, Santa Eulalia del Rio and Marlborough had absolutely no common denominator between them.

I had to start at the beginning. That there were newly opened UFO Research Centres in all the locations except Santa Eulalia was most certainly odd and a lead to follow up. That they were all opened within a period of three to four days of each other was definitely another lead to follow. But the ever-mounting mystery surrounding these ten European locations led to intangible suggestions. What they had in common would give me the answers. Recent sightings in all ten locations, abductions and other related events confused and obscured the riddle. Reports coming in from the ten centres thrust us into a whirlwind of bewilderment. There was a cluster of brilliant lights—a group of UFOs flying low over Paris. UFOs were spotted in Istanbul, flying in an inverted echelon formation. Over fifty-five targets—areas where UFOs had landed—had been traced on very sophisticated radar systems. A mysterious and peculiarly shaped apparition was escorted by an entourage of seven metallic UFOs…and so on.

All ten locations have something in common…What was it? I kept repeating this to myself. Nothing…nothing…I drew at least a dozen maps of Europe, linking up the ten spots shown on the map. Nothing. I was hoping to get a shape or diagram of some sort. Some pattern that would have a meaning…Still nothing. I drew a blank on whatever I tried. The map and its locations had taken on a mysterious force, and the sheer complexity of trying to find a common denominator in all the cities and towns on it demanded expert deductive reasoning. I had to wait for the completion of all the research findings. If the deadlock continued, then I would have to act. But how? That was the question. Researchers resorted to various explanations which focussed on very bright lights in the skies of all these locations. One investigation reported a very bright, star-like object had appeared at a ninety degree angle to all the spots shown on the map. These lights appeared between 9.30 and 1.00 at night.

Of course, it was interesting, the fact that there was a large bright light above all the locations. But no conclusions were drawn. There was one more development which seemed to be inexplicable. An astrophysicist at the British Space Research Centre was now certain, after a long, careful study, that the British were now far more advanced in space technology than they had been a couple of years back. He said that the massive Grey extraterrestrial presence in Wiltshire might well be the reason for these exceptional scientific giant steps towards a new way of life. "Something beyond the pure material plane of reality. Perhaps we are witnessing a new aspect of science, one based on spiritual and mental awareness." He added, "This new technology, an unbelievable new intellectual acumen capable of performing miracles, could challenge the destructive trend of the Eridanians."

None of this gave me a final answer. All the corrosive, evil plans of the Eridanians had been brought to fruition, up until now. But the starkly vivid, sudden appearance of Tamor the Grey extraterrestrial leader provided our only source of hope for the moment. The daring magic of the Greys in Wiltshire was quite evident to all those who had experienced abductions in the Marlborough and Warminster areas. Now Tamor claimed they had the power to get rid of the Eridanians.

I was enshrouded in a trancelike silence, sitting in a large armchair in the corner of the room, where all the others, including Emma and Clayton, received reports one after the other, and assessed their findings. I questioned myself about the powers bestowed on me by the Grey extraterrestrials. It was always instinctive, a power telling me to do the right things. The telepathic communication with the Greys was always a mental and spiritual process. All of a sudden, an idea about a person or a place would present itself in my brain. A curious and constantly exciting new mixture of realism and fantasy would lead me into a world of the unknown and there I would try and seek out the truth.

The more I struggled with my inner self to solve the mystery of the ten locations on the Harris map, the more I realised that every single aspect of this final episode led to Marlborough in Wiltshire. The so-called axis, all the lines from all the spots in the map of Europe, ended directly in that Wiltshire town. I was consumed by a sudden urge to return to Marlborough. "You are on the verge of a revelation," said a voice in my head. "And you will find it in Marlborough." Strange but true. But what of the common denominator? Where was it? What was it? I poured myself another bottle of beer and drank it.

"Turan," Emma called out, "quick! Come and have a look at this. I think we've found something."

She pointed to computer where there was a map of Europe with large black dots indicating the ten locations. Right next to each black dot, a long vertical line appeared.

"The vertical lines you see in all ten locations are antennae beaming out signals into the sky."

"After a careful look, I saw that the vertical line near Santa Eulalia was much shorter than the others."

"What about Santa Eulalia? Why is the line there so much shorter?"

"Believe it or not, we have found the explanation for that, too."

"Come on. Don't keep me in suspense," I said, eager to find out whether indeed she had solved the mystery.

"Information has just reached us about Santa Eulalia," she explained, "an antenna is being erected there at this moment. It will be operational by tomorrow."

"Well, now, I wonder if the Eridanians have anything to do with these antennae?"

"I think they must be operating the antennae."

"Why do you think that?" I asked her.

"Turan, we've contacted NASA and they have monitored the beams going into space. Our own people here at the British Space Research Centre have reached the same conclusions. These are interstellar communications. Strange beams emanating from all those ten locations. Somehow, new huge antennae have been built on old ones within a short period of time," she said.

"But you said these antennae are beaming out signals into space. We were, on the other hand, expecting the opposite: energies coming into these ten locations from the star systems shown on the Newbury map."

"You're right. But that was only an assumption. I don't know, Turan. It's very confusing. But at least we have now found a common denominator."

"You're brilliant!" I told her, giving her a kiss on the cheek.

"So what do we do next?" asked Emma.

"Since there are no incoming energies, then we have to find out what they are sending out. Only NASA can help us out on that one. They are able to decode complex transmissions sent out from these antennae. Since they have many employees there, the chances are that the messages may be in English or any other European language. But then again, what is the point of sending out transmissions in an Earth language to these star systems? I don't know. We shall see. But the messages must be very important indeed, since they are beaming them out to all the star systems in Newbury's map."

"Correction. We assume they are sending the signals to those star systems." said Emma.

"Yes, it is an assumption, of course."

Extraterrestrial civilisations like those of the Eridanians and the Greys must have made considerable headway in interstellar communications. I had in fact witnessed the Eridanians making contact with their distant planets within days, which meant that they had broken the great time and distance barrier. NASA decoded the messages within days. There was a rime number visual transmission and a voice modulated sound broadcast. The decoded messages simply said: "Eridanian and Grey extraterrestrials must unite…" I was very shocked when I first read this message from NASA. How could this be possible? The Greys who were supposed to save us from the Devil collaborating with the enemy? I did not want to believe this. So I contacted the NASA people and asked them again whether there was a possibility of a misinterpretation of the message. But they told me that their interpretation had been correct.

Then I thought about the message again. "Eridanian and Grey extraterrestrials must unite…" This could be an appeal from the Eridanians as they now knew they would not be able to defeat the Grey power. Whatever the reasoning behind this message, there was nothing special about the ten locations in Europe, except that they were operated by the Eridanians and were in fact sending out these messages to outer space. The British Space Research Centre, on the other hand, concluded that these messages had been intercepted somewhere near the planet Mars. If true, this could mean two things: either there was a large fleet of Eridanian spacecraft in the Mars orbit ready for action, or they had bases on the planet itself. Either way, any such development would point to a possible massive attack on Earth. Once again, I was moving around in the realms of fantasy. But was it fantasy?

The technology on earth was unable to overcome receiving problems. In other words, we were still unable to receive and decode any messages sent to us from outer space. Obviously, there was some kind of energy transport from the star system Epsilon Eridani and the other star systems on the Newbury map, but my assessment of the situation pointed to an earth-based extraterrestrial problem. Despite extensive investigations in Wiltshire and in particular in and around Marlborough, nothing was revealed. I felt I had to return to Marlborough. In the meantime, General Harris had disappeared without trace. Draco, the leader of the Eridanians and his two deputies—De Medici and Gonzaga were not to be seen anywhere in Britain either. That was odd, too.

The appeal, as I saw it, from the Eridanians to the Greys which beamed out of the antennae in the ten locations in Europe was not so important for the moment. The fact that Newbury's map was a perfect match with that of General Harris did not mean much either. Although I did not know what Harris planned to do next, the axis he mentioned were lines heading straight for Marlborough. Reports of accelerated alien activity in Marlborough prompted much wider research in that area in Wiltshire. But there was no incontrovertible answer as to what was really happening. Both Grey and Eridanian UFOs were seen in Wiltshire by the dozen.

The voices I heard through telepathic communication with the Greys told me to go to Marlborough. When one talks about hearing voices, one usually assumes that the person involved must have a psychological problem. The experience I had with my telepathic communication with the Greys was totally different. Suddenly a thought would enter my brain and that was it. The moment I had that particular thought, I somehow sensed it was coming from the Greys. I had a feeling something would happen in Marlborough, something that could destroy all the resistance against the evil Eridanians. I had no idea what it was. A raging inner fear dominated my whole being as I stepped out of the car and headed for the door of the house I was renting in Marlborough.

I looked up into the sky, trying to transmit messages to Tamor. I needed his help. The moon was brilliant and white. I switched on the light and gazed across the sitting room. I paused momentarily. I felt a presence in the house. I looked around. There was no one. But my blood was like ice in my veins as I searched for the intruder. I lit a cigarette to steady my nerves, and took a deep breath. Then I put on my shield hurriedly and took out my gun. Why did I have the feeling that someone was in the house? My pulse was racing and I felt I was trapped in a nightmare.

All of a sudden, all four of them—Draco, De Medici, Gonzaga and General Harris—appeared from nowhere and stood before me. Now I had to face the dark evil of Satan and his companions.

"Good evening, Mr Akova..." said Draco in his deep voice, his eyes glittering with triumph. "You see? We know every move you make."

"I'm not surprised," I replied coolly, trying to keep calm.

The power of darkness descended upon the room. I felt this was the time to unlock the mystery. But how? And what mystery? Four against one. Frankly, I did not have a chance. Unless...Clearly there was desperation in their moves. Their plans to take over Britain has been checked. During the months I had spent in Britain, somehow I had managed to keep them at bay. This was largely due to the power I possessed through the Greys. And the knowledge through which I succeeded in confusing them to the point of madness. But the major setback to their plans materialised when the Greys, through some miraculous operation, had managed to surpass their technology in a very short period of time. With extraterrestrials, anything was possible.

It was quite obvious, for the time being anyway, that the Greys had the upper hand. But that was by no means a guarantee for the safety and security of humankind. With the extraterrestrials, the development of technology occurred so fast that within days, the Eridanian devils might become superior to the greys once more. Such expansion and domination was absurd and very strange indeed, and yet it proved that we, as humans, were moving from one reality to another. The integration of alien wisdom into the human brain was not yet complete. But the race of the Greys and the Eridanians to dominate each other was perilously near the borderline of extraterrestrial war.

This was an eternal cosmic struggle between the two extraterrestrial civilisations and the outlandish implication of such a war would be disastrous for Earth and for mankind. The indomitable courage of those who fought against the Devil and his cohorts was simply not enough. I had taken a glimpse of the great cosmic design, but the intriguing puzzle of the great unknown was far from being solved. I possessed the power of the Greys. But this dangerous gift had to be used with discretion rather than profligacy. It was not possible to challenge them in a superficial or haphazard way. My only chance against the might of the Eridanians was probably an initial casual response and the surprise element.

Despite his transformation, General Harris was still an army man. He would always want to annihilate the enemy. He remained unusually quiet in Draco's presence. He was like a bull in a china shop and I felt Draco did not approve of that at all.

The Eridanian Harris was just about ready to attack me once again, when Draco intervened:

"General Harris," Draco took his arm solicitously, "I think you ought to go home and rest for a while."

"But why?" blustered Harris, "he is the enemy. We can do away with him now."

"Just do as I say and go home," said Draco softly, a glint of steel behind his words. Harris looked round the room bewildered and angry for a few seconds, and then he left. I was still holding my gun in my right hand.

"There is no need for the gun, Mr Akova."

"Why are you here? Go on, Draco, tell me: why?"

"I'm here to talk," he said.

"What is there to talk about?"

This was the beginning of a long, painstaking effort to dig out the truth of what was happening in Marlborough.

"We are not here to destroy human civilisation, Mr Akova. We are here to share our technology, the essence and wisdom of the universe."

"You have a funny way of doing that. Many have been murdered in the last few months. You want to control humanity. Many millions in Europe have already become slaves of the Devil. So how can you possibly say you want to share with us the wisdom of the universe?"

"Mr Akova, human civilisation is very backward. We have to control humans until such a time that they are fully equipped to reach the highest level. They are being trained in Europe to reach that level."

There was no point in arguing about the Devil's mission here on Earth. My mind was fixed on how to stop them. I had become familiar with all Draco's behavioural mannerisms, and I sensed he was once again being diplomatic. He wanted peace, not war. An agreement to take over Britain.

"Mr Akova, you are the most powerful human I have met so far. I know you are endowed with Grey power, and I respect that. But there is a much larger dimension behind the so-called fight to gain control over this country."

"And what is that?" I asked.

"It's obvious, isn't it?" he asked, "there is a distinct possibility of an extraterrestrial war."

"But why Marlborough, of all places?"

"Mr Akova, Wiltshire is full of alien energies. I must say we are winning the war of the energies. You see, extraterrestrial technologies develop within days, even hours, Earth time, that is. We are on the verge of becoming superior again," he said, "so don't fight us. Join us."

Draco, De Medici and Gonzaga disappeared, and I was left stumbling in the dark, not knowing what he would do next. Marlborough was the place where the Devil could be stopped. Burt how? I was fast moving into a much wider enigma. What was the war of the alien energies? Every tiny second was filled with suspense as I decided to evaluate the situation once again. Draco's initial response to my question about Marlborough had been evasive. He had said they were winning the war of the energies. What did he mean by that? I had no idea. I examined all and everything in and around Marlborough, but I could find nothing. Then finally, I decided to visit the Count's Mansion.

My heart thumped as I walked through the gate. The winds howled around the mansion. There was a strange abandoned silence throughout the place, as I opened the door and entered. But I knew they were here. Later, I heard noises coming from the basement, so I followed them down the stairs, where I saw blue smoke shrouding the whole room. I wandered frantically towards the middle.

There were beams of light crossing one another all over the basement. There was a shadow running from one corner to the other. I remembered Draco's words: "The war of the energies…" But surely that bore no relationship to what was happening here. Or were these the energies he was talking about? Suddenly, I heard a hissing and I saw three figures standing before me…By now, I was shaking with fear. I had placed myself into a trap. This time round, they were mere shadows, barely visible in the blue smoke. The Grey power I possessed took control of my brain. I was taken over by it. My nose stung as the smoke in the room entered my nostrils. All three had instruments in their hands, and they were projecting bright, white beams towards the floor.

The hissing increased while the three Eridanians took up position encircling me. Gun in hand, I moved behind the door, trying to take cover. There was no turning back. I had to find the energy and destroy it. My brain worked swiftly, sending messages to Tamor. The beams of very bright white light were coming from above somewhere. I fired two shots at the beam nearest to me. The bullets went through, but the beams continued piercing the floor of the basement. I was now defenceless against the power of the devils. The beams also came from their instruments. All three pointed their instruments at me. But the shield protected me from the power of the devils. I did not understand how that could happen, as the deadly beams from their instruments would be fatal to others.

I felt the presence of the Grey power in that basement, but I had no idea how long I could hold on. Then I lost consciousness completely. When I woke up, I was lying on a white metal table in the middle of a room. The creatures all around me were very tall (more than eight feet) and ugly, very ugly. The face nearest to me reminded me of the features of the face I first saw on the window pane in Salzburg.

The Devils were all around me. At first, I had no idea where I was, then I spied the stars through the large circular window to my left. I had been abducted by the Devils and I was in their UFO high above the Earth. My body was paralysed, but I could move my head. The ugly creatures seemed to be discussing something in their own language. The UFO bounced and wobbled in the air, heading further out. Suddenly, I had the strength to move both hands. I struck out at the nearest ugly thing with both fists. But I could not reach him.

I could see computer-like electronic equipment in a long panel against the white wall. I felt the contents of my brain and thoughts were constantly being revealed to the aliens. I looked across the large, white room. Draco appeared through an opening. He was in human form as always. He smiled, his white teeth shining.

"Mr Akova, you are now with us, and you will receive the energy."

"What energy?"

"Ah, that will be a surprise for you. You will become a powerful Eridanian."

"Nonsense," I said, "just because you have me lying here powerless and unable to move does not mean you can control my mind and will."

"Well, we shall see about that. We shall see how strong is the Turkish Cypriot from the island of Cyprus."

"Tell me, Draco, what do you hope to achieve by this?"

"Oh, a lot. First of all, you'll be the leading Eridanian down on Earth. You'll persuade those silly people in Britain to cease their struggle and join us."

Suddenly, the UFO began to shake. Then I saw Tamor, together with two other Greys, standing in front of me. Within seconds, I was floated down from the Devil's UFO and onto the ground. There was nothing Draco and his men could do to stop Tamor. This incident raised my hopes once again. Once at my home in Marlborough, Tamor explained.

"It's an energy you cannot perceive or understand. Their source is there in the mound near Marlborough. You were right in the first place. The Eridanians have a lot of energy stored at the mound. We've destroyed most of it. But there's lots more energy coming from their UFOs. It will clearly be an uphill struggle."

Tamor disappeared without warning, as always. I did not know what to make of his assumptions. He had said the Greys had destroyed Eridanian energies at the Mound. But he also stressed the fact that the energies kept reproducing themselves not only in the mound, but elsewhere in Marlborough. It was quite clear mankind did not have the technology to destroy Eridanian energies. We needed Grey help. Marlborough looked completely deserted the next morning as I walked down into the main street. The hotel I stayed in on my first visit to Marlborough looked empty except for the middle-aged lady at the reception. She was packing her suitcases.

"What's happening? There's hardly anyone left in town."

"We're all moving out," she said, quite frantic, "I suggest you do the same."

"Why? What's happening?"

I felt her gaze on me. "Now I remember. You're the pianist/composer who performed here at the music festival some years back. I heard you're involved with the aliens. Well, some officials told us to leave town for the time being.

They said there was a lot of alien activity in and around Marlborough and that it was not safe to stay here."

"But why? You can't just up and leave, and abandon your home because of alien activity here. There's always been alien activity in Marlborough. I don't understand."

"Well, the officials said it was dangerous."

"But who are these officials? Are they from the police?"

"I don't know, Mr Akova."

I left the hotel, wondering about this new development. Who were these 'officials'? What was the danger they were talking about? Why would they say it was no longer safe for people to stay in Marlborough? With its four arched doorways, the Police Station in Marlborough looked like a church. I tried the first door. It was locked. A car had pulled up alongside the curb. One of the men inside called out.

"Mr Akova?"

I stopped. Two men got out of the car.

"Yes?"

"You'd better come with us," said one of them.

"Why? Who are you?"

"We are the police."

"No. You've got it all wrong. I'm helping the government with their investigations."

"I'm afraid that's no longer the case," said the other man.

"You are mistaken. Call Major Blount. He'll tell you who I am."

"There is no need to do that, Sir. Major Blount asked us to take you in. Here," he handed me the phone, "you can call Major Blount and ask him if you like," said the first man.

"I'll do that." I called Major Blount immediately.

"Hello, Major. What's happening? Am I under arrest or something? If so, why?"

"Turan, I'm afraid it's out of my hands. But don't worry; you're not under arrest. I'll give instructions to the two men to let you go. You see, I received instructions form the new Higher Authority, asking me to terminate your involvement with government investigations on alien activity. As I said, I can't do anything about that. They also asked me to tell Emma at the UFO Research Centre that they can no longer be involved in any government activity or research. The UFO Centre, you and Emma can continue your investigations independently as long as you don't interfere with any official investigations."

"This means we can no longer expect any cooperation from the government. Tell me, Major. Who is behind this decision? Who is the new authority?"

"Turan, all I can tell you is that there is now a new executive body making these decisions. They are above the government. The Premier and his Minister of Defence are now mere puppets. At MI6, I'm powerless to make a decision on my own."

"By the way, everybody's left Marlborough. It has become a ghost town. Is that the decision of the new authority as well?" I asked him.

"Yes. Listen, Turan. Perhaps we can have a private talk later."

"I'll call your home," I said.

"Now let me talk to one of the men there." After a short exchange on the phone, they told me I was free to go. They drove off, leaving me in the empty street. I walked down the High Street of that town, once so full of life and prosperity. Alone in Marlborough, I walked back home and straight into the garage, where I had left my Daimler. So far, I had been able to do nothing. It was a disquieting thought. But I had to search; to search for something happening in Marlborough. The tone of Major Blount's voice had been mournfully jocular. I knew him only too well. There was something very wrong and what he called the 'new Higher Authority' had something to do with it.

Why would it not be safe for anyone to stay in this town? What was the danger? I drove through almost all the streets of the town. I even went back to Draco's twin mansions and parked there for at least fifteen minutes in case someone turned up. Then I drove back home. I made myself a sandwich. Later, I called Emma and explained to her what had happened earlier. She was shocked to hear of Tamor's appearance. I felt a presence deep inside my body. But I did not know what it was. Together with that feeling, the power within me was growing stronger.

I was tired and slept for a good three hours in the afternoon. When I awoke, I took a shower. Now I felt much stronger. It was really strange. A power seemed to enter my body at almost regular intervals. Although I had experienced something of the kind when Grey power was first bestowed on me, I was fascinated by the enormity of my strength.

My search continued in the dark, deserted streets of Marlborough. The street lights were off and I could see two or three shadows moving about in the darkness. This added to my fears of possibly the police or Eridanians following me. I was beginning to lose the faintest hope of finding anything at all, when the headlights of my Daimler hit a large house to the north of the town. I was determined to make contact, but with whom? My overburdened brain kept repeating the same words: "You will make contact…"

The lights were full on in this old house. I could hear the familiar voice of Frank Sinatra singing 'My Way'. I parked the car just outside the house. The curtains of the windows were open and I could see many people inside. I walked closer to the window. A group had formed a large semi-circle around an open fire. Some were dancing. It looked like a party. How cold these people be partying when everybody had left town?

The human sounds coming from the house reached fever pitch. There was definitely high excitement inside. I peered through a window before I rang the bell, and it was obviously a joyful occasion. Two young girls in their twenties opened the door. They were twins.

"Good evening, Mr Akova," welcomed one of them.

"Good evening. But how do you know me? Whose house is this? What's happening here?" The room was very large and airy, full of English colonial furniture.

"You are famous, Mr Akova, that's how we know you. Please come in. all your friends are here," she said, smiling. Was this another one of Draco's tricks? I walked inside, my nerves on edge. Then I saw Clayton approaching, his hands deep in his pockets. I felt more relaxed. But seeing him here in Marlborough was a complete surprise.

"Turan!"

"What's happening?" I asked.

"We're all here," he said, "all 36 of us. We've been summoned by Tamor."

"You still haven't told me what's happening."

"Turan, Tamor says he's found a way through the spiritual high level of the Chosen 36."

"And what does that mean? How will that stop the Eridanians?"

"Turan, just join the party. Emma is here. Tamor is here as well. He will explain everything," he said.

A high level of spirituality and powers of telepathic communication were given to the Chosen 36 by the Greys. Spiritual advancement was their strong point and only they possessed that ferocious drive to reach that level of great spiritual fulfilment. But I failed to see how such spiritual climaxes could stop the Eridanians.

Another question occurred to me. If there had been such an important development, then why had Tamor neglected to inform and summon me to the house, after all, I was the leader of the Chosen 36 and the most powerful of them all? Suddenly, a vibration perceptible only by myself filled the large room. It was definitely foreign, and only I had the power to discern it. I searched for Emma. When I found her, she was laughing hysterically, but shivering at the same time.

"Turan, I knew you'd come. Isn't this wonderful? Now we can stop the Eridanians!" She gasped between laughs. I pulled her away from the crowd and whispered into her ear the bad news.

"Something wrong here, Emma. You stay close to the door. We may have to leave in a hurry."

What was happening here? A man in his late thirties approached me from the bar. He smiled vacuously, a cigarette dangling from his mount.

"Isn't it wonderful?" he asked.

"What's wonderful?" I replied seriously.

"That we've finally defeated the Devil, of course," he answered, surprised by my sombre attitude.

"Don't be so sure about that," I told him.

"But why? Tamor is here and he's given all of us extra power. Now we will no longer have to fear the Devil, and—"

I could not wait for him to finish. The creature who had managed to disguise himself as Tamor was approaching. There was a strange elation in the air. Everybody seemed happy and content, but I felt as if on the edge of a precipice. Something was wrong.

"Why didn't you inform me of this meeting?" I asked him. He looked at me coldly. Tamor's eyes were not cold, I knew. A spasm of fear rippled through my entire body...Then I saw another Tamor, the real one, suddenly materialising across the room. They approached each other slowly and deliberately, and the tension was such that the room went completely silent.

I hurriedly stole away from them towards Emma, pulling Clayton with me.

"Quick! We must leave immediately," I whispered hoarsely to both of them. But neither of them moved an inch; they were as if paralysed.

The real Tamor was every bit as cunning as Draco, perhaps even more so. He attacked the evil Satan with both hands. Draco shouted in anguish, clenching his teeth. He was now on the defensive. I herded the crowd through the front door. I wanted to save them. As we all went out into the rainswept street, I realised that Tamor had effortlessly erased the Eridanian illusion from all the Chosen 36. Not only that, but I was astounded that he had strengthened their already powerful intuition. How on earth had all thirty-six of them been brought to a house in Marlborough? That was a mystery to me. Emma told me they had been summoned to this particular house by Tamor. He had told Emma that the strength and power of the Chosen 36 now posed as a significant obstacle to the Devil's progress. Wiltshire was the place for a confrontation. The Greys were far more effective in Marlborough than were the Eridanians.

Now there was a real chance to cripple the Eridanians. Emma heaved a sigh of relief when she saw Tamor walking out of the house. His power, his authority over the situation and his growing mysteriousness gave us a lot of confidence.

"You are the special ones," he told us, "but you should stick together. Draco and his demons are gone for the time being. But this is by no means the end of the struggle against evil. One thing is certain. All thirty six of you pose a threat to Draco's existence on Earth. So stay together. Akova is your leader. He can seek out the Devil and try to destroy him on his own. He has been endowed with other special powers which you do not possess. But do not fear. Even when he is gone for a while, no harm will come to you from the evil ones. One more thing you must remember. There is always a possibility that the powers of the Eridanians can surpass our own within hours or days. In alien civilisations, technological developments occur with unbelievable speed. Humankind will never be able to comprehend such developments. Today the Greys are ahead, tomorrow the Eridanians may take over. The struggle for supremacy is eternal. Mr Akova, take your friends back to your house."

There were many unanswered questions, but it was quite clear to all—at least for the time being—that we had the upper hand, through Tamor's assistance, of course. Nevertheless, we were in an unsettling situation. Spirits had soared at the anticipation of a definite and final check on the advance of the Eridanians but the uncertainty now continued. Would the Chosen 36 be able to contain the power of the evil deities from Epsilon Eridani? Would they be victorious against the unbreakable sword of the Devil?

As we entered the house I noticed a small man among those entering. He was a total stranger and I could not remember ever having met him before. He took a breath and then looked me in the eye, asking meekly: "So what do we do next, Mr Akova?"

I looked searchingly into his hooded eyes. Was he really one of us? I could not tell. I detected in his manner something like guilty discomfort which overlaid an air of profound disappointment.

"I don't remember seeing you in any of our previous meetings," I commented.

"We never had a chance to meet, Mr Akova," he replied apologetically, "I'm a lawyer. I work in London. I did visit the Centre on a couple of occasions, but you were not there."

I was attuned now to encounter the strange and horrible, and this man definitely gave me the creeps.

"What is your name?"

"Henry Reynold," he said.

"Pleased to meet you, Henry." I extended a hand and at last he smiled, grabbing my hand enthusiastically. I did not know what to make of him, but I felt a certain antipathy. There was really no reason to suspect him.

Later, I asked Emma and Clayton about him. It began to drizzle, as we stepped out onto the porch.

"Yes, I remember him," said Clayton, "he is one of the twelve British chosen ones of the thirty-six. Why do you ask?"

"I don't know. He seemed strange and a wee bit unbalanced. But maybe I'm just imagining things." I replied.

Who would have thought that we, the Chosen 36, would become the saviours and guardians of mankind. At first, we all looked upon this new development as an event of the first magnitude. But after our enthusiasm had died down, we realised—despite Tamor's assurances that Grey presence in Wiltshire was stronger than that of the Eridanians—we were in fact in the midst of a stronghold of evil forces. Mere incantations and brave challenges would not be enough to fend off the Devil and his armies.

Tamor had said that the Chosen 36 should 'stick together'. But it was impossible to accommodate all these men and women in my house. A man from Marlborough suggested they moved to a fairly large hotel about a mile away.

"The whole place is deserted, anyway," he added. Clearly all thirty-six, including myself, had been reinforced with extra Grey power. It was impossible to probe for evidence of this new power, but it was there and we all felt it. It was a highly spiritual refinement and combative energy which was now in the soul and body of the Chosen 36. The wicked, demonic evil could be challenged and the divine celestial light of the Greys, loyal and dependable, would prevail. But would the concentrated, renewed power of the chosen 36 be enough to challenge and defeat the openly gruesome, ghoulish and blood-curdling horror of the Devil? I didn't know. As we prepared to move to the hotel, Tamor materialised once more.

"You must stay in Marlborough," he said in his dignified way. His direct and sharp intelligence reaffirmed the superiority of the Greys over the Eridanians. His adroit handling of the situation was no match for the Devil. But for how long...? I had encountered all the escalating stages of horror during the last few weeks, but somehow managed to survive with or without Tamor's help. Politicians in Whitehall who had considered making a deal with the Devil had already given up the idea, not so much because they had 'seen the light', but because the Devil Draco and his men had suddenly disappeared and there had been no one to sign the agreement with. At any rate, it was impossible to bargain with the powers of darkness.

Now was the time to consolidate our positions in Marlborough. But how? Tamor did not tell us why, after all these investigations and subsequent efforts to stop the spread of Eridanian energies and pinpoint the source of demonic energy itself, we—the Chosen 36—possessed the real power source to prevent the Eridanians. How could this be? How could a mere group of thirty six people challenge a whole army of demons? It seemed like an impossible task. Also, the speed with which the extraterrestrial technologies developed, whether Grey or Eridanian, left me and my colleagues gasping. It was not possible to compare human intelligence and emotion with the actions and behaviour of the extraterrestrials. They were not robots, they were dynamic and alive, in ways that were quite different from our own. Nonetheless, I could detect a quiet determination in Tamor's behaviour, and also a certain kind of passion. He would almost always appear at the right moment. Despite a lingering uncertainty and gloom in the back of my mind about the possible reversal of affairs in favour of the Eridanians, I was, as always, optimistic.

The urge to find Draco was still there, but he had obviously gone into hiding. I had the feeling he was somewhere in Marlborough. Actually, it was not just a feeling, it was something I had deduced. It was now obvious that the Eridanians base could be nowhere else but in Wiltshire. In a whirlpool of confused admiration for Tamor and the Greys and the miraculous way in which I had been endowed with the power, I felt ready to seek out and destroy the Devil once and for all. I was now immune from the dangers that lay ahead. But I was determined not to divulge the enormous powers that I possessed to the other thirty-five. I had sufficient reticence not to confide a secret of such mammoth importance.

I told Emma that I was going out for a drive. I said I wanted to see if there were any people in Marlborough. I drove past Draco's twin mansions and stopped at the back of them. There was no light and no sign of life whatsoever in either of the mansions. Further west, I drove up into a road leading out of town. There, all of a sudden, I was dumbfounded to find myself in a world of unreality. I remembered how I had experienced the same trick by Draco when the whole landscape had changed. There in front of me near the forest that led up towards a small hill, stood an almost derelict castle which seemed unlived in. This old castle seemed familiar. Five years before, I had performed in a piano recital of my own works in Bucharest, and I had found time to visit Count Dracula's castle in Transylvania—not the one built especially for tourists, but the read castle where Prince Vlad had actually lived, and fought the Turks. I went in and climbed up the stairs.

It was very dark inside. A second flight of steps led to a narrow marble terrace, shielded by a long, thick curtain. Peering through a chink, I saw Draco, standing on a pedestal in a large hall, growling something in his own language. The place where he was standing was faintly lit by about five large candles, and he was surrounded by five naked women, beautiful women. Murmurs of ecstasy filled the hall as they prepared to make love. The old Count raised his voice and gazed up at the sky. A full moon and the stars were visible through a heap of ruins.

The thunderous voice and the genius of a thousand shades of the King of the demons—Satan—extinguished all the candles and I was embraced by pitch darkness. Draco's uncontrollable rage seemed to die down. The light from the full moon shone into the hall and I could see the five figures of the women now closing in towards him. His evil laughter seemed once more to pronounce the superiority of the Eridanians over the Greys. Once again, the spectre of uncertainty cast its evil shadow over my whole being. Was this really the moment when the superiority of the Devil was established over the Greys? I stood behind the curtain, transfixed, observing and experiencing some tyrannical torments. The frequency of technological change in the lives of these extraterrestrials was awesome. I had no doubt that Draco now had the upper hand. Yet an indefinable spiritual wealth and power was growing ever stronger in my body; the enchantment of the enormous power of the soul. That was it: the power of the soul, the power which emanated from my body was distinctly human, but of course, reinforced immensely by Grey power.

The interplay between these two powers, the power of the human soul and the power of the Greys were mysteriously linked together and towered with spiritual and physical strength. Under the ruined, moonlit hall of the ancient castle, I was confronting Lucifer. Flames in all four corners of the hall cast a flickering orange light on the proceedings, and I could clearly see Draco waving both hands as if preparing someone to be condemned to death by burning. The eerie and at the same time arousing screams of the women sauntering from one corner to the other transformed the hall into a horrific, monstrous stage of the supernatural. And I was in it.

I felt a sudden sharp sensation of pain with the fiendish leer right behind me. There stood two other naked women, relishing their cruelty and their lust. They were menacing, threatening evil and harm. I heard an enormous roaring thunder and the wind howled through the chinks in the ceiling. I was now ensnared by the tricks of the Devil, my limbs trembling with fright. He rippled with horrible delight and pleasure as the two beautiful women pushed me down near the pedestal where he was standing. Draco's spine-chilling slanting, lustrous dark eyes were now visible in the flickering light. He surfeited himself with the pleasure of the company of the women. His right hand firmly gripped a peculiar instrument which looked like a short Roman sword, and he shook his head violently from side to side as the women scampered about and around us both.

While I lay near the pedestal, a brilliant sparkling light appeared in the part of the night sky I could see through one of the openings of the ceiling. Now I had to confront what I feared most: the re-establishment of the Eridanian authority over the Greys. A gust of wind blew out the candles and the flames in the hall. I was in terrifying darkness with hands reaching out for my body. I had to grapple not only with Draco but with the women also. A slender hope still flickered within me. I was in a strange and abnormal state of mind. Was there really any hope of saving humankind from this horrendous fate? The dazzling swiftness through which the Eridanians had become superior to the Greys and vice versa was the one dominant development which hampered not only our chances of survival, but killed off any permanent final blow to the Devil.

With a diabolical expression on his face, Draco shouted at the top of his hoarse voice.

"We are the masters. Nothing can stop us now."

At that moment, Tamor appeared and stood facing the Devil.

"Get up and challenge him," he told me. "Remember you have the immortality of the soul. The soul of humankind not only survives after death, but it is in fact an energy power within the body. The soul within the body is the basic, fundamental and ultimate strength of mankind which the Eridanians do not possess. The evil power of the demons is inferior to that human faculty. This is the time. Strike him. Do not be afraid. Challenge him and he will go away. Your soul is the power."

I did exactly as he told me, and struck Draco twice with all my strength. While on the floor, a white beam emerged from his instrument. It hit me and I fell. The beautiful naked women surrounded me, moving about playfully. Summoning the last of my strength, I got up and grabbed the instrument he was holding in his right hand.

The white beams from the instrument hit him and he fell again. The women ran up to him, caressing the evil Satan. Then I heard Tamor once again.

"Now is the time to leave. Just leave. He cannot touch you. He will go away."

I ran out of the derelict castle and fell to the ground. Rain fell in torrents. When I looked up, I could see two saucer-shaped spacecraft hovering just a few feet above the ground. There were red and white lights emanating from both UFOs. I recognised the Grey extraterrestrial machine, the rays of which hit the black UFO of the Eridanian devils. This was, in a way, a show of force. Neither seemed to be damaged in any way by the rays. But they continued to emit bright flashes of intense white light. Minutes later, they both shot skyward and disappeared.

The rain and thunder stopped abruptly, and Count Dracula's castle vanished with it. I raised myself from the ground and walked slowly towards the road. This was the time to reflect on the sadistic brutality of the Devil. The retreat of Draco and the Eridanian UFO was the beginning, perhaps, of a new chapter in the history of mankind. The whole world was now aware of the presence of two kinds of extraterrestrials: the Greys who had been visiting planet Earth for the past sixty-five years from three star systems, Alpha Centauri, Tau Ceti and Zeta Reticuli; and the Eridanians who arrived on Earth from their star system Epsilon

Eridani. The whole history of the Devil described in many religious books including the Bible and the Koran was now in question.

The Devil was in fact an extraterrestrial. Humankind was now much more devil-conscious. The Devil had finally been identified as a creature from another star system. All conspiracies, abductions and silly terms like 'little green men' could now be abandoned in favour of the truth: the factual existence of the Devil. The EU was still under Eridanian control, but Britain had somehow survived. The human soul was powerful enough to check the advance of the Devil. But for how long, no one knew. The inexplicable Eridanian devil incursion had been repulsed.

I walked back to the spot where I had parked the Daimler. All of a sudden, Tamor appeared again. He stood just a few feet away from me. Then I heard the long passages from my two 'space music' compositions. The first was Alpha Centauri and the second Zeta Reticuli. The Grey UFO appeared above Tamor. He lifted his hand and pointed to it.

"The great music of a great composer. No composer on Earth has been able to harmonise chords by setting them in different and discordant keys like you have. Your avant-garde new music and your improvisations have no limits. Your liberty is unequalled, your freedom so original. You know, of course, that the inspiration for your music comes from above. But your music has been our inspiration also. Your musical genius is so special. Your compositions will live forever. The combination of your sounds is exquisite. You are not a mathematician like some other composers. Your music comes direct from the soul. Your music is not a mathematical assemblage of notes and chords. We are always desirous of its mysteries. Now go home and let the other Chosen Ones go home. Let me assure you that I will be back." With a final wave of his hand, Tamor disappeared. I walked back home, to Emma.